Making Spirits Bright

Books by Fern Michaels

Books by Elizabeth Bass

Wherever Grace Is Needed

Miss You Most of All

Books by Rosalind Noonan

The Daughter She Used To Be

In a Heartbeat

"Miracle on Main Street" (in *Snow Angels*)

One September Morning

Books by Nan Rossiter

The Gin & Chowder Club

FERN MICHAELS

Making Spirits Bright

ELIZABETH BASS
ROSALIND NOONAN
NAN ROSSITER

ZEBRA BOOKS
KENSINGTON PUBLISHING CORP.
http://www.kensingtonbooks.com

ZEBRA BOOKS are published by

Kensington Publishing Corp.
119 West 40th Street
New York, NY 10018

Copyright © 2011 by Kensington Publishing Corporation
Making Spirits Bright copyright © 2011 by MRK Productions
Fern Michaels is a registered trademark of First Draft, Inc.
Runaway Christmas copyright © 2011 by Elizabeth Bass
Home for Christmas copyright © 2011 by Rosalind Noonan
Christmas on Cape Cod copyright © 2011 by Nan Rossiter

All rights reserved. No part of this book may be reproduced in any
form or by any means without the prior written consent of the Publisher, excepting brief quotes used in reviews.

If you purchased this book without a cover you should be aware
that this book is stolen property. It was reported as "unsold and de-
stroyed" to the Publisher and neither the Author nor the Publisher
has received any payment for this "stripped book."

All Kensington titles, imprints and distributed lines are available at
special quantity discounts for bulk purchases for sales promotion,
premiums, fund-raising, educational or institutional use.

Special book excerpts or customized printings can also be created
to fit specific needs. For details, write or phone the office of the
Kensington Special Sales Manager: Attn. Special Sales Department. Kensington Publishing Corp., 119 West 40th Street, New
York, NY 10018. Phone: 1-800-221-2647.

Zebra and the Z logo Reg. U.S. Pat. & TM Off.

ISBN-13: 978-1-4201-0836-1
ISBN-10: 1-4201-0836-0

First Printing: November 2011

10 9 8 7 6 5 4 3 2 1

Printed in the United States of America

CONTENTS

Making Spirits Bright

FERN MICHAELS

Chapter 1

Placerville, Colorado
November 2011

Melanie McLaughlin positioned her cursor on the SEND icon, double-clicked, and waited for the window telling her that her mail had been sent to pop up. She signed off her e-mail account, then moved her mouse to exit the complicated graphics program she'd helped design last year. It was her biggest job to date, and she was happy to be finished. She didn't want to work during the upcoming Christmas season. Fortunately, she was her own boss, so she made the rules. She just wanted to enjoy the holidays without any professional commitments, no last-minute all-night projects to finish. She'd worked diligently through the Thanksgiving holiday to make sure her schedule was completely cleared until after the new year.

She'd promised Stephanie Marshall, her best friend, that she'd watch her girls, Amanda and Ashley, today, so that Stephanie and her fiancé, Edward Patrick Joseph O'Brien, "Patrick" to his friends, could spend Black Friday Christmas shopping. She thought it very courageous of the couple to tackle the crowds. Melanie had promised the girls she would take them skiing at Maximum Glide, then they would come back to her condo, where they would spend the afternoon learning to knit.

Melanie had been an avid knitter since junior high, long before it was fashionable. Both girls were eager to learn, telling her they wanted to learn to knit so they could give their mother handmade Christmas gifts. Melanie smiled, remembering the first scarf she'd made for her own mother. Uneven stitches and a horrid fluorescent orange; her mother had been delighted with her gift. She'd kept the scarf packed in a shoe box in the back of her closet all these years. For safekeeping, her mother'd said. Personally, Melanie thought her mother kept it out of sight to prevent temporary blindness to those unfortunate few who'd been forced to *admire* her handiwork. At the time, Melanie had reasoned the color would stand out on the slopes, her mother easily spotted in case of an emergency.

She'd made sure to purchase plenty of red and green yarn for the girls' first project, a pot holder. No way would she subject Stephanie to such a horrific color as her mother's!

She pushed the POWER button to turn off her computer. For the entire month of December and what was left of November, she vowed not to turn it back on unless it was a dire emergency. That didn't mean she couldn't check her e-mail. She'd just do it from her cell phone.

Melanie rolled her chair away from the desk and almost ran over Odie, her three-year-old boxer. "Hey, bud, don't sneak up on me like that. You're liable to give me a heart attack."

"Woof, woof!" Odie stood up on all four paws, his shiny brown eyes beseeching her not to leave him behind.

She gave him a quick scratch between the ears. "You're

a lucky boy today. I promised Candy Lee I'd let her dog-sit, so there." Candy Lee, a high school student who worked part-time at The Snow Zone ski shop was a die-hard animal lover. Melanie brought Odie to the store whenever she knew Candy Lee was working. Today would be crazy busy, but Melanie knew there were three staff members on loan from their ski-lift positions to assist Candy Lee since both Stephanie and Patrick had taken the day off.

An ear-piercing meow directed her attention to her newly adopted cat, Clovis. He had a rich butterscotch coat and giant jade-colored eyes, which were staring at her to demand her attention. Another ear-splitting meow. She reached down and scooped up the giant ball of fur. "I guess this means you want to come, too?" Another meow, and two quick slaps from his bushy tail, and Melanie knew she couldn't leave Clovis alone.

Weighing in at twenty-seven pounds when she'd spied him at the local animal shelter, he'd caught her attention two months ago when, on a whim, she decided Odie needed a pal. Though her intent was to adopt another dog, Clovis had glowered at her from his cage as she'd walked through the shelter. She'd heard his manlike meow, and decided a cat would be a perfect companion for Odie, who was docile and lived for belly rubs and the occasional bit of rare steak. A cat would be perfect given the boxer's disposition.

When she'd taken the husky feline out of his cage, he'd licked her face just like a dog. He'd captured her heart on the spot. The dog and cat had taken to each other like jelly to peanut butter.

She rubbed her nose against Clovis's before placing him on top of her desk. "Let me load up the ski equipment, guys," Melanie said, sure both animals understood her.

Odie dropped down on his haunches, and Clovis perched upright as though saying, "Okay, but speed it up."

She made fast work of getting her skis, poles, boots, and helmet from the front closet. She grabbed a tote that held her ski pants and all the miscellaneous gear one needed when skiing. She peered inside the bag just to make sure she had a full bottle of sunscreen. The morning sun blazed like a giant lemon in the powder blue sky. Given that and the blustering winds, sun- and windburn was a sure thing without proper protection.

That day, Melanie was thankful her condo had its own private garage. The temps were supposed to be in the low teens. Her Lincoln Navigator took forever to warm up when left outside. After stuffing her equipment in the back, she tossed her tote on the front passenger seat.

She made three trips to the condo and back to the Navigator before she had all her supplies. Since she was bringing Odie and Clovis to The Snow Zone, she'd brought their beds just in case Candy Lee needed them out of the way. Odie didn't like being shifted to the small office at the back of the store. Melanie was sure he understood the difference between the rows of sweaters and ski coats and the actual ski equipment. She'd often commented to Stephanie that if she were ever in a pinch, Odie was sure to be a great assistant. Neither animal liked being relegated to the back office, yet they seemed to make the best of their situation. Both animals got along famously. So far, they'd remained in the office without any signs of mass destruction.

Once they were all secured properly in their seats, Melanie made the short drive to Stephanie's little ranch house in Placerville. She grinned at the memory of last year's Christmas. She had purchased the little ranch home for Stephanie and the girls. She'd placed the deed and the rest of the paperwork that goes along with purchasing a house in a plain envelope as though its contents were unknown to her. Stephanie still told anyone who would listen what a grand gesture Melanie had performed.

Melanie had inherited millions when her grandmother died. Her parents had bought real estate when the market was hopping, before she was born, and they, too, weren't lacking in the financial department. This made their lives and that of many others better. Her mother always told her you get back what you give, tenfold, and it wasn't necessarily a monetary return. Melanie tried to practice on a daily basis what her mother preached. So far, she'd never been disappointed.

Melanie had come to love Stephanie like the sister she'd always dreamed of having. Adding her two adorable daughters, Ashley and Amanda, they completed the rest of the family she didn't have. Settling the three of them into a home of their own was the least she could do given all they'd been through. Married to an abusive husband, Stephanie had found Hope House for her and the girls. The secret shelter was for battered women and their families. Melanie's mother had long been a financial supporter of Hope House. It was there that Melanie found Stephanie and her girls. Grace Landry, the founder and a therapist, had taken the family of three under her wing and given them their first real chance for a normal life. The little garage apartment Grace had secured for them was owned by Melanie's parents. Melanie lived right down the road. And, as they say, the rest is history.

Melanie adjusted the heater controls on the dash, then stretched her arm over the seat to reach for a large blanket, which she placed over Odie and Clovis. Both readjusted their positions, allowing the blanket to drape comfortably around them.

She smiled from ear to ear as she engaged the four-wheel drive and skillfully maneuvered the steep winding road leading to Stephanie's. Careful not to slide off the side of the mountain, Melanie safely pulled into Stephanie's freshly shoveled driveway ten minutes later.

Patrick. It was his new mission in life to take care of Stephanie's every need, no matter how great or small. And the girls had him so tightly wrapped around their little fingers, their wish was his command even before they asked. Patrick of all men. A confirmed bachelor, he'd always intended to remain single. And then Stephanie Marshall entered the picture. Though they'd had a few rough patches, anyone who saw them together knew they were madly in love.

One evening after Stephanie had invited them all over for dinner, making her specialty, three-cheese manicotti and her famous homemade garlic-knot rolls, Melanie, Grace, and her husband, Max Jorgenson, who brought their new baby daughter Ella, listened intently as Patrick told them about Shannon, his niece. She had died of an extremely rare blood disorder on the day she was supposed to graduate from high school. Suddenly, Melanie had understood his fear of getting close to Stephanie and the girls too soon. He was afraid of being hurt all over again.

But Patrick, being a truly decent guy, had taken another look at Stephanie and her girls. And just as his best bud Max Jorgenson, famous Olympic Gold Medalist skier, had proposed to Grace, Patrick asked Stephanie to marry him. On New Year's Day, they were planning to take their vows at the top of the slopes and, together, as man and wife, they'd ski down Gracie's Way, and at the bottom of the run, all would celebrate the much-anticipated union of the couple.

* * *

Melanie hopped out of the Navigator, stomping her tan-colored Uggs on the cleared pavement. "You two sit tight. I'll be right back," she called out to her menagerie. She hurried up the short steps to the front porch, where she grabbed the doorknob, only to have it slip from her grasp before she even had a chance to twist it.

"Auntie M, Auntie M, are you really taking us skiing today? Are we still gonna go back to your house and learn how to . . ."

"Shhh, Amanda. We're not supposed to tell, remember?" Ashley chastised her little sister.

Stephanie chose that moment to join them at the front door. "Seems like I almost overheard a secret."

Amanda and Ashley looked away, not meeting their mother's stern look. Melanie broke in before the girls revealed their afternoon plans. "I'm teaching the girls a new skill. We're just not telling what it is," Melanie said.

"Good. I don't know what I'd do if you were to . . . to . . . do something like you did last year."

They all broke out in laughter, even the girls. Melanie tossed her long blond braid over her shoulder. "I don't think I'll be able to top that gift, at least not for a while. At the rate you're all going, I'll be a hundred and six before you stop ragging me about that."

"It is the best, Mel. Have you seen the bathroom since I painted? Patrick installed granite counters, and it's just absolutely to die for, not that it wasn't in the first place, but this just feels so . . . elegant. Come on and have a look-see."

"As much as I would love to, Odie and Clovis are waiting in the Navigator. They're staying with Candy Lee while the girls and I ski. I hope that's not a problem."

"Of course not. Candy Lee says Odie directs the customers to the ski equipment. Tell Candy Lee if Odie keeps this up, her job might be in danger."

"Mom!" Amanda shouted. "She needs this job. She's saving up for college."

Stephanie took her younger daughter in her arms. "Oh, sweetie, we're teasing. Candy Lee has a job forever if she wants."

Melanie knew the girls were a bit on the sensitive side. They'd seen so much violence from their father that, often-times, when the girls thought they or someone else was being wrongly disciplined or spoken to in a harsh manner, they spoke up for themselves and others. Melanie knew Stephanie was pleased with this, but didn't want them to take every word she said quite so literally.

"I would bet my last nickel Candy Lee gets that soccer scholarship she's applying for. She's a straight-A student and a killer soccer player," Melanie stated.

"How come you know all this, Auntie M?"

Melanie observed Stephanie as she lowered herself by her daughters and placed a hand on each of their pink-and-purple padded ski jackets. "It's not always polite to ask questions about situations that don't concern us. I'm sure Candy Lee will manage to get to college, so let's leave it at that. Now, Clovis and Odie are probably freez-ing their fur off in the Navigator. You two grab your bags, and I'll take care of your skis and poles." Stephanie looked at Melanie. "Keeping up with them wears me out some-times, but it's the best worn-out you'll ever experience."

Melanie squinted her eyes and scrunched up her nose. "As Mom keeps reminding me, I don't have a man in my life, no children, and I just don't see either one happening anytime in the near future. At the rate I'm going, I'll be lucky to adopt another animal from the shelter, so I'll just take your word even though the time I spend with the girls is the best ever." She teared up at the thought of not having the two little sprites in her life. She was content to remain Auntie M.

For now.

With Odie and Clovis relegated to the rear cargo area and both girls safely ensconced in their seat belts, Melanie glanced in her rearview mirror one last time, making sure they all were where they should be. She recalled the last time she'd taken the girls skiing. They'd wound up lost in a snowstorm and had delivered a litter of pups. Now she could smile at the memory. Grateful that Stephanie still allowed her within pitching distance of the girls, she shrugged her thoughts aside, focusing on their plans for the day.

Black Friday was usually one of Maximum Glide's busiest days. Melanie dreaded the crowds, the long lines at the chairlifts, but spending the day with the girls was worth the hassle. Both girls were excellent skiers. Max, Grace's husband, had taught the girls how to ski properly. Black diamond runs were easy for both, but Melanie wasn't that comfortable with them, so they'd tackle the blue runs.

She steered the Navigator carefully down the narrow road, mindful of the wet slushy conditions. Growing up in Colorado had its advantages. She'd learned to drive in foul weather at an early age, and while she wasn't excited at the prospect of driving up the mountain in such bad conditions, she was quite confident in her ability to do so safely. Snow chains and four-wheel-drive vehicles had nothing on her.

"Auntie M," Ashley called from the backseat. "Do you think you'll ever get married?"

Melanie almost lost control of the Navigator. She cleared her throat, needing the extra seconds to come up with an answer appropriate for an eleven-year-old. "I'm sure that someday I will." Lame, Melanie, lame, she thought as she glanced in her rearview mirror. Ashley wasn't buying it; Melanie could tell by the look on her face.

"That's not an answer! You sound just like Mom. 'Maybe' and 'someday' aren't real answers," Ashley stated in that clear and concise matter-of-fact way eleven-year-olds have.

Melanie chuckled. Ashley was right. "Truthfully, I don't know when or if I'll ever get married because I haven't dated anyone long enough to fall in love, so marriage hasn't been my number one priority."

"What's a priority?" Amanda asked.

"It means something that is very important, right Auntie M?" Ashley replied.

"Yes, that's exactly what it means. And right now my top *priority* is to arrive safely at The Snow Zone so we can drop Clovis and Odie off. I need to focus my attention on the road. It's incredibly slick."

Again, Melanie glanced in her rearview mirror. Ashley rolled her eyes.

"That means we're not supposed to ask any more questions about Aunt Melanie's personal life."

"Why?" Amanda asked.

With her engagement to Patrick, Stephanie talked about marriage constantly. It seemed the girls had acquired an avid interest in the topic as well.

Melanie wanted to tell the girls it was okay with her to ask such questions, just not while she was driving on an icy road, but this was Stephanie's rule, and she would respect that.

"You ask too many questions," Ashley informed her little sister. "Doesn't she?"

Melanie peeped in her rearview mirror again. "It's okay, Ash. All little girls like to ask questions."

"Mom says Amanda talks too much, but I would really like to know if you plan on getting married sometime in the future, because Krissy Haygood—she's a girl in my class—all she talks about is her big sister getting married this summer. She's the maid of honor and said it was highly unusual for someone her age to act as maid of honor, and, well, I sort of thought if you were to get married, or think about it, maybe I could . . . you know, be your maid of honor."

For once, Melanie was at a loss for words. She never remembered having such desires or thoughts when she was eleven, but times were different, kids matured earlier nowadays. She took a deep breath, fearing she was about to put her foot in her mouth, but decided if she did get married, there would be absolutely no reason that Ashley couldn't act as her maid of honor.

"When I get married, I promise to ask you to be my maid of honor."

Chapter 2

Melanie wrapped a thick towel around her wet hair, swooped her old worn-out yellow terry-cloth robe off the hook on the back of the bathroom door, slipped her arms inside, then secured the belt around her waist. She hurried to the kitchen just in time to hear the microwave's bell *ding*.

After spending the morning skiing, and the afternoon instructing the girls how to make a slip knot to cast on, Melanie was pleasantly worn out. Too tired to make a proper dinner, she'd popped in a microwave meal while she showered. Clovis and Odie were curled together beneath the kitchen table, waiting. She smiled at the sight.

"I know you two had more than your share of treats today, so what is it?" Melanie asked as she removed her lasagna from the microwave, placing the black plastic container on a dinner plate.

Odie yawned, and Clovis gave her his "don't-mess-with-me" look. Sure that Clovis had been an emperor in another life, Melanie turned around and gave the feline a quick bow. She did a double take when Clovis nodded his furry head, then reclined against Odie's belly. *He really does think he's an emperor.*

I am definitely spending too much time alone.

This reminded her of Ashley's earlier question. Would she ever marry? Have children of her own? She certainly didn't have any prospects, but that was her own doing. Since she'd started working from her home, she'd devoted most of her spare time to caring for her pets and to Stephanie's little family. She loved the excitement on the girls' faces when she surprised them with a visit or an unexpected treat. She often wished for a family, a child of her own, but knew until she met the man of her dreams, it was not to be. She was still young, still had enough time to pick and choose the right man. Thing was, the man supply had grown very slim since college. Most of the guys she'd met and dated in college were married with families of their own, and those who weren't already taken were not her type. Whatever that was.

So, she thought as she grabbed a can of soda from the refrigerator, *what exactly is my type?*

Tall, dark, and handsome? No.

Sensitive and shy? No.

Alpha male? Definitely a no.

She took a drink of soda. After several seconds' contemplation, Melanie decided she didn't have a type. She'd dated winners, a few losers, but none that knocked her socks off or made her feel like "he's the one." Nope. *Nada.* So, that left room for all those guys out there who were just waiting to beat her door down. Zero in that department, too.

For a young, well-to-do woman, she wasn't doing all that well. Yes, she had a condo to die for here in Placerville, another in Telluride that she kept rented for most of the ski season, and she was considering buying a house with a big yard, a white picket fence, the whole nine yards. She'd put that big purchase off, telling herself she didn't need that much space. Her condo in Placerville was perfect for her. She scanned the kitchen. While not as large as her condo's kitchen in Telluride, it was decent. Large enough for a table for six, an oak butcher-block island in its center, Sub-Zero refrigerator, a top-of-the-line Wolf stove and oven, all stainless steel. She'd softened the sterile look with cheery yellow accent pieces: canisters, local pottery, yellow and red Fiestaware, accentuated by cherry red place mats and matching curtains she'd had custom-made.

She'd chosen pale pinks and cream for the master bedroom, and a neutral gray and maroon for the guest bedroom. Both bathrooms had Jacuzzi tubs and walk-in showers large enough for two. The living room needed some color; she'd just never gotten around to finishing the decorating. Two beige sofas with a matching love seat and two overstuffed chairs filled the room. A fireplace on the main wall had been used only once since she'd bought the place, but Melanie told herself it was too much of a hassle, since she spent most of her time in the third bedroom she used for her office. She had a gas fireplace there, and, when needed, all she had to do was flick a switch and boom, within minutes, the room was as toasty as a wood fire. She did miss the smell of wood smoke, but figured the lack of a mess was worth the sacrifice.

She finished her lasagna, rinsed the plate, and placed it next to the others in the dishwasher. Sometimes it took her more than a week to fill the dishwasher. *Sad,* she thought as she removed the box of Cascade from beneath the sink. She either needed to cook more, have company over more often, or acquire a big family. There it goes again! Why couldn't she stop thinking about a family of her own? Was she spending too much time with Amanda and Ashley? Was she subconsciously envious of Stephanie?

Growing up an only child, she'd longed for a brother or sister. Melanie had been a change-of-life baby, much wanted, her mother always added, and she knew that to be true, but she had also known that the chances of her acquiring a sibling were slim to none.

She wondered why her parents hadn't adopted another child. They were certainly financially able, they'd both been in good health and still were. Maybe it was a blood-is-thicker-than-water kinda thing. No, no! Her parents weren't like that. They would have welcomed another child. Maybe they'd never considered it. Whatever, she told herself, it didn't matter now as she was a grown woman. She knew that her parents were counting on her to provide them with a houseful of grandchildren to spoil someday. She hoped they weren't holding their breaths.

Rolling her eyes at the path her thoughts were traveling, Melanie grabbed a damp cloth, swiped it over the countertops, then washed and refilled Odie's and Clovis's water dishes. She folded the dishcloth in half, placed it on the counter, and grabbed another soda from the refrigerator.

Odie emitted a low growl, which was followed by a junglelike meow from Clovis. "Come on, you two, it's time to call it a day." She said this every night to the pair of mismatched animals. Like clockwork, they wiggled out from under the kitchen table and followed her to her office.

She'd promised herself she wasn't going to work the rest of the holiday season, said she wasn't going to turn her computer on until the year had ended, but she hadn't voiced the promise out loud, so that was okay. As long as she hadn't verbalized the commitment to anyone else, she wasn't really worried about being accountable to anyone for breaking her promise, something she normally wouldn't do. Without another thought, Melanie went to her desk, clicked on the lamp, then hit the ON button to her high-end Titanus computer. A slight hum from the machine was the only sound in the room. Odie and Clovis had found their favorite spot by the fireplace. There wasn't anything or anyone to prevent her from doing what she was about to do.

She logged on to the Internet, typed Google into her browser, then typed three words and hit SEARCH.

Adoption in Colorado.

Her heart raced, and her stomach fluttered as though a thousand butterflies were dancing inside her. So many Web sites appeared, Melanie was sure she'd misspelled something. She typed the words a second time, this time watching her hands as they moved across her keyboard.

A-d-o-p-t-i-o-n-I-n–C-o-l-o-r-a-d-o. She hit the SEARCH icon.

Again, hundreds and hundreds of Web sites appeared on her screen.

"Okayyy, I can do this," she said out loud.

Melanie clicked on the first blue hyperlink at the top of her screen. She scanned the Web site, knew she didn't want to travel across the globe to China, and clicked on the second link. She perused the contents, then moved on to the next site.

After two hours of reading about Colorado's many adoption agencies, Melanie leaned back in her chair and twisted her stiff neck from left to right, her mind wondering at all the possibilities she'd just examined.

Is it possible?

She thought of all the tabloids she'd scanned while in line at the supermarket. It seemed just about every superstar in Hollywood was adopting a child. Many of them were single. If they could do this, why couldn't she? She was financially able to provide for a child, and she certainly had lots of love to give. Her parents would be surprised at first, but Melanie knew that once they got used to the idea, they would be as thrilled as she was beginning to feel.

Yes! She could do this! She *would* do this. First thing tomorrow morning, she was going to call World Adoption Agency in Denver, a local orphanage. Out of all the Web sites, this one held the most appeal. Children of every age, every race, some with health issues, some with emotional troubles, resided at the state-funded home. Yes, this would offer her a wide selection of children from around the world. Sex or age didn't matter to her. Melanie sensed she would know exactly which child she would adopt when the time came.

Chapter 3

At one minute past eight, Melanie dialed the number for World Adoption Agency. They opened at 8:00 A.M. according to their Web site and were open on Saturdays. It was meant to be, she figured, because it was Saturday, and she had absolutely nothing planned.

She wasn't going to waste another minute worrying about the timing of her phone call. Her mother always told her the early bird catches the worm. She'd been unable to sleep last night as thoughts of adopting a child filled her brain. Finally, around four in the morning, she'd given up all hope of sleeping, took a long, hot shower, and dressed in her old denim jeans and her favorite University of Colorado sweatshirt. She'd taken Odie for a short walk throughout the complex.

Impatient now that she'd decided to act on what she thought of as her newly budding motherly instinct, she didn't bother with the greenway behind the condos. Odie knew something was awry when she rushed him through his morning routine. He barked as though he were asking what did she think she was doing, then dropped his head to his chest.

"I promise we'll take an extra-long walk later," she told him. That had seemed to cheer the boxer up.

Back inside, Melanie made bacon and eggs for breakfast, giving half to Clovis and Odie. After she cleaned up, she stripped the sheets from her bed, tossed them in the washing machine, and mopped the kitchen floor. When she couldn't find anything else to distract her, she'd taken Amanda and Ashley's knitting needles from the baskets she'd given them. She removed several knots, rewound yarn, then tucked the beginner's instruction booklets neatly beside the balls of red and green yarn. On the verge of climbing the walls, Melanie brewed another pot of coffee and sat at the kitchen table watching as the hands on the clock turned more slowly than they ever had. Or so it seemed.

Just what I need—more caffeine. As if I'm not wound up enough.

And now that she had made the call, all she heard on the other end of the phone was an answering machine asking her to please leave her name and number, and they would return her call as soon as it was convenient. How dare they do this to her!

Melanie wanted to scream. This was ridiculous. There are hundreds of children just waiting for a home, and she's told to wait! Maybe she'd picked the wrong agency. If she owned such a business, if one even wanted to call an orphanage a business, she would make sure she never missed an opportunity to place a child. Deciding she would search for another agency, Melanie practically ran to her office.

The ringing telephone stopped her dead in her tracks.

The kitchen or the office? She was in the middle. The

kitchen. She raced the few feet back to the kitchen, and grabbed the phone. Exhaling, she spoke into the receiver. "Hello?"

A heavily accented voice said, "I am returning your phone call."

Without asking, Melanie knew this was the adoption agency.

"Uh, yes, I called. I wanted to . . . I was thinking of adopting—"

"Madam, that is why most people call us."

Madam?

"Oh, well, of course." Now that she had the agency on the phone, she was suddenly at a loss for words.

"Miss," the woman with the accent said. "I am a very busy woman. You called the agency, I am to assume that there was a reason."

It took Melanie a second to recover. "Yes, I would like to know what the procedure is for adopting a child."

There, she'd said it; she couldn't take it back now!

Melanie heard the woman's sharp intake of breath. "This is not the way we practice. You must schedule an appointment with the office first. If we decide to consider your application, then you will be given the proper instructions."

Melanie visualized the woman on the phone. Tall, stern, with waist-length hair pulled back in a tight bun. She thought of the children in her care. She decided to act quickly.

"Then I would like to make an appointment as soon as possible."

Another deep sigh, then the fluttering of paper. Melanie wondered if the woman was actually looking at an old-fashioned appointment book. Had computers not made their way to the adoption agency?

"You are in luck," the woman said. "We have an opening in the morning on Monday. Nine o'clock sharp. We do not tolerate tardiness."

Melanie's eyes practically bulged out of their sockets. She couldn't believe the way the woman spoke to her. She wasn't a two-year-old. She wanted to tell her that, but bit her tongue. Now wasn't the time to be a smart aleck. Briefly, she had the passing thought—if she was so punctual, why didn't she answer the phone at *eight o'clock sharp*?

"Of course not. I will be there promptly at nine."

"Of course you will," the woman admonished. "I will need some information from you first."

Melanie was on the phone for the next few minutes, giving the woman, who hadn't bothered to give her name, all the pertinent information one would need to run for president of the United States. When she hung up, it took a couple of minutes for Melanie to reacquaint herself with her surroundings. She was home in Placerville, in her kitchen. Images of prison camps kept flashing before her eyes. Those poor children!

The woman reminded her of a female version of Scrooge. Wired from too much caffeine, Melanie decided it was a good time to take Odie for that promised extra-long walk. The cold morning air would clear her head, plus she could burn off all her excess energy.

"Odie, let's go take that walk I promised you," she said as she grabbed her jacket from the front closet and removed his leash from a hook on the back of the front door. Upon hearing his name, Odie came running from his spot underneath the kitchen table before sliding to a stop in order for her to attach the leash to his collar. When all was in order, he jumped in circles, practically dragging her out the front door. Clovis remained perched on the windowsill in the living room, his nose in the air, apparently content to watch.

Melanie pushed the door aside and was greeted by an icy gust of frosty air. She drew in a sharp breath. It was much colder than yesterday. Even colder than it had been a few hours ago. Single-digit temperatures were predicted for the day's high.

The condo's greenway provided twelve miles of biking trails and hiking paths to satisfy all of the residents living at Pine Ridge Condominiums. As Melanie carefully wound her way down the main trail, she saw that the picnic tables were covered with a thin sheet of ice, and the dog pond that Odie loved to visit in the summer months was completely frozen over.

Once inside the off-leash area, Melanie unhooked Odie's leash, and he ran freely. Often they would see coyotes and the occasional fox, and Odie would go berserk upon catching their scent. Apparently the cold weather hadn't kept the wild animals away from the area, because Odie had his nose to the frozen ground, sniffing ninety miles a minute.

Melanie allowed Odie a few more minutes to do his business before calling to him. "Okay, bud, let's take that walk I promised." The dog would've been content to stay in the off-leash area, but Melanie knew from experience that if she let him stay too long, it would take forever to guide him back to the hiking path.

Several inches of thick-crusted snow flanked the path leading to her preferred route. Expertly, Melanie and Odie ascended the icy mound leading to her favorite trail, where in the fall one could view a pumpkin farm along the hillside. Spring green vines dotted the mountain in late summer, after which the hillside became infused with varying shades of orange in the fall. It never failed to take her breath away. Even in the stark bareness of late fall, Melanie could appreciate the Colorado beauty. Tall pines scented the chilled air, and she detected a faint hint of wood smoke. Briefly, she had a flash of herself running through the pumpkin fields with two small children at her side.

Two?

Not wanting to get her hopes up, she'd tried to close her mind to this morning's earlier conversation with the woman from the adoption agency. The possibility of one child more than excited her, but two? She allowed herself to imagine her life with two children. If the opportunity arose, she wouldn't deny herself or the children. She'd taken care of Amanda and Ashley quite well if you excluded their getting lost on the mountain last year. The image cut off further thought. What if the woman from the adoption agency asked for a reference? What if Stephanie told the woman that she wasn't ready for a child of her own? What if . . . what if . . . what if? Melanie knew her life would be closely scrutinized, she'd learned that much on her Web search.

Could one innocent mistake ruin her future chances at adoption?

Resigned that she might have to give up her dream of adopting a child, Melanie led Odie toward the condo. Maybe she'd just call and cancel Monday's appointment.

Maybe.

No!

Melanie was not a quitter.

She'd cross that bridge Monday morning. Nine o'clock sharp.

Chapter 4

Melanie spent most of Sunday morning scrubbing her condo from top to bottom. With two animals in the house, she was constantly vacuuming and dusting. She planned to spend the day curled up with a book and a pot of tea. It was minus three, too cold to venture outdoors. She wanted to get to bed early. Rather than drive six hours to Denver the next morning, she'd hired a private jet to fly her there. She was meeting the pilot and copilot at 6:00 A.M. She'd arranged for a rental car to make the drive from the airport to the adoption agency. She'd scheduled her return flight for two forty-five, so she would be home by early evening.

She phoned her mother asking if she could stop over around lunchtime to let Odie out. As always, her mother was glad to help. When she'd asked why she was flying to Denver, Melanie had clammed up. She didn't want to tell anyone what her plans were just yet, but she didn't want to lie to her mother, so she explained that she was taking a personal day to do something she'd been planning on for a while. A generic answer, but it was all she could come up with. Her mother didn't pry, and, for that, she was glad.

Melanie located her briefcase in her office, then added most of the important documents she would need to prove she was who she said she was and a dozen other papers she might need. She added her passport, just in case. She wanted to be prepared. It wasn't like they were going to look at her bank statement, and say, "Pick a child." No, the adoption process was much more detailed than even she could imagine.

Mandatory legal criteria had to be met, plus each individual agency had its own criteria as well. Melanie was amazed at the amount of paperwork required, but something as important as adopting a child *should* take a lot of paperwork. Once her application was accepted, *if* it was accepted, then the lengthy process would begin. She wasn't in a mad rush, but she knew in her heart that it was right for her. Felt it in her bones. Patience was required, and she was a very patient woman. Melanie knew one of the first requirements would be a home study, and if she was lucky enough, she would be able to bring a child home, where she would then be allowed to help the child make the transition from the orphanage to the new home.

Odie and Clovis had positioned themselves beneath the kitchen table. Melanie removed the teakettle from the stovetop, filled it with tap water, then placed it back on the burner. She took three chamomile tea bags from a bright yellow canister on the counter and dropped them in the small china teapot given to her by her grandmother when she was a little girl. In order to keep the tea warm, Melanie placed a cosy, one she had knitted years ago, around the teapot.

Maybe when Amanda and Ashley finished their pot

holders, she would teach them how to make tea cosies. She knew that Stephanie loved to drink tea and would appreciate such a gift from her girls.

Melanie's tea ritual was old-fashioned, but she loved it. Her grandmother had taught her the proper way to steep loose leaf tea, how to pour properly, and also how to hold a delicate teacup. Though she didn't practice this all the time, whenever she had company, or the occasion called for it, she returned to the ways taught by her grandmother. The kettle whistled, and Melanie filled the delicate china pot with boiling water. She placed the teapot along with a bright red mug on a tray and carried them into the living room. Odie and Clovis followed.

As soon as she settled herself on the sofa with her tea and favorite author, the telephone rang.

"Why did I know this would happen the minute I got comfortable?" Melanie asked her boon companions. As usual, Odie and Clovis answered her question by trailing behind her as she returned to the kitchen to answer the telephone.

"Hello," she said into the receiver.

"Oh good, you're there," Stephanie said.

Melanie smiled upon hearing her friend's voice. "What's up?"

"I wasn't sure I'd find you at home," Stephanie explained.

Melanie leaned against the island in the center of the kitchen. "Where else would I be?" She looked at the clock and realized she was usually in church at this time. Because of bad weather, Melanie had decided to stay home today. She said this to Stephanie.

"Same here. Patrick and I both took the weekend off. We wanted to take the girls skiing again, but it's really too cold. You're never going to believe who's coming to visit this afternoon."

"Why don't you tell me?" Melanie teased.

"Grace and Max are bringing baby Ella. The girls are so excited."

"Cool," Melanie said without much emotion. She'd just seen Grace, Max, and Ella a couple of weeks ago.

"Bryce is coming with them. Apparently, he's taking a month off from teaching, and he's planning to spend his time helping Grace and Max at Hope House," Stephanie said.

Melanie knew where this was leading. She had met Bryce, Grace's younger brother, a few times. He was a professor of history at the University of Colorado in Boulder. He was a couple of years older than she, and very easy on the eyes. With his raven black hair, and sea green eyes identical to his older sister's, Bryce Landry personified hunkiness if there was such a thing. If she'd met him without knowing his academic background, never in a million years would she have pegged him for a history professor. He looked more like the ski bums that hung out at the ski resorts. Melanie knew he was an avid skier; he'd been a big fan of Max's when he won the Olympic gold medal. Grace told Melanie how excited Bryce had been when he discovered his older sister was dating such a legend in the ski world.

"That's nice," was the only comment Melanie could come up with. She must sound like an idiot, she thought, as she eyed her pot of tea in the living room.

"I'm having an impromptu Christmas party this afternoon. Do you think you can make it? I know it's short notice," Stephanie added.

Melanie didn't really have any plans other than reading and getting ready for tomorrow's flight to Denver. Why not? Stephanie lived right down the road from her; it wasn't like she had to travel on I-70, which was treacherous during the winter months. It would take her mind off the adoption and help pass the time.

"Sounds like fun. What can I bring?" Melanie asked, looking around the kitchen for something to bring, a store-bought pie, anything that didn't require cooking or baking. Seeing nothing, she remembered she had a frozen black forest cake in the freezer, courtesy of a happy client.

"You don't have to bring anything, just yourself," Stephanie assured her.

Melanie would bring the cake anyway; she could not eat the entire chocolate concoction herself. It would take hours of skiing to burn off the calories. "I'd love to see the girls. What time are the festivities?"

"Any time after noon," Stephanie said. "The girls are bursting with energy at the mere thought of a Christmas party," Stephanie continued. "We've never hosted a Christmas party, so I figured the earlier, the better. Amanda is already mixing the ingredients for sugar cookies. If the kitchen's a disaster when you get here, you'll know why."

Just thinking of the visual, Melanie grinned. Stephanie was very neat and tidy, yet when it came to Amanda and Ashley, she was more than willing to allow whatever made them happy. Both girls loved to tinker in the kitchen, just like their mother. In time, they would learn how to clean up as they worked.

"Okay, I'll see you in a few," Melanie said, and hung up the phone. She gazed longingly at her now-cooled pot of tea and the new book she'd been dying to sink her teeth into. There was always another day to do nothing but lounge around and read.

But maybe not, she thought as she scooped up the tray carefully and placed the treasured old teapot and her mug in the sink.

If she were lucky, soon she'd be too busy to lounge

around. Hopefully, by this time next year, she'd have a family of her own to take care of.

She crossed her fingers and said a quick prayer.

A child of her own. Could life get any better? she thought as she raced through the condo like a kid at Christmas.

Chapter 5

Cars and four-wheel-drive vehicles were filling the driveway as Melanie parked her Navigator on the street at the edge of the snow-and-ice-covered lawn. Balancing a plastic-covered cake container in one hand and her purse and car keys in the other, she lifted an Ugg-booted foot to close the car door.

The small sidewalk leading to the front porch steps had been cleared of all snow and ice, courtesy of Patrick. Before Melanie had a chance to figure out how to press the doorbell, Ashley opened the front door.

"Auntie M, you came! Ella is here and so are her mom and dad," she said excitedly, as Melanie stepped inside the warm, festively decorated house.

Melanie laid her purse on an antique bench, careful to keep a tight grip on the cake container. She stooped down to Ashley's eye level and gave her a one-armed hug. "Of course I did. I wouldn't miss your Christmas party for all the money in the world," Melanie said. Ashley grabbed her free hand and led her to the kitchen, where Stephanie was standing in front of the sink.

"Look, Mom, Auntie M brought a cake."

Stephanie rinsed her hands off, and dried them with a paper towel. She took the cake container out of Melanie's hands and placed it on the counter next to three other cakes.

"Should've kept it, huh?" Melanie said as she spied the desserts.

Stephanie leaned in for a quick hug, then stood back, grinning at her friend. "Nah, Patrick's here. He'll take care of whatever leftovers we have," Stephanie assured her. "Bryce has been asking about you."

Blushing, Melanie shook her head. "He's just being polite, Steph." She wished everyone would stop trying to throw her and Bryce in one another's path. She'd met him more than once, and, yes, he was attractive, and, yes, she liked him, but she had a feeling Bryce wasn't into the "healthy, outdoor type" such as her. No, he probably preferred tall, skinny blondes with little or no brains. He was just too good-looking, she kept thinking. Men like him didn't date women with brains. She looked at her faded jeans and snow-covered Uggs. Definitely a Colorado kind of girl. It didn't matter that she wore a Stella McCartney sweater, or that her blond hair was really *her* blond hair. Guys like Bryce went for the glamour girls.

"Melanie, how are you? It's been too long," Bryce Landry said as he entered the kitchen.

Melanie's heart did a double beat when she felt him come up behind her. She took a deep breath. She could actually smell him. He smelled like winter. Pine and something else she couldn't identify. She felt her face turning ten shades of red. Thankful he couldn't read her mind, she turned to face him, and said, "Thanks, it's nice to see you, too, Bryce. You're right, it's been too long." She cringed at her words. What if he thought she'd been fantasizing about him?

Melanie couldn't help but admire Bryce's good looks. He certainly wore them well, she'd give him that. Dressed in a black turtleneck sweater and black jeans, his ebony hair hanging over his ears and down the back of his neck, he was extremely sexy, certainly not the look of a history professor, or at least any that she'd had in college. He stepped away from her as though he just realized he'd been standing in her personal space a bit too long. He had both hands out in front of him, fingertips upward, palms splayed up and out, as though he were trying to physically push himself away from her.

Melanie felt his gaze. She glanced at him before turning back to Stephanie. She could still feel his eyes boring a hole into her back. Without thinking, she whirled around and turned to face him.

"Is there something else?" The words were out of her mouth before she had a chance to stop them.

Bryce smiled at her. "Yes, actually there is. I want a piece of that cake you brought. I didn't know you were a baker. Thought it might be nice to sample the wares."

Melanie felt sucker punched, right in the middle of her stomach. Was he implying what she *thought* he was implying?

Sample the wares . . .

Apparently he caught his faux pas. He nodded at the row of cake dishes on the countertop. "There are four cakes to choose from. I wanted to try yours first."

Before Melanie or Bryce could put their feet into their mouths again, Stephanie removed a saucer from the cabinet and a fork from the drawer and handed them to Bryce. "Try them all."

He took the saucer, fork, and a cake knife Stephanie held out for him. He sliced into the black forest cake, hefting a giant slice onto his plate. Digging his fork into the chocolate confection, he crammed his mouth full.

Melanie couldn't take her eyes off his mouth. Why hadn't she noticed before how sexy his mouth was? A full upper lip, and the lower, slightly thinner. And that one front tooth, it was slightly crooked. Mesmerized, she stared at him while he devoured the cake.

Stephanie cleared her throat so loudly it startled Melanie. She took a deep breath and started coughing, which then turned into choking. She bent over gasping for air. Taking as deep a breath as her coughing would allow, she inhaled and exhaled a few times before getting her throat to open up again. Drooling like a thirsty dog, Melanie wiped her mouth with the sleeve of her Stella McCartney sweater. Stephanie handed her a glass of water.

"I must confess, I don't always have this effect on women," Bryce said.

Melanie looked at him over the rim of her glass. Before she could stop herself, she tossed the rest of the water in Bryce's face.

"Oh my gosh, I'm so sorry! I don't know—"

Bryce lifted his clingy black sweater over the top of his head, revealing a most perfect six-pack. He slung the garment over his shoulder, a grin the size of the moon on his handsome face.

"I'm not going to ask why you did that because I know you're going to tell me."

Mortified, humiliated, and *ashamed* didn't begin to describe what she was feeling. "I don't know what . . . I am so *sorry*! I have no clue why . . ." There wasn't anything she could say to defend her action. She was as baffled as the next person.

Stephanie passed Bryce a wad of paper towels. He mopped up the remaining drops of water on his face.

I should have stayed at home with my book and my teapot, Melanie thought. Appalled by her actions, she tried to come up with an explanation, but couldn't. Maybe it was just one of those knee-jerk reactions, something in her subconscious. Whatever it was, she'd never been quite as embarrassed as she was now. Shaking her head from side to side, Melanie looked at the floor, then her gaze traveled up a pair of heavily muscled black-clad legs. When her eyes came to rest on his flat abs, she looked up quickly and focused her gaze on Bryce's sculpted face. "I'm sorry. I have no idea why I did that." Lame, she knew, but she had no other explanation to offer.

Bryce tossed the crumpled paper towels in the garbage can, then slipped the black sweater back over his head. Melanie could see the darker spots where the water had soaked the wool. On the positive side, at least no one but Stephanie had witnessed her act of stupidity.

"Stop apologizing," Bryce said with a sly grin. "It was only water. I'm just lucky it wasn't coffee."

Melanie focused on her surroundings, because she had a fear that if she didn't, she might do or say something else out of character: oak cabinets. Dark brown granite countertops, flour scattered all over the top. Cream-colored curtain above the bronze sink. Stove. Refrigerator. Dishwasher. Cake containers on the countertop. A burning smell.

Okay, she was focused. Now if she could keep her hand under control, she'd survive until she could safely come up with an excuse to leave! Fire, the place was on fire!

"Something's on fire," Bryce said casually as though he were talking about the weather.

"Oh my gosh! The cookies!" Stephanie grabbed two oven mitts, and yanked the oven door open. Gray smoke billowed out in one giant puff. She carefully pulled a baking sheet topped with little black mounds of what must've been meant to be cookies out of the oven. Stephanie dumped the ruined cookies in the sink. "I can't believe I forgot the cookies! I promised the girls they could decorate them." Stephanie shook her head and began scrubbing the burnt mess off the baking sheet.

"It's my fault, Steph. I'm sorry. I'm going to visit the girls and Ella, then go home. I can't seem to do anything right these days," Melanie said, irritated at herself. If she hadn't tossed that water at Bryce, the cookies wouldn't have burnt.

"Oh stop it, you two," Bryce said. "It's cookies. I say let the girls start a new batch. Let's air the place out first." He leaned over the sink and raised the window. A small gust of icy-cold air filled the room.

Bryce grabbed a kitchen towel, fanning the smoke toward the window. Melanie grabbed a place mat off the small table and followed Bryce's moves. Stephanie backed away from the sink, allowing them the room they needed to fan the smoke toward the window.

Melanie hoped this scene wasn't indicative of her future. If so, her hopes of adopting would surely go up in smoke.

Chapter 6

The early-morning air was bone-chillingly cold. Melanie parked her Lincoln Navigator inside the hangar and followed the airport attendant to the small jet waiting on the tarmac. Holding her documents against her chest, she climbed the small steps leading inside the plane.

She was seated and buckled in when the copilot offered her a cup of coffee from a thermos.

"Thanks, I needed this." He handed her a Styrofoam cup full of the steaming-hot brew. She breathed in the aromatic scent, loving the smell of it. She had overslept and hadn't had enough time to make a pot of coffee or much of anything else. She'd grabbed her makeup kit and a bright red sweater to put on later in addition to the jeans she'd barely had time to slip into. Grateful she'd showered and washed her hair the night before, she hoped she wasn't going to be judged on her appearance. Because if that was the case, she could forget about adopting a child.

If she couldn't dress herself, why would anyone think her capable of dressing a child? Or anything associated with a child. Maybe the whole idea was a pipe dream and nothing more.

No, it was not a pipe dream. She was ready for this, knew in her heart this was the correct path for her. If the agency didn't approve her application, she would just accept that now was not the time for her to make a life-changing decision.

Melanie felt the pressure as the jet lifted off the tarmac. Takeoff was her favorite part of flying, giving her an instant rush. Once they had reached their assigned altitude, she relaxed. The flight was only one hour, just enough time to ponder last night's dinner with Bryce. She still couldn't believe she had gone to dinner with him, let alone made plans for a second date. Yesterday was just full of surprises.

She still had no clue why she had tossed a glass of water in his face. That would have to remain a mystery for a while yet. Once they'd cleared the kitchen of all the smoke and mess, she had helped the girls make a second batch of cookies, the slice-and-bake kind, but they'd had fun in spite of the smoky start.

She'd had a great visit with Max and Grace. Baby Ella was just starting to walk, and seeing the little girl convinced her even more that she was making the right decision. They'd spent the remainder of the afternoon laughing, talking, and sharing their plans for the upcoming holiday. When Melanie was reminded that Bryce was going to be hanging around until after the first of the year, she couldn't help but feel a little bit excited. After she'd gotten over her initial bout of mortification, courtesy of Bryce's easygoing manner, she'd relaxed. They'd talked about everything from the ski conditions to their preference for dark or light turkey meat.

Melanie couldn't believe she'd never taken the time to

learn much more than superficial things about Grace's younger brother. They'd been around one another long enough to get to know each other, but Melanie had made the assumption that he was not interested in her or anything she had to say, so she'd kept her distance.

Now, here she was about to make a drastic change to her life, and all she could think about was their upcoming date, midmorning tomorrow. They'd planned a day of skiing, and both decided if they weren't too tired, they'd try out that new Italian restaurant everyone was raving about.

Melanie grinned. Life was good, and if she had anything to say about it—and she did—it was about to get even better.

The plane landed as scheduled, and her rental car was parked where it should be. She'd asked that the car be equipped with a GPS. She recalled the woman from the adoption agency's words: *Nine o'clock sharp.* So far, everything was going according to plan.

She programmed the GPS with the adoption agency's address. While she waited for the information to reach some satellite in space, she checked her hastily applied makeup in the rearview mirror, tucked a few loose strands of hair back into her topknot. She'd changed into her red sweater before getting inside her rental car. Yes, things were going just the way she wanted them to. Smooth as silk.

It was already 7:30 A.M., and the traffic was bumper to bumper on Denver's I-70. Miles of red taillights stretched out on the road before her. At this rate, she'd be lucky to make her nine o'clock appointment. Slowly, she crept down the heavily trafficked highway. Twenty minutes later, she looked again at the bright green digital clock on the dashboard, then back at the GPS stuck to the windshield. According to the directions, she would arrive at World Adoption Agency in fifty-seven minutes. Somehow this didn't seem possible with all the traffic, but she knew the GPS also tracked your speed, so she would trust the gizmo to do what it was supposed to do.

In her peripheral vision, Melanie saw where several of Denver's large businesses had decorated their office buildings with elaborate displays of colored lights, giant blow-up Santa Clauses, snowmen, and the usual array of decorations. If she'd had more time, she would have taken the exit to get a closer look at some of the outrageous decorations, but she would do that another time. At the moment, she had more important things to do. If she were lucky, this time next year she would have a child of her own to take to view the elaborate Christmas decorations.

Briefly, she wondered what Bryce would say about her plans. She shook her head; it didn't matter what he or anyone else thought. She'd made a decision, and she would do her part to see that her plans came to fruition.

The traffic started moving faster, and thirty minutes later, the electronic female voice told her that her exit was one mile on the right.

Butterflies danced in her stomach as she weaved her way through the back streets that led to the adoption agency. The female voice told her she had arrived. She didn't know what she had been expecting, but she knew she hadn't expected what she was seeing. She pulled into the asphalt parking lot and turned the engine off, wondering if she'd been given the wrong address.

A flat-roofed brick building, which at one time might have been an old school building or a county government facility, was surrounded by a tall wire fence. There were no swings in the side yard, no merry-go-rounds, no type of equipment that would indicate children lived here. Her heart sank. This picture certainly did not match the one she saw on the Internet. Thinking it was possible the Web site designers had gone a bit overboard when they'd created the Web site, in hopes of luring potential parents, Melanie walked down a cracked sidewalk that led to a steel door with faded black and gold letters that read OF-FICE. She looked at her watch. She was a few minutes early. Not knowing if she should knock on the door or simply step inside, Melanie went with her gut and opened the door.

Melanie stepped inside to a dimly lit reception area. A grayish green metal desk, clear of the usual clutter, with a sturdy wooden chair tucked beneath it stood in the center of the room. Behind the desk on the wall facing her were several tall gray metal filing cabinets. She looked to her left and right in hopes of finding another desk, maybe a desk with a computer on it, but saw nothing except for a few small wooden chairs pushed up against the wall. It was obvious the chairs were for children, not guests.

As Melanie was about to wander down the long hall-way to her left, she heard the *click-clack* of heels coming from the opposite end of the hall. She remained in place, smoothed any imaginary wrinkles from her jeans, and took a deep breath. It was now or never. Exhaling as she'd been taught in her yoga class, she let her breath out slowly. She watched the tall figure make her way down the dark hallway toward the front reception area.

Where were all the children? she wondered. Surely they were up and about by now. But then she realized that they had probably already left for school.

In the same nasally accented voice she'd heard on the phone, the tall figure called out as she made her way over to the desk. "You must be Mrs. McLaughlin."

She was the exact image that her voice and manner projected over the telephone. Sturdily built, steel gray hair pulled back in a bun so tight her eyes were pulled up-ward. She wore a brown wool suit, thick stockings, and ugly black shoes with large square heels. It was the sort of outfit that brought to mind a warden in a medium-security prison for women. "Well, are you going to answer me or not?" she asked.

"Yes, I'm she . . . I am Melanie McLaughlin."

"Follow me," the still-unnamed woman said.

Melanie did as instructed. She traveled the length of the dark hallway, the woman's broad back blocking her view of what lay beyond. At the end of the hall was a small office, this one a bit more personal. There was a wooden desk with a banker's lamp placed to her right. And two matching chairs, both of which might have been light blue at one time but were now as gray as the rest of the surroundings, were placed on the opposite side of the desk.

The woman walked around and slid her chair from beneath the desk. She sat down, rifled through a stack of papers on her desk, then gave Melanie a nod, indicating she should sit.

"You have all of your paperwork in order?" the woman said flatly, her voice displaying not the slightest bit of emotion. Melanie was beginning to regret her choice of adoption agencies. This woman was simply rude—not having bothered even to introduce herself.

She placed the file folder of papers she'd brought, along with her passport, on the desk. "I think so. I brought along a few extra things." The woman stared at her as though she could see right through her. "Just in case," Melanie added in a small voice.

"You think? If you're not sure you've brought the required documents, how is one to assume you're capable of caring for a child?" The woman, whose name she still didn't know, reminded her of the assistant principal in the movie *Uncle Buck*. John Candy in his role as Uncle Buck had told the hateful old woman to take a quarter and pay a rat to gnaw the giant wart off her face. Though the discourteous woman across from Melanie lacked the giant wart, she might as well have been that character come to life. Just thinking about the comedic scene made Melanie smile.

"You think this is funny?" the woman asked, her voice rising in anger.

Melanie wasn't going to allow herself to be treated this way one second longer. "Not that it's any of your concern, *madam,* but I was smiling at a memory that has absolutely nothing to do with my paperwork."

There, now, if the headmistress, or whatever this harridan was called, asked her to leave, Melanie would just take it as a sign that this wasn't the right agency for her.

"This isn't the place for silly thoughts, Mrs. McLaughlin. World Adoption Agency requires our prospective parents to be serious and mature. If you feel you cannot meet these requirements, please don't waste any more of my time than you have already."

Melanie was minute by minute becoming more convinced that this shrew had come directly from central casting, an exact replica of the much-hated character in the *Uncle Buck* movie. But having traveled all the way to Denver, Melanie decided that she might as well play out what was rapidly turning into a farce to the end, no matter how rude and bossy the woman was.

Practically biting her tongue, Melanie said politely, "Of course not, *Mrs. . . .*" Maybe before she left, she'd at least know the woman's name.

"Olga Krause," the woman said.

Surprised at her name, Melanie almost fell out of the sagging chair. She hoped this wasn't some kind of joke, some new adoption-based reality television show. Because if it was, she wasn't laughing. This was too unreal to be real. This was starting to sound crazy.

"Mrs. Krause," Melanie said as *maturely* as she could,

"I am more than ready to start whatever proceedings are required by this agency. You asked me to bring those documents." She nodded toward the manila folder in Mrs. Krause's hand. "And I did. If there is anything more I need to bring, I assume you will inform me. I've never attempted to adopt a child before. I'm not practiced in this procedure, but will be once we get through this initial screening."

Melanie waited while Mrs. Krause went through the paperwork. She glanced around the small room, looking for a picture, a knickknack, anything that would show some personality, but she observed nothing that would indicate the room was someone's personal space. She decided that the faded blue chairs were as personal as it was going to get. She waited for another few minutes.

"I'm going to need to make copies of your documents. I will be right back," Mrs. Krause inched away from her desk.

"Those are your copies. I have the originals here if you need to see them," Melanie added, thinking *anything to speed up the procedure.*

She'd yet to hear one sound that would indicate there were children present.

"Well, that was very thoughtful of you, I must say." Mrs. Krause slid her chair closer to the desk. She stacked the papers until the edges were perfectly aligned.

Shocked at the positive words, Melanie remained silent, fearful that if she said anything, it would disrupt Mrs. Krause's train of thought.

After several uncomfortable minutes, the woman spoke up. "Your paperwork appears to be in order. Before we can proceed, we must first run a criminal background check. Once those results are in, and if they are in order, we will proceed to step two."

Melanie wanted to roll her eyes, but refrained. Images

of needy children kept flashing in front of her. However, she didn't want to stay in the room any longer than necessary, so she spoke up. "And may I ask what step two consists of?"

"I can tell by your question you did not fully read through the information provided on our Web site."

And here we go again, Melanie thought, as she waited for Mrs. Olga Krause to enlighten her.

"Each agency has certain criteria that must be met as you know since you read all of the fine print." Mrs. Krause paused, her wicked brown eyes staring at Melanie as though she'd committed a crime. "Since this agency receives state funds, we require a private meeting with your husband before we can schedule an interview with both of you together as a couple."

Melanie felt like she'd just been slammed with the old proverbial ton of bricks.

A husband.

Olga Krause was absolutely correct. She had missed *that* part of the fine print.

Chapter 7

Melanie inserted her key in the front door and hurried to unlock it. Odie was reclining against the door. Melanie slowly pushed the door inward, letting the dog know it was safe to move.

She let the boxer jump up and lick her face. Clovis rubbed against her leg. *The best part of owning pets*, Melanie thought. Returning home. They were always glad to see you no matter what kind of mood you were in. And she was in a very, *very* rotten mood. She'd stewed on the drive back to the airport, stewed on the short flight to Placerville, and continued stewing on the drive home.

"Give me a second, Odie, and we'll make a quick trip outside." She kicked off her black leather boots and replaced them with the Uggs she always kept by the front door. She hung her purse on the knob next to Odie's leash. "Clovis, you wait right here." She rubbed the cat's head before snapping Odie's leash to his collar.

Being late afternoon, it was almost dark. Melanie didn't like this part of late fall, *but it is what it is*, she thought as she led Odie to the greenway. A walk in the frigid air would do her good. Clear her mind a bit.

Shivering, Melanie led Odie to the off-leash area. She unhooked him. "Three minutes, bud, and that's it. Too cold for animals and humans," she muttered to herself.

While she waited for the dog to make his rounds, she revisited the scene at the adoption agency. Mrs. Krause— *Miss* Krause, she'd informed her as Melanie was leaving—told her not to expect a phone call from the agency unless her background check came back clean. She'd treated her like a criminal, but Melanie knew it wasn't personal. The old woman was a spinster, probably treated all prospective parents the same way. Still, she didn't see how she could've missed such vital information on the Web site. She was going to reread every bit of fine print. Twice.

"Okay, Odie, your three minutes are up." Like the obedient animal he was, he came out of the off-leash area, stopping in front of her when she held the leash out.

It had to be at least twenty below, she thought, as she jogged back to the condo. No one in their right mind should be out in this weather. At the moment, however, she wasn't in her right mind. She felt like a total and complete idiot. Of course she had forgotten to mention to Miss Krause that there wouldn't be a need for her to run that background check since she didn't have a husband. But something had stopped her from revealing that important bit of info to the old woman. Why? She didn't know, but went with her gut instinct and simply said good-bye before racing out to her rental car. Once inside, she'd almost had a panic attack! *How could I have missed such vital information?*

Inside, Odie shook off the wet snow before resuming his position beneath the kitchen table. Clovis jumped on the countertop in search of his evening meal. Melanie removed a can of cat food from the pantry, flipped off the aluminum lid, and dumped the stinky contents in Clovis's bowl before placing the bowl on the kitty mat by the back door. Odie dragged himself out from under the table, apparently remembering it was dinnertime. Melanie scooped a large portion of kibble into his bowl. "Okay, you two. Now let's see what the human is going to have for dinner."

She opened the refrigerator, but didn't see anything that appealed to her. Not that she was hungry. She grabbed an apple out of the bowl in the center island. She wanted to cool down, to wait a bit before she went back to the agency's Web site, but she couldn't.

Inside her office, Melanie munched on her apple while she waited for her computer to boot up. Did it always take this long? A few seconds later, she heard the familiar hum. She clicked onto the Internet and found the agency's Web site. She read all the fine print, then read through it a second time. And a third time, just to make sure she wasn't losing it. Nowhere did it say one had to be married to petition for an adoption. She clicked on all the pages a fourth time, went through all the links one by one, and still didn't see anything stating that only married couples could adopt.

That Miss Krause was a true old bat, she thought as she clicked through the pages. Spiteful. Maybe she had an unhappy life and wanted to make those around her as miserable as she was. Knowing all hope wasn't lost, if push came to shove, she would have the law on her side since there was absolutely nothing saying a potential parent had to be married. Miss Krause was mistaken, there was no other explanation.

Stay hopeful, that's what she would do. If this agency

didn't work out, she'd simply find one that would. Single parents adopted children all the time. Maybe Miss Krause was new to the job. "Nah, I doubt it," she said out loud. The poor old woman was probably childless, with no family to speak of. Melanie did a mental three-sixty.

That could be me, thirty years down the road.

Chapter 8

The sun shone like a brilliant goldenrod. Though the temperatures were in the mid-teens, Melanie wasn't the least bit cold. She wore the latest in outdoor wear, her favorite top-of-the-line Spyder Gear, which promised to keep its wearer warm in temperatures much colder than that day's.

She'd dropped Odie and Clovis off at The Snow Zone, knowing Stephanie was there by herself. Candy Lee was out of town with her parents, so Melanie knew that the animals would keep Stephanie company. Not that she'd have much time for them, because the store was jam-packed with customers when she'd dropped the pair off, but Melanie knew having Odie around was an added comfort for Stephanie.

She'd agreed to meet Bryce at the chairlifts at ten o'clock. She glanced at her weatherproof wristwatch. Ten of. She'd left early, allowing herself the extra time needed to drop the animals off. She put her skis and poles on the metal rack alongside dozens of others. In all the years she'd been skiing, she'd never had anything taken. Ski bums were good people. Skiing was not a poor man or woman's sport. The equipment was extremely expensive, the price of the lift tickets outrageous. The food in the lodge was quadruple the normal rate. But it was a sport that one either liked or not.

Melanie loved to ski, loved the freedom, and, more than anything, loved being outdoors. Her work kept her rooted to her desk, so when she had the opportunity to get away from it all, she took it.

She supposed you could call today a date. Sort of. Not a traditional date, where the guy knocked on your door with flowers, walked you to the car, and held the door open. In all honesty, Melanie couldn't recall ever having a date like that, but the fantasy was nice. No, she and Bryce had agreed to meet right here at the chairlift. She paid her way, he paid his. She liked it better that way because she didn't feel the slightest bit obligated to "pay back" in a manner she wasn't comfortable with.

Even though it was still early by ski-bum standards, the lift lines were longer than normal. While she waited, she observed the beginners at the bunny hill. People of all ages dressed in every color of the rainbow were either wedging, or, as the instructors taught the little ones, "pizza-ing" down the small hill. Those who were better balanced positioned their skis side by side and "french-fried" their way up and down the mini slope. The unlucky ones lay sprawled on the snow, struggling to bring themselves upright, so they could try one more time to make it down without falling.

"I remember those days well," Bryce said. He'd come up beside her without her noticing. He tapped her on the nose. "Earth to Melanie." Wearing his skis, he couldn't get much closer to her without tripping over them.

Melanie whirled around. "Hi, Bryce. You sneaked up on me, no fair! I don't have my skis on yet. Give me a second," she said, then raced over to the racks, where she removed her skis and poles and placed them flat on the ground. She clicked each boot into the proper position and adjusted her gloves before poling back to the chairlift.

"Okay, now I'm fair game," Melanie said as she slid into place beside him.

"Blue or black?" Bryce asked as they poled their way to the front of the line.

Melanie raised her eyebrows. "A daredevil now, are we? I never would've guessed. Let's start with a blue run, then we'll see how things progress. I'm not as young as I used to be," she said teasingly.

Bryce laughed, showing that one crooked tooth. *Sexy as ever,* Melanie thought as she laughed with him. Why hadn't she noticed that before? *Doesn't matter,* she thought, as they stood waiting for the chair to tap the back of their knees. *I'm here now.*

In one giant swing, they were airborne. Bryce lowered the protective railing before sliding closer to her. "I'm scared."

Both burst out laughing. "A college professor, and you can't come up with a better pickup line than that?"

He inched closer, so close in fact that she could smell his minty breath. Melanie was glad they had on their heavy outerwear. She did not want to see those flat six-pack abs, or his well-muscled chest, not even a hint at what he looked like under all that down. At least not yet.

"I thought we were past that," Bryce teased.

The lift stopped midway up the mountain. They were dangling on the topside of a mountain, and neither seemed to notice. The gears ground, then they resumed the climb.

"You did, huh?" Melanie replied.

"Yeah, I did," Bryce said, "so let me see what I can

come up with." Bryce placed his index finger on his cheek as though he were in deep thought. "How about a little Shakespeare?"

He cleared his throat, then began,

Shall I compare thee to a summer's day?
Thou art more lovely and more temperate:
Rough winds do shake the darling buds of May,
And summer's lease hath all too short a date:
Sometime too hot the eye of heaven shines,
And often is his gold complexion dimm'd;
And every fair from fair sometime declines,
By chance or nature's changing course untrimm'd;
But thy eternal summer shall not fade
Nor lose possession of that fair thou owest;
Nor shall Death brag thou wander'st in his shade,
When in eternal lines to time thou growest:
So long as men can breathe or eyes can see,
So long lives this and this gives life to thee.

"How's that?" he asked when he'd finished.

"If you don't hurry up and raise the bar, we're gonna be in trouble," Melanie said as they came within a few feet of their drop-off point.

Bryce slid across the seat, checked to make sure their skis and poles were out of the way, then raised the bar. They inched as close to the edge of the seat as possible, raising their ski tips. As soon as they could feel the heavily packed snow beneath them, they shoved off the lift and skied to an area where they wouldn't be in the way of the other skiers and snowboarders. Skiing had its rules.

Both adjusted their goggles and helmets. Bryce pointed to an easy blue run. Melanie nodded, then shoved off. The run was packed with people, and Melanie had to use every ounce of her skill to maneuver between them without tripping over the fallen skier or snowboarder. She whizzed through a group of students, then heard a loud thump behind her. She slowed down to look behind her, but all she saw was a flash of royal blue as Bryce practically flew past her.

"So he wants to play rough. I'll show him rough." Melanie leaned down and forward, increasing her speed. Seeing that the bowl ahead was scattered with skiers of every skill, Melanie made a quick decision, turning left on the trail, which would lead her to a shortcut. Not many knew about it, but this was an emergency. Kind of. She laughed. Yes, it was off the map, but no way was Mr. Landry going to beat her to the bottom. She flew down the hill, slowing down when she saw a fallen skier. He or she—one could never tell, bundled up in all the clothing—gave her the thumbs-up sign to indicate there was no injury, so she used her poles to regain speed.

Passing through the tall evergreens, Melanie was suddenly grateful to be alive. She inhaled the familiar pine scent mixed with a touch of wood smoke; this was life in Colorado at its finest. Seeing that she was almost at her destination, she leaned forward, legs practically touching one another as she soared to the bottom of the mountain. Hurrying to get back in the lift line before Bryce, Melanie hit a patch of ice. Before she knew what happened, Bryce Landry was helping her get back on her feet.

"Hey, just because I recited you a love poem doesn't mean I expect you to fall at my feet," Bryce said, his verdant gaze full of mischief.

Melanie removed her goggles and helmet. "If I had a glass of water right now, I'd toss it squarely in your face." She looked at him and gave him a genuine ear-to-ear smile. Again, for the second time, she was thrilled that she and this hunk of burning love were friends.

And who knew, maybe it would turn into something more. Today, for some reason, she believed that anything was possible.

Chapter 9

Melanie and Bryce stopped once for a quick lunch before heading back to the slopes. She was tired, but in a good way. They were on the chairlift again, and this time she slid closer to him. "For the record, I liked your poem."

"It wasn't original, but I could write you one if you like," Bryce said, nudging his helmet to hers.

"Okay," she murmured. "I like."

"Good. I was hoping you'd say that."

"Really?" She leaned back in order to see his face, or at least the part that wasn't covered by his helmet. She saw nothing but honesty reflecting back at her.

"Yes. Really. Because that means you'll have dinner with me tonight even though you're probably going to be too tired. I'll need some more inspiration."

Melanie shook her head. "Okay—you left me at the last hill. I'm not getting something here."

"The more time I spend with you, the more inspiration I'll have for the poem I'm going to write."

"I see," Melanie said. "I thought you were a history professor."

"I am, but I'm also a lover of words."

Just then, they reached the top of the mountain, preventing her from responding. Again, they flew down the trails, this time side by side, as though they'd practiced it a dozen times.

This time, when they reached the bottom of the mountain, Bryce removed his helmet and goggles, kicked his skis aside, and wrapped his arms around her bulky jacket. Without giving her a chance to remove her helmet, Bryce dipped his head forward, slightly tilting it to the side, and touched his lips to hers. She leaned back and closed her eyes, savoring the warmth from his mouth.

It was the best kiss she'd ever had.

They stood silently for a few minutes, kissing one another. Little nips, light smacks, nibbles. Suddenly sensing a presence, Melanie gently pushed him away. "We have an audience." She gestured to a little girl no more than five or six years old, staring at her. The child couldn't seem to take her eyes off them. Melanie removed her helmet and shook out the long braid she'd wound up on top of her head. She lowered herself to the child's level. Before she could ask a question, the little girl screamed, "You're not my mommy!"

Melanie turned when she heard a shrill cry coming from behind.

"Penelope! There you are! I told you to meet me in the lunchroom with your instructor. Where is your instructor?" the woman asked, cupping a hand across her forehead in search of the missing instructor.

The woman, who was obviously Penelope's mother, wore ski attire identical to Melanie's. Red-and-black Spyder jacket and black pants with red stripes running down the leg. No wonder the little girl had mistaken Melanie for her mother.

Melanie stood up as Penelope slid into her harried mother, attaching herself to her mother's legs. "I had to pee, and that man said I had to wait till it was time to eat. I hate skiing, Mommy. I want to go home now!" The little girl started to wail, her cries attracting the attention of the other skiers at the base of the mountain.

"Don't ever leave your instructor, do you understand?" the mother admonished. "We discussed this before."

Melanie wanted to intervene on poor little Penelope's behalf, but it really wasn't her place. She stood next to Bryce while the little girl pitched a fit that could have earned her an Oscar nomination.

When the mother realized they were being watched by a large crowd, she grabbed the child by the hand. "She doesn't like to ski," she said to those gathered around. Without another word, she pulled Penelope alongside her and headed for the main lodge. The little girl continued to cry.

"Poor kid," Bryce said. "If she doesn't like to ski, she shouldn't be forced. That can be dangerous. Grace never cared that much for skiing as a kid, and Mom and Dad never forced it on either of us."

Surprised that Bryce would even comment on the child, let alone have an opinion about the mother's treatment, Melanie gave a mental high five. This guy was turning out to be much more than she'd hoped for. He was not just another pretty face.

"It's part of the Colorado heritage," Bryce said. "If you live here and don't like to ski, you're not right in the head. Speaking of which, I have had enough skiing for one day. I'm pooped."

Bryce fastened the binders of his skis together and tucked them under one arm along with his poles. Melanie followed suit, suddenly glad she wasn't parked in the spillover lot.

They walked to the parking lot in silence, the crunching of their heavy boots on clumps of brown snow on the asphalt the only sound.

"So, are we still on for dinner? Grace and Max say that new Italian restaurant downtown is to die for."

Melanie wanted to appear as if she were considering his question even though they both knew the answer. "Odie and Clovis are with Stephanie, so I have to go to The Snow Zone before I go home."

"Okayyy," Bryce said. "I'm assuming they're your pets," he stated flatly.

Maybe strike one. "You don't like animals?" Melanie said. They reached her Navigator, and she removed her keys from her pocket, opened the hatch, and put her ski gear inside. She sighed with relief when she removed her heavy ski boots. Stepping into her Uggs, she smiled as Bryce watched her. "So, you didn't answer my question. Do you like animals or not?"

"I have three dogs, so I guess you could call that a yes."

Scratch strike one. Another mental high five.

"Really? You never mentioned them." Melanie felt so comfortable with Bryce, more so than she had with any guy she'd known for such a short length of time. After the water incident, she'd relaxed, letting down her defenses. Whatever will be, will be. She closed the hatch and twirled her keys around, smiling. "So, what breed?"

Bryce chuckled. "Mutts, all of 'em. I volunteer at an animal shelter in Boulder every Saturday. When we can't find a home for any of the strays, I take them in. So for now, I just have the three. In the future, who knows?"

She couldn't believe someone hadn't snatched this guy

already. He was just about perfect. Figuring she was on a roll, she asked, "What about children?"

He switched his skis to his other shoulder. "What about them?"

She laughed, shaking her head from side to side. "Do you like children?" There!

"Of course I like children. Ella is the best niece in the world, as I'm sure you've heard. Grace and Max are lucky. I hope to have a houseful of my own someday."

Standing in the parking lot, Melanie started to feel the cold. At least that's what she thought she was feeling. The more Bryce talked, the more she wanted him. And not just as a date.

"What about you, do you want children?" Bryce asked, all traces of his earlier humor gone. He leaned his skis against her Navigator, careful not to scratch the paint.

They were having a serious talk. In the parking lot at Maximum Glide. *Okay, I can handle this.*

Should she tell him about Miss Krause, and her desire to adopt a child? Would he want to take her to that little Italian restaurant if she had a child? She knew about Stephanie and Patrick's beginnings, and Patrick's fear of loss where kids were concerned because of his niece. Patrick hadn't been too keen on kids at first because of this fear. But Bryce wasn't Patrick, and she wasn't Stephanie.

Melanie took a deep breath, the icy air burning her lungs. "Yes, I do, I've always wanted children. Being an only child, I always swore I would have at least four, but I'd settle for one or two. You know, being practical. I don't want to be another Octo-Mom. Fourteen might be tough to handle." She laughed. "Look, I would love to continue this discussion, but I'm freezing. My toes are numb."

"Why didn't you say something? Here." Bryce took her

keys from her hand, unlocked the driver's side door, and hauled himself into the driver's seat. He adjusted the heater controls on the dash, then led Melanie to the passenger side, where he opened the door for her, just like in her fantasy.

"Let's go get Odie and Clovis, then you can drop me off at my car. We can finish this discussion at dinner."

Chapter 10

Max and Grace were right. Giorgio's served the best chicken marsala she'd ever tasted. Bryce had chosen the linguine and clam sauce. Both ordered caesar salads with their meal. The waiter brought a basket of homemade garlic bread that smelled divine. For a solid hour they did nothing but eat. When Bryce asked the waiter for a second bottle of wine, Melanie knew it was time to call it a night.

"I'm afraid I'm already a little bit tipsy," she said. "Any more, and I won't be able to drive safely. I can't remember the last time I ate so much."

He nodded his acquiescence. "How about dessert? Are you sure you don't want any tiramisu?" Bryce asked. "Grace said it was the best she'd ever had."

Melanie doubted she could take so much as a sip of water without exploding. "Nothing for me, thanks."

She had picked Odie and Clovis up from The Snow Zone and driven home happier than she could ever remember. After she'd taken care of the animals' needs, she'd soaked her aching muscles in the hot tub, washed

and dried her hair, and even attempted to apply her
makeup with a professional hand. She had agreed to meet
Bryce at the restaurant because it was easier for both of
them.

Now that the temperatures were dropping quickly,
Melanie knew from experience that the back roads would
ice over in a matter of hours. Back roads were always the
last to be cleared. She didn't want Bryce driving off the
side of the mountain. If one didn't know the road by the back
of one's hand, it could happen, *had happened.* More than
once.

Ever the gentleman, Bryce took care of the check even
though Melanie offered to pay her share. "Real men don't
accept money from their dates. Or at least this is what my
father taught me before he passed away. And I always listened to my father; his advice hasn't failed me yet."

Melanie didn't say it out loud, but she gave Bryce another mental high five. One to his father, too. The man
just kept getting better and better. Surely there was something wrong with this guy, something she'd find out when
she got to know him better. But then again, maybe not.
Nice guys still existed, they were just extremely hard to
find these days. Not that she'd spent much time looking.

After Bryce settled up with the waiter, he walked her
outside to her Navigator. "I don't want the evening to
end," he said. "It's been . . . let's just say it's been one of
the best days I've had in awhile. A very long while."

Melanie wanted to dissect his words, take them apart
one by one, searching for a hidden meaning, but now
wasn't the time. She'd leave those thoughts for later. She
wanted to be one hundred percent in the moment when
she was with Bryce. She was falling in love with him.
She'd never felt so alive, so excited to be with a man. That
was love, or at least the beginning of the falling part. In
spite of the chilling temperatures, she felt a warm glow

flowing through her, like a brilliant ray of sunshine. Yep, this was love, had to be.

"I feel the same way, but as you know, I've got a couple of guys waiting for me at home, so I'd better head back."

Without the bulky ski coats between them, Bryce captured her small waist, then pulled her as close to him as their winter dress would allow. He kissed the sensitive part of her ear, then trailed light butterfly kisses down the side of her neck, along her jawline, before touching her mouth with his. No longer on public display, Bryce covered her mouth hungrily. Melanie accepted his kiss and allowed herself to feel the passion. His tongue teased hers, and she teased back. He tasted of red wine and mint. He pulled away for a nanosecond, then his lips recaptured hers, but this time they were more demanding.

If they weren't in the middle of the parking lot, Melanie knew this would lead to something much more intimate. And she wanted that, but not yet. She stepped out of his arms, a hand touching her lips. She smiled, suddenly feeling shy like a schoolgirl.

"Hmm, that was nice," she said with a grin.

"That's it, just nice?" He wrapped his arms around her neck and touched his cold nose to hers. "How about that? It's the way Eskimos kiss."

"I'm not going to feed your ego, Mr. Landry. I think you enjoyed that kiss as much as I did, and that's all I'm going to say."

"Okay, I admit it. I was fishing."

Sighing contentedly, Melanie said, "You know what they say about men who fish?"

He cradled her head against his chest. "No, but I'm sure you're about to tell me."

"I just made that up. I have no clue what they say about men who fish."

He gave a hearty laugh. "You don't play fair. What if I said, 'men who fish are excellent lovers,' would you agree with that?"

Oh boy, she thought. "I've never slept with a fisherman, so I wouldn't know."

"Fair enough." A streetlamp provided just enough light for him to see her clearly. "What about a college professor?" He looked at her, and the double meaning of his words was very obvious.

She fought the urge to rip his clothes off, right there in the middle of the parking lot, but the cold and the fear of getting arrested prevented her from taking action. This certainly wasn't the time or the place.

Taking a deep breath, and letting it out as slowly as humanly possible, Melanie spoke, her voice soft, seductive. "I'll put that on my bucket list." And without another word between them, Melanie unlocked the door and got inside the Navigator. She cranked the engine over and was about to turn the heater on when she saw Bryce tapping on her window. She hit the POWER button to roll the window down halfway. "What? It's cold out there!" she said, even though she didn't care how cold it was. Bryce didn't want to leave her any more than she wanted to leave him.

He looked down at his ice-covered boots, then back at her. "This might sound . . . well, never mind how it sounds. I'm asking anyway. I planned on taking a trip to Las Vegas next weekend. Believe it or not, I've never been there. Would you like to come along? I've got two tickets to see Cher."

That was the last thing she had expected to hear from him. Vegas, of all places. And why did he have two tickets? Had some other woman canceled at the last minute? Was she just a convenient stand-in?

Before she could stop herself, the words flew out of her mouth. Sort of like the water incident.

He threw back his head and let out a great peal of laughter. "Actually, Mom was going to go with me but had to cancel at the last minute."

His mother? This guy was good. Really good.

"I planned to decorate my Christmas tree this weekend." She did, but also, what if the adoption agency called and she was out of town.

She'd given Miss Krause her cell number.

"Okay," he said. "I can see where decorating your Christmas tree would take precedence over a trip to Vegas." He turned away from the window, heading toward his Jeep.

Melanie rolled the driver's side window down as far as it would go. "Bryce," she called out to him, and he turned around. He appeared to be amused, not angry as she'd thought. "Do you want to come over and help me decorate my tree tomorrow? I need to do this before the weekend. I'm going to Vegas with a friend."

He stared at her, then burst out laughing. "I knew you would see things my way."

"Careful, a girl can change her mind in a split second. How's noon sound? It's about an hour's walk from the condo. I have all the equipment." She watched him and tried to suppress a giggle.

"You cut down your own tree?" he asked, apparently amused by this.

"Every year as far back as I can remember. You game or not?" She put her foot on the brake, shifted into reverse slowly, and eased the SUV out of her parking space. Bryce walked slowly along the side of her vehicle.

"Rest assured, I am game. I'll see you at noon."

Melanie smiled and punched the accelerator a bit too

hard, fishtailed, and caught herself just in the nick of time, before pulling out of Giorgio's parking lot. She looked in her rearview mirror. Bryce stood in the middle of the asphalt lot smiling from ear to ear.

Merry Christmas to me, she thought as she drove home to her condo.

Chapter 11

Melanie wanted to tell someone about her and Bryce's evening but saw it was almost midnight. Too late to call Stephanie, too late to call her mother. If Mimi were still alive, she would've called her no matter how late. She'd had an extraordinary relationship with her grandmother and knew that Mimi was looking down on her from the heavens above. Melanie smiled at the image. Mimi would've told her to pack her best undies and bring her most expensive perfume.

And that's just what she did after taking Odie out for an extra midnight potty break. Inside, she was too wired to even think about going to sleep. The animals sensed there was something different about her. They hopped on top of her bed and watched her as she went from closet to chest of drawers to luggage, their heads moving in perfect unison.

"Mom will take you two for the weekend. Dad might even grill you two a steak, but don't tell him I know he does this, or I'm sure it'll stop. Now, what's left to pack?"

She spoke to Odie and Clovis like they were people. She swore sometimes they could understand her.

She checked the contents of her luggage once more, making sure she had double of everything. Just in case. A slinky black dress, a slinky black sheer blouse, a slinky pair of formfitting black slacks. Black bikini undies with a matching bra. Yep, this would do for a weekend. She would wear her black leather boots on the flight, so she didn't have to pack an extra pair of shoes. Seeing there was nothing left to do, she closed the luggage again, placing it on the floor next to her bed.

She couldn't believe how her life had changed in just a matter of a few days. What a fantastic Christmas season. Now all she had to do was wait for Miss Krause's phone call confirming that her background check was clear, which she knew to be a fact since she'd never had so much as a speeding ticket. Then she could honestly say that her life was close to perfect. Well, if you didn't add that one teeny little element about marriage, then her life would be as close to perfect as it was ever going to get.

Odie yawned, reminding her of the late hour. Too keyed up to sleep, she retrieved her novel from the living room, then washed her face and brushed her teeth. She stripped down to her undies, slid into her favorite pair of sweats, and an old T-shirt from her high school days. Once she'd gently moved Odie and Clovis to their side of the bed, she opened her book and began to read about the latest saga in the vampire world. Within minutes, she was sound asleep.

Bryce finally gave up. In bed tossing and turning for the past two hours, he couldn't have stayed still if his life depended on it. Shoving the heavy covers aside, he decided to get up and go downstairs in search of a snack.

Grace always had some type of baked goods just waiting to be sliced into. Thankful there were no residents staying at Hope House, he didn't bother putting on a shirt.

Downstairs in the kitchen, he poured himself a glass of milk, then spied a plate of brownies sitting next to the stove. He grabbed a saucer from the cabinet, stacked three large brownies on top of one another, and headed back upstairs.

It was going to be a long night, he thought as he entered the guest room. Switching on the lamp next to the bed, he placed the glass of milk and plate of brownies on the night table. Grace usually had a stack of fiction novels tucked inside a drawer. He opened the drawer on the night table and was not disappointed. James Patterson's, Vince Flynn's, and Harlan Coben's latests were neatly lined up side by side. Grace must've known he wouldn't be able to sleep, because those were three of his favorite authors. He hadn't read any of the three novels, either. He picked up Vince Flynn's newest. He read the jacket copy, read the dedication, then the prologue. When he realized he'd read the prologue but hadn't a clue what he'd read, he closed the book.

Normally, after a day on the slopes like the one he'd had today, he would've crashed hours ago. Instead, he felt renewed, like he'd just run an easy marathon and won. It was Melanie. He couldn't stop thinking about her. He'd met her casually a few times, thought she was a knockout, but for some reason hadn't pursued her. When she'd tossed that cup of water in his face, well, it'd been an opening for him. Not having a clue why she'd acted in such a manner, he was glad she had. Of course, he wouldn't tell her that.

He couldn't believe she'd accepted his invitation to spend the weekend with him in Vegas. It almost seemed too easy, but he wasn't going to question his good fortune. Tomorrow, he would help her chop down a Christmas tree; heck, he might even chop one down for his room. Then they'd go back to her place and decorate. He'd never been inside her condo and found himself suddenly curious about her. Did she prefer the right or the left side of the bed? Tea or coffee? Sugar or cream or both? Such inconsequential things. But he found he wanted to know all about her. He wanted to feel her next to him when he woke up in the morning. He wanted to wrap himself around her, wanted to make love to her until they were both pleasantly exhausted. And he would, as soon as he felt the time was right.

He wasn't the man-about-town a lot of women thought he was. Not that Melanie had implied this to him, but he knew what his so-called reputation was on campus, and somehow he knew it would follow him for the rest of his life. If only he'd had such luck in high school. Gangly and tall, with crooked teeth and the beginnings of acne, he didn't seem to appeal to any one particular girl. He'd dated in high school and had his first serious relationship in his second year of college. He'd thought Diana was the love of his life until he caught her sleeping with his dorm mate. In his bed. A life lesson, Grace had said, and she was right.

Since Diana, he'd dated a few women, even slept with a few that he thought he cared about, but he'd never felt such instant attraction for any woman, nothing like what he was feeling for Melanie. Until now, he'd never believed in love at first sight, or rather, at first splash. He suddenly realized he'd never believed in it because he hadn't experienced it. And now? He looked around the bare but quaint bedroom. Pine chest of drawers, two twin beds with the night table separating them. Max's magazine covers framed and hung neatly on the wall opposite the beds. Everything looked the exact same way it had the last time he'd slept in this room.

The only difference: now he was seeing it through the eyes of a man in total, absolute love.

Love. He'd fallen head over heels. Big-time.

Chapter 12

"I can't believe you've spent your entire life in the fine state of Colorado and never chopped down your own Christmas tree. It's practically unheard of," Melanie joked, as they trudged through ankle-deep snow. The day was bitter cold, but at least the sun was out. A perfect day to cut down a tree.

"Yeah? Well I know something else that's unheard of," Bryce said.

Winded, Melanie stopped to catch her breath. "What's that?"

Bryce dropped the canvas bag of tools on the snow-crusted ground next to his sturdy boots. "This." He wound his hand around her loose hair, something he'd been wanting to do all day. With his free arm secured firmly around her waist, Bryce kissed her with all the pent-up emotions he'd spent the past forty-eight hours confronting—kissed her because he wanted to and because he could. Her response matched his. Both were eager to take their passion one step further, but Bryce wanted to wait until the timing was right. Or that's what his brain kept telling him. Another part of him said, forget timing, but that part would have to wait. He drew away from her but kept both arms wrapped around her waist. "You taste like chocolate." He licked his lips, teasing her.

She grinned the grin of the cat that ate the canary. "Think it has anything to do with that cup of hot cocoa I drank before we left?"

He nibbled at the tender spot where her shoulder met her neck. "Mmm, I've never done this," she muttered between kisses, "while searching for the perfect tree."

"There's a first time for everything," Bryce whispered, sending chills down her spine.

Melanie nodded in agreement. "This isn't the place . . . it's too cold." She visibly shivered. "Let's go find my Christmas tree before I turn into an icicle. I don't remember it ever being this cold, do you?" She moved away from him and grabbed the bag of tools by his feet. He took them from her, and she let him. He was a true gentleman, and she found that she liked that about him. Kind of an old-fashioned sort of guy. Women's libbers would not approve, that's for sure. She laughed out loud.

"What?" he asked. "Tell me what you're laughing at."

Melanie plodded along, content to have Bryce by her side. "It might not be funny to you. But I can see you're not going to let me brush it aside. Actually, I was thinking how nice it is to be with a man who has manners. You know, you're sort of old-fashioned. I like that about you. Not something a modern woman admits to these days."

She glanced at him, surprised at the tenderness in his expression.

"I guess I should say thanks. And you're right, I am a bit old-fashioned. My dad was adamant when it came to treating women with respect. He always treated Mom and

Grace like they were a queen and a princess. I just followed in his footsteps. Are you telling me you dated a bunch of ill-mannered slobs?"

They came to a clearing, one Melanie was quite familiar with. Tall pine trees flanked the clearing, their pungent odor refreshing. Even though cutting one's own Christmas tree down in Colorado without a permit was illegal, Melanie's parents had owned this particular piece of property for at least twenty years. Her father always replanted what they took. It was kind of like their own personal Christmas tree farm.

Spinning around hoping to catch a glimpse of just the right tree, Melanie watched Bryce watching her. "Hey, you're not looking. You have to spin around like this." She twirled around, both hands splayed out at shoulder level. "When I was little, I would use this method, and whatever tree my right hand pointed to, that's the one we would chop down. Didn't matter the shape or size, Dad can work miracles with a pair of clippers, so . . . well, that's what I did—actually, still do. Look." She pointed to a small blue spruce about fifty feet away from where they were standing. "What do you think?"

Melanie watched Bryce closely as he came up next to her. He didn't touch her, he simply looked at her, his forest green eyes shining as bright as the sunlight that filtered through the massive pines. "I think I'm falling in love with you, that's what I think."

A soft gasp escaped from her lips, her breath caught in her lungs, then she exhaled.

"I think I am, too. Falling in love."

There. She'd said what she'd never imagined she would say to a man she'd practically just met.

Bryce wrapped his arms around her, pulling her down on the snow-laden ground. "Ever make a snow angel?"

Chapter 13

Olga Krause normally wasn't one for theatrics, but that day she would make an exception. It was, after all, the time of year one showed goodwill to one's fellow man. Besides, she really didn't have a say in the matter.

"I want you to know this is highly unusual," she said to the police officer and to Carla Albright, a social worker she'd known since coming to work at the orphanage twenty-seven years ago. "Come inside; you'll let out all the warm air the state has to pay for." Olga Krause opened the back door for the pair. Highly out of line, they were.

"I know it is unusual, that's why we're here," Carla stated matter-of-factly.

The policeman, who couldn't have been a day over thirty, held a small infant carrier by its sturdy plastic handle, while in his other hand, he gripped the hand of a little boy. The child's face was red, his bright blue eyes cloudy and puffy, as if he'd been throwing a temper tantrum. Miss Krause peered inside the carrier. Practically a newborn. And she did not accept newborns under any conditions. Or she wouldn't if given the choice. They cried constantly and were never satisfied. Fortunately, the state agency rarely saw a newborn. It seemed adoptive parents wanted them. She did not understand why. Why would one willingly want a baby? She had eleven children at the agency ranging in age from nine to fourteen. Not that she liked them, but they were much easier to manage than infants. Babies required constant attention.

"Follow me," Olga Krause said to the two unwelcome visitors. "Let's go to my office."

They followed her down the dark hallway.

"You would think the state would spring for some lights," Carla said to Olga's back. "It's as dark as a cellar in this place. And it's too quiet. Where are all the children?"

When they reached the office, Olga Krause turned the desk lamp on. She nodded toward two old blue-gray chairs. "Sit."

The small boy hiccupped, then stuck his thumb in his mouth. "Take your thumb out of your mouth right now, young man. You'll have an overbite, and the state will be responsible for the bill."

Carla Albright practically flew out of her chair. "How dare you speak to a child that way! He's only three years old, and he just lost both of his parents in a terrible car accident! Why do you care what the state has to pay for? It certainly doesn't come out of your paycheck."

Carla reached for the little guy's hand. She gathered him in her arms and sat down, holding him tightly in her lap. She dabbed at his eyes with the sleeve of her blouse. "Officer Rogers, please sit down. You're making me nervous."

"Yes, ma'am," he said. At least six-foot-three, Officer Rogers looked like an oversized child in the small chair. Careful so as not to wake the little girl resting peacefully inside, he balanced the carrier on his lap.

"Now, tell me exactly why you're here," Olga Krause demanded. "It's after eight o'clock. We normally don't allow visitors at this ungodly hour." She crossed her arms over her more-than-ample bosom, waiting for an answer.

"You need to retire, Olga. You're too old for this job," Carla said through clenched teeth.

"How dare you tell me what I can and cannot do! Now, get on with it before I ask you both to leave. Explain." She directed her hateful gaze at the little boy and his infant sister.

"Every state agency except yours has reached its maximum occupancy. It's Christmas, Olga. Where is the Christmas tree the state allocates its tax dollars for?" Carla smoothed the little boy's damp hair. "I'm serious, Olga. Something is not right here. I'm sure you have an explanation, but before you say another word, hear me out. Officer Rogers, would you mind taking Sam—that's his name, by the way—to the restroom, wipe his little face off, and see if he needs to potty. It's my understanding he has been trained for quite some time now," Carla said.

"Uh, sure . . . but," Officer Rogers looked at the baby in his lap.

"I'll take her." Carla gently helped Sam off her lap, then took the infant carrier from Officer Rogers. Sam looked like he was getting ready to cry again. Carla was so sad for the two children, she was tempted to take them home herself, but it was against state policy. If something didn't change soon, she would have to risk the state's wrath.

"Where are the children?" Carla demanded as soon as they were alone. "And don't you dare tell me they're sleeping, because no one puts a child to bed this early anymore, unless they're sick. And where is the Christmas tree? I'm not going to ask you again." Had she not had the

infant seat in her lap, Carla would've reached across the
desk and smacked Olga Krause right upside her homely
face. Thank goodness for the baby, she thought as she
fought to control herself. No wonder World Adoption
Agency never ran at capacity. Who in their right mind
would send a child to this . . . this *prison camp*?

"The children are in bed. I don't know if they are
asleep; if they aren't, they should be. Bedtime is seven
thirty, prompt. No exceptions. I have used the funds allo-
cated for a tree for another purpose, which is none of your
concern. Now, what is it you expect me to do with these
two . . . kids?" Olga Krause gestured toward the baby as
though she were garbage.

Carla was a calm woman. Never married, she'd devoted her life to finding homes for children who needed
them. At sixty, she wasn't quite ready to call it quits, but
after this experience, she wasn't so sure. Olga was in her
midseventies and as mean as a belly-crawling snake.
Carla prayed she never became as bitter and hateful as the
woman sitting across from her. The state should have
fired her years ago. Why they hadn't remained a mystery.

Forcing herself to bite her tongue, Carla spoke between gritted teeth. "Two days ago, these 'kids,' as you so
eloquently call them, were made wards of the state when
their parents were killed in a car crash on I-70. It was on
the news—I'm sure that if you watched the news, you
would have heard about the pileup. Eight cars were involved. Sadly, Sam and Lily, she's three months old, in
case you're interested, were left without any family. Both
parents were adopted and had no family to speak of. They
were young and apparently they hadn't made . . . arrangements for their children, which is the worst injustice in
the world. Now, does that answer your questions?"

"You want to leave them here? I am not equipped for
an infant, I'll have you know. We don't have a crib, and

certainly there are no baby bottles to be found. I'm sure one of our sister agencies is much more equipped than I." Olga Krause drummed her fingertips on the desk.

"Trust me, if I had a choice, we wouldn't be here. There is nowhere else, Olga. You have to take them. Unless you've a family willing to foster them on such short notice. My fosters are full, especially during the holidays. Poor little things," Carla said.

Olga cleared her throat. "Well, I have a young couple who might take them in, but I can't say for sure until I speak with them. The woman was just here; we haven't even completed her background check, though I'm sure she passed. I haven't counseled her or her husband. Never mind, they're not qualified. Forget I brought this up."

"No. Let's call them. I'll see to it that their paperwork is expedited. Give me the information before I do something I'm not proud of." Carla made a mental note to check on the other children before she left. This was worse than she'd imagined.

Olga removed the single file from her desk drawer. She hadn't placed a child in over twenty years. With luck, that was about to change.

Chapter 14

With a slight screech, the plane touched down at Las Vegas's McCarran International Airport at precisely 1:40, just as scheduled.

Melanie and Bryce were seated in first class and had been given the royal treatment, courtesy of Caesars Palace and Bryce's checkbook. When he'd originally booked the trip, he'd had his mother's creature comforts in mind. Now he was glad he'd sprung for the extras. Melanie looked like a kid at Christmas when he'd picked her up this morning. She'd brought a small Louis Vuitton carry-on and nothing else. A woman with taste, he thought as he'd watched her at the airport in Denver. A true class act.

"What?" Melanie asked him while they waited for the cabin doors to open. "You've got this funny look on your face."

Bryce placed his hand on her cheek. "It's just the look of a guy head over heels in love, that's all." All the corny, lovey-dovey stuff he'd made fun of in his younger days wasn't corny anymore.

"Oh."

"Yeah, *oh*."

Melanie giggled. "Sorry. You just looked funny to me. Guess I've never seen what a guy in love looks like."

A flight attendant's voice came over the intercom, telling them they were allowed to unfasten their seat belts but should remain seated.

"I know it's crazy, but I've never felt this way. Ever," Bryce said. He'd told her about Diana, and she'd told a few stories of her own. Both were on equal footing in the romance department.

Another flight attendant told Melanie and Bryce their limousine was waiting on the tarmac.

"Top of the line, Bryce, top of the line."

"Only the best." He grinned.

Since they were going to be in Vegas for just two nights, both had brought only carry-on luggage so they wouldn't have to wait at the baggage claim. Bryce carried both pieces of luggage in one hand.

In a cordoned-off private section on the tarmac, a sleek white Lincoln Town Car limousine waited for their arrival. Inside the limo, they found a chilled bottle of Cristal with two crystal goblets. With expert skill, Bryce removed the cork. He filled each goblet, the creamy white foam overflowing. "Let's make a toast."

Melanie nodded, holding her flute aloft. "Cheers." Bryce touched her glass with his. "To the future."

"To the future," she repeated.

If anyone would have asked Melanie a week ago what she would be doing a week later, she certainly could not have told them she would be drinking champagne while riding in a limousine with a man she was madly in love with. She still hadn't told Stephanie or her mother and dad about her blossoming relationship with Bryce because it was still so new to her. They hadn't even slept together. Melanie was a patient woman, and she knew for a fact that Bryce was a patient man. They'd had more than one opportunity to throw all caution to the winds, yet they hadn't.

Lost in her daydreams and expensive champagne, Melanie reclined into the soft leather seat, suddenly too tired even to think about anything romantic, let alone act on it. She closed her eyes. She was almost asleep when her cell phone rang. Fumbling through her purse, by the time she located her phone, whoever was calling had hung up. She didn't recognize the number, so she assumed it was a new client. She wasn't even going to think about work until after New Year's.

She and Bryce were on the same page in that department for sure.

"Anyone I know?" Bryce asked as she put her cell phone back in her purse.

"I don't recognize the number, so it's probably just a new client."

"Spoken like a woman of means," Bryce teased.

She winked at him. Though she hadn't gone into avid detail about her finances, she had told Bryce that her grandmother had made her a very wealthy young woman. He told her that was fine with him, but he wasn't interested in her money.

When they arrived at Caesars Palace, a uniformed attendant actually rolled out the red carpet for them as they entered through a private entrance reserved for VIP guests only. He took their luggage and followed them at a discreet distance. Melanie felt like a movie star.

"A girl could get used to this kind of treatment," Melanie whispered.

"I have no clue where I'm going," Bryce remarked. The young man with their luggage revealed a small card in his hand. "If you will follow me," he said politely.

Bryce and Melanie stepped aside, allowing him to take the lead. Roman elements with a contemporary style made the elegance at Caesars Palace stunning. Everywhere one looked, there was marble, sculpted statues, and chandeliers that glistened like diamonds.

A replica of Michelangelo's statue of David stood eighteen feet high in the center of the grand lobby, adding a more imperial atmosphere. Melanie had only been to Las Vegas once, with a group of girlfriends right after she turned twenty-one. They'd spent most of their time lounging by the pool drinking wildly mysterious looking cocktails. (That's probably why she didn't remember the trip that well.) So in a way, Las Vegas was as new to her as it was to Bryce.

The young man used the card to open the door to their room. They were staying in the Palace Tower Deluxe suite. After their luggage was put away inside a closet, Bryce gave the guy a wad of cash, then closed and locked the door behind him.

"This is awesome," Melanie said as she gazed around the room.

Decorated in brown, gold, and several shades of cream, the suite boasted a living room complete with sofa and contemporary end tables with exquisite lamps atop each one. A small dining area close to the balcony gave one a bird's-eye view of the famous Las Vegas Strip.

"So, what to do first?"

Melanie laughed. "Now that's a loaded question if ever I heard one. This hotel is humongous. It'll take days to see everything. It's a shame we only have two. I don't remember much about my last trip here. I guess I wasn't old enough to appreciate the concept."

She walked over to the sliding doors that led out to the small balcony and stepped outside. The December air was dry and cool, similar to that at home, but not nearly as cold. She had forgotten to pack a bathing suit, but somehow she doubted she would have time to visit the various swimming pools at the luxurious hotel.

"Let's go to the casino while you decide what you want to do first. Remember, this is my first time here."

"Okay. Let's go."

If anyone were to see them together, odds were good they would pass as a happily married young couple on their honeymoon. Certainly not a man and woman who, until last week, barely knew the other existed.

They spent the next six hours in the casino, Bryce at the blackjack tables while Melanie tried her hand at the roulette wheel. Deciding too much thinking was required, Melanie had wandered over to the slot machines, content to lose her winnings. She'd draped her purse shotgun style across her shoulder. Reaching inside to grab another twenty-dollar bill out of her wallet, she spied her cell phone. Flicking it open to check her missed call list, she saw that the same telephone number she'd seen in the limousine had called her numerous times. Highly unusual. Melanie felt a tinge of alarm. For someone to make so many phone calls, it must be something important. She clicked on the number and pushed the SEND button.

What she heard sent shivers down her spine.

"I've been looking all over for you," Bryce said. "I was starting to think you ran out on me. Hey, are you okay? You don't look so good. Melanie?" The sudden change in his tone brought her back to reality.

Not knowing what to do, or say, Melanie opted for the truth. At the bar over lattes, she told him about her desire to adopt a child. She explained that her reason for not telling him was that their relationship was too new, too fresh. Tears pooled in her eyes when she said, "I think I should just go home."

"Why would you even think such a thing? So, you want children, you're willing to adopt, become a single parent. What's not to like about that? Hell, I admire you even more than I did already." He blotted her tears with the tip of his finger.

"Really?" she asked, surprised at how easily he accepted her choice. He really was the most perfect man alive. Almost. They still hadn't slept together, but that didn't matter. When the time was right, she knew it would be worth waiting for.

"Yes, really. Now dry those tears, because we've got tickets to see Cher. You still up for that?" he asked, a wicked grin revealing his sexy white teeth.

When did I start thinking of teeth as sexy?

"Of course I am, but, Bryce, there's more."

"I'm listening."

Five hours later, they were on a flight to Denver. Only this time, as man and wife.

And what happens in Vegas stays in Vegas. They still hadn't slept together.

Chapter 15

Melanie looked at the fake, cheap, metallic gold ring on her finger. Then she looked at the fake cheap metallic gold ring on Bryce's finger. Then she looked at the marriage certificate printed on cheap, plain white paper. Then she looked at Bryce, who was still in a state of semishock.

They were married. Husband and wife. Till death do them part. The old ball and chain. She had married Bryce Landry. She was Melanie *Landry* now. She had to admit, she liked the sound of her new name.

Unlike the flight to Vegas, they were unable to purchase first-class tickets on such short notice, so the only seats available to them were those in coach at the very back of the plane. By the restrooms. The stench was atrocious.

Melanie had barely uttered a word since she'd confessed to Bryce that, even though she had been told by the horrible woman at the adoption agency that she wouldn't be able to adopt a child unless she was married, she'd gone ahead and had her application processed anyway. She said that she knew it was selfish and foolish of her.

She was flabbergasted when he told her there was no time like the present, that he would've married her anyway. He said it was his destiny.

"I told Ashley when I got married she could be my maid of honor."

Bryce took her hand in his. "Let's worry about one problem at a time. We can always have another wedding. Now, tell me again what this woman Carla said."

Melanie's eyes flushed with unshed tears. "It's like something right out of a fiction novel. Apparently there was an eight-car pileup on I-70, nothing new there. A couple in their early thirties died at the crash scene. Carla said there were no relatives, no foster parents available. So I guess the next step was World Adoption Agency.

"According to Carla, Olga Krause has been stealing the state practically blind. She believes Olga is hoarding away money for when she retires. There are eleven other children in need of a home. Those poor little kids; I should've known something was wrong. And to think that old bat was in charge of all those innocents! She reminded me of Scrooge—I remember thinking that at the time. She just had a mean look about her. I hate to judge, but I hope that woman is prosecuted to the fullest extent of the law. Let her live the remainder of her life behind bars. Carla said the children were malnourished and frightened. Oh, Bryce, what in the world have I gotten myself into? And you, too."

Bryce squeezed her hand because, for once, he really didn't know what to say. The only thought that kept beating against his skull was the fact that he'd married Melanie. They'd been dating for less than one week, and he'd married her. What he couldn't get past was the fact that he'd never felt such pure and complete happiness. Yes, it had been a crazy thing to do when Melanie told him she wouldn't be able to adopt a child unless she was married. Like the gentleman he was, he'd quickly made arrangements for a Vegas-style wedding, and now they were on their way home to Denver. Melanie had called her parents, telling them she was returning sooner than planned and that she would pick up Odie and Clovis as soon as she could. She had neglected to mention she was coming home a married woman.

Bryce had a feeling this Christmas was going to be unlike any other. Past and present.

"We'll work things out. I have lots of friends in Boulder." What he didn't say was that he wasn't sure if any of them would be willing to take in thirteen children.

Less than twenty-four hours after leaving Denver International Airport, they'd returned to Placerville. Seated in the rear seats of the private jet Melanie had engaged, they were the last ones to exit the plane. Neither spoke while they waited for the other passengers to retrieve their book bags, diaper bags, and the like from the storage compartment.

Bryce would've been happier seeing Cher, but Melanie and the thirteen kids were much more important. Being in academia, he was around young adults most of the time. Of course, he was beyond thrilled to be Ella's uncle, but would he pass muster as a parent if it came to that? He could only hope. Now more than ever, he wanted to be the stand-up kind of man his father would've been proud of.

After they had gotten to Denver, Carla had explained that there was no prohibition on single-parent adoptions in Colorado—that Olga must have deliberately misled Melanie on that score, because anytime a child left the orphanage, the funds available for Olga to embezzle decreased. But neither Melanie nor Bryce had the least regret about the solution Bryce had come up with for Melanie's adoption woes. Married they were and married they would remain. Till death do them part.

With a renewed sense of purpose, Bryce vowed those thirteen children were going to have the best Christmas ever.

He would make sure each and every child found a home, and, maybe, if he was lucky, each and every one of them would have a home before Christmas.

Epilogue

One week later . . .

Melanie quietly closed the door to the spare bedroom, careful not to shut it all the way, just in case Sam or Lily needed her during the night. This was their second night together, her first night as a legally certified foster parent. Carla had expedited her application given the circumstances. Normally, she would be required to take parenting classes and undergo an extensive background check, but her circumstances were anything but normal.

Bryce and her parents were waiting for her in the living room. She'd invited them over to thank them for their help locating temporary homes for the other eleven kids. It hadn't been easy, but they'd managed.

World Adoption Agency had been permanently closed. Olga Krause had dozens of charges filed against her. She'd been jailed, then released on her own recognizance. It would take years before her case was heard in court. Melanie rather hoped that the old woman would die first, saving the taxpayers money. Melanie knew that was callous, but she didn't care. The children in her care had suffered greatly on her watch, and who knew what kind of psychological problems they would endure in the future? Her mother always told her that children were most resilient. She hoped this was true.

And now it was time for her and Bryce to tell her family they were married. They'd decided to wait until all the hoopla died down, since the story of the orphanage had made headlines.

She took a seat next to her husband, still amazed at the changes in her life in such a short span of time. Bryce kept reminding her, saying over and over that you only live once. She agreed with him.

"Melanie, you've been dancing around all night. I know you're happy you have Sam and Lily—your father and I adore them already—but something is bothering you. Am I right?" her mother asked with the sweetest smile. She was the best mother in the world. Melanie loved her so much at that moment, she had to close her eyes for a few seconds to compose herself. She was truly the luckiest woman alive.

"You're not sick, are you, kiddo?" her dad asked. "If you are, we'll get you the best doctors in the world."

"Dad, you're such a riot. No, I am not sick. At least, I don't think I am." She turned to Bryce. "Do I look sick to you?"

"You look beautiful, Melanie," Bryce said, his voice laced with love. And longing.

"Mom, Dad." She paused. "There is no other way to say it, so I'm just going to say it: Bryce and I got married in Vegas."

There.

She looked at her parents, waiting for their reaction. When they said nothing, she repeated herself.

"Bryce and I are married, and we're going to adopt Sam and Lily."

Her parents looked at one another, then at Bryce, and back at her. They high-fived each other. Then came the congratulations.

"Wonderful news! I knew something was up." Her parents hugged her; her dad shook Bryce's hand so long that she was sure it would fall off. That old guy thing. Mother and daughter hugged each other, tears puddling in their eyes.

"I couldn't have handpicked a better man for you, Melanie dear. Now, why didn't I see this coming?" her mother whispered loud enough for the others to hear.

Bryce laughed. "We didn't see it coming, either, but it's the best decision I've ever made."

Melanie kissed her husband on the cheek.

"So you're both okay with this? You're not going to have me committed?"

They all burst out laughing.

Bryce nuzzled her neck, whispering in her ear, "If I don't have you tonight, they'll commit *me*."

"Patience, Bryce. Patience," she whispered back.

Then Melanie giggled like a kid at Christmas. Right now at that precise moment, her world was absolutely perfect.

Merry Christmas, world!

Runaway Christmas

ELIZABETH BASS

Chapter 1

Christmas was only a few days away, but you never would have known it from sitting in the living room at Sassy Spinster Farm. A tree? No. A carol or two on the radio? Heaven forbid. The scent of gingerbread? Not at Aunt Laura's, not this year.

Erica had really been hoping for a tree at the farm. It would have been cool to see all her mom's old ornaments again, and remember happier times.

Two miles away, at her father's house, her stepmother, Leanne, had started decking the halls the second the Thanksgiving dishes were cleared. Every corner of every room was crammed with Christmas junk, and *The Nutcracker* had been on a constant loop for three weeks now. There was Christmas galore in the place Erica didn't want to be, and a big Christmas black hole in the place she usually loved.

The trouble was babies. The world was a wonderland for a baby. For a thirteen-year-old, not so much. Adults turned the world upside down for babies, even when babies threatened to turn the adults inside out.

Her aunt sagged in the recliner chair where she now lived twenty-four-seven, her eyelids droopy. When Erica suggested they make a batch of Christmas cookies, Laura's skin turned a weird color. In Crayola terms, she'd be Screamin Green. "Just the thought of a cookie makes me ill."

"How can a cookie make you sick?" Erica asked. "Cookies make people feel better."

"Because everything makes me sick," Laura said, readjusting the washrag on her forehead. "The succubus doesn't want me to eat anything but mint-chocolate-chip ice cream. And bacon."

The succubus was Laura's baby-to-be, which wasn't going to be born until May but was already dictating everyone's life, the same way that one-year-old Angelica did at Erica's dad's house. Usually Erica came to the farm to escape the tyranny of Leanne and baby Angelica—or Angel Baby as she was often nauseatingly called—but now all the good times at the farm had been hijacked by the unseen being Laura alternately called the succubus, the critter, or Hortense the Creeping Terror.

"If I can pass just one nugget of wisdom on to you, youngster," Laura said, "let it be this—don't ever get pregnant."

Erica, who was sitting cross-legged on the floor, pursed her lips. As if anyone had to tell her *that*. "Once the kid's born, it'll be all you think about. Like Leanne and Angelica."

Laura scowled. "Leanne's just putting on an act to trick you into making the same mistake she made. Don't be fooled. Don't have kids. Don't even think about boys. Go find a cave and live by yourself. Keep a cat for company. Or a chicken."

Laura's husband, Webb, who was sitting across the

room quietly reading a mystery, looked up from his book, smiling. "She'll make a great mom, won't she?"

Laura roused herself enough to shoot a threatening look his way. "*You* don't get to say a word on this subject. You're not the one incubating the critter."

"Really?" He laughed. "Your bitching and moaning makes it all so real for me, I sometimes forget."

"Secondhand suffering doesn't count for squat."

Erica sighed. It used to be fun to come to the farm and listen to Webb and Laura's scrappy way of communicating, which provided a refreshing contrast to the bored silence sporadically broken by real scrapping between Leanne and Erica's dad. At the moment, though, she just wished everyone in her family talked like normal people. "I'm supposed to bring something to the youth group's Christmas party at church later this afternoon," she said. "Something like cookies."

"Why don't you take a plate of bacon to the party?" Laura asked. "It's more nutritrious."

"And what's more festive for kids than a platter of Christmas bacon?" Webb asked.

"It's got protein," she shot back.

Erica couldn't help rolling her eyes. "Well, if we don't make cookies, what are we going to do?"

"I don't know about you," Laura told her, "but I'm going to sit here and make up new critter names. What do y'all think of 'Vomitia'?"

In contrast to Laura's words, a whole room had already been transformed with primary colors and stuffed with toys and furniture, awaiting the baby's arrival. The critter was probably going to be the most spoiled baby that ever crawled the earth.

"Wouldn't it be fun to put up a Christmas tree?" Erica asked.

"The stench of cedar right now would send me straight to the hospital," Laura said.

Of course. Erica glowered at the carpet. "I wish Heidi had decided to come and visit."

Laura shot to an upright position. "That would be *all* I need right now."

"I *like* her," Erica said.

Heidi had been her mom and Laura's stepsister when they were teenagers, and now Erica thought of her almost as another aunt. She hadn't visited the farm since the summer Erica's mother had died, but she wrote Erica all the time, and had sent her a really cool outfit on her birthday, and had invited Erica to come visit her in New York someday. *New York City!*

Well, Brooklyn.

Erica had hoped that Heidi would visit the farm for the holidays. But Heidi had said she was too busy with work this year. She'd just opened some kind of café.

A café was better than a baby.

"Why don't you go ride Milkshake?" her aunt suggested, evidently eager to change the subject from Heidi, who she'd only ever learned to tolerate.

"It's cold and drizzly."

"Wimp," Laura muttered, closing her eyes.

Webb guffawed. "You're one to talk. One little baby's sent you into a monthlong swoon."

"Every time you make a crack, that's one more onerous chore in your future," Laura warned as she rearranged the rag over her eyes. "I've already got you slated for eighteen months of diaper duty and *Disney on Ice.*"

It was going to be another awful Christmas, Erica realized with despair. Maybe not as bad as last year—nothing could be that bad again. Last year was the first Christmas

after her mother had died, and though everyone had tried
to be nice to her, nothing could make up for the fact that
the person she'd most wanted to celebrate with wasn't
there. And, of course, her half sister, Angelica, had been
born two weeks early, on Christmas Eve, which Leanne
and Erica's dad had insisted was a Christmas miracle.

But this year was shaping up to be a strong runner-up
for worst Christmas ever. Laura was completely consumed with her morning sickness, and Webb was all
about catering to Laura. At home, with Leanne and
Erica's dad, the house was gearing up for Angelica's first
birthday and baby's second Christmas. *Erica's thirteenth
Christmas* didn't seem to be on anyone's radar. No one
was thinking of her. It was as if she'd disappeared from
her own life.

In the old days, her mother had always been there to
make her feel special. But now she felt so lost—an un-
formed blob of a person—and there was no one she could
turn to. None of her friends at school understood. She'd
never felt so alone.

She unfolded her legs and stood up. "I should go
home."

"You just got here." Laura sat up a little. "Wait—you
want to watch a movie or something? Maybe we can
stream *Mommie Dearest* off Netflix. I could bone up on
my parenting skills."

"No thanks." Watching movies was something they
used to do with her mom. It wasn't quite the same with
only Laura and Webb. Nothing was the same. The big
house, which once had been so full of life, felt empty. In
her mom's day, there had been paying guests living in the
rooms, and music playing in the kitchen from sunup to
bedtime. Now sometimes it was hard to believe that her
mother had ever been here at all. Then Erica would catch

a glimpse of something to remind her—her mom's boom box in the kitchen, an afghan, the muffin pan that had made a thousand trips to the oven.

Erica fingered the ring that hung on a chain around her neck—the ring that had been her mom's last gift to her. Tears stung her eyes and she grabbed her denim jacket. "I'll see y'all later."

Webb stood up. "I'll run you back."

"Bye, Laura," Erica said as she shrugged into her jacket. "I hope you feel better."

Her aunt grunted.

Outside, Webb put Erica's bicycle into the back of his truck. They climbed into the cab and, as he drove the blacktop roads at a more leisurely pace than usual, he glanced sidewise at her. "I hope you're not upset with Laura."

She shrugged. "I get the feeling that Fred the Chicken rates higher than I do these days." Fred, a one-legged rooster, probably was the apple of Laura's eye. Erica didn't resent Fred, but it would have seemed silly to say she was jealous of a little baby who wasn't even born yet.

"She's been knocked for a loop by the pregnancy," Webb explained. "She'd never been sick a day in her life before this."

"Yes, I remember," Erica said.

As if she didn't know her aunt as well as he did! Webb might have been friends with Laura since junior high school, but Erica had known her forever and had lived with her for several years after her mother had gotten divorced and moved back to the farm. Laura had always seemed almost as much of a friend as an aunt. But of course now Laura had Webb . . . and in a few months there would be Hortense.

Everyone had someone. Except for her.

Could it be that the older she grew, the more she shriveled in importance to everyone who mattered to her? It probably wouldn't have been that way with her mother, but . . .

Her lip started to tremble, so she broke off the thought.

"Christmas can be the hardest time of year," Webb said.

She nodded.

"Next year things will be more normal," he added.

Normal? Was he insane? Next year he was going to have a little baby. Erica knew what that meant: diapers, colic, teething, never sleeping, short tempers. Breast-feeding. All focus on the baby. Baby constantly monitored. *Did it say a word or was that just gas?* Babies meant you couldn't go out, or, if you did, you had to carry along so much baby junk—diaper bags, strollers, bottles, sippy cups, binkies—that it almost wasn't worth the effort.

"Life takes a little patience sometimes," Webb told her.

Patience. Webb could have been the poster boy for that quality. He'd waited forever for Laura to agree to marry him.

But it was unfair of him to preach to her. "It's not like I'm *impatient*," Erica said in her own defense. "It's just . . ."

"Just what?"

I can't wait to be grown up. So I'll matter again.

She tried to find the right words—ones that didn't make her sound like she was impatient. Which she supposed she was . . . although it was more complicated than that. "Is it selfish to want something good to happen?" she asked. "To happen to me?"

He shook his head. "No. You're overdue, I'd say."

She growled in frustration. "So, *when*?"

"I guess you need to keep your eyes open for an opportunity to happen along—something you want. And then grab it."

Great. How often did opportunities happen along for a thirteen-year-old girl in Sweetgum, Texas?

When they reached Erica's dad's house, Webb got out and lifted her bike out of the back of the truck in one swipe and rolled it to her side. He gave her a quick, bracing squeeze on the shoulder. "Hang in there, E."

She bit her lip. "What else can I do?"

"Remember, you're coming out to the farm Christmas Day and staying till New Year's. You and me'll make that batch of cookies. Let the Grinch sit in her chair and squawk all she likes."

She smiled tightly. He meant well. *But I need those cookies for the Christmas party* today.

She took her bike around to the back and then trudged toward the kitchen door, mentally bracing herself for several scenes with Leanne before it was time to go to the party. Whenever Erica tried to bake anything, Leanne was always convinced she was going to burn the house down.

The moment Erica opened the door, however, it was clear something had changed. The air was charged. The "Dance of the Sugar Plum Fairy" was blaring through the house, but this time the music was accompanied by the sounds of footsteps scurrying, doors slamming, and Angel Baby wailing at the top of her lungs.

Leanne came winging into the kitchen with her screaming daughter on her hip. "There you are! We couldn't find you."

"I was at the farm. I told you I was going."

Leanne handed Angelica over to Erica. "See if you can get her to be quiet."

"Me?" Erica asked.

"Yes, you. I'm asking you for help. We're having a crisis here, in case you haven't noticed."

"I just walked in the door," Erica reminded her over the piercing screams.

Her excuse didn't hold water with Leanne. "Well, catch up—we're leaving."

"*Leaving?*"

"My sister's got appendicitis and we're having to go to Houston ASAP to take care of her kids. We'll be spending Christmas there, so pack enough to get you through the holidays. And please see what you can do about Angelica. My head is throbbing!" She hurried out of the kitchen.

"Wait." Erica trotted after her, confused. "*I'm* going to Houston?"

"Of course."

"But what about my party this afternoon?"

"You'll have to miss it."

Erica's face flushed at the injustice of that. Missing the party wasn't what bugged her the most, though. Now, instead of a week at the farm, she was going to have to spend her Christmas with Leanne's family? People she wasn't even related to.

Her father came out of his and Leanne's bedroom with a suitcase. "Are you ready yet?"

"Hello?" Erica said. "I just now walked in."

"Well, get packed. We're hitting the road in fifteen minutes."

Fifteen minutes? Were they crazy? "But I'm supposed to spend Christmas at the farm!"

"The farm and Houston are two hundred miles apart, Erica. I can't drive you back and forth," her father said in exasperation, even though she hadn't asked him to drive her anywhere. "Decide where you want to be and then stick with it."

Where *she* wanted to be? Really wanted to be?

Deciding took her about half a second.

"I'll call Aunt Laura," she said. "They'll come pick me up. Y'all won't even have to worry about driving me over."

Her dad stopped and raised his brows, as if this solution hadn't occurred to him. But of course it hadn't, because he hadn't realized there was a problem. He'd assumed Erica would fall into step with whatever was going on.

"Webb and I were just talking about my staying over there," she assured him. "He and Laura won't mind if I come a couple of days early."

"Well, go make your call."

She nodded, hurried into her room, and shut the door. Still holding her sister, she flopped down on the bed, hugging the kid to her chest like a squirmy pillow. Erica considered getting on the phone, just for show, but decided against it. Instead, she lay there with Angelica, absorbing her fussing, and breathed in her baby shampoo scent.

A plan began to form in her head. She could call her friend Rachel and say she needed a ride to the party in Carter's Springs. Then, at the right time, she could tell everyone her aunt had come to pick her up, and then she would leave. No one at the church—Leanne's new church—really knew Laura, so they wouldn't want to say hello to her. Best part of all, the church was in the middle of town . . . not far from the bus station.

After a few minutes, she stood up. Angelica was calmer now, which was more than Erica could say for herself. Anxiety and excitement buzzed in her chest. She took Angelica out and handed her off to her dad, who'd put on his jacket to leave. "Everything's cool, Dad," she said, surprised at how calm her voice sounded. "Webb said he'd swing by and pick me up just as soon as he runs a couple of errands."

"Good. That makes things simpler." He gave Angelica back to his wife.

Now that they were about to leave, Leanne pursed her lips in concern. "It's going to be Angel Baby's first birthday—Christmas not having her big sis with her," she cooed, pouting.

Erica tried to muster the appearance of regret. "Yeah, well . . ."

"C'mon," her father said to Leanne. "Traffic on the interstate's going to be a bi—bear."

They hurried out.

Erica ran after them at the last minute. "Dad!"

He turned as he was opening the driver-side door. "What?"

"Can I have some money?"

For a second he looked as if he was going to lecture her, but then he surprised her by reaching for his wallet. "I was going to give you a hundred dollars anyway, for your Christmas present. So here it is."

He forked over five twenties, and she was so thrilled she practically launched herself at him in a hug. "Merry Christmas, Dad!"

"Merry Christmas, Erica. Be on your worst behavior for your Aunt Laura."

She laughed. There had never been any love lost between those two.

"I'll give her your regards," she promised him.

Leanne, who had strapped Angelica into her car seat and already was settling into the front, got out again and poked her head over the roof. "Don't forget to lock up the house."

"I won't," Erica promised.

"And leave the porch light on."

"Okay."

Her father installed himself in the driver's seat, buckled up, and pulled out onto the road, but Leanne made him stop a few yards from the drive. She lowered her window and called out to Erica. "Make sure the appliances are turned off. And the Christmas tree lights are unplugged. Oh! And it would be great if you could come by and check on the house while we're gone . . ."

Her father accelerated, forcing Leanne to duck her head back in.

Erica stood in the front yard in the drizzle, waving at them until the car disappeared.

And to think, a half hour ago she'd decided that opportunity never came along in Sweetgum. Now a big fat Christmas miracle had dropped right in her lap.

She hurried inside to check airfares.

Chapter 2

"I hate to think of you spending Christmas all alone," Dinah said.

She simultaneously frowned at Heidi and hacked off a slice of carrot cake for Clay, who, if he wasn't the Sweetgum Café's best customer, at least had the best attendance record, probably because he lived three doors down. Already tonight he had been planted on a stool next to the counter for an hour, nursing his after-dinner cup of coffee and mooning at Dinah. When the waitress slapped the piece of cake in front of him, he stared lovingly at that, too.

"It's my Greta Garbo Christmas," Heidi explained for the hundredth time. "I *vant* to be alone. I've been looking forward to a quiet 'staycay' for months. I've got a pile of books to read, and my Netflix copy of *Avatar* has been sitting on my TV stand for five months."

Dinah rolled her eyes. "You could come to my folks' place in Chippenhook—we have DVD players there now."

Clay interrupted them. "A front's coming in tonight. Maybe you shouldn't plan on going to Vermont tomorrow, Dinah."

"The ticket's bought," Dinah said. "Snow or no snow, I'm going to be on a northbound train tomorrow night."

She had been talking for weeks about going home for Christmas—not because she was homesick, but because she'd heard that her old flame, Dan Janacek, the boy next door—or from the farm next door—who was now an investment banking prince in the city, was going to be home for the holidays, too.

"If he works on Wall Street," Clay asked with a hint of bitterness, "right here in the city, why haven't we ever seen him? And why isn't he offering to go home with you?"

Heidi had wondered the same things. From what Dinah had said, it seemed as though it was only when this Dan guy knew he was going to be stuck on a visit home that he paid her any attention.

"He has a car," Dinah said. "People like Dan don't take Amtrak."

"But if he has a car, it would be all the more polite to ask you along," Clay pointed out.

Dinah put her hands on her hips and glared at him. "Do you intend to eat that cake or just stare at it?"

Actually, he had been staring at *her*—not that Dinah ever seemed to notice.

"Of course," he said, giving the cake his attention at last. "This looks great, Dinah. Like my grandmom used to make."

Heidi slanted a skeptical glance at both Clay and the dessert. She had made the cake herself, but Dinah, who had been on holiday overdrive for weeks now—no doubt thinking of a certain investment broker under the mistletoe—had put green food coloring in the icing. "I don't

know how they do things in Boggy Bottom, Arkansas,"
Heidi said, "but green icing on carrot cake is just wrong."

"Bog Hollow," Clay corrected her quietly.

"You're an old Scrooge," Dinah told Heidi, wiping
down the counter. "All the customers have mentioned the
icing."

"Of course they have," Heidi said. "It's peculiar."

"I think it's . . . festive," Clay said, taking a bite. After
a few cautious chews, his face broke into a relieved smile.
"And it tastes the same."

Dinah rounded on Heidi in triumph. "There! See? You
have no Christmas spirit."

"Which is another reason you don't want me anywhere
near your parents' place on Christmas," Heidi said. "I intend to lock myself in a room completely devoid of evergreen, gift wrap, and candy canes. No offense to anyone
with visions of sugarplums dancing in their heads, but I
just don't want to have to think about Christmas this
year."

Mostly, she didn't want to have to think about the fact
that it was Christmas and she was alone. Her mother was
spending the holiday in Cancun with her new husband,
Tom. The two had actually invited Heidi along, but after
having had last Christmas consumed with being her
mother's maid of honor—elf of honor, her mother had
joked—she certainly didn't want to tag along this year for
their first anniversary celebration. And she also had been
invited—by Erica, at least—to visit Texas. But fly down
for two measly days to inflict herself on Laura and be reminded that even her cranky, misanthropic ex-stepsister
had managed to achieve a happily-ever-after ending for
herself? No thanks.

Anyway, she couldn't afford it. The café kept her bank
account running on empty.

Maybe some might think self-imposed isolation was a

weird way to try to forget she was all alone in the world at Christmas. But Heidi had decided the best and most restful approach to the holiday was to pretend it was a regular weekend, the kind normal people had—people who didn't own their own businesses. This would actually be her first real weekend since deciding to open the Sweetgum Café had plunged her into a nonstop cycle of work, worry, and near-destitution.

And yet, she loved the café. It was her pride and joy. She just needed a mother's day out, and Christmas was it.

Dinah sighed in frustration. "So you're going to hole up in that shoe box?"

"Yup."

"All alone?"

"All alone in my shoe box. Sounds cozy to me."

Dinah shook her head as the bell over the door jingled. "You're pathetic." She turned to greet a new customer, but her smile disappeared when she saw that it was only Patrick and Marcus, two of the neighborhood cops who stopped by regularly. Having had brushes with the law, Heidi understood the importance of good police relations. As long as she owned a café, cop coffee would be free.

Dinah, who was eight years younger than Heidi and had a comparatively uncheckered past, was less in awe of the boys in blue, especially since some cops equated free coffee with freedom from tipping. "Would you two please tell Heidi that she's pathetic?" she asked them by way of greeting. "She's still insisting on being a total Christmas refusenik. It's not normal." Dinah appealed to Patrick. "Please tell her it's not normal."

His gaze sought Heidi's and immediately she turned away to join Sal by the sink. She tried to avoid drawing attention to herself in front of policemen—especially when someone was crowing about how abnormal she was—and

Patrick's way of looking at her was particularly unnerving. He was imposingly tall, with striking green-blue eyes. Hypnotic eyes. The kind of eyes that could probably make a suspect confess to anything.

Sal flicked a sympathetic smile her way. He was supposed to be their dishwasher, but the title didn't begin to describe him. Busboy, baker's helper, short-order cook, plumber, electrician, bouncer—he was all of those things at the Sweetgum Café, and, icing on the cake, he had grown up working in his uncle's restaurant in Bay Ridge, so he knew way more than Heidi about the ins and outs of the business. He'd even informed her of the proper amount to bribe an NYC health inspector. She vowed never to use the information for her restaurant . . . although she'd keep it in mind the next time she dined out in Bay Ridge.

Sadly, Sal also knew something about robbing fast-food joints—or, as he insisted, had fallen in with a crowd who did—which was why he'd spent eight months of his nineteenth year on Riker's Island. Heidi had taken pity on him when he'd come around looking for a job. Having ended up as a key witness during her ex-boyfriend's trial for embezzlement a year ago, she knew all about keeping company with the wrong people and coming to grief. She was a firm believer in second chances.

And since hiring Sal, she was also a firm believer in lugging the cash box home every night.

"The no-decorations thing is why we're here, Heidi," Patrick confessed. "We found you a Christmas tree."

Puzzled, Heidi turned. "We already have one."

Festooned with lights, ornaments, and tinsel, the restaurant tree stood next to the fireplace, which had stockings bearing all the employees' names hanging on the mantel. Between the café and Heidi's apartment, the café was by far the more festive place to hang out. Which was good, since she seemed to spend most of her life here. The café was situated in a brownstone just off Court Street that had been zoned commercial a few years before. Its recent roots as someone's living room made it homey and warm—and, at the moment, thanks mostly to Dinah, it was so Christmassy it could have been the set for a Bing Crosby special.

"Thanks, guys, but we couldn't squeeze any more decorations in here," Heidi told the policemen.

Patrick suddenly seemed very interested in his shoe. "Actually, this tree's for your apartment."

She tilted her head. "How did you know there's no tree in my apartment?"

Dinah snorted. "Because for the past month you've been telling everybody that you're not going to do anything for Christmas but sit in an empty room and watch *Avatar.*"

Marcus grinned at her. "But if you don't want it, no problem. Leave it dumped on the sidewalk. That's where we found it."

"You *found* a tree on the sidewalk? Abandoned?" She rushed forward to take a look. Sure enough, through the glass of the restaurant's door, she spied a fully decorated tree—lights, shiny ornaments, and tinsel—leaned up against a parking meter.

"We lugged it over here from Clinton Street," Marcus explained. "Someone must have gone on vacation early and decided to ditch it. Save them from depressing-dead-tree syndrome when they get back."

She shouldn't have been surprised. People in the city left their possessions on the sidewalk all the time. Even their valuable possessions—couches and chairs, desks and televisions. Abandoned street items accounted for a significant portion of the furnishings in her apartment. But tossing out an almost-new, fully decorated Christmas tree two days before Christmas? That seemed cold. It was as if the tree were being deprived of its destiny, its big chance to shine.

Dinah crept up behind her and peered over her shoulder. "Aw, look at it, Heidi. It's saying"—she spoke in a faint, shivery voice—"*I'm so cooooooold. And so aloooooone. And I've never seen* Avataaaaaar."

Heidi rolled her eyes and steeled her heart against the homeless . . . tree. It was just a tree, for Pete's sake. "That's very nice of you guys, but, really, I can't take it."

"Oh well," Marcus said, seeming almost relieved. "It was worth a shot."

Patrick's eyes were still locked onto Heidi's face so intently that she pivoted toward the cash register. "I'm sure someone else will want it, though," she said. "It'll probably disappear by the time we close up."

After Patrick and Marcus filled their to-go cups and left, Dinah rounded on Heidi. "You are really taking this no-Christmas business to a nutty extreme."

"What are you talking about?" Heidi pointed around the café. "I've got more lights strung around this place than Rockefeller Center!"

"What would have been the harm in accepting their tree?"

"Because I could see the next step—Patrick and Marcus would offer to take the tree to my apartment. Maybe even *inside* my apartment."

"So?" Dinah blinked. "You got a collection of severed heads in there or something?"

"No! But I don't want . . . I mean, I've been trying very hard to distance myself from the law."

Dinah laughed. "Are you sure you weren't Lizzie Borden in another life? You seem to think you're going to be dragged off to jail whenever a person with a badge comes within ten feet of you."

"Haven't you noticed the way Patrick looks at me?" Heidi asked. "Doesn't it strike you as odd?"

"Yes. It seems odd that someone could be so utterly clueless that a guy has a crush on her." She frowned at Clay, who was looking up at her with a gooey expression. "What's the matter with you? Are you saving that cake for a rainy day?"

Dutifully, he took another bite.

"A crush!" Heidi said, feeling her cheeks flush in spite of herself. "No way. You don't know my history. He probably sees me as a shifty character—someone to slap handcuffs on."

"Paranoid much?" Dinah chortled. "He might dream of handcuffing you, but not because you're shifty."

Could that be? Heidi didn't believe it, even while she realized she wanted it to be true. "I can't imagine having a relationship with Patrick. One look from him makes me want to blurt out every infraction I've ever committed, starting with shoplifting the candy bracelet from the dime store when I was five. Of course, maybe if I could see him out of that uniform . . ."

Dinah laughed, and Clay choked on his coffee. Even Sal at the sink sniggered.

A blush crept up Heidi's neck. "Not what I meant, guys." Although, now that she thought about it . . .

Dinah sobered as she peered into the maw of their large tip jar, which had only a few thin layers of spare change at the bottom. "Well, one way to test what's really going on is to stop giving the boys in blue free coffee and muffins. Cops are like bears—once you feed them they keep coming back around."

Heidi wasn't going to change her policy, but she took comfort in Dinah's words. "Of course. See? I'm sure that's all Patrick is—a nuisance bear."

For the rest of the night until closing, she kept catching

streetlight flashes of tinsel from Patrick's tree, which still leaned against the parking meter. As she was shutting down the register for the night, a bitter wind kicked up, blowing the tree over so that it partially blocked the sidewalk. It was as if the Christmas fates were daring her to walk past it on her way home. Which she might have had no trouble doing—if only the poor tree had stopped twinkling at her.

Chapter 3

By the time she finally flopped into an airplane seat that night, Erica's mood soared from exhaustion to elation. Finally—she was on her way on her first-ever plane trip. The closest she'd ever come to flying before this was when her mother had planned a trip to Mexico for them. But then her mom had been diagnosed with cancer, and they'd been forced to cancel.

The past eight hours had been such an ordeal—first the party, then the hour-long bus ride to DFW Airport, always with the clinging fear that something would go wrong when she tried to check in. Even once she'd had her ticket in hand, she'd expected the men on the other side of the walk-through metal detector thingy to haul her away to the airport equivalent of the principal's office. Instead, they'd joked with her about not knowing to take her clunky necklace off, and one sent her on her way with a friendly wink after Erica had slipped her sneakers on again and asked him the way to her gate.

Of course, she would have been happier to be on a plane if she were headed directly to New York. The cheapest ticket she'd been able to find routed her from Dallas to Phoenix, Phoenix to Chicago, and Chicago to New York.

As the plane lifted off, her stomach fluttered both at the queasy sensation and the finality of what she'd done. No turning back now. She closed her eyes, trying to still her wobbly nerves. What if someone had realized she was missing already? They might be able to trace her. Maybe when she landed in Phoenix, there would be policemen waiting for her to take her back to Texas, where . . .

She would be in mega ginormous trouble. That worry had lurked at the back of her mind ever since the airline's automated machine had accepted the bar code on the receipt she'd printed out at home after she'd bought the ticket online. That and a scan of her never-used passport and she'd felt she was home free. Except that she wasn't, really. The ticket, plus taxes, had come to six hundred and twenty-eight dollars. When her dad and Leanne found out about that, they would kill her. Or lock her in her room until she was eighteen. Or make her spend the rest of her life babysitting Angelica.

Maybe after the trip, she'd have some of her spending money left over. She could give her dad that as a down payment. She could promise not to ask for anything for the entire next two years, and she could do without her allowance completely. Her allowance was ten dollars per week, when her father remembered.

She did some rapid calculating. To pay off her six-hundred-and-thirty-dollar debt, she would have to do without her allowance for sixty-three weeks, which was just a year and eleven weeks. So, really, any way you looked at it, she would have it all paid off by the time she was a sophomore in high school. That didn't sound too bad.

Anyway, Webb had told her she needed to seize her opportunity for adventure, and now she'd done it. It didn't make sense to do something exciting but then ruin it all by worrying.

The flight attendant arrived at her row and asked what she wanted to drink. The woman next to Erica ordered a Bloody Mary and handed over seven dollars. Seven dollars for a drink in a little plastic cup! Erica panicked. If she threw away money like that, she'd be broke by the time she arrived in New York. She needed to save a little money for fun spending and other stuff. Like a taxi from the airport in New York to Heidi's place. That was bound to set her back at least ten dollars.

"I don't want anything, thank you," she told the attendant.

The flight attendant raised a thinly plucked brow at her. "You sure, hon?" she asked in a syrupy tone.

Erica sat up straighter. *There's no reason to talk to me as though I were six years old.* She was a year over the airline's age limit to qualify as a minor traveling unsupervised. She should at least be given credit for knowing whether she was thirsty or not. "I'm sure."

"You visiting relatives for Christmas?" the woman next to her asked as she upended a tiny bottle of Smirnoff into some tomato juice.

Erica nodded. "My aunt. Well, she's sort of my aunt. She would have been my step-aunt, I guess, if her mom and my grandfather hadn't got divorced."

"Does she live out west?"

"No, she's in New York."

The woman frowned. "You realize you're going the wrong way?"

"It was cheaper to get there through Phoenix."

An earthy laugh rumbled out of the woman. "Oh, sweetie. Sounds like you'll be lucky to get where you're going by New Year's."

Erica frowned. "It's only three flights."

"Sure, but you might want to look at a weather report. At some point, one of those flights will be heading you straight into a blizzard."

Ten o'clock found Heidi trudging through snowfall with her messenger bag slung over one shoulder and the café's cash box tucked inside an old, plain shopping bag in her left hand. She always carried the cash box this way, with the expectation that any sane mugger would go for the leather bag rather than the paper tote. Of course, any sane mugger wouldn't be out on the streets tonight, but better safe than sorry.

Her right hand was clasped around the trunk of the Christmas tree, which she dragged behind her, leaving a Hansel-and-Gretel tinsel trail in her wake. She hadn't been able to pass it by. Especially since, when she'd locked up for the night, the Christmas tree was still in front of the parking meter, looking even more forsaken beneath a layer of newly fallen snow.

Now, as she approached her block, she could feel enthusiasm growing, as if she were bringing home a stray kitten, not a soon-to-be-dead tree. Tomorrow she would need to run out and buy a stand for it. She imagined herself cozying on the couch, staring at twinkling lights, and falling asleep surrounded by the scent of evergreen, with dreams of . . .

Uh-oh. Here was the problem. Dreams. That's what these sneaky trees did to a person. They awakened memories of being young and having all sorts of impossible wishes—of waking up Christmas morning and discovering Santa had made all your dreams come true. It might be a dream that there would be a puppy under the tree, or the dress you'd whined about for weeks, or the dream that the next year would be the best year ever. When you were mesmerized by blinking lights and shiny tinsel, it was easy to forget that dreams were usually chased by disappointment.

But there was no reason she had to get carried away now. It was just a tree. Having it didn't mean she would have to make wishes or glut herself on eggnog or waste a night weeping over Zuzu's Petals. Just a tree.

It wasn't as if she wanted anything, anyway. She had her café. Of course, she'd hoped to have money to buy a new, larger mixer. Also, it wouldn't be terrible to meet someone and have a mad passionate love affair, which would turn into happily ever after . . .

Just a tree. Just a tree. Just a tree.

The snow swirled down in fat flakes. Movie snow. The fresh white coating made Brooklyn look sparkly clean. There weren't many drivers out, and the quiet combined with the streetlights gave her block an ethereal, almost magical quality.

A sharp series of barks drew her gaze to her building. On the sidewalk, yapping and straining at his leash, was Mrs. DiBenedetto's Pomeranian, Marcello. Seeing her landlady standing above him on the stoop, Heidi had to suppress a groan. No one could kill a magic moment faster than Mrs. DiBenedetto.

The old lady was planted on the second step, fists on hips as she watched Heidi dragging the tree up the street. Mrs. DiBenedetto was small, but she was adept at using her stocky, bread-loaf body and baggy, brown eyes to intimidate. Relations between them had been cordial when Heidi first moved into the building's basement apartment, but things had deteriorated after Mrs. DiBenedetto read in the newspaper about Heidi's testimony at her boyfriend's embezzlement trial. After that, she couldn't be convinced that it hadn't actually been Heidi who had stolen money from the Bank of Brooklyn's geriatric depositors. If Heidi forgot the rent on the morning of the first day of the month, at noon Mrs. DiBenedetto would be rapping sharply on her apartment door, threatening legal action.

And then came the begonia incident.

"Where did you get that?" the old lady asked darkly, nodding at the tree. She had a hint of Sicily in her voice, although Heidi doubted that Mrs. DiBenedetto had ever been to Italy, even as a tourist. She suspected the woman just had Corleone in her soul.

"I found it on the street."

Mrs. DiBenedetto let out something between a snort and a snarl.

"It's true," Heidi insisted. Marcello's yaps came every few seconds and were sounding sharper—probably because the taut leash was strangling him. Most of his tiny canine fury was aimed at the tree. He growled at it as if it were an approaching menace.

"Always finding things on the street, aren't you?" Mrs. DiBenedetto asked in a not-so-subtle reference to the begonia.

Heidi rolled her eyes. "I swear, I thought you were throwing that begonia away. It was right next to the trash."

Another snort of disbelief.

Honestly, who in their right mind in Brooklyn left pots of begonias sitting on the sidewalk in front of the stoop? And it had been right next to a sack of garbage. But nothing would convince Mrs. DiBenedetto that Heidi wasn't an evil flower snatcher.

From the look in her eye now, she evidently assumed Heidi had escalated her thieving to include Christmas trees. Big game.

"Marcello! Get away from that tree," the landlady said sharply. As if it were tainted.

"Seriously, Mrs. DiBenedetto—a cop found the tree and gave it to me."

A penciled-on eyebrow arched at her. "You said you found it in the street."

"Well . . . the cop found it." She cursed herself for caring what the old battle-ax thought anyway.

"Marcello!"

Marcello had worked up the courage to actually lunge at a branch. A one-sided battle ensued—dog versus blue spruce; it wasn't pretty—and Mrs. DiBenedetto was tugged down a step.

Heidi decided the smartest thing to do at that point was to take her tree and go inside, but, pivoting toward the entrance to her basement apartment, she failed to notice that Marcello's leash had snagged on a branch. When she yanked the tree toward the basement entrance, she unwittingly sent Mrs. DiBenedetto flying off the porch.

At first Heidi caught the catastrophe out of the corner of her eye—the initial jerk a confusingly swift move for a seventy-year-old lady. As Heidi turned, she saw her landlady's feet slip on the slick stair, sending her sailing down to the sidewalk. The moment the woman hit the pavement, Heidi could almost hear the snap of brittle bones. She surged forward.

"Mrs. DiBenedetto!"

The woman let out a moan of pain.

"Oh my God." Heidi reached for her.

"Don't touch me!" the lady yelled at her. "You'll kill me!"

Hearing the angry rasp was a relief. For a terrifying heartbeat, Heidi had been afraid she really had killed her. "Are you all right? Can you get up?" she asked.

"Of course I can't get up! Something cracked!"

Heidi reached into the shoulder bag she'd dropped on

the sidewalk and dug for her cell phone. Marcello had stopped barking and was now lifting his leg next to a Christmas tree branch. Heidi called 9-1-1 and frantically relayed what had happened and the address. The dispatcher's calm, almost bored voice gave her the impression that there were old ladies all over New York slipping off their stoops. She only hoped they had ambulances enough for them all.

Waiting on that ambulance felt like the longest fifteen minutes of Heidi's life. Especially since Mrs. DiBenedetto wasn't shy about telling her that it was all her fault. Heidi didn't know what to do or say, so she took off her coat and covered Mrs. DiBenedetto's shivering body with it. "Murderer," her landlady muttered between clenched teeth.

"I'm sooo sorry." As apologies went, it sounded anemic, but Heidi didn't know what else to say. ("I honestly didn't mean to cripple you"?)

Without her coat, she stood awkwardly by, teeth chattering   even Marcello with his fur was shivering in the cold. The snow was coming down more heavily now and Mrs. DiBenedetto wouldn't let Heidi touch her to flick the flakes off, so by the time the ambulance stopped in front of the building, the woman looked flocked. The EMS guys gaped at Heidi as if she was an awful person for standing there while snow accumulated on her landlady. And of course it didn't help matters that Mrs. DiBenedetto was pointing at her and yelling *assassin*.

Heidi smiled and tried to explain what had happened, but the paramedics were understandably more interested in getting Mrs. DiBenedetto off the sidewalk. Heidi decided the best thing to do at that point would be to take Marcello into the house. She scooped up Mrs. DiBenedetto's keys from where the woman had dropped them on the stairs and then hurried with the dog into the landlady's apartment. A stale, meat-loafy aroma hung in the air.

Marcello crept along the wall, trembling and freaked out, and kept up a constant growl at Heidi that periodically burst into a full-fledged bark. In the kitchen, she threw open cabinets until she spotted his dog chow, which she poured into the food bowl on the floor. He sniffed it and then growled at her as if she were trying to poison him. Heidi sighed and sloshed fresh water into the neighboring bowl.

"There, I'm done. You can relax now and I'll be back in the morning." She reached down to pet him and he bared ferrety little teeth at her. When she let herself out and locked up the apartment, he started barking in earnest.

On the way back out, she dashed into her apartment to grab a dry coat—a hideous beige puffy coat that she'd bought for thirty dollars at Costco, thinking that if she ever had to wear it, it would be practically in whiteout conditions and she wouldn't care if she looked like a giant broiled marshmallow. For once she'd been right.

Outside, the paramedics had given Mrs. DiBenedetto a shot of morphine to kill the pain so they could load her onto the stretcher. The drugs must have addled her mind a little, because as they were hoisting her into the ambulance, the woman's arms started flailing and she pointed at Heidi. "You take care of my Marcello!"

Five minutes earlier she had been calling Heidi a murderer.

"You take good care of my baby!" she slurred.

"Of course. He'll be fine."

"You take care of him or else!"

The EMS workers were ready to close the back of the ambulance. "Wait," Heidi said. "I'm going too."

"Sorry—you'll have to follow."

She didn't believe him at first. People rode along in ambulances all the time in the movies. "But I don't have a car!"

"I'm sorry. Family only. You'll have to hail a cab."

"But where are you taking her? I need to go with her."

"If you want to check on her, she'll be at Methodist." Heidi's blank expression must have spoken for her, because he added, "New York Methodist—it's in the Slope."

It wasn't that she wanted to spend her night in a hospital emergency room, but it would be awful for Mrs. DiBenedetto to be stuck in emergency, drugged, with nobody to speak for her.

Reluctant to let the EMS vehicle out of her sight, Heidi snatched her snow-covered purse and the shopping bag off the sidewalk and ran after it, nearly falling a few times before she reached the corner of Court Street. The ambulance was long gone by the time a cab slid to the curb to pick her up.

"Can you take me to Methodist Hospital?" she asked the driver.

"You called me, right?"

She blinked, confused. "Well, no, I didn't—"

"Yes, you did. Otherwise, this trip would be illegal, because only yellow cabs can pick people up on the street."

"Oh." She sighed. "Right. I did call. What took you so long?"

He nodded. "Methodist Hospital, coming right up."

Heidi sat back and watched the near-deserted, snowy streets glide by as she frantically prayed that Mrs. DiBenedetto would be okay. It seemed likely the woman had broken something, since she hadn't been able to get up. But sometimes old people fell and there were complications. What if she'd hit her head on the way down? People could seem fine after a bump on the head and then die hours later.

Suddenly, any dreams of shiny industrial mixers, true love, or just a quiet day in her jammies watching *Avatar* evaporated. All she wanted for Christmas now was not to have killed her landlady.

Chapter 4

By the time Heidi dragged herself back home again, it was past one thirty. She was unlocking her door when her neighbor Martine appeared, dressed in a wool coat over a pair of satiny-looking pajamas, her hair pulled back in a haphazard ponytail. The French girl worked as an au pair for Janice, a woman who rented the apartment that took up the second and third floors of Mrs. DiBenedetto's house. Janice, who traveled for her job with the UN, wasn't around half the time to enjoy her luxurious spread. Money was wasted on the rich.

"What is happening!" Martine yelled as if Heidi were a half a block away instead of a mere foot from her face.

"Come in," Heidi said. The snow was still coming down, and it was too cold to be talking in the doorway.

She led the way into her apartment, and Martine scrunched her face as she glanced around. Whatever was bugging her evaporated momentarily in the face of Heidi's primitive conditions. *"Mon dieu!"*

The apartment was one room, really—a straight shot from the front door through the living room to the back wall, except that about three-quarters of the way, futons and old chairs gave way to an ancient refrigerator and a stove that Heidi still didn't entirely trust after a year. A bathroom with a leaky shower, an addition tacked on by the late Mr. DiBenedetto to make the space rentable, was located off the kitchen.

"It's not the Waldorf," Heidi agreed.

Whatever was disturbing Martine, this peek at Heidi's living conditions didn't help. All at once, she put her hands over her ears and let out a shriek. *"Je n'en peux plus!"* When Heidi stood blinking at her, she stamped her foot and translated. "I can't take any more!"

"Any more what?"

Martine bugged her eyes and pointed to the ceiling. "You cannot hear it? The barking constantly of the dog?"

Heidi tilted her head. Now that she was listening for it, Marcello's yapping upstairs was hard to miss. She'd been too glad to be home—and too distracted by Martine—to notice the noise.

"It's been going on for hours!" Martine cried. "He will not stop. I knocked on the door of Mrs. DiBenedetto, but she does not answer."

"Oh—Mrs. DiB had an accident. I took her to the hospital. She fell down the front steps and broke her hip. Sprained her wrist, too—but the hip is going to be the big problem."

Martine sank onto the futon as if boneless, buried her head in her hands, and started bawling like a baby.

Heidi gaped at her. She'd never gotten the sense that Martine liked Mrs. DiBenedetto—or anyone, really. "I'm sorry—I had no idea you'd take the news so hard."

Martine shook her head. "I'm crying because my father is in hospital. In Lyon."

"Oh." She understood the problem now. Or thought she did. "That's awful."

"He is so sick, Heidi. I think maybe he might not get well. Maybe I won't see him again, ever."

Heidi sank onto the sofa next to her. Slumped there, her eyes red, Martine looked about eighteen years old. Which she might have been. Heidi wasn't sure. When she'd first met her, Martine had been with Janice, and Heidi hadn't wanted to say, "You look too young to be taking care of someone's kid." But it was true. Right now, she looked like a child herself.

"Oh, Martine. I'm sorry."

"And I cannot go home," she continued, snuffling. "I cannot leave Wilson."

Wilson was Janice's baby. Well, he'd been a baby when Heidi moved in. Now he had to be one and a half, maybe going on two.

"Because Janice is . . . where, exactly?"

"Darfur."

"Oh." Not within easy reach, then.

"I cannot sleep." Martine's face squinched up as she tried not to cry again. "And then the dog starts barking and the kid cries and cries."

Heidi straightened. Wilson. He must be up in the apartment by <u>himself</u>. Heidi knew nothing about kids, but she was pretty sure leaving them alone in an apartment wasn't kosher. She got up and attempted to rally Martine. "It'll be okay. I'll fetch Marcello and make him shut his yap, and you go back up to Wilson and try to get some sleep. Things will seem better in the morning than they do now."

Martine stood on a sigh, and dragged to the door. "Thank you, Heidi. I have no one else here."

If Heidi was all she had, she was in bad shape. They barely knew each other. "It'll be okay, Martine," she said, trying to sound reassuring.

She grabbed her own keys and Mrs. DiBenedetto's

thick key ring and headed for the apartment upstairs. Through the door, Marcello sounded ferocious, but when she stepped into the living area, he bleated and streaked toward the kitchen. Heidi gave chase. The little fur ball growled as she scooped him up, but she was too tired to care about getting bitten. All she wanted now was sleep.

Holding the Pomeranian under one arm like a football, she grabbed a bag of dog food with her free hand and made her way back downstairs. The unfamiliar surroundings in the basement succeeded in shutting Marcello up, but if he did start kicking up a fuss again, at least there would be an empty apartment as a buffer between him and Martine.

Heidi slipped into the first flannel pajamas she could find—ones with Snoopy in a Santa hat all over them, the cuffs of which were trimmed in white faux fur. They had been a gift from her mom and were still stiff from non-use, but they were warm. Not bothering to make up the bed, she pulled her comforter out of the closet and crashed on the futon as it was, still folded into a couch. She rolled toward the backrest until she hit a tiny body behind her. Marcello snarled a warning, sending Heidi scrabbling back to the edge.

But this was ridiculous. She wasn't going to be dictated to by some furry little piranha. She sat up to explain the rules of the apartment to Marcello, but was interrupted by a knock on her door. Marcello launched himself off the futon and skidded to the door in full Pomeranian bray.

Heidi hitched the comforter around her shoulders and tromped toward the door, expecting to find Martine again.

Instead, she swung the door open and came face-to-face with Patrick. He was still wearing his uniform topped with a dark coat that had reflective patches all over it. He took off his hat, shedding snow in the doorway.

Heidi gaped at him, confused, until the instant that gaze of his locked onto her.

She gulped. Of course. She knew why he was here.

"I saw your light on," he began.

She blurted out, "I wasn't trying to kill her."

He blinked as if he didn't know what she was talking about—as if he hadn't come by to wring a confession out of her.

"Mrs. DiBenedetto?" she said, in answer to his clueless look. Oh, he was good. She turned to let him into the apartment, although Marcello had no intention of being such a pushover. "Marcello—quiet!"

The dog growled at her.

"That's why you're here, right?" she asked, shutting the door after Patrick had batted more snow off himself and stepped inside.

He glanced around, his squint indicating he was no more impressed by her apartment than Martine had been.

"We heard there was an EMS call to your building," he explained. "I came by to see . . . well, what happened."

"The EMS workers probably told you about Mrs. DiBenedetto calling me an assassin, but it was all just a mix-up with Marcello's leash—he got stuck in the Christmas tree."

"The one on the sidewalk?" Patrick's eyebrows arched. "The one Miss Scrooge swore she didn't want?"

Heat zipped into her cheeks. "Okay . . . I brought it back with me. Seemed stupid to waste a perfectly good tree." She tugged the comforter more tightly around her, in the vain hope that he hadn't noticed she was wearing fur-trimmed Snoopy-Santa pajamas.

He nodded slowly, a smile tilting his mouth. "And so you were dragging the tree home, the dog got tangled in it, and this woman, this—"

"Mrs. DiBenedetto, my landlady." Heidi gave a blow-by-blow account, going back to the accidentally pilfered begonia and Mrs. DiB's crazy notion that Heidi had stolen the tree. When she was done, she was close to certain she'd convinced Patrick that she hadn't intended to kill or maim anyone.

Patrick leaned down and petted Marcello, who, having accepted that the intruder was here to stay, fell on his back for a belly scratch.

Heidi looked on, amazed. "He hasn't done that for me."

Patrick mumbled some doggie-speak at Marcello and angled a smile at her. "Maybe he still sees you as a mad assassin."

"So . . . are you going to write this in your report?"

"What report?"

"The incident report."

He stood. "Actually, I'm off duty, but since I was passing by, I wanted to make sure that everything was okay here. That you were okay."

"Oh." For the first time since he'd come through the door, Heidi began to breathe easier. He wasn't about to toss her in the hoosegow, then. Except . . .

He'd come to see *her*?

She swallowed. "You want some . . ." She tried to think of something she had to offer. "Hot chocolate?"

"Sure," he said, looking around again. He kept his expression neutral, but she could tell he was thinking what any sentient being would. *What a dump.*

She hurried to the stove to boil some water. From the back of the cupboard, she pulled out a box containing hot cocoa packets—God knows how old, since she didn't remember buying them—the contents of which had solidified into thin slabs. She knocked a couple of packets on the counter to break them up before tearing into them. "So you just finished work?" she asked.

He leaned against the fridge, watching her preparations. "Till tomorrow."

"You work the holiday? You don't mind?"

"Nah. The duty sergeant tries to let the guys with families have a little free time. And since I'm single . . ."

Those eyes lasered in on her, and she shifted uncomfortably in her comforter cocoon. She drummed her fingers on the frigid counter tiles. "Is it too cold in here?"

"It's nippy, for sure. I guess that's why you're bundled up."

"Uh-huh."

"I was worried you'd already be in bed, but it looks like . . ." He frowned and scanned the room again. "Don't you have a bed?"

"I fold down the futon," she explained, pulling the kettle off the stove. She tossed the petrified cocoa powder chunks into mugs, sloshed the hot water in, and gave the liquid a few stirs. Then she rearranged the comforter, tossing one corner over her shoulder, toga-style, to free up a hand.

"Thanks," Patrick said as she handed a mug to him.

They drifted back to the futon, each perching on either side of it, and took cautious sips of cocoa. It was on the weak side, with sad, desiccated marshmallow chips bobbing on the surface.

"So . . . all alone for Christmas," he said.

Marcello darted into the space between them, sidling closer to Patrick. Heidi laughed. "Not as alone as I'd anticipated."

"Doesn't your mother live around here?" he asked.

"She lives in Connecticut, but this year she's in Cancun with her husband. Christmas Eve is their first anniversary. I was invited to Cancun, actually, but, you know . . . three's a crowd."

Great conversation. She took another swig from her

mug and wished there was rum in it. Why did she feel so nervous? He was just a guy. Just an incredibly good-looking guy who'd dropped by at two in the morning.

"It's officially Christmas Eve day right now," he said.

"That's right." She remembered last year. "Last Christmas Eve was all about my mom's wedding—I was maid of honor. Then she and Tom flew off on their honeymoon and I came back here and glutted myself on wedding cake and watched the Turner Classic Movies' Christmas marathon. It wasn't pretty."

"Last Christmas I got shot," Patrick said. "That wasn't pretty, either."

She gasped in a breath, nearly choking on her cocoa. "You got shot? How?"

"Fast-food robbery in Bed-Stuy. Christmas is a big time for armed robbery. Lots of money pressure on people."

"But you came out of it okay, right?"

"Sure—Marcus and I even managed to catch the guy. The bullet only nicked my arm, but it still got me a few days off."

"I don't like guns," Heidi said with a shiver.

"Hopefully, you'll never have one pointed at you."

Too late for that hope. Images flashed through her mind of being hunkered down in a horse stall in Texas with a gunman firing at her. Laura, of all people, had rescued her. Laura, who had always seemed to want her dead. It was tempting to tell the story to Patrick, but she wasn't sure explaining that her ex-boyfriend had hired a thug to kill her because she'd discovered his embezzlement racket would put her in the best light.

She sipped her watery cocoa. "So . . . do you have a big family?"

He laughed. "Huge. Five brothers and sisters, uncles and aunts and nephews all over the place. We're the kind of family that has to set up card tables in two rooms to squeeze everybody in at holiday meals. And I can't even remember the number of Lego sets I wrapped up for Christmas presents for my nephews in the past week."

A stupid grin seemed to have frozen itself in place on her face. A real family. One that actually liked you. What would that be like?

"And so your mom's it?" he asked.

"Well . . ." She cleared her throat, mentally fishing for some angle that would make her life seem less isolated and desperate. "I've got a couple of ex stepdads, and some ex-stepfamily in Texas. That's where the café's name comes from. Sweetgum, Texas."

He nodded.

"Sometimes I dream of having more family—*real* family—but I'm not sure I would know what to do with them. Maybe I should kidnap a few kids, give it a trial run." She felt her face go scarlet. "That is, I wouldn't *really* kidnap anybody."

Those eyes skewered her. "Like you wouldn't actually yank an old lady off her stoop?"

"Oh God."

He laughed and put his hand on her shoulder. The touch startled her. She hadn't realized how close he was. His eyes, which had laughter in them at first, darkened. His entire expression changed, and a charge snapped in the apartment's frigid air. She pulled her gaze away from his eyes, but it landed on his lips. She'd never noticed how full they were.

Marcello growled.

"It's late," Patrick said, standing abruptly. "I should get going."

She followed him to the door, the comforter requiring a geishalike mince. She still felt dazed from being so close to him, from sensing they were a moment away from . . . from what? What would have happened if Marcello hadn't intervened?

"Good night, Heidi," Patrick said at the door, putting his hat back on. "I'll see you tomorrow at the coffee shop."

"Actually, you'll see me today at the coffee shop."

"Right." He grinned. "Love the Snoopy jammies, by the way."

She closed the door and sagged against it. Her fleeting romantic notions faded as she looked around her—the crappy apartment, her bizarre outfit, the watery hot chocolate with cocoa film floating at the top. If Dinah's first theory had been correct, and Patrick wasn't just a nuisance bear, this visit had probably cured him. No wonder he'd fled.

What an evening.

She deposited the mugs in the sink and stumbled back to the futon. Marcello hopped up ahead of her, settling into the center against the backrest. She lay down, attempting to perch on the edge and not squish the dog. As she closed her eyes, a curious question popped into her head.

How had he known when he'd heard the EMS report that it was her apartment building?

How did he know where she lived at all?

Interesting.

Yawning, she flipped over and was immediately hurtled back to the edge by a series of rapid-fire snarls.

Chapter 5

She awoke to someone pounding against her skull with a mallet.

Except, when she listened more closely, she realized the mallet was Marcello. Marcello barking. And that pounding? Someone was at her front door.

Heidi lumbered off the futon and stumbled toward the door, tripping on the comforter she still hugged around her for warmth. God, it was cold. Was miserly Mrs. DiBenedetto controlling the thermostat from her hospital bed with thought rays?

"Marcello, shut up."

He didn't like that. The dog turned his frantic attention from the door to Heidi, as if *she* were the intruder.

"Shush!"

When she swung the door open, letting in a blast of wet freezing air, he was still barking . . . and Martine was standing in front of her, still weeping. It might have been two in the morning all over again. Except Heidi felt more tired now, even after sleeping. What time was it?

"Will you take him?" Martine asked.

"Who?"

"Wilson. I must go."

Heidi gave herself a mental slap in an attempt to wake up. Something told her she needed to have her brain firing on all cylinders. *Take Wilson?* She hadn't babysat anything since she was a teenager. And that had just been one time, for a desperate neighbor, and it had not resulted in success. Due to a Jiffy Pop disaster, she'd ended up with fire trucks surrounding the house.

Sometimes it amazed her that she'd made it to adulthood. So-called. The jury was still out on whether she would actually make it *through* adulthood.

Still, Martine looked frantic. She couldn't not help.

"Of course I'll take him. Let me wake up a little . . ."

"I must go. Now."

"Now?" Heidi tried to kick-start her head. "Okay—I guess I can take him to the café with me. He doesn't move around much, does he?"

The French girl's brows beetled. "What?"

"The kid. He mostly just sits there, right?" Heidi had really only seen him in his stroller, with Martine pushing him.

"He's a toddler."

"Oh." Toddling. She supposed she could handle that. The incipient cry coming out of Martine's throat made up her mind for her. "No problem," she assured the au pair. "Bring him down."

The girl was gone in a flash. Heidi turned back to the apartment and tried to pull herself together. Marcello's vocal output shifted from annoying barks to a constant whining hum. Heidi hurried to the kitchen and got out some cereal bowls, filling one with water and putting it on the ground. The dog trotted over and started slurping it up.

Maybe she should have put a bowl out for him last night. She opened his bag of food, shook some kibble into the other cereal bowl, and placed it on the floor next to the water. Marcello switched to it immediately, inhaling the dog food in such a frenzy that he seemed to be choking and swallowing at the same time.

Before Heidi had finished dressing, another sharp knock sounded at the door. Martine was back, this time lugging a lot of stuff with her, not the least of which was Wilson, who she pushed inside the apartment in his stroller. The little boy looked a lot bigger than he'd seemed the last time Heidi had seen him. Like a little human, really. He was half covered in a puffy snowsuit, although she could see he was dressed in jeans and a green corduroy jacket and matching hat underneath. Martine dropped a duffel bag on the ground and tossed a manila envelope and some keys on the kitchen counter. "It should be okay."

Heidi frowned at the keys. "Are those to Janice's place?"

"Of course. But please don't mess anything. The maid has come yesterday."

"Yeah, but . . ." How long did Martine intend to be gone? Heidi assumed she was going to the hairdresser's or something. Or to a Christmas brunch with some fellow au pairs. But the duffel indicated something longer than a morning.

"Thank you so much, Heidi. I know we have never became good friends . . ."

"Wait a sec," Heidi interrupted the farewell message with a frown. "Where exactly are you going, Martine?"

The girl blinked. "Lyon."

"Lyon?" Heidi repeated. "In *France*?"

"Yes, of course. My home. I told you."

Crap. "But—" What about Janice? What about Wilson? Heidi eyed the kid again. With each passing second, he looked bigger, more labor-intensive.

Her small hesitation was all it took to set Martine off again. She not only started crying, she was quivering. "I *must* go home! My father, he is dying, do you understand? Doesn't anyone understand what it means to be so far from him now?"

Heidi remembered hearing about the death of her own father, long divorced from her mom and living on the other side of the country. She had seen him a few months earlier, but she never had a chance to say good-bye. "Yes, I understand. Really, I do. But Janice—"

"Janice is coming back."

"When?"

"For Christmas."

Christmas was tomorrow.

"But I have to leave, now, because of the ice," Martine explained.

"Ice?"

Martine nodded. "Otherwise I will never get home until it will be too late." She pushed the envelope toward Heidi again. "It's all there. All instructions. It will all be okay."

"But won't Janice be pissed?"

Tossing the fringed end of her scarf over her shoulder, Martine said, "I don't care. I will be in France." She was already heading for the door. "Thank you for doing this thing for me, Heidi. I never believed Mrs. DiBenedetto when she called you *une criminelle.*"

Lovely.

Heidi was still trying to make sense of what Martine had said before—about the ice. "What did you mean about ice?"

"There is a storm on the way," Martine said, opening

the door. Her suitcase was waiting outside. She wasn't wasting any time, evidently. When she took hold of the handle, Heidi began to panic.

"Wait—what should I do with Wilson? I mean, what does he eat . . . and *do* all day?"

"It's all in the envelope," Martine said, flipping up her coat collar. "You can take him with you everywhere. He likes people."

Without further adieu—literally—Martine headed up the walkway and turned onto the street. In a flash, something red streaked out the door past Heidi's knees.

Wilson!

She reached out in time to catch him by the hoodie. When he realized he wasn't moving anymore, and that his nanny was disappearing down the street through the snow at a quick trudge, the kid started screaming his lungs out. Martine whirled, yelled something that was lost in the wind and the distance, and blew a kiss at him. Wilson shrieked her name as she turned away and grew smaller. "Tiiiiiiiiiinne!"

It was like the end of the Western, *Shane*—the scene when Shane rides away, leaving the boy, stuck on his parents' bedraggled ranch, yelling after him. Heidi felt she was playing the part of the bedraggled ranch.

When she couldn't take any more of the drama or the cold, she pulled a shrieking Wilson back indoors and flipped the lock.

She had to think. But the dog was barking again—at Wilson now—which in turn made Wilson scream louder. Or maybe he was crying because it had sunk in that Martine had left him stuck in Heidi's incompetent hands. Come to think of it, she felt like crying herself.

The kid stood in the foyer, frozen, except for his mouth in full cry. Then he began to stomp-hop across the living room, weeping and raving. "Pee pee pee pee pee!"

Those syllables set alarm bells clanging inside Heidi's skull. Especially once she caught the first strong whiff of urine.

"You need to pee?" she asked in a voice that sounded unnaturally loud and upbeat. Then her slippers skidded beneath her and she noticed glistening little boot tracks all across her polyurethane plank floors.

She swept Wilson off the ground, holding him at arm's length, and skidded toward the bathroom. He was wailing and she was letting out a keening sound, and Marcello was right at her heels, yapping. She deposited the kid in the bathroom and had started peeling the snowsuit off of him when it occurred to her that his clothes were dry. And that even if the kid had peed in his pants, he was probably wearing some kind of diaper. Which meant the offender had to be . . .

She glared at Marcello, who sensed immediately that the worm had turned. He yelped and fled to the living room, scooting under the futon.

Maybe that was the real reason he'd been whining this morning, she realized. She had a lot to learn—about dogs and kids.

Unfortunately, dogs were probably easier. At least she knew what to feed them. A quick look in the bag told her that Martine hadn't left her a bag of toddler kibble. There was a sippy cup in there, however. She put a kettle of water on for hot cocoa for the kid and set about mopping up the floor damage. Then, once the water was tepid, she mixed in the cocoa in the sippy cup, sloshed in some milk, and put the kid on the futon with it.

While he was slurping, she frantically went through the information Martine had left. Amazing—Janice was into helicopter parenting even from a continent away. She'd written up rules about how much television Wilson could watch (none), what music Martine could listen to in the child's presence (no rap, hip-hop, or anything with foul language or dissonant chords), and what foods he could eat. Nothing but organic produce was supposed to pass baby's lips. Best not to think of the five inches of un-pronounceable chemicals on the ingredients list on the cocoa box. Already she was failing.

But Martine had sworn Janice was coming back for Christmas. That had to mean today or tomorrow. How much damage could she do in a day?

She hoped it would be no more than a day. Heidi scanned the complicated contact sheet Martine had left. Although she doubted Darfur was on her calling plan, she picked up her phone and dialed a number in Africa.

Thirty minutes later, it was clear that tracking down someone in Darfur was no easy matter. She had finally reached a woman speaking on a satellite phone in a village, who had informed her that Janice had left there over a week before.

So where was she? On her way home, Heidi hoped. *Please let her be on her way home.*

What Martine had meant about the ice storm became clear as soon as Heidi left the apartment. Earlier, when she'd hurriedly walked Marcello up and down the street, the sky was partly cloudy. Yet by the time she'd rebundled Wilson, packed a backpack full of emergency supplies—extra clothes and Pull-ups—and wrestled him into the stroller to head out for the café, sleet was coming down steadily. A film of ice covered the snow, making walking an extra challenge. With every step, her boot would crunch through the ice and she would have to pick her foot out of the snowy trench.

Sal, Clay, and Dinah were hunched on the café's stoop when she walked up. Seeing the stroller, Dinah's eyes widened. She shouted something through her muffler, but Heidi shook her head in incomprehension as she dug for her keys and opened up the café. Talking in the open air required effort, and she was already exhausted from picking her way across five blocks of the slippery ice bog to get here.

Once they were inside, everyone began to unpeel their outer layers and gathered around the stroller. "What is that?" Dinah asked, dropping the suitcase she'd brought with her on the floor.

Clay laughed. "I'm guessing it's a boy."

"But where did he come from?"

The kid gaped at them all shyly. He'd kept up a constant semi-intelligible babble all the way from the apartment, but now he didn't appear willing to give these people any information, even under torture. Which, judging from his wary expression, he expected at any moment.

"He's a neighbor's kid," Heidi explained. "His name's Wilson."

She was going to make introductions, but Wilson wasn't paying attention to them at all now. He gazed at all the stuff on the walls—Christmas decorations, mementos from Texas, pictures of Sweetgum, and the television mounted on the wall near the counter. And, of course, the Christmas tree. The moment she unbuckled him, he hopped out of the stroller and took off running to inspect the tree, falling halfway there.

Heidi braced herself for a piercing cry that didn't happen. Sal cut it off at the pass.

"Watch out, Wilson!" He picked the kid up and swung him to his shoulders. "Wanna see the angel on top?"

"Wilson reminds me of that Tom Hanks movie," Dinah said. "You don't think the kid's parents named him after a volleyball, do you?"

Heidi shrugged. "It might be a family name. Who knows?"

"I was assuming *you* would," Dinah said. "Since you volunteered to take him."

"I didn't volunteer. His nanny up and ran away to France this morning."

"Holy cow," Clay said. He was over at the coffeepots now, loading up the Bunn for its first round of the day. In this morning of chaos, Heidi didn't question a customer crossing the counter barrier. "When's the mom coming back?"

Heidi lowered her voice. "Not sure about that."

She had brought the list of phone numbers and an e-mail address, in hopes that she would be able to track Janice down today. "She's supposed to be on her way back—I think so, at least—but with this weather . . ."

"This weather sucks." Dinah took out an apron from behind the counter, unfolded it with a snap, and tied it around her waist. She glared at Clay, who was watching over the coffeemaker. "You want an apron, too, Clay?"

"I'm just trying to get things started."

"The automat is dead." Dinah pushed him toward a chair. "Go sit down like you're supposed to."

"Speaking of weather," Heidi said to her, "shouldn't you be getting home?"

"My train doesn't leave till this evening."

"Maybe you should take an earlier train."

Dinah rolled her eyes in good-natured disgust. "Please! This isn't Texas or Arkansas. New York doesn't shut down because of a little snow."

"They're predicting intermittent freezing precipitation through the day," Clay said. "Ice-pocolypse."

Dinah rolled her eyes at Heidi. "One stretch of bad weather and he's Al Roker."

"I'm serious," Heidi said, though it touched her more

than she could say that Dinah would risk her meet-up with master-of-the-universe Dan Janacek to stay and help. "I know you're not a wimp. I know Vermonters are used to living in the tundra. But Amtrak has gone haywire over smaller problems than this."

"So what am I supposed to do—leave you here with nobody?"

"I'm here," Sal said.

"Me, too," Clay added.

Dinah rounded on the latter in exasperation. "You don't work here. Your only job here is to hand over your hard-earned money."

Clay looked offended. "Well, if that's the way you feel, I'll pay for my coffee and leave right now." He pulled out his wallet. "And you won't see me again." He fished around the bills and finally handed over a twenty. "Not till lunch."

Dinah laughed as she snatched the bill and took it behind the counter. "Hey, Heidi—we need to open the register."

Heidi hurried over. Her brain was still in outer space. Or Darfur. She keyed the register open and also unlocked the cabinet under the counter. She opened it, reached in, and . . .

Nothing.

Heat flashed through her—that fevered realization that something huge had been forgotten. The test, the mother's birthday, the tax deadline. *The cash box.*

She carried the box home every night and lugged it back each morning in a shopping bag, and then unlocked the cabinet like she was doing now and put it back. But she'd forgotten to do that this morning because she hadn't brought the box back from her apartment.

Another wave of heat hit her, making her light-headed. She hadn't brought it because . . . well, because everything this morning was all screwed up. But, also, she hadn't seen it. The shopping bag hadn't been sitting under the kitchen table, where she usually kept it stowed overnight. She couldn't remember having seen it at all since . . .

Last night.

Heart thumping, she went over the events of the night before. She had taken the cash box home in the shopping bag. Mrs. DiBenedetto had fallen. Heidi had called an ambulance. She'd run indoors to lock up Marcello, and then . . .

Oh God. Oh God. She'd left it sitting on the sidewalk.

But then she remembered. She *had* picked up the bag off the sidewalk! She recalled that very clearly. In her hurry to follow the ambulance, she'd grabbed both her leather messenger bag and the shopping bag. She'd had her hand around the two handles when she'd run to Court Street to get the cab.

But then what had she done with it?

Lost it. And because she hadn't made it to the bank yesterday before it closed, that meant she'd lost . . . she calculated rapidly, roughly . . . over eleven hundred dollars.

She stumbled backward and sank down in a chair with a thump.

All eyes were on her now, including Wilson's, peering down at her from high atop Sal's shoulders. Two round, worried orbs among all the others.

"I don't have the cash box," she said. "It's gone. All that money's gone."

Chapter 6

She probably could have flown to China by now. Instead, she was still stuck in Chicago.

Lots of people seemed to be stuck here. O'Hare Airport swarmed with travelers, some frantic, many just plain cranky, but a lot, like Erica, wearied numb. If the loudspeaker at the gate had announced that they were routing passengers to New York through Australia, most people probably would have lumbered onto the plane without a question.

It was a struggle to stay awake. She'd already drunk so much Coca-Cola that she felt as if the blood in her veins had turned to corn syrup. Walking through the airport to keep from conking out, she had discovered this really cool long hallway that was all flashing neon. She'd spent thirty minutes going from one end to the other on the moving sidewalk until finally all the sugar in her system and the blinking light made her twitchy. She'd bought another Coke and sat down.

And then, with forty-five minutes to go until they

promised—absolutely promised—that her plane to New York was finally going to board, she remembered something vital. So vital she actually groaned aloud. She didn't have a present for Heidi! She couldn't show up empty-handed on Christmas. Her mother had always said it was rude to stay at anybody's house without bringing some kind of gift. And here she was, about to show up on Heidi's doorstep without warning on Christmas Eve. And no gift.

She shot out of her chair, wondering what she could buy with her rapidly diminishing funds. Food and drink and bubble gum had eaten up almost twenty-five dollars already.

She'd mulled over spending some of that money to call Heidi and warn her that she was coming. Or maybe calling Laura. It could be that everyone in Texas had figured out she was missing by now. They might be really worried—might think that a serial killer had gotten her or something. In Phoenix, she'd stopped at phone booths several times, her hand poised over the receiver.

But Heidi might tell her to go back home to Sweetgum, and that was something that Erica absolutely didn't want to do. Or maybe Heidi would feel duty-bound to call Laura on Erica's behalf, or—even worse—her dad. The thought of that happening made her skin flash cold and hot, and Erica suddenly felt overwhelmed by the crowds around her, and the stupidity of what she'd done.

Those calls were going to have to be made eventually. She knew that. The farther she got from Texas, the more she dreaded the inevitable moment of truth. In the movies, runaway or lost children were always welcomed back home with tears of happiness and sometimes guilt on the part of the parents, who now understood that they hadn't really appreciated the missing kid. Maybe that was the image she'd had in her mind when she'd boarded the bus to DFW Airport nearly twenty-four hours ago. A lifetime ago.

But who was she kidding? All anyone was going to feel toward her was pissed off. Her father was going to be spitting mad—even before he found out that she'd used Leanne's credit card information to buy her tickets. Best case, her father would ground her for a few years. Worst case, he would forbid her from going to the farm ever again and send her off to live at a boarding school for juvenile delinquents.

Either way, Erica was in no hurry to find out exactly how mad they all would be. And they would be just as angry whether she actually made it to Heidi's or not, so she might as well have her Christmas in New York before being condemned.

She hurried through the airport, hunting for something that might make an okay gift. Options were limited. For a moment, she considered decorative coffee mugs and coffee—but then she remembered that Heidi owned a coffee shop. Definitely not a good idea.

One store offered stuff like weird alarm clocks, back massagers, and motorized wine-bottle openers. But it was all real expensive and sort of weird. She wanted to get Heidi something she'd actually like. She looked in a place that sold sunglasses and tried on fifty pairs before deciding that was a stupid idea, too. How could she know if they'd even fit Heidi's head?

Twenty-five minutes to go—they might have already started boarding her plane. She reached an area set by for selling stuff like liquor and perfume. Evidently the airport believed all its patrons either stank or needed a drink.

There were other items, too—chocolate, for instance. Lots of chocolate. You couldn't go wrong with that, could you? She bought a gigantic triangle-shaped chocolate bar.

But once she'd spent the money, the chocolate bar seemed lame. It was a kid's gift, something *she'd* like. Heidi was more of a girly girl kind of person.

Erica was heading out of the duty-free area when her eye snagged on a perfume counter. Chanel. She remembered that her mom had bought Laura some Chanel powder once. "Known me all my life and you're *still* confusing me with Zsa Zsa Gabor," Laura had said.

But Heidi was Laura's opposite. So she'd probably like it.

Trouble was, the prices made Erica's stomach knot up. She wouldn't be springing for many meals while she was in New York, that was for sure. A measly little bottle of eau de toilette set her back sixty-five dollars. It hurt to fork over that much money for something called toilet water.

But it came in a foily prewrapped box, and she was able to sprint back to the plane in time to board carrying two gifts that she was sure were bound to please. Which was good, because she had a hunch that Heidi might be the only person to defend her when the poop hit the fan.

Heidi retraced her steps of the night before. Though she was in a panic, she had to go slowly because she had Wilson in tow. The sleet pelting against her hood caused a steady drumbeat in her ears as she picked her way down the sidewalk. The stroller wheels had frozen, so she pulled the thing behind her like a dray. She probably should have left the kid at the café—he'd already bonded with Sal—but now that she had taken responsibility for him, she didn't feel she could dump him on someone else. Although dumping him might have been preferable to dragging him around in an ice storm.

Finally Wilson pitched such a fit that she decided to let

him try to walk along with her, but for every three steps he took, he fell once. She expected him to explode in tears; instead, he couldn't have been more thrilled. "Snow" and "oops" became his favorite words. She tried to explain that this was *ice,* and that if he wasn't careful, there would be lots more oops ahead, but slipping was a game. It was all snow, all fun.

After a block of chasing after him and pulling him up-right, she decided she needed to keep a closer eye on the sidewalk instead of the kid, and so she forced him back in the stroller. Tears ensued, including her own as she reached her apartment block without finding the shopping bag with the cash box in it.

What had she expected? That a strongbox containing over eleven hundred dollars would sit untouched on a New York sidewalk overnight, waiting for her?

How could she have been so careless? Granted, it had been a traumatic night. But—eleven hundred dollars! The reality of her near-empty bank account tempted her to hurl herself onto the ice and let the sleet bury her alive. But now she had Wilson to be responsible for . . . not to mention Marcello . . . and she probably wouldn't die anyway. With her luck, she would only lose an ear or a nose or something. And then she'd have to spend the rest of her life not only poor, but noseless.

It had been idiotic for her to be running around with all that money in the first place—and all because she'd been paranoid about Sal. Sal, who had never been anything but honest with her. Who was unfailingly helpful, in fact. Who this very morning had settled Wilson down like the second coming of Mary Poppins.

Smart, Heidi. That great instinct for people strikes again.

As she approached Mrs. DiBenedetto's house, she noted the buried Christmas tree, its decorations now dull points of color beneath the ice. If she had simply left the tree in front of the café last night, her landlady wouldn't have accused her of stealing it, Marcello wouldn't have gotten his leash tangled, and Mrs. DiBenedetto wouldn't be in the hospital. And she wouldn't be chasing after her lost money.

She turned in to her brownstone at the same moment Patrick was emerging from the steps leading down to her door. She flushed with awareness that she probably looked a wreck in her Costco coat and her muffler and hat caked with sleet. Not to mention her dribbly nose and eyes rabbit red from worry, exhaustion, and stinging cold.

"Do you ever sleep?" she asked him.

"Do you?" His voice conveyed a smile even as his expression remained dead serious. Then he looked down at the stroller. "You weren't joking about kidnapping a kid for Christmas, were you?"

Damn. She had forgotten saying that—and here she showed up with a stray toddler. "No, I swear," she said, "he's the neighbor's son. I never would have—"

"I know," he said, smiling. "Marcus and I were just at the café."

"Oh." She felt foolish now. *Of course* he wouldn't think she'd actually kidnapped anybody.

She hoped he wouldn't, at least.

"We heard about what had happened with the money, too." His smile faded into a sympathetic frown. "I don't suppose you found the cash box?"

"No." She shrugged. "I shouldn't have expected to, I guess."

"How much money was in it?"

"Over eleven hundred dollars. I should have taken it to the bank, I know, but . . ." She stopped, knowing Patrick didn't want to hear about her bank's hours, no matter how patiently he heard her out. No doubt he listened to dozens of hard-luck stories every week using that same sympathetic stare. "Well, I screwed up. I suppose the next step is to call the cab company—but it was cash. Do people turn in found cash?"

"Sometimes. You'd be surprised." This, from the man who had been shot during a Christmas robbery. "What about the hospital?" he asked. "Did you have it then?"

She pinched her brow in concentration. "I don't remember. I know I was carrying my leather bag . . ."

"I'll check the hospital for you," Patrick said.

"Aren't you working?"

"Hey—this might have been a theft, right?" He assumed a Jack Webb deadpan. "That's where I come in. I carry a badge."

She couldn't help laughing, although she wanted to throw her arms around him and give him a boa constrictor squeeze of thanks. Her hero! Or at least he was trying to be. "Thank you, Patrick."

"Don't thank me yet."

"Just knowing there's someone else who cares makes me feel better."

"I do care." He hesitated a second, then began to blurt out, "In fact, I—"

Wilson started screaming and managed to scoot out of his seat. He took one step and fell smack on his butt. "Oops!"

Distracted, Patrick laughed and scooped him up. "Hey—watch it, buddy."

"It's a good thing he has that snowsuit, or he'd be black and blue by now," Heidi said.

Patrick walked with them to her apartment, but he didn't finish whatever it was he'd been about to confess to her. He deposited Wilson on the rectangle of mostly snow-free pavement at her doorway. "I'll get back to you this afternoon," he said. "Right now I've got to swing by the café again and pick up Marcus—he's on lunch break."

"And probably being abused by Dinah."

"Do you want a ride?" he asked.

It was tempting, but she shook her head. "No, I think I need to ransack my apartment thoroughly, to make sure the cash box isn't there. But thanks. Again."

Patrick hurried to the patrol car that was parked up the street. She couldn't remember feeling such a rush of love for anyone in a long time. Of course he was only being nice, but she felt so grateful, so aware of what an incredibly generous man he was, that she had the mad desire to run after him and promise to devote her whole life to making him happy, whether he wanted a hausfrau or just a lifetime supply of free coffee. His wish would be her command.

Fortunately, she restrained herself.

Or unfortunately, as it turned out.

Chapter 7

She and Wilson returned to the café, where a smattering of customers had gravitated to the tables nearest the television. Someone had turned it to The Weather Channel. In front of the register counter, Dinah leaned on the bottom of Heidi's rickety, paint-splattered aluminum stepladder. On the top of the ladder perched Clay.

"What is going on?" Heidi asked.

"Clay's hanging mistletoe."

"What for?"

"I think it's his last-ditch effort to get lucky," Sal muttered to her as he deposited fresh-from-the-oven gingerbread on the counter.

"As if we didn't have enough problems with the icy stoop," she grumbled, hoping there was some rock salt in the supply room. "Nothing says lawsuit like a customer on a ladder."

"It was my idea," Clay said, tacking the sprig in place by a silver ribbon tied around its stem. It stood out in the empty overhang—Heidi had been meaning to do something there, but couldn't decide what.

Clay looked hopefully at Dinah. "What do you think?"

"Isn't that stuff poisonous?" she asked.

Sal laughed. "It depends on who sees you standing under it."

Clay climbed down and waggled his brows at Dinah. "You're right under the mistletoe, Dinah."

"Close your eyes," she said.

Like a fool, he complied. Dinah reached behind her and pulled a piece of gingerbread off a tray. She smashed it into Clay's mouth and then arched a brow at Heidi. "You can take it out of my pay."

After catching the avalanche of gingerbread that crumbled down his sweater, Clay blinked in surprise. "That's really good," he said. "Did you make that, Di?"

"No, Sal did—and please don't call me Di," she said. "I'm not a princess, or something that gets rolled down a craps table. At least, not usually."

Heidi reached for the television remote. She was as transfixed by the weather as anyone, but having it on made her feel as if she were in an airport lounge. She flipped it to TCM, which was showing a Robert Mitchum movie. The black-and-white images worked on her nerves like a tonic.

"Maybe you should go home now," she suggested to Dinah.

"Why?" Dinah tossed a glance at her watch. "Does it take five hours to get to Penn Station these days? My train doesn't leave till six thirty."

"There might be trouble with the trains."

"The sleet's let up."

"The weather guy was saying it's going to start up again in the evening," Heidi warned her. "You might need to change your reservation to another train."

Dinah laughed. "Do you think there are dozens of alternatives to the Ethan Allen Express? On Christmas Eve?"

"Maybe you won't get out at all," Clay said. "If you need someplace to go on Christmas . . ."

"I don't," Dinah said. "I'll leave work this evening, catch my train, and be in Chippenhook by midnight." She smiled and repeated, "Chippenhook by midnight—sounds like poetry, doesn't it?"

"Not to me, it doesn't," Clay grumbled.

Dinah ignored him and studied Heidi. Worry must have shown in her face.

"I didn't find the money," Heidi told her in a low voice.

The younger woman put a hand on Heidi's shoulder. "We know. Patrick told us awhile ago when he came by to pick up Marcus. I'm sorry."

"It wasn't in my apartment, either. It could still show up, though," Heidi added. "I'm going to start calling cab companies."

"I can do that," Sal said, taking out his cell phone. "I have an uncle who's a dispatcher."

Heidi's heart picked up, then sank again. "It was a gypsy cab."

"No worries," Sal assured her. "Uncle Nick knows all these outfits. We'll find it."

Patrick, now Sal. Heidi felt so grateful to these people trying to keep her hope alive. Especially since there was only a chance in a million that the money was still out there.

She spent the rest of the afternoon serving up the usual lunch fare and baking way too much. She tried not to think about what the loss of that money would mean to her in concrete terms. Good-bye, new mixer and new sink in the café's bathroom, which was rust-stained and pulling away from the wall. Come the new year, she would really be flying by the seat of her pants—one payroll away from disaster, really. It wasn't as if there was a lot of fat that could be trimmed from her operation. She had Sal and Dinah, and she couldn't imagine the Sweetgum without either of them. Short of putting all her belongings in storage and sleeping in the supply closet, she couldn't think of many ways to cut corners.

Not baking more than she needed would probably be a good start. But if she wasn't baking, she would be worrying. Sal was parked on a stool by the sink, still trying to find the car service that had picked her up—and having no luck, if his mutterings and occasional outbursts in Italian were any indication.

Dinah stayed all afternoon, even though there were never more customers than Heidi could have handled alone. She had the feeling that the waitress was hanging around to see if the money ever turned up.

At one point, Sal hung up the phone, clapped Heidi on the shoulder, and ran out. She and Dinah grinned at each other. Maybe she was finally about to run into some luck. The mood in the café lifted higher still when Clay got Wilson to say *mistletoe*. It came out as "mizzletoed," but he said it—often—with gusto.

As daylight drew to a close, the sleet started falling again. More heavily this time.

"I better leave," Dinah said, reluctantly picking up her suitcase.

Clay hopped up. "Walk you to the subway?"

Dinah looked him over with exasperation.

He upped the ante. "Treat you to a cab?"

A smile spread across her lips as she shook her head. "It's a free country. You can waste your time and money if you want."

He scooted to her side and helped her on with her coat as if she'd just agreed to a date.

"Have a Merry Christmas," Heidi told her, pressing some cookies on her to take on her trip.

Dinah smiled. "You, too. Enjoy *Avatar*. And babysitting. And dog-sitting."

When they were gone, Heidi sat Wilson in the chair by the fireplace with a ball of cookie dough, which during the course of the afternoon had become his obsession. He not only liked the taste, it also served as makeshift Play-Doh.

As afternoon surrendered to Christmas Eve, Heidi sold lots of to-go things to people who were obviously headed to some holiday gathering. They came in for a dozen cookies, or a whole pie, or a loaf of pumpkin gingerbread. Some seemed happy, some frenzied.

The customers kept her busy enough that she'd almost forgotten about Sal until he appeared again. He didn't come running in with the same enthusiasm as when he'd left. In fact, he seemed morose, and was hiding something under the arm of his jacket.

"You found the cab?" she guessed.

He nodded.

"And they hadn't seen anything?"

He shook his head and slowly unfolded the bag that had been tucked under his arm. She recognized it right away as the shopping bag she'd used to haul around the cash box. It was intact . . . except for the gaping hole in the bottom.

"Dude said it was like this when he found it."

Heidi nodded as she inspected the bag—as if it would tell her anything other than the fact that her money was gone.

She reminded herself that she never really expected to find it. But that didn't make losing eleven hundred dollars any easier to accept.

"I'm sorry, Heidi. When I found the right cab, I thought for sure it would be there if we searched—that maybe it could have slipped under the seat. But there was nada. Zip. Maybe the box fell out of the bag and one of his later fares found it."

"Or maybe the bag broke before I got to Court Street." In which case, the money really was gone, because it hadn't been there when she retraced her steps.

Any way you looked at it, it was gone. Gone with the wind. *Get over it, Heidi. You're broke. So are a lot of people. Move on.*

Sal dug his hands into his pockets and surveyed the empty café. "Dinah take off?"

"A little while ago."

"Clay go with her?"

She eyed him sharply. "How did you know?"

"Guy looked like he was going to stick to her like glue."

"Poor Clay. She has her heart set on the master of the universe from Chippenhook."

"Don't write Clay off yet," Sal said. A dough missile whizzed past him and he pivoted toward Wilson. "Hey, man! What have you got there?" Before he could take a step, the kid hurled another wad of dough through the air.

"Mizzletoed!" Wilson yelled, which apparently now was toddler-speak for "bombs away!"

He had surprisingly good aim. The buttery, sugary blob landed a few inches to the right of the mistletoe sprig, where it stuck to the wall.

"Mizzletoed!"

Heidi flinched—she wondered if she would ever hear that word again without wanting to duck. "Maybe I could make some extra cash marketing my cookie dough as an adhesive."

"I'll get the ladder," Sal said.

He hurried to the storage closet and came back with

the stepladder. Before he could start to climb, she stopped him. "I don't need to accompany anyone else to the hospital this holiday."

He tilted his head. "You have to be careful, though. You have a kid now."

"Just on loan," she said, gently nudging him out of the way. She climbed the few rungs with a rag in her hand and reached for the blob of dough. Gallant Sal stayed where he was, holding the base steady, so when the blob fell before she could grab it, he was in a perfect spot to get it splat on his head.

His face froze in an expression of comical disgust as he picked the sticky lump out of a stray lock of hair. "Exactly what I needed."

Heidi laughed and reached over to wipe the residual grease spot on the other side of the mistletoe. At the same time, Sal stepped away from the ladder, which wobbled precariously. For a moment she worried that she would be joining Mrs. DiBenedetto in the hospital, but Sal turned and caught her before calamity could strike. He put his hands around her and hauled her off the step, which might have been a seamless maneuver if she'd weighed forty pounds. As it was, Sal staggered and the two of them nearly went down together before regaining equilibrium.

After more than twelve tense hours, Heidi finally found some release, laughing at the awkwardness of their Laurel-and-Hardy antics with the ladder. Sal was laughing, too, but when he looked into her face, he evidently saw the strain there. He brushed her hair away from her eyes.

"Hey," he said. "You okay?"

She nodded.

They were still standing that way when the bell rang

again. Sal crooked a brow at her playfully. "Just when we were finally alone at last."

She snorted again and stepped away to right herself before facing the newly arrived customer.

Only it wasn't a customer. It was Patrick.

His skin flashed from wind-burned red to pale shock and then back to red again. He looked as if he wanted to speak, but his lips remained clamped together.

"Patrick!" Heidi said, stepping farther away from Sal.

Whatever Patrick had been thinking—and it wasn't hard to guess—apparently her action only made him think it more. "I came by to tell you that there was no news." His voice came out clipped, strained. "About your cash box. At the hospital."

"I didn't think there would be," Heidi said. "Sal found the shopping bag—but it was empty."

Patrick narrowed his eyes on Sal.

Honestly. From the way he was acting, anyone would think finding clues to the cash box was some macho competition. It was ridiculous.

She crossed her arms, deciding not to dignify his petty jealousy with stammered excuses or explanations.

Sal, watching them, blurted, "We were just getting some cookie dough off the wall." When no one responded, he added, "The kid threw it."

Patrick glanced at Wilson and then buried his hands in his coat pockets. The shadow of sincere disappointment that crossed his features made Heidi question who was being petty. She wanted to laugh and jolly the tension away, but Patrick was already turning toward the door.

He pivoted back to say something, and Heidi's heart lifted. "Mrs. DiBenedetto told me to tell you that the vet's number is on her refrigerator. In case of an emergency."

After the bell had jangled his departure, an enormous

sense of letdown overwhelmed Heidi. He actually liked her. Or had. She could see that now.

It was always easy to see things clearly when they were all over. Her power of hindsight had been honed to laser sharpness.

Sal let out a sigh. "I hope this doesn't get back to my girlfriend. She doesn't trust me as it is."

"I doubt she'd consider me much of a threat."

Sal reflected on this and nodded. "Probably not."

Heidi whacked him on the arm. "Wrong answer!"

He blushed and stammered, "Oh, hey, you know—"

"Yes, I know. I'm in my thirties. Old enough to be your grandmother."

"I didn't say that. Anyway, I always liked older—"

She cut him off before he could do more damage. "It's okay, Sal." A glance at her watch told her it was almost six o'clock. "Let's get out of here." She went behind the counter and started filling a box with day-olds. "Here—I'll give you some stuff to take home."

"Thanks," he said, taking the box from her. She expected him to breeze out the door as he usually did at the end of the day, but instead he swallowed and looked down at his feet. "Thanks for everything—for giving me the job, I mean. Taking a chance."

"No thanks required," she said, meaning it. "This place couldn't get by without you."

When he was gone, she turned her attention to Wilson. "Hey, Wil. You feel like going home?" He blasted a yell into her face. "I'll take that as a yes."

She did a quick clean-up, wiping the tables, sweeping, and tossing all the pans in the dishwasher. Then she boxed up leftovers to lug back to her apartment. Christmas dinner. Of course, she might have to go root around in Janice's apartment to find some real food—or real baby food—for Wilson. So far he'd been surviving on split pea soup and cookie dough. She wasn't sure if that was a well-balanced diet or not for a little kid. She knew there were certain things they weren't supposed to eat, like honey. And popcorn.

God, there were probably a million things. What was she going to do if Janice never came back? A disastrous string of headlines scrolled through her mind like the newsfeed at Times Square. What if Janice got kidnapped, or her plane went down over the Atlantic Ocean? Had she unwittingly signed on to a lifetime child-care commitment just by opening her front door this morning?

After a short struggle, she managed to get Wilson bundled up again. The kid could squirm away from a sleeve like nobody's business. As she was turning to shut off the CD player, the café's door opened, causing her to twist back as an overstuffed backpack dropped to the ground. Its owner let out a sigh that was half triumph, half exhaustion, as if she'd just summited Pike's Peak.

"I made it!"

Heidi stared at the tall girl in black jeans, high-top sneakers, and a blue denim jacket. She knew who this was, but her mind stubbornly refused to accept the idea that Erica—daughter of her late friend, Rue—could possibly be standing in her café. In Brooklyn. It was all wrong. She blinked twice, certain the figure was only a person who looked like Erica.

"Well, aren't you going to say something?" The Texas twang was undeniable.

"Erica?" Heidi's voice came out as a squeak. "What are you doing here?"

"Surprised?"

Erica's face broke into a hopeful expression that had so much Rue in it that tears sprang to Heidi's eyes. She lurched forward and nearly squeezed Erica to death in a hug. It felt as if she'd grown half a foot in the past year and three months since Heidi had last seen her.

"Where did you come from?"

"Where do you think?" Erica asked, as if dropping in out of the blue was the most reasonable thing in the world. She extracted herself from Heidi's death squeeze and stepped into the middle of the room, where she turned in a circle. "Wow!"

A picture in the corner caught Erica's attention—a black-and-white photo of Rue, Laura, and Heidi as teenagers, sitting on the bench in front of the store in Sweetgum. Rue and Laura were leaning against each other, laughing, while Heidi sat apart, primly, with a lapful of schoolbooks—the odd girl out, stepsister, dweeb— her blond hair cut in bangs and sprouting from one side of her head in a poofy ponytail.

"That's the Sweetgum store, isn't it?" Erica asked. She didn't wait for Heidi's nod before adding, "Look at Mom! She was so pretty."

The photo had been snapped the year before the car accident that had scarred Rue's face. The accident had scarred Laura's psyche, too, although in Heidi's opinion, Laura had never been the poster girl for good mental health.

The café had other pictures from Sweetgum—including one of Erica and her horse, Milkshake, by the cash register—mixed in with eight-by-tens of movie stars. Erica walked around, taking it all in. Then she tilted her head, listening to Dean Martin singing "A Marshmallow World" on the CD player.

"Mom would have loved this place!"

Heidi swallowed. "That's the best compliment any-one's ever paid me." She had conjured up the café as a sort of tribute to Rue, and the way she had taken Heidi into her own kitchen when Heidi had been at her low-water mark, morale-wise, before her ex-boyfriend Vinnie's trial.

Erica sank down on a chair. "I was starting to believe that I was the only one who remembered Mom anymore."

"Not a day goes by that I don't think of her," Heidi said.

Erica sniffed. "I miss her so much. Laura never talks about her. Nobody does."

The mention of Laura jolted Heidi a little. *Where was Laura?*

Laura had been Heidi's tormenter in her teen years, and the possibility of her being in New York, on her own home turf, didn't exactly fill her with Christmas cheer. She returned to her original question. "Erica, what are you doing here?"

"Visiting you."

Her brain attempted to digest those two words. "Who brought you?"

"No one."

"You mean . . . ?"

"You said you couldn't come to Sweetgum," Erica explained, "so I've come to spend Christmas with you!"

Though enthusiasm suffused Erica's voice, Heidi could tell she was nervous about how that announcement would be received. A host of new doubts and worries swirled through Heidi's brain, but she tried not to let them show.

Erica, however, wasn't so good at hiding her surprise—and dismay—upon finally spotting Wilson. Which she didn't do until Wilson chucked a tiny glove at her. "What's *that*?"

"It's Wilson."

"A *baby*?"

"Toddler," Heidi corrected, envisioning another ten minutes of struggle to get that glove back on. "He's . . . well, he's sort of spending the holiday with me, too."

Erica lowered herself into a chair with a groan. "There's no escaping them, is there?"

"I didn't really run away," Erica said after devouring her second bowl of soup and her second turkey sandwich. "I just sort of took off."

As she listened to the story of Erica's journey, including the tricky way she'd gotten to the bus station, then the ride to the airport, and the many delays thereafter, Heidi wasn't sure which was stronger—her awe for what a thirteen-year-old had managed on her own, or her sense of impending doom. Erica might not think of herself as a runaway, but Heidi was pretty sure her father wouldn't see her Christmas journey as a big adventure.

"The most awful part was sitting on the runway for *hours*." She frowned. "No, actually, the hardest part was when I got to the city, on account of the cabs were so expensive. I was almost out of money, so the guy dropped me at a subway and told me to go to the Carroll Street stop. It sounded easy when he said it, but I think I went the wrong way first. It took forever. But everybody was pretty nice, actually. After the way Laura always talked about this place, I was expecting to get mugged."

"And Laura had no idea you were coming here?" Heidi asked.

"Gosh, no. She might be a little mad, actually," Erica admitted. "I was supposed to spend Christmas on the farm with her and Webb."

Oh. Oh. Oh.

Erica perceived her growing panic. "But she didn't

want me there—not really. I swear, all Laura does now is whine."

"*Laura?*" One thing Heidi couldn't associate with her ex-stepsister was whining. Laura was as tough as old boot leather.

"She's got morning sickness."

"Laura is *pregnant*?"

"Didn't she tell you?"

"No!"

"Yeah, well, she's sort of cranky these days."

Heidi snorted. "*These* days?" Laura's first reaction after slipping out of the womb had probably been a huff of irritation.

"Most of the time she's vegged out in her recliner chair, moaning and thinking about the baby." Erica eyed Wilson again. "Babies have taken over my world."

Hearing that Laura was La-Z-Boy-bound did not soothe Heidi any. If anything, the idea of a sick Laura frightened her more than Laura in tip-top health. Sick, she became an even more unpredictable animal. The only thing certain was that she would freak when she discovered Erica missing. And when she discovered she had run away to spend the holiday with her once arch-nemesis, she'd be doubly pissed.

"We have to call her," Heidi said, dreading it. "And your dad."

Erica's face fell. "Can't we wait till tomorrow?"

Heidi shook her head. "Now."

"How about tonight?"

"Erica, when they figure out you're missing they're going to be frantic with worry. They might already have reported you missing to the police. There could be Amber Alerts and all sorts of searches going on!"

Erica laughed. "I left a note."

Thank heavens for that, at least. "Where?"

"At the house."

"Whose house?"

"Dad's."

Considering that she herself had forgotten to do as much for Janice, Heidi gave her points for clearheadedness. "Do Webb and Laura have a key to your dad's house?"

Erica's face collapsed, and Heidi had her answer.

"Oops."

Chapter 8

Erica slipped and fell on her butt twice within two blocks before she got a clue and slowed down. High-top sneakers weren't the best footwear for hockey rink sidewalks. And her denim jacket was a joke in twenty degrees. Not only her teeth but all of her bones were chattering with cold, even though Heidi had made her put on an extra old sweater she kept at the restaurant.

Still and all, it was sort of cool to be here. It would have stunk if she'd come all this way and everything had seemed exactly like Sweetgum. No way could anyone confuse the two places. The world here was so vertical, just block after block of three-story houses smooshed together. All the buildings seemed ancient—as old as or maybe even older than the courthouse in Carter's Springs, a building from so far back that people sometimes drove hours just to take a picture of it. That kind of person would go crazy here. Except for the ice-encrusted vehicles that appeared more like larva than actual cars, the city around her looked like something out of another century.

Heidi, who was ahead of her, pulling the stroller, stopped outside a row house identical to every other one surrounding it. "This is it."

Thank God. Erica shivered and stared at the long lump under the ice by her knees. "What's that?"

"My Christmas tree, sort of."

Erica frowned. Now that she looked more closely, she could make out shadows of color under the ice. "Why's it out in the snow?"

"It's a long story. We had an accident here last night." She gestured for Erica to follow her. She didn't head for the porch thing that led up to the building's entrance, though. Instead, she went toward a recess under it, where there were some steps down from ground level and then a smaller, less impressive doorway.

"Was the accident the reason you ended up with Wilson?" Erica asked.

"No, that's another story." Heidi had to take off her glove to fish her key from her coat pocket. Through the door, a dog barked at them.

"I didn't know you had a dog."

"I'm just taking care of him for a while." She made an attempt to open the door with a flourish. "Ta-da! Cave, sweet cave."

Erica slid down the steps to the door, knocked some of the ice off of herself, and followed Heidi inside. Immediately, the little dog circled her, barking as if she were an intruder. It didn't seem any friendlier to Heidi, she noticed.

"Marcello, calm down!" Heidi said, ineffectively. Marcello continued to yap. Then he peed on the floor. "Damn," Heidi muttered. She sent an apologetic glance Erica's way as she clicked on some lights. "I think Marcello has a bladder control problem."

Erica was too distracted by Heidi's apartment to think

about the dog. On TV, New York apartments didn't look like this.

"Wow . . . it's . . ." Erica frowned. The long narrow room had wide, chipped wood floors and brick walls that made it seem like a cellar. From somewhere in the back—which had been converted into a makeshift kitchen—a faucet dripped. There were no holiday decorations, if you didn't count the Christmas card Erica had sent Heidi weeks ago, which she'd propped on a plastic stacking shelf unit next to an old-fashioned, boxy television.

"I know it's not the Plaza," Heidi said, scrambling toward the kitchen area to grab some paper towels to clean up the floor. "But the size is fantastic. That's why Brooklyn is so great—you get so much more space."

Apparently she didn't realize Erica had been sucking in her breath ever since walking through the door. "Where's the bedroom?"

Heidi gestured to the futon couch. "There."

Okey-doke. Erica reached back to her mom's training from when she was four and was going to her first birthday party. Her mom had told her that when you went into someone's home, even if it was a dump, you were supposed to pick out something to compliment, something that made it special.

"This is incredible," Erica said. "I've never been in a place so, so"—she spun around—"so totally without closets."

Maybe that wasn't a good compliment, but she must have gotten the tone right, because Heidi smiled. "I don't need one. That's what the wardrobe is for." She gestured to a banged-up wooden cabinet hulking in one corner. The doors hung crookedly, so that they overlapped where they met and didn't quite close properly. Heidi had fixed this problem by connecting the door pulls with a rubber band.

The Laura in Erica shook her head, but her mother's training kept the smile pasted on. "That's a big . . . thing."

"Isn't it impressive?" Heidi said. "It came with the place. Really sold me on it, actually."

"You *own* this?" Erica asked, horrified.

"No such luck. I just rent."

Erica deposited her stuff on the futon and asked if she could take a shower. She felt grimy from her trip. Also, a hot shower might help her thaw out. The temperature in the apartment wasn't that much of an improvement over the weather outside.

Luckily, though the shower was an icky contraption with painted metal walls and pebbled flooring—the sort of thing you'd expect at a public pool, not in someone's house—the hot water worked fine. Erica stood under the spray, the warm water at first making her cold skin prickle in protest, and wondered what she was doing here. For the past day and a half, her sole aim had been to get to New York. Now she'd arrived, and it seemed weird. Heidi's apartment wasn't any more Christmassy than the farm had been. Plus, there was the little kid and the yappy, house-training-challenged dog. Worst of all, it suddenly struck her that Laura and Webb might be hurt that she had abandoned them for the holidays.

And then she was going to have to explain to her dad about Leanne's Visa card . . .

When Erica came out of the shower, Heidi was bustling around the kitchen. Wilson, still in his snowsuit, sat on the floor with Marcello, who didn't seem to know what to make of him. At least he'd stopped barking. He was actually cute, although she was so used to the big dogs at the farm, he seemed more like a rabbit. She wadded up a Kleenex, threw it, and watched him skitter across the floor to race after it.

Definitely a dog. Marcello's goofiness cheered her up a little.

Steam poured out of a kettle on the ancient stove. "How about some hot chocolate?" Heidi asked. "I found this mix last night." She whacked a stiff white envelope on the counter. "It's perfectly good."

"Sure," Erica said. "Thanks."

"I'll have it all ready after you call Laura," Heidi added pointedly.

Erica groaned.

"Or your dad," Heidi said. "Whichever you feel up to tackling first."

Easy decision. She decided to call her aunt.

When Laura answered the phone, she sounded relieved. "Where've you been?" she asked. "I've called your house three times. Has the wicked stepmother revoked your phone privileges?"

No, but that's probably coming.

Erica swallowed. "There's sort of been a change in plans."

A pause came over the line. "What happened?"

Here goes nothing. "Well, see, Leanne's sister was in the hospital, so she and Dad had to go to Houston . . ."

"When was this?"

Erica swallowed. "Yesterday." Had it really just been yesterday? It seemed like weeks ago, actually.

"Yesterday! You should have called us. Are you staying with a friend?"

"Yeah." Erica darted an anxious glance at Heidi. "A friend."

"Where? We'll come pick you up."

"That's not possible."

"Why not?"

"Because I'm with Heidi."

"Heidi who?"

"Heidi Bogue. You know—*Heidi*. That person who used to be your stepsister."

The silence that crackled over the line made Erica nervous. But what came next proved worse. She had to hold the phone away from her ear and cover the receiver with her hand to muffle the tinny sounds of Laura's hollering.

Heidi crossed the kitchen in two steps. "Here—let me talk to her," she said, taking the phone.

Erica handed it over gladly and listened as Heidi tried to smooth things over.

"Laura, she's here. She's safe. Everything's fine." More angry bleats emanated from the receiver before Heidi continued, "I didn't *lure* her over here. Believe me, I was as surprised as you are now. The only difference was, for me, it's a nice surprise." She smiled at Erica. "No, I don't know how she did it . . . just got on an airplane, I guess. . . . No, I don't know where she got the money." She held her hand over the receiver and asked Erica, "Where did you get the money?"

"I charged it over the Internet, on Leanne's Visa card."

Heidi's brows shot up. "Laura, she used Leanne's Visa card. . . . Yeah, I think she's worried about how it's all going to go over." She listened to Laura's response, nodded, and looked up at Erica. "Laura says your days are numbered."

Erica took the phone back. "I'm sorry, Laura. I didn't mean to upset y'all."

"I'm still too stunned to be upset," Laura replied, conveniently ignoring the fact that she'd just spent five minutes yelling. "Though I guess you couldn't have been looking forward to our holiday together very much. Not if you'd steal from your stepmother and brave a blizzard to fly all the way out to see Heidi instead."

Erica cringed, but then felt an answering indignation

billow up. "You two didn't seem like you were all that into Christmas, anyway. You didn't even bother to put up a tree!"

"And what's Heidi got in her place—eleven lords a-leaping?"

Erica gave the apartment an uncomfortable second glance. "Her café is really incredible. There's a huge tree there, and stockings hanging, and garland. And it's got pictures of you and Mom when you were young, and the farm and everything."

Laura snorted. "I bet that pulls in the customers."

"I thought it was neat," Erica said defensively. "I *like* remembering Mom."

A heavy pause followed this last statement, and she could almost hear the tension as Laura struggled over how to respond. "Look, Erica," she said in a more measured tone. "Someone's going to have to break the news to your dad that you've flown the coop—with the help of Leanne's credit card. I figure that someone might as well be me. He already hates me."

Erica suddenly felt bad for getting huffy. Her aunt had always been on her side, and probably always would be, even through this. "Could you?"

"Sure, but you'd better prepare for some serious blowback."

"I know. At first he'll tell me that he's been worried sick about me, but I'll bet he never even knew I was gone. And then he'll yell at me about the money and probably ground me for life."

"Well . . . maybe the storm won't be so bad if I call him first. I'll be your barrier island."

After Erica had stepped through the door at the Sweetgum Café, a mild hysteria had taken hold of Heidi. A dog, a toddler, an unexpected guest—all hope of a holiday of relaxation and solitude evaporated. Now, not only did she have to worry about the missing money and Wilson's mom never showing up, she had to figure out what to do with a runaway teenager.

But Erica's arrival turned out to be a godsend. She might profess that she didn't like little kids, but she actually knew something about taking care of them. Watching Erica playing with Wilson, handling him, bossing him, brought home to Heidi how clueless she herself was. For instance, when Wilson had gone nuts, running around red in the face, screeching in unintelligible toddler-speak, Erica pinpointed the problem immediately. "He needs a change." She grabbed him and sniffed. "Wilson, when was the last time you had a bath?"

Heidi felt embarrassed. Martine had left her with a perfectly clean kid twelve hours ago, and now she'd let him get dirty. "I don't really have a bathtub," Heidi said.

"I noticed." Erica surveyed the kitchen. "We could use the sink."

"Should I run some water?"

Erica seemed to have sussed out Heidi's child-care incompetence already. "You'd better let me. It can't be too hot."

After Erica had been set up with baby supplies and was working her magic with Wilson, Heidi went outside and attempted to chip the tree free from the ice. Giving Erica a few Christmas trappings, including a Christmas tree, would repay her efforts to some extent. But the only tools at Heidi's disposal—a broom handle and a half-empty container of Morton's salt—failed to break through the two inches of ice over several inches of snow that encased the tree.

She trudged back inside, wondering what else she owned that was Christmassy. From her feeble bag of wrapping supplies, she found a red ribbon left over from last year, which she tied around the rabbit ears on her television. Also, she pulled out a Santa hat. She put it on and set about making some tea. In the kitchen, which was filled with Wilson's chatter and Erica's laughter, she changed the radio to a local station that was playing Christmas tunes. Jackson Browne sang "The Rebel Jesus" as Erica stuffed her newly scrubbed charge into jeans and a flannel shirt.

"I can't wait till Angelica is a little older," Erica said. "Wilson's a lot easier to deal with than my sister. And smarter."

"He is?" Heidi found him baffling.

"Sure—he already knows my name. Don't you, Wil?"

Wilson smiled. "Ca!"

She looked over at Heidi. "See?"

"Does he know my name?"

Erica asked him. "Wilson, who's that?"

"Mizzletoed!"

Heidi laughed.

Erica was trying to get him to say Heidi's name when the phone rang. It was William, Erica's father. Heidi recognized his voice right away and did her best as "advance man" to smooth things over. "Erica's doing great—it's so fun to see her. Can you believe she made it here all on her own? That was *amazing*. You must be so—"

"I'd like to speak to her," William grumbled.

"And she's being so helpful," Heidi said. "I don't know what I would have done without her this afternoon. I—"

William interrupted in a spiky, impatient voice. "Can you put her on the phone, please?"

Reluctantly, Heidi handed the phone over to Erica, who took it with a look of dread.

"Hey, Dad."

A full two minutes passed before she got another

chance to speak. Heidi turned away, pretending not to listen, but shutting out the conversation in such a small space was impossible.

"But what does it matter?" Erica lifted her arm in an impatient shrug, as if her father could actually see her. "I got here okay, didn't I? I'd think you'd be relieved!"

That angle, apparently, didn't go over well.

"But nothing *did* happen." Erica listened for another long stretch, then said, "I'll pay Leanne back. I swear. You can hold back my allowance for two years, and the debt will all be paid off. I promise."

When Erica finally hung up, she looked depressed. Her dad must have agreed to her terms. "Well, looks like I'm broke for the forseeable future."

"Welcome to the club," Heidi said.

While they ate a small dinner of leftover soup and saltines, Heidi filled Erica in on all the things that had happened in the past day before she showed up.

"What are you going to do if you never find the money?" Erica asked.

"I'm assuming at this point that I never will."

"That's terrible!"

Strangely, it felt good to have someone say that. Someone to commiserate with.

"So when's Wilson's mom going to come home?" Erica asked.

"I don't know. She hasn't responded to any of the messages I left for her in Africa, or on the number of her phone I have listed for her here, or the e-mail I sent her at the address Martine gave me. If she doesn't show up tonight, I guess I should leave a note on her door telling her I've got Wilson down here, in case she comes back in the middle of the night and freaks out that he's gone."

They cleaned up the dishes and deliberated on what to

do for the rest of the evening. "It's Christmas Eve," Heidi said. "You've come all this way to New York. We should do something special. We could go to a caroling service at one of the big churches."

Erica's nose wrinkled. "I have to go to church at home. Plus, what would we do with Wilson? He'd get fussy in a church, I'll bet."

"Oh, right." That thought hadn't occurred to her.

"What did you have planned?" Erica asked her. "I mean, maybe you have parties or something to go to."

"No, I don't."

"But you must have had something in mind for the holiday."

It was time to fess up.

"Have you ever seen *Avatar*?"

"That movie that came out years ago? About the blue people?"

Heidi explained that she'd been too busy with the restaurant to completely catch up with her Netflix queue. Then a troubling thought occurred to her and she hurried over to check the box. "I better check to make sure it's not R. I wouldn't want your father to be mad . . ."

Erica laughed. "After I've run away from home and stolen six hundred twenty-eight dollars? I don't think he's going to worry about me seeing a movie that's not PG-13." Erica scurried to her backpack and rummaged around until she came up with a gigantic chocolate bar. "I brought you this. I'm saving your big present for tomorrow, but we can have some of this with the movie."

The bar was big enough that she would be munching on it during movies for weeks, but Heidi adhered to the philosophy that a person could never have too much chocolate. She accepted the present with a hug, then a worried frown. "I mailed your present to East Texas. You probably didn't get it yet."

"That's okay. I'll have something to open when I get home. I'll probably need something to cheer me up."

They prepped for the movie. First, they got Wilson ready for bed. Once he was in his jammies, they plopped him down in the center of the futon, where he promptly fell asleep. God knows the day had probably been more stressful for him than it had been for them. They wrapped themselves in blankets and sat on either side of him.

The moment he heard the chocolate bar being opened, Marcello jumped up to join them.

"Dogs can't have chocolate," Erica warned Heidi.

"Right," Heidi said. "I knew that."

But would she have remembered it if Erica hadn't been here?

She punched PLAY on the DVD player and they settled back for an evening's entertainment. This was good. She'd planned to be alone, relaxing, but it was nice to have Erica here. Heck, it would have been nice with just Marcello for company. Another warm body, even a dog body, made the place seem homier.

Maybe she should get a cat.

Or a boyfriend.

The memory of the hurt in Patrick's eyes when he'd seen her and Sal together under the mistletoe flashed through her mind. Oh well. That probably wouldn't have worked out. A cat would be a lot easier to maintain than a boyfriend, anyway.

For now, she wasn't going to worry about it. She wasn't going to fret over the money, either. Or anything. She was going to have a good Christmas and hope that nothing else bad happened.

After the third preview, there was a sharp *click* and the world went black.

"What was that?" Erica asked, invisible in the darkness.

Heidi folded her arms. "That was the electricity going out."

They remained on the couch, waiting for the lights to snap back on. When a minute passed and nothing happened, Heidi got up and started rummaging around for matches. She lit the only two candles she had.

Erica tugged her blanket more tightly around herself. "Is this a blackout?"

"Uh . . . I guess so. I suppose something's happened to the line because of the ice."

Brilliant deduction, Sherlock. Heidi half expected Erica to sneer at her, but when she looked at the girl's face in the flickering candlelight, her brow was pillowed in thought. "It was already cold in here, but I can feel the temperature dropping by the second. Can't you?"

Now that she mentioned it . . . Heidi jumped up and walked to the ancient radiator that sat under the front window. The thing was an iceberg.

"Is the heat electric?" Erica asked.

"I think it's steam . . ." She tried to tamp down panic, but any effort to sound knowledgeable failed. She didn't know squat about stuff like this, and Mrs. DiBenedetto was gone. "Maybe it's not on because of the boiler . . ." She wasn't even sure where it was, or how to get to it.

After a moment of silence, Erica asked, "So, how cold does it have to get before bad things start happening?"

"Bad things like what?"

"Like . . . freezing to death?"

"We'll be fine," Heidi assured her.

After another half hour, however, she decided it was time to pack up everybody and find refuge somewhere else. She didn't get any arguments from Erica.

"Where are we going?" she asked while Heidi loaded a sleepy, fussy Wilson into the stroller.

"The café." Even if the electricity was out there, at least they could use the fireplace.

Erica shivered. "I might have known I'd end up spending Christmas in Sweetgum, one way or another."

Chapter 9

"I think my dad's more angry about the money than anything."

"I doubt that's true," Heidi assured Erica as they trudged toward the café.

Brooklyn had never felt more eerie. Some streets would have been plunged into inky shadow and rendered utterly unnavigable if the world hadn't been a glistening white. Despite the clouds overhead, there was enough atmospheric light, or spillover from the rest of the city that still had power, to make the sidewalks almost seem to glow. A group of snowmen stood as rigid sentry in the neighborhood park, vestiges of the fluffy snow from the storm's early hours. No kids played outside now, of course, and trees released groans as the bitter wind hit their ice-coated branches.

At least the sleet had stopped.

The strip of Court Street nearest the café had lights, but the road itself was a mess. Cars people had attempted to parallel park jutted into the street like crooked teeth. The city's salt was doing battle with the ice, but not always coming up the winner. Only the most intrepid vehicles were still out.

Of the few people they encountered during their trek, the happiest was a man in mountaineering attire cross-country skiing down the unplowed side streets of Carroll Gardens.

Kids might be staying up in hopes of getting a peek at Santa's sleigh this evening, but Heidi imagined their parents would prefer to see the lights of a Con Edison truck. She wouldn't place any bets on which was likelier to show up.

Erica edged her way along the sidewalk in thoughtful silence. When she spoke again, her words indicated she was still preoccupied by her family troubles. "My dad spends lots of money, but whenever I want to buy some little thing, he goes nuts."

"Well, a plane ticket's not exactly a little thing," Heidi pointed out.

"No, I guess not," she admitted.

Erica's problems led Heidi to think of her own. In the months since the café opened, she'd tried not to dwell on the fact that she owed more money than she'd ever earned in her life, or that the café barely broke even most months. Keeping her head in the sand would become harder now. Eleven hundred dollars didn't seem like all that much compared to the amount she'd borrowed, but it still left a gaping hole in her finances. What if it proved to be the tipping point? If every journey began with a single step, surely every bankruptcy commenced with a single irretrievable dollar. She had over eleven hundred of them. Perhaps next Christmas there would be no Sweetgum Café.

As they approached the café's block, Heidi's heart beat a little faster in suspense. Would there be lights? So much of the neighborhood was dark, she braced herself for disappointment. Even with the fireplace, the café would still be cold with no electricity, but it might keep them from having to seek refuge at an emergency shelter. The idea of crowding into a church basement with a teenager, a toddler, and a dog seemed grim. Plus, a shelter might not let her bring Marcello, and she had promised Mrs. DiBenedetto she would look after him.

She turned the corner onto the street where the café was situated, and almost wept in relief. The entire block appeared surprisingly normal. Tree lights twinkled through windows and from stoops that owners had taken pains to decorate.

In the café they took a moment to absorb the wonderful heat—the sixty-five degrees Heidi had set the thermostat to seemed almost sultry. She released Wilson from his wheeled prison and unhooked Marcello's leash. Both boy and dog immediately started running.

Erica hopped the feeling back into her feet and then flopped into a chair. "I don't think I've been warm since we left this place four hours ago." She eyed the fireplace greedily. "Can we have a fire? Please?"

"Of course."

"I can do it," Erica said. "I make them at the farm sometimes."

"Knock yourself out."

At Erica's suggestion, Heidi had grabbed several toys and picture books from the duffel Martine had brought down for Wilson. Now while Erica was stacking firewood with scientific precision, Heidi unpacked a clunky Thomas train from a tote bag and let Wilson push it around on the rug running from the door to the cash register.

She fired up the drip coffeemaker for herself and put some milk on low heat on a burner. Despite being pulled away from her place on Christmas Eve, she wasn't unhappy. In a way, the café felt more like a home to her now than her apartment. She put in a CD, and when Louis Armstrong started singing "Christmas Night in Harlem," Erica jumped up excitedly.

"I *love* this song!" she said. "I haven't heard it since—"

Heidi nodded. She might have known this had been one of Rue's favorites. Funny, she had never imagined what the farm had been like at Christmastime while Rue lived there in later years. When Heidi had been there as a teenager, during her mom's short-lived marriage to Laura and Rue's cranky dad, the farm had been a joy vacuum. But in later years Rue had snapped the place up and given it new life. That's how Heidi tried to remember it now.

"What did you guys usually do on Christmas Eve at the farm?" she asked Erica.

Erica draped her torso over the counter. "Mom always fixed this really great shortbread. With pecans. It was *so good,* and it made the entire house smell like butter. I helped her a couple of times, but I wouldn't remember how to do it."

Heidi smiled and tilted her head toward a lone shelf on the wall. On it, in a place of honor, sat the recipe box Rue had given to Heidi before she died. "We don't have to remember. We'll let her tell us."

Erica's face lit up. "Can we make some? Do you have all the stuff for it?"

"Oh, honey, I've got enough ingredients here to make all of Brooklyn smell like butter."

The doorknob rattled and Marcello exploded. He made like a furry bullet for the door and barked himself hoarse at the threatening figure of Clay peeking through the glass. Heidi tried to calm him down and let Clay in.

"I saw the light on," he said, scooting inside. "You open?"

"Not exactly, but come on in. I've got a fresh pot brewing." She introduced Erica to Clay, adding, "You'll probably be seeing a lot of him."

Clay stomped his feet on the carpet. "This is crazy, isn't it? I hope Di's okay."

"Did her train leave on time?"

"It was delayed—she made me take off after an hour. I bought her some sandwiches to take on the train."

"Sandwiches?"

He shrugged. "Vermont's a long way. What if the train got stuck somewhere?"

"Then she'll freeze to death and won't need the sandwiches."

"That's what I figured," Clay said. "So I also got her one of those cashmere pashmina shawls. And wool socks. And mittens."

"Clay . . ."

"What?" he asked. "Mittens are warmer than gloves."

"Maybe you should have loaded her up with a portable stove and Sterno cans while you were at it."

He shook his head as he helped himself to coffee. "They don't sell anything like that in Penn Station. Place has more magazines than you can shake a stick at, but nothing really practical."

She laughed. "On trains, reading material sometimes comes in handy."

He shrugged, then glanced over at the baking project in progress. "Hey—what are y'all doing?"

"Making pecan shortbread," Erica said. She was getting ready to grind pecans in the food processor.

"Can I lend a hand?"

Heidi zapped a few bricks of butter in the microwave to soften it up. "If you want, you could unload that coffee into one of the thermoses by the sink. And fill one with hot water." In case the café lost power, too.

"Good thinking!" Clay hopped to it, and in fact filled

two thermoses with coffee, which struck Heidi as overkill. It was already after nine. How much could they drink?

It began to seem more practical after a few people filtered in. These weren't necessarily regulars, but people Heidi recognized from the neighborhood. All came loaded with stories about being stuck in their dark apartments, some without heat, unable to track down friends or family in luckier, less electricity-deprived areas.

Heidi placed steaming cups of coffee in front of them. She turned the television on and switched to the news station, where a man in a parka was standing in downtown Brooklyn with a microphone, announcing that sections of the borough were without electricity, and that people should be careful because the ice was slippery.

"They should stop calling it *the news* and rename it *the obvious*," Heidi said.

The first batch of shortbread came out of the oven as an old man entered the café. He was bundled up and carrying a blanket and a plastic sack that contained his pillow and a dopp kit. He'd been heading to his church to see if they'd set up a shelter yet, but had seen the lights on in the café and decided to stop. Heidi handed him a steaming mug and a plate of cookies.

"How much?" the man asked. "You've got a situation ripe for price gouging here, you know."

What an idea. "I could change the name from the Sweetgum Café to Scrooge's."

"You could clean up," he told her.

"And in a few years, I'd have ghosts giving me guilt trips. No thanks—put your money away." Eleven hundred dollars plus change, she'd already lost. What the heck—it was Christmas. She'd kick *go for broke* up to a whole new level.

"Everything's on the house," she announced.

A little after eleven o'clock, her cell phone rang. She leapt for it, hoping it would be Wilson's mom, but instead Dinah's name appeared.

"Where are you?" Heidi asked.

"Back in my apartment." She sounded demoralized. "My apartment, where there is *no electricity.* I was better off in Penn Station with the irate Amtrak customers and the homeless man who smelled like a discarded Styrofoam meat tray sleeping next to me."

"What happened to Vermont?"

"I got tired of waiting for my train to board. Every other train seemed to leave eventually except mine. I started to wonder if Clay had paid off Amtrak to keep me here."

Heidi smiled. "You can ask him, if you want. He's standing right here."

"Clay's in your apartment?"

"No, we're at the café. There's electricity here. We're drawing quite a crowd, actually."

"Really? What is this crowd doing?"

Heidi looked around the room. Wilson had crawled back into his stroller and fallen asleep. Two people were dozing in the comfy chairs by the fire, and about half the tables had people at them. Some were eating, some were watching the movie *Holiday Inn* on the television, and, at one table, a couple was playing backgammon.

"Mostly they're just hanging out."

"Do you need help?"

"I don't know . . ." She looked over at Clay, who had installed himself in the kitchen. "Clay is acting as short-order cook right now."

"*Clay?* Clay is a CPA."

"I know—a CPA who makes a mean grilled cheese."

"This I have to see."

Heidi made a tour of the kitchen, checking on supplies. Because she had planned to be closed on Christmas, she hadn't restocked the perishables that day. She did have a lot of eggs, and two gallons of milk. But as far as vegetables went, she only had onions and two tomatoes. She doubted anywhere in the neighborhood would be open tomorrow . . . but hopefully the electricity would be back on by then anyway.

Just in case it wasn't, she was making dough in preparation for the next morning, when Patrick and Marcus came by.

"What's going on?" Marcus asked. "You running a mission now?"

"Sort of."

Patrick glanced around the kitchen for a moment, pausing to squint at Clay, before turning his usual smile on her. She wondered if he'd been scanning the premises for Sal.

"These aren't your usual hours," he said.

"It's not a usual day—well, night. My apartment didn't have any electricity, so I brought Wilson and Erica over here."

"Erica?" he asked.

Heidi nodded to the figure curled up in an armchair by the fire. "That's Erica." Then she pointed to a picture on the fridge of Erica with her horse, Milkshake. "From Texas. She's staying with me over the holidays."

"Kidnapped another one, did you?" Marcus asked. When her mouth dropped, he smiled and added, "Uh-huh. Patrick told me."

"She just showed up," Heidi said in her own defense.

Patrick laughed. "Your 'staycay' of solitude is history, I guess."

"History that never was."

Marcus studied the people sitting at the tables. "Do these customers plan on staying here all night?"

Heidi shrugged. "They're not really customers. And I'm not going to kick them out."

"But you can't stay open till all the lights in Brooklyn come back on."

"Why not?" she asked. "Is there a law against it? I'm not selling anything."

Patrick and Marcus exchanged befuddled glances.

"Why don't I go ask some of these people if they need help getting to a shelter?" Marcus ambled around the tables to see if there were any takers.

Patrick leaned toward Heidi, close enough that she could smell the woodsy scent of his cologne. She closed her eyes for a moment, blotting out the surge of whatever it was that rushed through her. Desire. Or delirium, maybe.

"You okay?" he asked.

"Fine. A little tired."

He took in the mess of flour and dough on the counter. "What is this?"

"I'm going to make quiche tomorrow morning."

"You intend to make this an all-nighter, then?"

"I guess so. We'll see. Dinah's going to be here, I think. She can take a shift."

He shook his head. "I'll check back in on you later. Maybe I can pilfer some blankets from somewhere."

She smiled at him. "Thanks."

"Merry Christmas," he said.

She looked at the clock on the wall. It was a quarter past twelve. "That's right—Merry Christmas, Patrick."

He hesitated for a moment, his eyes staring at her so intently that she could see herself reflected in their depths. She swallowed. *About Sal . . .* she wanted to say.

Before she could blurt the words out, Patrick repeated, "I'll be back." Then he smashed his cap on his head, and left with Marcus.

Chapter 10

Erica awoke with a start. She'd been up and down all night, but sometime during the early morning she'd fallen asleep in a chair, facedown on a table like naptime in kindergarten. Now bright light poured through the café windows.

"Merry Christmas," Heidi said, handing her a mug of hot chocolate.

Erica pushed herself semi-upright. The drink looked frothy and warm, and she could barely wait to mutter a Merry Christmas back at Heidi before taking a sip. This stuff tasted milky and rich—not like the watery mix they'd had at Heidi's apartment. The sugar helped clear her groggy brain. In her dreams, she'd been back on the farm, but now she stared around the café in a daze. One of those old-man singers her mom had liked was singing "O Come All Ye Faithful."

"What time is it?" she asked.

"Almost nine thirty," Heidi said.

Erica was stunned. This had to be jet lag. Usually she

liked to be up and doing things early. "What time does the café open?"

Over half the tables had people, most sitting with blurry stares fixed on the mugs in front of them, or on their laptop screens, or the television on the wall. Most had lugged items they hadn't been able to bear leaving in their apartments. A couple was installed at a four-person table, with several overflowing tote bags taking up the spare chairs. A pudgy guy tapping away at a netbook had leaned two violin cases against the wall near the Christmas tree. At another table, an older woman with a carry-on suitcase by her knees sat calmly dipping a tea bag into a steaming mug.

"We weren't supposed to be open at all," Heidi explained, "but turns out, we never closed."

"You stayed up all night?"

"Dinah kept watch over the place for a stretch while I napped."

Dinah. The woman who had come in late. Erica took another long slurp of hot cocoa. She felt better. "That's yummy."

"Good. I'm afraid it's going to have to stand in for your Christmas present for the moment."

Christmas. It was hard to believe. She thought back on all the Christmas mornings of her past—mornings of impatient waiting by the tree for the adults to get themselves out of bed so the assault on the presents could begin. She'd been such a greed-head, always hoping whatever package she opened contained joy—toys—and not something practical. Her mother had always insisted on getting her a boring piece of clothing, like a nightgown. Erica had hated the nightgowns. She'd always assumed her mom bought them to give her practice acting happy about something boring.

When she was younger, it had never occurred to her that the biggest gift of her life was sitting a few feet away—her mom herself, who she'd always assumed would just be there. She would have given anything to be opening a boring nightgown this morning.

She blinked away tears, adjusting as she always had to when memories of her mom snuck up on her. There was a lot of reality to adjust to this morning. She felt a brief stab at the strangeness of it, then glanced at Heidi's smile and felt one spread across her own face. "You're letting me stay with you for a few days—that's a huge present."

Heidi burst out laughing—a shooting fountain of sound Erica remembered so well from the summer she'd stayed with them on the farm before her mother died. "Huge! You get to sleep in a chair."

The old woman looked over at them, smiling, and Erica noticed that behind the suitcase, there was a cat carrier. She moved instinctively toward the amber eyes staring at her through the metal grate.

"What's his name?" she asked the lady.

"Scamp."

Erica extended her finger and let Scamp rub his nose on it. She loved animals. Which reminded her . . . "Where's Marcello?"

"Clay and Dinah took him out on their expedition to see if there are signs of life—or electricity—back at Dinah's apartment." Heidi's lips twisted. "I wonder if mine is on, too. I had hoped we could do something fun today. You know—go see Rockefeller Center and skate, show you the sights, catch a movie. But now . . ."

Erica looked around at the people propped at tables with their coffees. None of them had expected to be here, either, but most seemed resigned, if not happy, to have a warm place to hang out.

"I don't mind hanging out here today," she said. "I can help out, if you tell me what to do."

Heidi leaned forward and gave her a grateful squeeze. "Excellent! You can be Sal today."

"Who's Sal?"

"He's the person who usually keeps this place going."

Throughout the day at the café, people came and went. Some came and never went. Occasionally a new arrival would announce that Such-and-Such Street had electricity back, which would spark an exodus. Sometimes the people wouldn't be back, but more often they would, looking either more grumbly or more resigned than before they'd left. Tempers flared, but then Erica would zip in and offer coffee, tea, cocoa, or cookies, or push a deck of cards at them from the shelf of games in the corner. People usually responded to a little attention, and sugary food never hurt.

By two in the afternoon, Erica felt a little bit as if she *was* keeping the place going. If something needed doing, she did it. She remembered her last dismal Christmas, how the day had dragged. She had spent it thinking about her mom, no matter what she had been doing. Even holding baby Angelica for the first time had made her burst into tears. Not, as Leanne had supposed, because she was so happy to have a little sister, but because this new life made her think of the life that had been lost so recently. Maybe the Disney song was right, and life was a big circle or whatever. That idea was meant to be comforting, but her mom had been irreplaceable, and to see evidence of the world chugging along without her had broken Erica's heart.

Today she thought about her mom, too. A lot. She was there in the music Heidi chose—Ella Fitzgerald, Frank Sinatra, and all those others Laura called geezer music—

and in Cary Grant's face when her mom's favorite Christmas movie, *The Bishop's Wife,* played on television. (Her mom would be so happy if Cary Grant really was an angel and she was up there with him!) But Erica was also reminded of her mom when she was able to do stuff for Heidi—unbending the mixer beaters that Heidi had mangled somehow, or stopping a table from wobbling, or delivering food to people who were on the edge of losing their tempers from the climate curveball life had thrown them this holiday.

At moments, Heidi seemed overwhelmed, but Erica managed, remembering what her mom would have done in each instance. For the first time, she began to see that she *was* her mom—a piece of her, maybe. The circle that had upset her a year ago now seemed more like a vitamin shot to her system today, giving her confidence, making her walk taller through the café.

Later in the afternoon, during a rare lull, Heidi pushed a sandwich in front of her. Erica appreciated the gesture, especially since she knew they were running out of cheese.

"You okay?" Heidi asked her.

"Better than okay." Despite her words, Erica frowned. "I guess I should call the farm, though." And her dad. "I have to wish them all Merry Christmas and let them yell at me some more."

But her dad seemed calmer today—almost jovial, actually, as if he'd sent her to Brooklyn on vacation. "Merry Christmas, wanderer. Having fun in the Big Apple?"

"I'm working in Heidi's café."

"Things don't close for Christmas up there?" he asked.

"I think everything's closed except us." She described the ice storm, the difficulties, and the scene at the Sweetgum Café.

"Sounds like a soup kitchen for stranded yuppies," her father said.

"I guess it is, sort of." Her dad probably imagined the whole city was peopled by folks that looked like the cast of *Friends*. She'd sort of expected that herself. And there were lots of younger adults who looked as though they'd logged serious time in coffee shops. Yet they sat calmly next to old Italian men in moth-eaten sweaters and a Russian family that was camped out at a corner table, where Wilson had gravitated, since there was another toddler to tear through the café with. The adults—young and old—played Trivial Pursuit or backgammon, or talked on cell phones to far-off relatives or friends across town, or stared at Bing Crosby on the TCM Christmas marathon.

"Have you called Laura today?" her father asked her with a hint of amusement in his voice.

"Not yet. Why?"

"No reason. When you do, make sure and tell her I said Merry Christmas."

That was strange. When Erica called the farm, though, no one answered. Webb's mother lived outside of Carter's Springs, so maybe they were over there. She tried Laura's cell phone number, but didn't get an answer. At that moment, Wilson hit his head on the side of a table and Erica put down the phone and went over to calm him down. She didn't think about her aunt again for another few hours, and by then Christmas was almost over.

The first time Heidi saw Patrick that day was when he and Marcus came by with firewood they'd "found" somewhere.

Heidi stood by Patrick as he stacked the wood next to

the fireplace. "Does the NYPD consider this official business?"

His broad shoulders lifted in a shrug. She could tell by the redness of his ears that he was freezing; maybe he'd only wanted a reason to come in from the cold. Marcus had wasted no time helping himself to hot coffee.

Patrick glanced up at her. "You might say it falls under the umbrella of community relations."

"Sort of like my free cop coffee policy in reverse," she said.

He stood. "Is that a policy? I thought you liked Marcus and me in particular."

She felt herself blushing. Weren't people in their thirties supposed to be beyond that?

He looked around, and she didn't have to guess who he was searching for.

"How are you holding up?" he asked.

"We're low on cocoa and eggs, but we should be able to make it till tomorrow on what we have."

"Actually, I was asking about you." He clasped his hand around her arm. "How are *you* doing? This isn't exactly the Christmas you expected."

"It's better," she said, and, strangely, she meant it. "If I was home all alone, I'd be worrying about money and having nearly killed Mrs. DiBenedetto." She frowned. "I hope she's okay."

"I'll go see her this afternoon."

Heidi brightened. "Will you? Could you take her some cookies for me? I made some I think she'd like—usually she complains that my cookies have too much stuff in them or are too chewy. Evidently she mostly eats supermarket biscotti. She must have molars like jackhammers. But I think these butter cookies Erica and I made have enough crunch for Mrs. DiB."

Was she rambling? Patrick grinned. She was.

Suddenly, Heidi became aware that he still had a grip on her arm. But just when she was getting used to the idea, he let go and stood back, looking around the room. "Where's Dinah?"

"She discovered her power was still not working, so she went over to Clay's to clean up someplace where she wouldn't turn into a human popsicle the moment she stepped out of the shower. That was"—Heidi glanced at, then gaped at, the wall clock—"over *two hours ago*! What could they be doing over there?"

Patrick laughed.

She shook her head. "Oh no. She's never liked Clay. In that way, I mean."

"Snowstorms make strange bedfellows," he said. "In nine months, the maternity wards will be overflowing."

Heidi had always heard that was true, but from what she'd witnessed at the café for the past eighteen hours, she was skeptical. There hadn't been much turtle-dovey behavior. Mostly the couples she'd seen had been cranky—sleep deprived, cold, and overcaffeinated.

Maybe her sampling was skewed. She couldn't deny Clay and Dinah had been gone a suspiciously long time.

"You ready to roll?" Marcus asked Patrick.

Heidi loaded the guys down with muffins for themselves and the butter cookies for Mrs. DiBenedetto. "Tell her that Marcello is doing fine," she said. "I sent him off with Dinah, so he's probably lounging in the warmth and . . ."

"And seeing some sights he never saw at your landlady's," Patrick finished for her.

Heidi laughed, but then she found herself looking into Patrick's eyes, and thoughts of what the two of them could do alone in a warm apartment flitted through her brain. A rush of heat swept into her cheeks again, making her almost glad when Marcus dragged him away.

It was another full hour before Dinah came back, freshly scrubbed and arm in arm with Clay. Looking at them, you would have guessed that she was as deliriously happy with the sudden change in their status as Clay obviously was. But the moment she and Heidi were alone, she grabbed Heidi's hand and dragged her back to the storage room.

"What am I going to do?" Panic was written all over her face, and she collapsed on a wobbly stool. "I don't know what came over me—I think it was the lure of a functioning radiator next to a warm bed. The next thing I knew, I was looking into those moony eyes of his and thinking that he looked sort of like Edward Norton, who I've always found sort of cute."

Heidi nodded. "He does, in a way."

"Right—the same way I sort of look like Scarlett Johansson," Dinah said. "In other words, not at all. It's ridiculous. What's the matter with me? I can't have Mr. Unattainable, so I'm hopping in bed with Mr. Overly Available, who vaguely resembles the guy from *Death to Smoochy*."

"He's really great, and he likes you." Unlike a certain someone Heidi could mention.

Dinah was up and pacing now. "The worst part is, if I break it off with him, I'll lose the best-tipping customer I have."

"You can't stay in a relationship with a guy because he tips well. Why would you even consider it?"

"Well . . . it turns out he does other things well, too."

Heidi would have gotten the drift even if Dinah hadn't arched her brows meaningfully. In fact, she could have figured it out from having seen the smile on Dinah's face when she was looking at him as they walked in. "So what's the problem?"

"The problem is it's *Clay*. The boy scout CPA who tells you to wear your mittens. Not exactly my dream man."

"Your dream man sounds like a jerk," Heidi laughed. "But I'm the last person you should come to for advice— my guy compass has always been out of whack. My ex-boyfriend is in a medium security federal lockup. I should be so lucky as to find a nice concave-chested CPA from Bug Tussle to fall in love with me." *Or a cop*.

"Bog Hollow," Dinah corrected her. "And it's not concave, exactly. He's one of those strong, wiry guys."

Erica skidded into the storeroom. The alarm in her eyes stopped Heidi's heart. "You'd better come quick. The police are back. I think they've come to arrest you!"

Heidi rushed out and found the lights from patrol cars parked outside strobing through the café's windows. Patrick's lips were turned down with tension. Marcus looked uncomfortable, too, and no wonder—between him and Patrick glowered Janice, Heidi's upstairs neighbor, her face mottled red and tear-stained.

"What have you done with my son?" she screeched.

The blood drained out of Heidi's face. Damn. She'd forgotten to leave a note.

"Janice, he's fine." She turned to the fireplace, where Wilson was curled up asleep in the armchair, like a cat.

Janice burst into tears and fell on Wilson with such ferocity that he woke up startled and began to cry.

"My poor baby!"

Heidi observed the tearful reunion with equal parts gladness and defensiveness. "Martine asked me to look after him before she went back to France—"

Janice broke off Heidi's sentence with a huff. "Martine! I'm going to sue her for child endangerment."

"I left messages for you," Heidi continued, "but you're a hard person to get a hold of."

"Nonsense! I have a dozen contact numbers."

"Yes, but some of them are in Africa, and you obviously weren't there. And if you don't check the others—"

"Are you saying I'm negligent?" Janice snapped.

Heidi stammered before spitting out, "N-no . . ."

"How dare you call me a bad mother!"

"Excuse me," Erica interrupted, Jeeves-like, slipping between Heidi and Janice with a steaming mug of coffee and a warm cinnamon scone on a plate. She held the plate close to Janice's face. "Scone?"

Heidi could tell the moment the whiff of cinnamon hit Janice's olfactory nerves. Her eyes widened and she pincered a scone, inspecting it only briefly before she took a nibble. Erica was still there with coffee at the ready when she needed it. Her performance was all the evidence Heidi needed of the soothing effect of superior service.

"Thank you," Janice said. The act of swallowing seemed to have calmed her down where words, and the obvious well-being of her child, had failed.

"I'm glad you can take him home now," Heidi told Janice. "You two will still have a few hours of Christmas together."

A look of cold fury crossed Janice's face, although this time it wasn't aimed at Heidi. "But I can't take him home. I came back all the way from Africa to discover there's no electricity here. And our street hasn't been plowed yet. What's the city doing?"

She directed this last question at Marcus, as though a police uniform made him stand-in mayor during a crisis. He kept a concerned yet placid expression on his face. "We have shelters."

Her eyes flashed in horror. "I am *not* taking my child to a *shelter.* I'll call hotels, is what I'll do." Janice flopped down in a chair and pulled out her cell phone.

Patrick took Heidi aside. "You handled that well."

She shook her head. "Erica handled it. I wanted to shake the woman." Still did.

"When Marcus and I arrived at her place after she discovered Wilson missing, I worried she was going to insist we have you booked for kidnapping, even though we assured her he was here."

"So arrogant!" Heidi said, stewing. "And not a word of thanks for taking care of Wilson. Not that I did much, but . . ."

"Maybe when she's calmed down a bit," Patrick said.

"I'm not holding my breath."

But, actually, she was. Because looking into Patrick's eyes, and smelling that woodsy cologne again, made it difficult to breathe normally. Her heartbeat quickened when he was standing next to her. It was difficult to tell whether her galloping pulse could be laid at Janice's door, or Patrick's.

"I saw Mrs. DiBenedetto today," he said. "She's feeling better—she even admitted she liked your cookies."

Heidi smiled. "That's good."

Tension showed in Patrick's brow as he looked down at her. "Heidi . . ." he said, his voice a husky whisper, as if lowering it would provide them some kind of privacy. "About yesterday . . . I felt like a jerk."

She swallowed.

"That is—"

One minute there were two of them huddled together, and, in the next instant, Marcus was between them. Heidi would have groaned with frustration at the interruption had it not been for the urgency in Marcus's eyes. "Sorry to break this up, but we gotta fly. There's been an incident."

Patrick straightened, all business. "Right."

Disappointment rose in Heidi's throat, along with an edge of panic. What was an incident? "Wait!" She felt a moment of shock when her hand clasped around muscle—she hadn't intended to reach out and stop him, but she hadn't been able to help herself. "Will I see you again?"

Something sparked in his eyes. "I certainly hope so."

She watched him go, wondering at the hollow in her stomach, the kind that couldn't be cured by a cinnamon scone.

The lights kept flashing as the patrol car accelerated down the street, which made her uneasy. Last Christmas, Patrick had been shot. What if they had been called to another robbery? *An incident.* The grating sound of Janice on the phone in the background, chewing out desk clerks who had the audacity to work at hotels that had no vacancies, punctuated her thoughts. The whole café probably felt relieved when the woman finally found a friend on the Upper East Side who could give her a room for the night.

"*They* have power, naturally," Janice said. "I never should have moved out to the boondocks."

It was harder than Heidi would have imagined to see Wilson go, even when he started screaming at being bundled up again and realized he'd be leaving. "Mizzle-toooooooeed!" he shrieked through tears as Janice wheeled him out.

Later, it seemed that that was the moment when the natives had become restless. Or maybe it was just the moment when *she* became restless. Wilson dragged away shrieking, bankruptcy ahead, Patrick called away to heaven only knew what kind of crime . . . all was not merry and bright. That others were suffering from flagging patience became clear when a fight exploded near the end of a viewing of *In the Good Old Summertime.*

"It's not even a Christmas movie!" yelled a man who was lobbying for a switch to The Weather Channel.

"Yes it is," said a woman, a relative newcomer near

him. "It's Christmas at the end of the movie, when Judy Garland discovers who Van Johnson really is. Just like *The Shop Around the Corner.*"

"Which we just saw!" A vein throbbed on the man's forehead. "What's the point in watching the exact same story twice in a row?"

"Well, what's the point in watching the weather?" someone else said. "We know what the weather is—bad."

"*Look!*" Erica ran over to the door and pressed her face against the glass. "It's snowing! Cool!"

Her enthusiasm wasn't shared by the rest of the residents of the café.

"What is this?" grumbled the cranky guy. "They said it was supposed to warm up."

"Really?" Heidi asked.

"Into the upper thirties!"

"It needs to be warmer than that to melt all this ice."

The Judy Garland woman claimed that it all depended on the humidity. "Even above freezing, it might not be humid enough to melt ice."

The first guy looked as though his head were going to start spinning. All Heidi's efforts to soothe the world with soup, buttery baked goods, and hot beverages had gone down the toilet in a matter of minutes. "Are you an idiot?" he asked the woman.

"Wait a second," Dinah said, leaping into the fray. "Don't call people names, asshat!"

Clay tugged at her elbow. "*Dinah . . .*"

"No," she said. "If this guy is going to call people idiots, let him say it to a person who has a carafe of piping hot beverage aimed at his crotch."

Heidi held her breath—it felt as if everyone in the café did—half expecting Dinah to make good on the threat. But instead of more insults, or a man screaming in agony as hot coffee made contact with his privates, the next sound she heard was a resonant, beautiful note from a violin. Everyone turned toward a heavyset man, one of the old-timers who'd been in the café since the night before. Closing his eyes, he began to play an achingly beautiful rendition of "Silent Night."

The sound of a violin so close, so expertly played, brought goose bumps to Heidi's flesh. Or maybe her reaction was due to the fact that music had halted the hostilities so abruptly. She scrambled to turn off the CD player and the television.

The next song he played was "We Three Kings." Some people started singing along. When the impromptu concert and singalong continued for a third song, she began to relax again, and retreated to the kitchen, where she found Erica leaning against the fridge. Her eyes were glistening.

"You know what this reminds me of?" Erica asked in a low voice.

Heidi knew. Rue's kitchen. Before Rue had died, Sassy Spinster Farm had taken in guests who wanted to experience living on a working farm. The house had always been full of music and movies and conversation. Sometimes bitter arguments had cartwheeled into laughter, or dancing.

She went and leaned against the fridge, too. "I love thinking about the summer I spent on the farm. Especially when things are rough here. I envy you having such a great place to call home. You've got roots."

Erica swiped her eyes with her sleeve. "God, I've really screwed up."

Heidi frowned. "Wasn't your dad in a better mood today?"

"Yeah, he was—but I know he'll never trust me again. And then, I called Aunt Laura and she wasn't home, and she never called me back. I guess I really teed her off."

"Of course you did." Heidi nudged her with her shoulder. "Everything annoys Laura. Why should you be any different?"

Erica smiled grudgingly and sniffled. "She's been better lately. She really has. Except for being sick—that's made her sort of cranky."

"I'll bet."

"I hope she'll forgive me. I guess I haven't shown much enthusiasm for Hortense—"

"*Who?*"

"That's what she calls the baby."

"She would," Heidi muttered. "Instead of a college fund, we should set up a therapy fund for that child."

"But I really am glad for her," Erica said. "I guess Hortense will seem a lot more interesting to me than Angelica. And Mom would have been so excited, don't you think? Hortense would have been her niece. She'd want me to do something nice for her—or him, if Hortense turns out to be a he. I wish I'd learned to knit . . ."

Heidi gave her a hug. "You can do better than knitting booties. When Hortense is bigger, you can give her rides on Milkshake. And when you're sixteen and you get your license, you can take her to movies and stuff. It'll give you a legit excuse to borrow your dad's car."

Erica grinned. "Or Laura's truck."

"Just think—it's not that far away. Two years."

"Two and a half," Erica said. "I might even have all the money paid back by then."

The word *money* pushed Heidi's worry button—about money, about Patrick, about everything—but she tried not to show it. She gave Erica another squeeze.

Erica tilted her chin up. "I'm not sorry I came, though."

"I'm not, either."

"Really?"

Heidi shook her head.

"That's good, because I started to think it might have been bad of me to barge in on you. Like, what if you'd made other plans, or—"

"Had a life?" Heidi laughed. "I don't. Still . . . it might be a good idea to call first next time."

By the time they left the kitchen area to return to the others, the concert had ended. Heidi dimmed the lights, and everyone settled in for the last Christmas movie in the marathon, *It's a Wonderful Life,* the movie Heidi had never been able to resist. But now as she watched the blips of angels speaking in heaven, previewing the lifetime of worries and woes that were about to squeeze poor Jimmy Stewart like an almond in a nutcracker, she started to fidget. She knew what was coming, and a story about missing money was too close to home for her to enjoy as entertainment. The movie had a happy ending, but her money was gone for good.

Almost as a reflex, she retreated to the kitchen to make . . . something. Anything to keep busy. The cupboards were emptying out, as was the fridge. She peeked into the hydrator and saw a few lemons rolling around. *When life gives you lemons, make lemon bars.*

The activity was soothing, even if it didn't put the brakes on her angst. What had happened to Patrick and Marcus? The looks on their faces before they'd gone worried her. So tense. What had they been headed for when they'd left—a robbery, a murder? Every life-and-death cop show or TV news scenario played through her head. Most of the time at the café, Patrick and Marcus seemed so laid back, it was easy to forget that they worked a dangerous job, day in, day out.

It made losing a cash box seem fairly trivial.

After she slid the lemon squares in the oven, Heidi went back, pulled out a chair next to Mrs. Lamberti's cat, and watched Jimmy Stewart and Donna Reed dance into the swimming pool.

She must have nodded off, because the next thing she knew, Mrs. Lamberti was poking her shoulder. "Hon, your timer's beeping."

Heidi jumped up and pulled out the lemon squares just at the perfect moment, when the pastry was beginning to brown. She set them aside to cool. But by the time they had cooled enough to be dusted with powdered sugar, it would be two in the morning, and no longer Christmas. The world would be swinging into its post-Christmas sugar stupor and starting to contemplate the celery-and-treadmill days of January.

"Those look good," a familiar voice behind her said.

She turned. It was Patrick.

She couldn't help herself—she threw her arms around him. "You're back!"

He laughed, but returned the hug. "Did you think I wouldn't be?"

"The way you guys ran out, and after what you said about last year . . ."

"Don't get me wrong," he said, his low voice almost a caress, "I liked your greeting a lot."

She crooked her head to look up at him. She should have stepped away, or he should have. But they remained just as they were, testing the closeness. "I guess the memorable stuff—shootings and mayhem—doesn't happen every Christmas," she said.

"Oh, I think I'll remember this Christmas, too." He looked into her eyes.

She felt as if the floor wobbled beneath her, and she had to move away from him. *He means because of the storm, not because of me.*

Doesn't he?

Her sweater was damp. "Your coat's wet," she said.

"The snow's turned to drizzle. It's a real mess out there now." As if it hadn't been before.

He unzipped his coat to take it off, and Heidi felt glad that he intended to stay awhile. She took his hat and coat and turned to hang them on the coatrack in the storage closet.

He followed her and, inside the doorway, after she'd hung up his things, she turned and collided with him. He took her arm, steadying her. "I didn't think you'd be worried, Heidi. I mean, I didn't really think you . . ."

She looked up. "Patrick, what you saw yesterday afternoon—Sal and I were just horsing around."

His expression turned momentarily sheepish. "I sort of figured that out today, when he wasn't here. I guess I acted like a nut."

"No—"

"I was jealous, seeing him with you." He leaned closer to her. "There's been something I've been wanting to do forever, you know."

Even if she'd needed to, she didn't have time to ask what that something was. He pulled her toward him and wrapped his arms around her back. She leaned into him, her heart hammering, amazed at the way he could take his time pressing his lips to hers, tasting her slowly, savoring the moment. She felt the opposite—all hopped up inside—and had to hold herself back from slamming the door on the storage closet and letting him have his way with her against the all-purpose flour. Good thing that one of them had restraint.

"You taste like ginger," he murmured, pulling her more tightly against him.

She moaned. "This is a bad time to start something, isn't it?"

She'd meant that anyone could walk in on them, but he was thinking more long-term.

"No, it's the best." He kissed her temple and squeezed her in a tight embrace before she could step away. "It'll make it easy for me to remember the date. Our first kiss—Christmas night, the year of the ice storm. Even when I'm old and gray and can't remember my hair's on top of my head, I'll remember this."

His words melted away the last of her reservations. Snowstorms might make strange bedfellows, but this didn't feel like anything that would be remembered as madness once the last icicle thawed. For one thing, they weren't hopping into bed, or onto the flour sacks. But even if they had, she couldn't imagine second-guessing Patrick. Maybe her guy compass had found true north at last.

After a few more achingly sweet kisses, she stepped back and took his hand. He allowed himself to be tugged back to the others. Two chairs next to each other weren't available, so they pulled a couple of blankets off the stack on one table and spread them next to the wall near the fireplace.

How long had it been since she'd slept? She was so tired, it was easy to lean against Patrick's chest and close her eyes, just for a wink. Jimmy Stewart was running through Bedford Falls, horrified that in this new nightmare world, his wife had never married and had become a librarian. Heidi couldn't help smiling, and then she thought again of Patrick kissing her and telling her she tasted like ginger.

"Hey," she whispered drowsily.

He leaned close, nuzzling her temple. "What?"

"Who's Ginger?"

The rumble of his laughter was the last thing she remembered before drifting off.

Chapter 11

Erica nibbled on a lemon bar and looked over the wreck that was the café. She had carried the dishes to the sink, but the tabletops were still littered with crumbs, old napkins, a stray glove, and other debris. She'd found a cell phone on a chair, a Hefty bag containing a Temper-pedic pillow, and someone's gas bill, stamped and ready to mail, on the floor and covered with boot prints. Chairs faced every which way, some draped with the blankets Patrick and Marcus had brought.

The place needed tidying and sweeping, but she had promised not to wake Heidi, who was curled up on the floor next to the fireplace, sleeping soundly for probably the first time in two days. Marcello, on the other hand, quivered from restlessness even though Erica had taken him out.

It hadn't been much of a walk, though—just up and down the sidewalk in front of the café. Erica hadn't wanted to let the café door out of her sight, since she and Heidi were the only ones there and she didn't have a key to lock it. Outside, the ice was melting, so that not only was there the constant drip of water coming off the trees, but occasionally there were chunks of ice dropping to the sidewalk or avalanching down from the eaves. At the corner of the block, when she looked down a larger street and spied skyscrapers in the distance, she'd become antsy to explore the city.

Maybe this feeling was where the expression "cabin fever" came from. If she had lived in pioneer days, they would have had to put her on Ritalin or something.

Eating sugary stuff probably wasn't calming her impatience any. When she thought she saw Laura and Webb standing outside the café, peering around the street and then into the glass part of the door, she began to regret that last lemon bar she'd inhaled. Great—sugar hallucinations. Her brain was really bugging out.

Then, in a surreal moment, her hallucination rattled the door, opened it with a very real jangle of the bell, and in walked Webb followed by Laura, big as life.

At first, astonishment rooted Erica in place, but in the next moment, a rush of joy propelled her across the room. She threw herself into her aunt's arms. "Laura!"

Laura wrapped her long arms around her in a tight hug. "Youngster!"

Marcello skittered over to the newcomers, letting out muttered *ruffs* as he sniffed Laura and Webb's shoes.

Tears streaked down Erica's cheeks. She hadn't realized how much she missed Laura until the moment she buried her face in the old barn jacket her aunt was wearing, which smelled of old leaves, soil, and maybe a little of Milkshake. Home.

"I'm *so sorry,*" she said, snuffling.

"Nothing to be sorry about," Laura said. "If anyone should apologize, it's me. I've been a jackass as usual."

"No you weren't. You just weren't feeling good."

"You must have thought I didn't want you around,"

Laura continued, "or that you weren't needed now that Hortense is on the way."

"I felt lonely," Erica admitted.

"I assumed you knew what you mean to me, Erica. That losing you would be like . . ." Her voice cracked. "Well, it's not going to happen, that's all."

Erica nodded, trying to pull herself together. It was just such a shock to see them here. She glanced over at Webb, looking so out of place here, but so welcome.

He winked at her. "How are you, E?"

Laura relinquished her hold and answered for her. "How do you think? All alone in this godforsaken place." She inspected the café with narrowed eyes. "What kind of a joint is this?"

"It's a café," Erica explained. "She sells coffee, dessert, and sandwiches. Stuff like that."

"And where is *she*? I might have known she'd get you up here to do all the work."

Erica pointed to the sleeping form in the corner. Heidi flopped over, disturbed by the voices but not quite awake yet.

"Weird!" Laura tilted her head. "Does she always bed down on the restaurant floor?"

In a low tone, Erica explained what they'd been going through these past two days. This morning, when they'd found out that the power had come back on in the neighborhood, all the people had gathered their things and gone home. Heidi had slept through it, though. The last to leave had been Patrick. He'd said he would be back, and he'd instructed Erica to keep the restaurant sign flipped to CLOSED in the meantime and to let Heidi rest a little longer.

"Who is Patrick?" Webb asked her.

"He's a cop."

"The police here go in for mollycoddling, do they?" Laura grinned at them and then swaggered over to Heidi's makeshift pallet. She toed Heidi's foot. "Heidi-ho. Wake up!"

She kept hearing that voice—that voice from her past. Gravelly. No-nonsense. Terrifying. For several minutes she twitched into wakefulness, and then something kicked the bottom of her shoe. Heidi opened her eyes to the vision of Laura looming over her, arms akimbo, eyes glittering with amusement. About the only thing different about her was the bump jutting out incongruously from her midsection, which made her look like a Who from Whoville more than a mother-to-be.

She sounded just like the old Laura, however. "Do y'all actually serve food in this place, or should we take our business elsewhere?"

Heidi lurched to her feet, gave Laura and then Webb quick hugs, and attempted to shush Marcello as he circled them, barking. "Of course I'll fix you something. I'm just so surprised. What are you doing here?" Although she knew. And the happy-mixed-with-sad expression on Erica's face told her that she knew, too. They'd come to get her.

It was so disorienting, as though they'd dropped from the sky. One minute she'd been asleep, and then . . .

She looked around."What happened to everybody?"

"All the people left," Erica explained. "The power's on most everywhere in the neighborhood now—at least, according to Patrick and Marcus."

Patrick! Heidi flushed. Where had he gone?

Webb smiled at her. "Looks like we arrived just in time to miss all the fun."

"All the chaos," Heidi corrected.

"Good," Laura said. "We decided to use Erica's going AWOL as an excuse to take a little vacation."

Erica gasped. "You mean, we're going to stay in New York a while?"

"A few days," Laura said. "Why not? We had a hell of a time getting here—my heart doesn't yearn to head back to the airport, I can tell you that much."

"Can we go and watch the ball drop on New Year's Eve?" Erica asked.

Laura's face slackened in dread, and she and Webb exchanged glances. He seemed amused by the idea, but Laura looked so torn at not giving Erica her heart's desire that Heidi took pity on her. Times Square on New Year's was no place for the easily nauseated.

"We could probably find something more fun to do," she told them, making her way back to the kitchen. "Now let's see—breakfast. There're all sorts of stuff left over . . ." A peek under the cellophane-wrapped trays and cake covers told a different story, however. Except for a few lemon bars, most of the baked goods were gone. She eyed the fridge critically. "We've got a half a carton of eggs, is about all."

"Just coffee for me," Laura said, her lips pursed. "Decaf."

While Heidi cooked the breakfast for everyone else, she got caught up on the news from the farm and Sweetgum, and then explained—or re-explained—what had been going on here.

Laura darted a skeptical glance at Heidi. "Let me get this straight. You lost a whole box of money, and so the next day you started giving out free food and coffee? Does that make sense?"

"Not really, but it felt good."

"Does it feel good to be even more broke than ever?" Laura followed up.

Heidi arched a brow at her. "I hadn't quite mulled that over yet. But thanks for reminding me."

Webb leaned back in a chair, inspecting the tip jar by the register. "What about that money? Doesn't it count?"

Heidi glanced at the jar for the first time that morning. Yesterday, she had noticed that some people had been putting change and even a few dollars into it. Now, though, it was crammed with bills.

"They passed around the jar last night," Erica told her. "And this morning, when everybody was leaving, most of them left more."

Heidi was amazed. "They shouldn't have done that. I didn't expect them to."

"But I think they *wanted* to," Erica said. "At least, that's what Patrick said."

"What happened to Patrick?" Heidi couldn't help asking.

"He said he was going to call you later this morning. He figured you weren't going to open the café today."

"No—I think I'll take a holiday."

Seeing Laura and Webb here, looking so much themselves, but so out of place, buoyed her spirits. They got another lift when Erica counted out the money in the tip jar and discovered it contained nearly four hundred dollars. "Wow! What are you going to do with that?"

"Split it between you and Dinah," she said.

Erica's eyes widened. "Seriously?"

"You did *a lot* of work," Heidi told her. "And maybe this way you'll be able to pay off your dad faster."

Erica jumped up and did a happy dance.

"Let me give you guys the grand tour of the neighborhood," Heidi said. "We can go back to my place. I could use a shower."

"Me, too!" Erica chimed in.

"And we can call around and see if we can find a hotel," Webb said.

Heidi locked up the café and led them all down the street. Webb and Laura strolled side by side carrying two duffel bags, followed by Erica walking Marcello on a leash. Despite the slushy sidewalks, Heidi felt a bounce in her step. The sun was shining at last, they'd survived the storm, and good things had happened: Three hundred and eighty-six dollars in a tip jar. Patrick.

Her phone rang inside her satchel, and she dug it out. It was him.

"You're up," he said.

"Yes, we're all headed over to my apartment."

"All?"

"Webb and Laura are here, from Texas. They're going to stay a couple of days. I was going to get cleaned up and then take them out to . . ." She frowned and turned to call back to them. "What do you want to do today?"

"Empire State Building!" Erica said excitedly. "Can we? I want to go to the top, like in the movies."

Laura turned a little green at the prospect, which made Heidi laugh. She nodded and spoke to Patrick again. "We're going to the Empire State Building."

"Do you need a guide? I've not only been there a zillion times, I've arrested someone there."

"Excellent!"

"Give me forty-five minutes," he said. "And Heidi?"

"Yes?"

"The only Ginger I've ever loved was on *Gilligan's Island.*"

She smiled as the warm feeling from last night returned. "So you don't mind hanging around?"

"Try and stop me."

Heidi hung up and was feeling close to euphoric when

they turned onto her street. As they approached her apartment, Webb and Laura both slowed down, their gazes drawn to the fully dressed Christmas tree lying on the sidewalk. The ice had mostly melted off of it, so that there was just a layer of gloppy snow crusting over it.

"What's that?" Webb asked.

"That's Heidi's Christmas tree." Erica looked up at Heidi. "If we shook the snow off and took it inside now, do you think the lights would work?"

Heidi frowned. "I'm not sure . . ." Now that she took another look at it, it seemed huge. She wasn't even sure where she could put it. And she'd have to take it down soon, anyway. That was always a bummer.

Laura, who had been inspecting the tree for the best way to extricate it from the snow and remaining ice, kicked something nearby. "What the heck?" She lifted a green metal box from the sidewalk and batted snow from it. "Is this what all the fuss was about?"

Heidi's face fell. *The cash box.* It must have been there all this time—buried. When she'd picked up the shopping bag to go to the hospital, the box had probably slipped right through the soggy bottom into the snow.

She ran over to Laura, nearly skidding into her in her excitement. She threw her arms around her ex-stepsister and let out a squeal of glee . . . much to Laura's dismay. "Thank you!"

"You idiot," Laura said. "Why thank me? It was right here all along."

"But you found it for me!" Heidi exclaimed. "You're my guardian angel and Santa Claus all rolled into one!"

Laura groaned and tried to bat her away.

"And now it's my turn," Heidi continued. "Anything you want, Laura. Your wish is my command. Ask and you shall receive."

Laura's brows darted up. "Really?"

Heidi nodded. "Anything. Even world peace—no guarantees, but I'll give it my best shot."

"I know what she wants," Erica said.

"What?" Heidi and Laura asked at the same time.

Erica and Webb exchanged glances. "Bacon!"

Heidi laughed and then hugged Laura again. "I'm going to smother you in bacon, Laura. All the way till New Year's."

Laura considered it. "You know what? I think I'm finally in the Christmas spirit." She shrugged Heidi off of her, brushed her hands together, and looked down at the tree, all business. "Now, let's get this monster inside. The youngster wants a tree."

Home for Christmas

ROSALIND NOONAN

For Karen and Dave Barretto,
who so kindly shared their New England homes,
their Red Sox caps,
their hearts.
You guys are wicked awesome.

Chapter 1

"I'm back!" Joanne Truman called from the back room of the Christmas shop. She closed the outside door behind her, pausing at the sight of Christmas in motion. Hundreds of dazzling lights twinkled in schemes from cool blues and silvers to warm cardinal, burgundy, and gold. There were trees dripping in silver icicles, trees decorated with miniature toys, trees decorated with gingerbread people. Carols were playing and the air was scented with cinnamon and spice. Surrounded by two girls she loved and radiant trees and ornaments that made the shop resemble the inside of a jewelry box, she soaked up the lights and the joy.

A handful of customers browsed in the store, one of the few places in town open this late. Jo could tell that the customers—an elderly couple and a group of women in ski parkas—were visitors in Woodstock. She pretty much knew everyone from these parts.

"Deck the halls with balls of holly," five-year-old Ava sang.

Jo grinned, loving the chipmunk quality of her daughter's voice.

"Follow lama la, la, la, la, la . . ." Ava stared intently through the long strands of her gold bangs as she straightened the gold threads of the wooden ornaments she was hanging on a low rack.

Toting a plastic bin from the back room, Jo paused by her daughter. "Honey, that's *boughs* of holly."

Ava frowned up at her. "Holly doesn't bow."

"It's different, like a tree bough."

"Balls sounds better. See what I did, Mommy?"

"Good job. Looks like you need a haircut, lovey."

"Nope." She held up a carousel horse and hung it on the peg with the others. Since the shop's opening last year, Ava had enjoyed helping out, and Jo was glad to have her daughter close for the portion of the day she spent here.

Jo brushed Ava's bangs back and headed to the front of the store, smiling as Ava crooned along with the music.

"Opening this shop was the best idea I ever had." Jo plunked the plastic bin on the glass countertop beside her cousin Molly.

"Mm-hmm." Molly didn't look up from the register tape and calculator as she tallied the day's sales. "But as I remember it, Cousins' Christmas Shop was my idea."

"It was your idea to pack everything we own and head west till we ran out of highway," Jo pointed out, untangling the hooks of three snowman ornaments dripping with white glitter.

"Ay-yuh. I remember now. You're the homebody who refuses to leave this cursed place."

"That's right. This is my home. And now it's Ava's home, too."

"We'll see about that. Once I finish nursing school and

get a real paying job in Manchester or Boston, you'll be calling me and begging me to get you out of Dodge."

"Nope. We've got roots here. We're staying put." Jo balled up her jacket and stuffed it under the register. She'd run across the street to help out at Woodstock Station, the restaurant inside the inn, for the dinner rush. Waitressing wasn't one of her regular gigs, but as her dad managed the place, she was willing and able to help out in a pinch.

"So, what did I miss?"

Molly bit her lip as her fingers tapped the calculator pads. "Earl came over, busting his buttons with delight. He's gotten loads of comments about those two trees we did for him." Earl Camden, owner of the Woodstock Inn, had paid them generously to decorate trees for the library and the lobby of the inn. "He was so impressed, he ordered two more for the Riverside and Cascade House."

"Yes!" Jo slapped her cousin five. "God bless that man."

"This town would be lost without Earl and the inn." Molly's brown eyes were sincere behind her black-framed glasses. "I hate the name 'Black Friday,' but I'm sure glad that Christmas shopping season has started. Do you know we sold five decorated trees today?"

"Really?" That alone would make this season profitable for them. "Well, Merry Christmas to us," Jo said as the brass horns sounded the intro to "What Child Is This?"

"Dave needs to deliver three of them. Two to the condos by Loon, and one to Pete's Pizza in Lincoln. The other two Earl is going to pick up himself."

"Fantastic." Hands on her hips, Jo walked through the rows of decorated trees, pointing to the ones marked with SOLD tags, which would need to be replaced.

"I see we have some decorating in our future. I wonder what time Target opens . . ."

"Psst!" Molly put up a hand to stop her. "Don't give away our trade secrets. Besides, it's Black Friday. The big stores are probably open twenty-four-seven from now till Christmas."

As if on cue, the bells on the door jingled and a woman in an elegant velvet-trimmed cap appeared. She waved in a boy who looked to be around Ava's age, maybe a year or two older.

"Now stay close to Mommy," she warned him.

The boy proceeded to turn away and disappear behind a tree decorated with Victorian fans and glittering ornaments in silver and lavender.

"Jason . . ." She fetched him from the aisle and pulled him toward the front of the store. "Stay here, where I can see you." She turned to the counter. "Sorry."

"No worries," Molly insisted. "They've all got minds of their own."

Jason meandered to the streetfront window, where ornaments, Christmas clocks, and novelties sat on staggered levels of gold, satiny cloth. Jo and Molly had built the display from a tablecloth with old books propped underneath, and, although the materials were cheap, Jo thought the final product, accented with red and gold ribbon and red balls suspended from fishing line, looked rich and quite grand.

"Look, Mom. A snow globe."

Joanne looked up from the bin of tangled ornaments to watch the little boy reach into the shop's window for the display item.

Everyone loved the snow globe.

Large enough to contain a person's dreams, yet small enough to hold in your hands, the globe looked down on the main street of Woodstock, New Hampshire, where the gabled Woodstock Inn sat next to the old firehouse that had been converted into an annex of rooms for the inn.

Across the street, one of the shops had been carefully labeled COUSINS' to match the shop where Joanne and Molly sold Christmas novelties all year round. Behind the storefronts arose a tiny version of the White Mountains, white peaks speckled with green trees.

"Lovely," the woman said, leaning over her son. "But you have to hold it still a second and let the snow settle. See? There's the inn where we're staying. And this is the shop we're in now."

"Cool." The boy's mouth ruffled in a pout as he stared at the globe, then began shaking it again.

"Jason, what did I say? You need to put it down." Tension tugged down the woman's voice, but her son turned away from her, hogging the globe.

Joanne was about to intervene when her daughter stepped out from behind the candy cane tree.

"Hey, that's not a toy." Though she was only five and thin as a string of licorice, Ava the disciplinarian could pack a wallop.

"I know." The boy looked down at her defiantly, but he held the globe securely now.

"I'll take that." The woman swept the snow globe out of his hands.

"Can we get it, Mom? Please?"

The woman tilted the globe so that the white snowflakes danced to the side. "I suppose so." She put it on the counter without checking the price. Which always floored Jo. Didn't she care whether it was a value or an extravagance? It was like shopping with a blindfold on.

"We can get the snow globe if you promise not to touch anything else in the store," the kid's mother said.

"That sounds like a tall order." Jo came around the counter and crouched to be on the little boy's level. "You may be interested in some of our toy ornaments. Do you like cars?"

He nodded eagerly.

Ava threw up her arms dramatically. "I'll show him where they are! Come on." And the two kids headed toward the back wall.

The woman turned to Jo. "Toys are just what he needs right now. We've been sitting on the interstate forever, and he's not too happy about having to leave home this weekend."

"It's hard for kids," Jo said as she went back to her bin of sorting. "Are you visiting family here?"

"Oh, no. My husband is here on business, and we decided to make it a family trip since it is Thanksgiving weekend." Even under the hat, which was too frou-frou for Jo's tastes, the woman radiated beauty, with eyes that sparkled like sapphires, and porcelain white skin.

"Well, I hope he enjoys his weekend in Woodstock." Molly glanced up from her notepad. "If we get some more snow, that'll be fun for the kid."

"Can I help you find something?" Jo asked.

"No, thanks. I think I'll just browse . . . and I want to check out your toy ornaments myself. Last year Jason and his dad pulverized a few of our glass ornaments with the Nerf gun he got for Christmas."

"Our toy ornaments are kid-proof," Molly said as the woman headed toward the back of the store. The older couple brought a basket of items to the counter for Jo to ring up.

"Have a Merry Christmas," Jo said as the couple left with their purchases.

The door bells were still jingling when Molly tapped Jo's shoulder and pointed to a number on her notepad, circled three times. "Would you look at that? Better than I thought."

Jo's heart leaped at the number. They had never had a thousand-dollar day, let alone two thousand.

"Are you sure?"

Molly nodded. "I'm telling you, it was a stroke of brilliance to start selling entire decorated trees."

"Wow . . ." They could pay their rent on the shop for the next three months and still have money left for groceries and gas, rent and heat.

"I might just up and quit my job on the mountain." In the past two weeks, Joanne had been working nights at the ski resort, cleaning floors and bathrooms in the off-hours after the resort closed. Though she didn't mind the work, the job made her miss Ava's bedtime, which broke her heart.

"Go for it. If things keep up, I'll have enough to take a full course load next semester. I'll be Meredith Grey before you know it."

"Isn't she a doctor?" Jo asked.

"Whatever." Molly pumped her fists in slow motion, dancing behind the counter to "Jingle Bell Rock."

"Next year, this time, you'll be coming to Boston to visit me in my new life."

"A very short visit. I hate to be away from Woodstock at Christmas," Jo said.

"But you'd come to see me, your BFF."

It was true. In their tight-knit family, she and Molly had been best friends since their mothers threw them into the same playpen in diaper days. Molly's desire to leave Woodstock was a thorn in Jo's side. Almost finished getting her nursing license, Molly was eager to get out of Woodstock and put down roots in a place where one job would pay the rent.

Jo was sometimes amazed at what opposites they were, since she couldn't imagine living anywhere but here. Of course, as a single parent, she needed to live near her family, and you couldn't get much closer than the apartment across the lane from your parents' house. The setup in the old carriage house was good for child care and easy on the budget—not so good for actually moving on with life. She never thought that when she turned twenty-five, her mum would still be doing her laundry. Correction—her laundry *and* her kid's, too.

"You work hard all day," her mother always said. "I'm happy to help out where I can." When it came to Ava, Mum and Dad were great. But sometimes Jo felt like her best wasn't good enough. Could you ever spend enough time with your kid?

"Hello?" Molly snapped her fingers in front of Jo's face. "Penny for your thoughts."

"I was just thinking of how much Ava and I will miss you when you're down in Boston next year, drinking wicked strong candy cane cosmos."

"What? You think I'm a party animal?" Molly snatched a fuzzy mouse with a Santa cap from the bin and launched it at her cousin.

Laughing, Jo caught the little mouse and was about to wing it back when the elegant woman appeared amid the lit trees.

"Need some help?" Molly asked.

The woman reached into her Coach bag and removed a slender card case. "It's so hard to choose. I think we're probably just better off taking the whole tree—the one with the Matchbox cars on it. We're renting the Cascade House for the next few months, and it could use some decorating. Do you know it?"

"Sure." Jo shrugged. Everyone in these parts knew the Cascade House. Built as a millionaire's mansion in the early 1900s, it had been turned into a bed-and-breakfast by the Seidel family. "But don't Teddy and Laura have their own tree?"

She waved the question off. "You can never have enough Christmas, right? The sign says you make deliveries?"

"Sure thing." Jo took the woman's credit card, which read *Clarice Diamond,* and tallied up her purchases. The total was another substantial sale, which increased even more when Ms. Diamond said she would toss in another hundred dollars to have the tree delivered tonight. Clarice Diamond said the lodge they were renting was dark and dreary, and it would help brighten the place up.

"I have to ask my brother Dave," Jo said. "If he's around, I'm sure he'll do it."

Within minutes they were covering the tree, with Dave on his way over. Clarice Diamond leaned against the display window, a slim cell phone pressed to her ear, while her son danced in the aisles, a car ornament in each hand. Ava manned the sticky-tape dispenser at the base of the tree they were wrapping, singing carols as she assisted.

"O come, o come, amen you well . . ." crooned Ava, her little legs huddled beneath the knit skirt of her dress.

My little bundle of Christmas cheer, Jo thought. Often she had to resist the temptation to drop everything and gather her daughter up in her arms. Ava was petite for her age, but she had gotten to the point where she did not want to be babied in public, and Jo tried to respect that.

Clarice joined them by the wrapped tree, sliding her phone into her purse. "Thank you so much for doing this so quickly. My husband will be so relieved to see Jason happy again." She looked around to see if other customers were listening. "He's Sid Diamond, you know."

Molly rose. "The real estate guy who's trying to trump Trump? The one who owns half of Boston?"

"Such a crazy reputation." Mrs. Diamond's eyes warmed a bit when she smiled. "We'll be here for the season while my husband makes one of his famous deals. He's looking at the base of Cannon Mountain."

"Mmm. Well, if you're going to be around, come back

next week," Molly said. "I hear Santa might be stopping by."

Ava's mouth dropped open. "Really?"

Molly shrugged. "Just something I heard."

"We'll be sure to check that out," Clarice said. "And I hear that one of you is somewhat famous, too. My girlfriend said one of the young ladies running this shop was engaged to Shane Demerit."

Awkwardness filled the pine-scented air, and suddenly Jo's palms were damp. Jo felt Ava's eyes on her, wide and eager.

"The famous skier?" the woman prodded, as if they needed reminding.

"Ay-yuh, that would be me." Jo raised her hand, but her smile was gone, the good mood drained from her. "I'm Joanne Truman."

"Clarice Diamond." She extended her hand. "It's so nice to meet you. Looking at you now, I remember seeing your photo back in the day. I was a huge fan of Shane's." She pressed a palm to her chest, biting back a smile. "Actually, I have to admit it. I had a crush on him. I saw him at a competition and though I didn't know him at all, he had such a presence. When I heard that he died, I was in shock for days. Such a devastating loss to the ski world."

And to the people who loved him, Jo wanted to say, as grief, cold and familiar, settled over her shoulders. In the five years since Shane's death, the pain had eased. But the scars still throbbed, especially at this time of year when symbols of the holiday she loved threatened to remind her of that dark season when Shane had died.

"I've always been haunted by Shane's story." Clarice locked her sharp blue eyes on Jo. "I guess it was his bad boy reputation that intrigued the world. What made him do it?"

Jo had nothing to say. She had learned that she didn't

owe the public any explanation as far as Shane was concerned. She stepped back from the woman and let her eyes drop to the floor, where her daughter perched, bright and curious. Ava was her inspiration for pushing on. Ava was the light of her life, the beautiful aftermath of her darkest days.

"Can you believe that was five years ago?" Molly said as she applied another piece of tape to the tree. "Time does march on. And look at Ava, here. Five years old now."

Ava frowned up at them, her eyes masked by hair. "Do you need any more tape?"

"I think that's it, kiddo," Molly said.

"Oh . . . she's yours?" Clarice looked from Ava to Joanne and back again. "This is his daughter? Oh, wow . . ." She pressed her palm to her chest again, as if her heart couldn't take the drama.

Jo reached down to Ava, pulling her to her feet. "Why don't you put the tape away?" she asked.

"But I want to hear about Daddy."

"Listen to your mum," Molly said in her stern aunt voice, and Jo was grateful when Ava marched off.

"It's all such a sad story," Clarice said. "My heart goes out to you."

Jo stared at the woman, wondering how such a thing of beauty could be so vacant. She wanted to point out that Ava had never met her father. She wanted to tell Clarice that they didn't need her pity.

But she kept her mouth clamped shut and went back to the register, grateful that another customer was ready to be rung up.

Later, when Ava was settled in with her grandmother, and the customers had cleared out, Jo's anger resurged at the thought of Clarice Diamond's dramatic scene.

"That woman really pissed me off," she muttered to her cousin.

"Still seething over Princess Diamond? She's just a pretty face."

"A pretty face in my face." Jo brushed glitter from the counter. "In my daughter's face. You'd think that a woman with a child of her own would be more sensitive to a kid who never got to meet her notorious father. It made me wonder if it's right having Ava here. With me working ninety jobs, I thought it would be a good way for the two of us to spend more time together, but now I'm not so sure . . ."

"It's fine," Molly reassured her. "Ava likes to hear about her father. You can't keep the truth from her forever."

"I'm just trying to protect her." Jo sprayed glass cleaner on the counter and wiped down the sides. "I never thought I'd have celebrity mongers in here, sniffing around my daughter. Gushing sympathy."

"The woman dropped a lot of sympathy here. A few hundred bucks' worth."

"Still . . ." The whole thing left a bad taste in Jo's mouth. "How do you tell a five-year-old the difference between famous and notorious?" she asked.

"You don't." Molly zipped the cash and receipts into a bag and went to the front door. "You say, 'Bet you didn't know your dad was so famous, did you, pumpkin?' And you leave it at that." She locked the front door. "It's late. We'd better get going, 'cause we're back open at nine tomorrow."

"Give Ava extra hugs and kisses for me," Jo said, wishing she was headed home, too. "And her Boo Bear is in the dryer." Ava never slept without it.

"Relax, Mama Bear. I've done this plenty of times before." Molly would walk Ava home from Jo's parents' house to the apartment in the carriage house that Molly, Jo, and Ava shared.

"I don't know what I'd do without you, cuz," Jo said as she started turning off light displays around the store. She went to the display window—the only lights they left on after closing—and paused by the Woodstock snow globe. Ava had reminded her to replace the window sample with a globe from the stockroom after the Diamonds had purchased it.

She turned the smooth globe upside down and watched as snowflakes danced over the town, landing on the mountains and the rooftops. Let Molly have her wanderlust; Jo loved this town. It was here in the circle of the White Mountains that she'd fallen in love, had her heart broken, then been given a brand-new life with the birth of her daughter.

On this Thanksgiving weekend, she was grateful for many things . . . her daughter, her family, her New England home. Thank God towns like Woodstock were still able to exist and prosper. Thank you, God. She turned the sign to CLOSED and followed her cousin out the back door to a real-life snow dance.

Chapter 2

The old window rattled as Sam slammed it shut and stripped off his sweater. Up on Dare Mountain, the falling snow would penetrate like slivers of glass, and the wind would freeze to the bone. It was crazy to go up on the mountain on a wicked cold night like this, but in the past few years, crazy had become the new normal for Sam Norwood.

Stripped down to his jeans, he turned and caught his reflection in the mirror over the dresser. A freakin' horror show. The old colonial furniture had served him fine when he grew up in this room, but since he'd returned from Afghanistan, it was all another reminder of days long past, childhood plans and alliances that had been shattered and torn. He grabbed a pillow from the bed and propped it up against the mirror to block the ugly truth.

He pulled the titanium shell over the tender area of his shoulder, pausing to massage the scars, braids of skin that twisted like maps of the chambers of hell. He didn't need the mirror to know the patterns of the wounds, the discolored skin that ran up one side of his neck, the distorted area where his ear had once been.

And to think, he and Cack really believed they were going to make it through in one piece. Cackalacky was the platoon's nickname for Floyd Miller, a North Carolina boy. "If something gits ya, ya gotta hope you git damaged just enough to send you home still walking and talking," Cack used to say. That was what Cack had wanted more than anything . . . to get home.

Bitterness stung the back of Sam's tongue as he slammed the drawers of the old dresser closed. That was the perverse irony, the sick joke of the universe—Cack had a family to return to and he went home in a body bag, while here was Sam sleeping in his old bedroom, with nobody who would really miss him, save for his ma, who'd made a life of her own.

Why was the person who had the least to lose always the survivor? Last man standing.

Not even thirty years old and he'd already outlived his two best friends. He'd joined the army to start a new chapter in his life. He'd been running from home, running from guilt, running from Shane's ghost. But in trying to escape the tragedy that had happened up on Dare Mountain, he'd run straight into a fiery pit of more agony, the kind that wakes you up bawling in the middle of the night.

One thing he'd finally learned: There was no escape.

It was time to point his head into the wind and let fate finish knocking the crap out of him.

Sam opened the closet door and dug into a bin of winter gear. Gloves. Hat. Insulated socks. It was all there the way he'd left it four years ago. Even a face mask. That would work.

He stuffed the gear into the big pockets of his jacket and turned toward the door. The wall there was bright with posters of the U.S. Olympic ski team, and his gut tightened at the memory of the dreams and plans that he and Shane had hatched in this room. The two of them thought they were going to ski with Bode Miller. They were going to be champions, Woodstock's first heroes.

A couple of idiots.

He flicked the light switch, thinking that it had ended that fast for Shane. One stupid decision on Dare Mountain and Shane was gone, leaving dozens of people to pick up the pieces and ask why as they reeled in pain. Missing him.

The house was tired and quiet around him. His mother had all but moved out, spending most of her time with Ted Provost, the groundskeeper down at the golf course. She probably should've sold this place while he was gone, given his stuff away to charity. One more way to erase the past.

Out in the shed, Sam found his ski gear, dusty, but the boots still fit and the bindings worked. He dumped the stuff into the back of the truck and headed out to the mountain.

Time to face the beast.

He hadn't planned on coming home. Four years ago when he left for Afghanistan, he figured he'd seen the last of these mountains. But yesterday, on his way home from the airport, he saw the rock cliffs rising on the horizon and knew he would have to do it.

Time to face the mountain.

Dare Mountain was the setting for his nightmares, the place where he watched Shane disappear over a rocky ledge. It was also the setting for the Humvee nightmares, which didn't make sense, since the hills of Afghanistan were carved from entirely different landscape.

But no one ever said dreams made sense.

On a clear day, from the top of the mountain, you could see four states and Canada, but most of the people in Woodstock never got that view. They kept their eyes on the road, on their kids . . . on the pasta they were cooking for dinner or the fence they were painting. Normal people living normal lives. As a kid, Sam had always wanted more. He wanted to be up on top of a mountain, looking to the future.

Now that he'd spent time in the craggy brown mountains of Afghanistan, he'd learned that tomorrow isn't on the next hilltop or valley, your future comes from the landscape within. That's how he knew he was on shaky ground.

When you were dead inside, the terrain of tomorrow looked flat and dusty. Very bleak.

Chapter 3

Swabbing the mop in time with Glenn Miller's version of "Sleigh Ride," Jo made short work of cleaning the ladies' room in the main lodge at the bottom of the mountain. Last Christmas she'd helped Les Benedict, the manager of the lodge, choose a few Christmas CDs after he'd read an article that said tips usually tripled when customers were jollied up by Christmas carols.

"Music calms the heart," she'd told him. "People want to be generous and share goodwill. It makes us all feel good. We just need a little cajoling."

Now as she backed out of the ladies' room, she swayed in time to the swing band's rousing climax of the song.

"I like a person who puts her heart in her work," Les said from behind her.

"With a selection of music like that, who can resist?" Jo swiped the hair from her forehead with the sleeve of her sweatshirt.

"You helped me pick those songs, Jo, and for that I'm very grateful."

"It was a great idea you had. Sure makes my work here go faster."

"That's what I'm meaning to talk to you about." Les tugged at the zipper toggle of his down vest. "What's this I hear 'bout you quitting on me?"

"It's true. Business has picked up at the shop, and Dad says they're going to need my help at the inn over Christmas. As I told Carla, I can give you another week, two if you need it."

"We're going to miss you, Jo. Good worker like you's hard to replace, but I'm glad your shop is taking off."

"Thank you, Les. I don't want to leave you in the lurch, but it'll be good to be home with my kid at night."

"I bet it will." The radio on his belt crackled, and Carla's voice called his name. "Excuse me," he said, turning away to answer.

As Jo sprayed the windows and wiped till they gleamed, she wondered if one of her cousins might be interested in taking on this job. She'd like to help Les out, and one of the high school–age kids like Lauren or Katie could handle the hours, at least over Christmas vacation.

When she wheeled her cleaning cart toward the snack bar, Les was still in the hall, pacing as he spoke into the radio.

"Ay-yeah . . . it's the only way to handle it. I'll send her up if she's willing. Be right there, myself. Ovah." Worry creased his face as he frowned. "Got some trouble up on the mountain. Ice storm up there has made our black diamond runs downright treacherous, and we need to close 'em off. Ski patrol is up there tending to an accident on the Crazy Eights Run right now, and with people out sick we're short-staffed. Carla suggested you grab some skis and head up there to help us out. Mostly we need people to stand at the entrance to the black diamond trails and divert skiers." He waved a hand toward the rest of the lodge. "If you can help us, I'll get someone else to finish the cleaning in the morning."

Jo felt her jaw drop at the prospect of heading up to ski on a night like this. "But . . . it's been years since I worked ski patrol. I was in high school." She pointed up toward the mountain. "I don't even ski anymore."

"It's like riding a bicycle. It'll come back to you."

"But I don't have a parka or any equipment or—"

"Drop into the rental shop and they'll fix you up with what you need." He clipped the radio back onto his belt and patted her shoulder. "Appreciate you helping us out, Jo. I'm going to head on up there. See you at the top."

Jo's pulse tripped quickly as she peeled off her plastic gloves and wheeled her cart to the supply room. This was not good. She hadn't been up skiing on this mountain since before she was pregnant. She hadn't snapped skis on since Shane had died, and she wasn't keen on getting back into the sport now.

Thirty minutes later she sat on the cable car decked in rental clothes from head to toe. Her feet and ankles felt mummified in the tight boots, and she couldn't believe the weight of the black helmet in her hands, which Andy in the rental shop had told her was required for ski patrol these days. A dark, cloying dread gripped her, and she kept telling herself she couldn't be afraid of skiing. She had grown up skiing. She used to give lessons. She could handle herself on the mountain. But then, Shane had been an expert skier, too. He'd placed in the World Championship and had been chosen for the 2006 U.S. team.

"Welcome to the White Mountains of New Hampshire," Drake, the cable car's operator, said as he closed the doors. "And tonight, as you can see, it's really white out there. We've had ten inches of snow in the past twelve hours. Apparently there's some ice mixed in with that, folks, because we have closed our expert runs. I repeat, the black diamond runs are closed due to icy conditions. Here at Dare our first priority is safe skiing."

Drake nodded at Jo, then surveyed the passengers. "Do we have some newcomers here? A handful. Skiing for the holiday weekend? Then I'll give you the short tour."

As the car began to travel uphill, he gave a brief history of the area. "Home to Dare Mountain, Cannon Mountain, and Franconia Notch, where a natural rock formation on one cliff side became famous in the early eighteen hundreds because it resembled the face of an old man. People came from everywhere to see the Old Man of the Mountain, and in nineteen forty-five the state of New Hampshire adopted it as its state emblem. We still have it on state road signs and license plates. When the rock formation collapsed in two thousand three, people were devastated."

Jo was sixteen when the rock face of the Old Man came tumbling down. She didn't think it was a big deal at first, but when Shane gathered a group to drive over and check it out, she'd ditched class without a second thought. At sixteen she'd been glued to Shane's side, whenever he wasn't off drinking or raising hell with his buddies. Shane had had a small, elite circle of friends, stand-up guys like Sam Norwood and Tim Healey, who would have given anything for Shane. After Shane's death, they'd been lost, too. Sam had joined the army, and Tim took a job somewhere in Massachusetts.

Trying to tamp down fear, Jo wiggled her toes in her boots and thought of Ava. She really should teach her how to ski. Ava was curious about it, especially since she'd heard that her father loved skiing.

Yes, skiing had been Shane's number one passion . . .

or maybe it was passion number two, just after drinking. She wondered if the oh-so-perfect Clarice Diamond knew about Shane's drinking problem when she had her crush on him. Or had Clarice been smitten with the media account of Shane Demerit, local legend?

Just before the 2006 Olympics when he was to be one of the top downhill competitors, twenty-year-old Shane Demerit had killed himself on a late-night run down the mountain. People called it a tragic accident, a great irony for a young skier to die on the brink of his success, a "perfect storm," with an ice storm making conditions hazardous. People failed to mention the obscene blood alcohol level that had made even a simple descent impossible. Shane had "liked his beer" as Jo's mother used to put it. A nice way of saying he was an alcoholic, an ugly drunk when he tied one on.

That was the side of Shane that Jo had always sought to hide from their daughter. But Shane had possessed endearing qualities, too. Despite his bouts of drinking and general craziness, Shane had a good heart, and Jo had thought their love could get them through the difficulties of her being a teen mother.

Unfortunately, Shane hadn't seen it that way. "Trailer trash," he kept saying. "I'm so sick of being trailer trash." He'd thought he had found a way out of that with his skiing, but he was sure that a baby was going to send them back to the hellhole he'd escaped. He was sure they'd be ruined.

Although the baby was an unexpected mistake, Jo argued that she couldn't destroy a part of herself and the man she loved. She would care for the baby and keep saving for their house. Her mom and Aunt Martha would help. They'd make things work, if he just gave it a chance. She had thought she could deal with his issues, help him, ease his pain. She had thought she could make him happy.

Jo had gone over that last conversation a million times; it played like a top forty song she couldn't get out of her head. But that night, talking to Shane was like talking to a wall. He was too drunk to process what she was saying, all liquored up like that.

She should have known that Shane had been drunk and "flipping out" as he used to say, but then, she'd been flipping out herself. Nineteen and pregnant and worried about losing the guy she loved.

Ay-yeah, she'd been wicked panicked.

As the cable car bumped into place at the top of the mountain, Drake gave a second warning about icy conditions and closed trails. Jo pulled the black helmet over her head, thinking that she really belonged home with Ava right now. She should be in her sweatpants and slippers, stringing beads for ornaments, peeking in on her daughter in the next room, checking for her soft, sweet breath as she slept peacefully.

Stepping out into the bitter wind reinforced that feeling. She clamped her goggles on so that she could see where she was going, tipped her skis over one shoulder, then tromped over to Les, who was easily identifiable in a red jacket with a red blinking light clipped to the front.

"It's wicked cold up here," Jo said, her voice raised against the noise of ice chips pelting her helmet. "I can't believe you have any skiers up here in this weather."

"People from the city want to get their ski time in on vacation weekends, and we attract a lot of them as we're open more'n most." He held out a gloved hand holding a dark disk. "Take this and head over to the entrance to Heartbreak Ridge. It's blocked with barricades, but there are always a few show-offs who think they can defy gravity."

Jo was well experienced with daredevils.

"The cable car stops bringing people up at eleven, so you've only got another hour or so. You got a cell phone?"

She pressed the pocket of the ski patrol coat, just making sure. "Sure do."

"Call Carla down at the lodge if you need anything. You should be fine, though. It's pretty quiet up here."

"Okay." Feeling a bit rusty, Jo snapped her skis on and herringbone-climbed the ridge to get to the main trail. Once she began to glide on the icy surface, it all came back to her. Her palms were sweating inside her gloves, but it wasn't terrible to be cutting an edge or gliding downhill. Although it had been years since she'd been up here, the trail map was etched in her mind. Even in the blistering ice storm, she knew where to fork left and when to veer to the right to reach the top of Heartbreak Ridge.

The entrance to the run was marked by two short gray lumps. The cones blocking the entrance were covered with icy gray scales, nearly obliterating the orange color. Jo stopped beside one of them and poked at it with her ski pole. It would take awhile to chip the ice away, but then, she had plenty of time to kill.

It took ten minutes to clear off one cone, and during that time only a handful of skiers passed by on their way to the intermediate trail. One woman stopped to ask if the expert trails would be open in the morning, but, otherwise, the mountain was quiet. Almost eerie.

As she hacked away at the ice on the second cone, she imagined Shane here, speeding down the runs. Did he stay low and tuck his poles in a racing stance, or was he so sloppy drunk that he wavered on his skis?

Hearing a noise behind her, Jo staked her poles into the ground and turned to look behind her.

And there he was . . .

A gray ghost of a man looming under the lights behind

the curtain of falling snow. He swayed casually down the slope, as if cutting an edge in ice was no problem at all.

Her heart pounded in her chest, her pulse roaring in her ears as he approached.

"Shane?" She wiggled around to face him, nearly crossing her skis in the process.

She wasn't so much scared of his ghost as she was alarmed that she could be losing her mind in a snowstorm at the top of Dare Mountain.

It couldn't be him . . .

Squinting through her goggles, she noted the way he leaned fearlessly, as if he knew the mountain would support him. That was Shane's style.

But then, as she watched him crouch, she saw that his stance was closer than Shane's. Closer and tighter.

It wasn't him.

Thank God. She would have felt like a total idiot, thinking she was talking to a ghost. The skier's face was covered by a black mask. Creepy-looking, though practical up here.

He didn't turn toward the intermediate trail but shot straight toward her, spraying ice and snow as he stopped.

"Hey, how's it going?" she called.

He stared at her in silence, and though the mask obscured his face completely, she sensed some undercurrent running between them, connecting them.

Then, he tilted his head, as if curious. "Jo?"

Her stomach lurched, and she had to remind herself it wasn't Shane.

"Yeah. Who are you? I can't tell with your mask."

He pointed one pole down Heartbreak Ridge. "How is it?" His voice was muffled by the mask.

"The trail is closed. Didn't they tell you? The icy conditions have made it treacherous."

As she spoke, he pushed off and moved to the top of Heartbreak.

"What are you doing? The intermediate trails just below us are open, but you can't go down Heartbreak."

He looked back at her, a picture of evil in the black mask. "I got it."

"No, you don't. Are you nuts? No one can handle themselves on an expert trail in sheer ice. It's like jumping off a cliff."

He didn't answer, but pushed off toward the edge.

"Don't be an ass!" Something sparked to life inside her and she burst from her spot, as if flying out of the gate in a downhill race. Within seconds she was on him, grabbing with her arms, tackling him as he loomed on the brink of the first big drop.

His body was hard under the ski clothes—all sinew and bone—but she must have hit some tender spot, because he groaned when she made contact and tugged him down to the ground.

For a moment they remained still, a tangle of arms and torsos, cold surrounding them, but a surprising source of heat at the core of the mass.

Well, sure . . . body heat.

And the hot burn of fury for this moron, who was reckless enough to break both their necks.

Jo pushed away from him and sat up. "Are you trying to get us both killed?"

"You were the one who tackled me." He lay back on the snow a minute, his right hand pressed to his left shoulder, as if applying pressure to a wound. He seemed to be in pain, but she was not unscathed either. Her butt hurt, and her hip, where she'd either rammed him or rammed into the ground, felt raw.

"I was trying to save your life," she said, "but you don't make it easy."

"It never is." He curled into a ball, lined up his skis, then rose. "Don't get yourself hurt, Jo. You got a kid to take care of."

She snapped to attention, amazed at the truth of his statement and surprised that he knew her this well. "Who the hell are you?" she asked.

He turned back toward her, pausing. "You wouldn't remember me," he said, then pushed forward.

"No, no! Wait!" One fist pounded the snow beside her, but she couldn't keep him from the black diamond run.

He didn't look back, didn't hesitate at the edge. Dread clutched her as he pushed off into the curtain of snow and dropped out of sight.

Despair.

Panic.

She pulled off one glove. Her hands shook as she took out her cell phone and scrolled to the number of the lodge. With a fake calm in her voice, she asked Carla what they could possibly do to save a royal jackass from the mountain.

Chapter 4

The sound of his skis scraping ice cut through the silent night, the only sound besides the whoosh of adrenaline firing Sam's body. At times he felt as if he rode the wind itself as he flew down, down, into the depths of the night.

The first landing was bone-jarring, but he bent his knees and rode the bumps to the next patch of air. He kept his body tight, his stance low. "It's all in the knees," old Vic, his ski instructor, used to say.

Though the run was closed, the resort had left the lights on; a good thing. Even as he hurtled down the mountain at a high speed, Sam could see that things had changed. Trees had grown taller. New moguls rose from the ground. Ice-covered drifts had formed lofty ledges, like a sloppily frosted cake. The landscape of his youth had changed. Not long ago he could have navigated this run with his eyes closed. He'd never expected it to change so dramatically.

But time had passed, the planet kept spinning.

And I return to the mountain and find Jo Truman working ski patrol at the worst possible time.

That was the damnedest thing, seeing her at the entrance to Heartbreak. He had recognized Jo Truman the minute he saw her, though she couldn't have guessed it was him under the mask. Damned noble of her to try and stop him. She didn't realize that, under the mask, he was already damaged goods.

Jo had been on his mind way too often in the past few years. She'd been there in the desperate moments of close calls, when shots whizzed past so close and exploded nearby patches of dirt to dust. And on quiet nights, when he lay on his bunk trying to tune out the snores of the other guys, Jo was the only good thing he could visualize. Like a star on the darkest night, she lit the darkness, reminding him there was still some good in the world.

"She's one of the good ones," Shane used to say. "Sometimes I think she's way too good for me."

And Sam had always jumped in with a string of objections, that no girl could be too good for his best buddy, because that was what guys did.

But Sam had seen how Jo had suffered when she lost Shane. He had held the sobbing girl in his arms, a girl pregnant with his best friend's child, and felt sick with love and compassion for her. He remembered how her dark hair, soft as corn silk, had slid over the back of his hand as he held her. How she'd stood, tall and responsible, but how the pink around her eyes and the feel of her compact, delicate bones had argued that she wasn't as strong and proud as she seemed.

She had sobbed in his arms, her face against the stiff shirt and borrowed necktie. Jo had cried her eyes out while all he could think of was the sweet smell of her hair and the way her body fit against his. And he'd hated himself for the attraction that had consumed him.

A hankering for his best friend's girl. His dead friend. Sam had his own girl back then, but once he'd held Jo in his arms he knew there would be no playing house with Stacey. That relationship was done once he'd touched Jo Truman. He may have seemed polite as he consoled Jo that day, but inside he knew he was sick and disgusting.

Vile.

That day at the funeral, he had made the decision to leave. He knew he had to get away, and if the army wanted to send him to the other side of the planet, well, that seemed like a safe enough distance.

Unfortunately, the distance had only amplified his thoughts of Joanne Truman. In the back of his mind, he'd known that he'd run into her when he returned to Woodstock. Jo and her family worked in just about every small business in these parts. He'd expected to see her; just not so soon, and certainly not up here.

She'd sworn off skiing after Shane's death. Maybe it was good that she'd bounced back and returned to the mountain. It had been five years since Shane died, and Jo deserved a chance for a do-over.

He whipped past a line of pine trees, veering dangerously close to the edge of the trail.

Pay attention. Stay on course.

Somehow, after seeing Jo, it was suddenly important that he make it through this run in one piece. He didn't want to be another ghost on the mountain for her.

As he *schussed* toward the bottom of the mountain, where the black diamond trail cut back into the intermediate run, exhilaration flared in his chest.

He felt alive again.

It was more than that blazing sense of danger, more

than the adrenaline rush of walking on the edge and cheating death.

As he tucked his arms and hunkered down low, he realized that he never needed to make peace with this mountain. And as for Shane, there's no making amends with a dead man.

This was about making things right with himself.

Time for a good, hard look at his own black soul.

Chapter 5

For as long as Jo could remember, her family had cele-brated Thanksgiving on the Monday after the actual holi-day. Bob and Irene Truman had always been pressed to work in some food service industry or another over the holiday weekend, and as soon as they were old enough to get work permits, each of their children had followed suit.

So Thanksgiving Monday had officially become "Thanks-giving II," or, as Jo's mother, Irene, liked to say, "Thank Goodness Thanksgiving is Ovah!" The five Truman off-spring and their children always assembled at Bob and Irene's home, just a stone's throw from the apartment where Jo lived with Ava and Molly.

With its cherry-paneled walls, bookcases, fireplace, and tall ceilings, the great room of the old house on Bull Moose Road was the perfect spot to assemble the large Truman family. Colored dots of cheery light—the lights outlining the frame of the old house—bobbed in the wind as Jo crossed the driveway with her contribution to din-ner. Pops considered anytime after Thanksgiving fair game to trim the place, and it was already looking good, with twinkling lights and garland made from trimmings brother Dave had left over from his landscaping business. Jo and Molly were not the only Christmas fanatics in the family.

Earlier that day, as soon as school had let out, Pops had taken all the grandchildren out in search of a Christmas tree, and from the tall pine that now graced the large picture window, Jo could see they'd had success.

"The Holly and the Ivy" was playing as Jo carefully juggled a tray of roasted sweet potatoes and a tin of cookies to press open the door. The smell of pine and roasting turkey and the bright faces of children reminded Jo that Christmas really was coming. Teenagers were sprawled on the sofas, and the little ones perched on the oriental rug between the tree and the fireplace, a few of them dipping and tiptoeing in time to the music.

Ava popped up from the cluster of cousins. "Mommy, Mom! Look what we cut down from the woods!"

"I see you found the perfect tree, as usual." Jo peered up at the tall pine that nearly grazed the ceiling. "Though you may need a cherry picker to get the star on."

"We'll figure it out. We always do," Jo's father said, crossing the room with strings of lights coiled on his wrist. At six-two, Bob Truman was a burly man who enjoyed his meals, as evidenced by the paunch that graced his argyle sweater. Jo and her sister, Fran, had gotten Pops's dark hair and big brown eyes. And though the girls had spent some nights in junior high worrying that they might grow to be giants, only Bob's sons had inherited his height.

He bent down to kiss her cheek. "Happy second Thanksgiving, sweetheart. Mmm, sweet potatoes."

"Matthew, Michael, get off your duff and help your Auntie Jo carry that stuff," Fran snapped from behind a big box of ornaments.

Immediately, seventeen-year-old Matthew was at Jo's side. "I'll take that for you, Aunt Jo." His gravelly voice belied his boyish face. He handed the cookie tin to his brother, Michael, and took on the heavier tray.

"Aunt Jo, we're doing white lights on the tree this year," thirteen-year-old Laura announced. "Dad says it looks classy."

"That and Costco was having a sale on white lights," Dave said as he plugged in a set to test them, and a hundred white diamonds sparkled to life.

Tommy and James, Jo's other brothers, entered the room carrying boxes.

"These are the last of the ornaments in the attic," James said.

"And we have extra hooks here." Dave's wife, Chloe, held up the box of hooks, a schoolteacher all the way. "Now as soon as the lights are on, you kids get to take over. It's up to you teenagers to help the little ones."

"We will," James's daughter Katie promised.

"We can get a boost from Matthew to reach the high branches," little Tommy Junior said. He was on all fours on the oriental rug, stretching like a cat.

Ava bunched the hem of her dress in one hand. "I want a boost from Matthew."

Matthew swooped down and lifted Ava as if she were a doll. "You're supposed to wait till we start decorating," he teased, and she giggled as at something hysterically funny.

Jo smiled, her heart warmed at the exchange. Molly could chase her dreams to the big city, but Jo was set and content right here, in the heart of her big, loving family. She shrugged off her down jacket and hung it on a peg in the little nook by the door, where enough boots were lined up to outfit an army.

"Easy on the appetizers there," Irene Truman told her

grandchildren. "Smell that turkey? It's been roasting all day, and it'd be a crime if you lost your appetite."

"But we're really hungry, Nanna," Laura said. "I was supposed to have hot lunch at school, but they ran out of pizza."

"Just stick to the veggies," Irene advised, offering a platter to Jo and Fran. "Cheese puffs?"

Jo grabbed two. "Thanks, Mum. Molly will be here as soon as her friend Meg shows up to take over the store."

"Good. Your Uncle Ted and Aunt Lisa are driving in from Haverhill. They should be here soon." A few years ago, Molly's parents had moved south, to Massachusetts, in pursuit of jobs, but they never missed a holiday or family event.

Jo and Fran went into the kitchen to help James's wife, Brittany, chop vegetables. They were joined by Tommy's wife, who came straight from the clinic in her scrubs.

Within the hour, the men had the lights strung and the ritual of family decorating began. Jo and her sister sank onto the sofa as the teenagers set up the open boxes and bins.

"I can't see! I can't see!" Chrissy, Tommy's youngest, shrieked. "What if I don't get to hang one?"

"You'll get a chance, Chrissy. Look at all these ornaments!" As the oldest grandchild of Irene and Bob, Matthew had become the unofficial facilitator, and over the years he'd begun to grow into the role. "In fact, everyone will get a chance to hang at least one of their favorites. And you can definitely hang any ornament with your name on it."

"I want to hang the blue snowflake!" someone cried.

"I want the Mickey Santa."

"You always get the Mickey Santa."

"Do not . . ."

"Don't you love the sights and sounds of Christmas?" Jo said.

"I love that the kids are old enough to decorate the tree on their own, but then you should *really* love it. You decorate all day long."

"But it doesn't feel like work." Working in the Christmas shop was a labor of love for Jo. "We have fun with it."

"Molly told me you had a weird encounter up on Dare Mountain."

Word traveled fast in the Truman family; Jo had known the story would get around when she told Molly early Saturday morning, but she hadn't been able to keep it to herself. The encounter had haunted her thoughts and disturbed her sleep.

"You know, it was my first time back on skis on Dare Mountain, and here comes an ace skier who reminds me of Shane. What are the chances of that?"

"You thought he was Shane?" Fran's eyes grew round. "Did he look like Shane?"

"I couldn't see his face. He was wearing a mask, but something about his style reminded me of him."

"That's scary."

Jo nodded and told her sister about how the skier had insisted on going down the closed trail, how she'd tried to get him to stop, but failed.

Fran smacked her forehead. "A raving lunatic. Did he break his neck?"

"By some miracle he made it down the mountain safely. Carla and Les checked the recordings from the camera at the base of Heartbreak Ridge, and they saw him skiing like a pro. Somehow my masked man made it down in one piece." It still bothered Jo to think about it, partly because it had to be someone she knew. He'd called her Jo, right?

What she hadn't shared with her sister or with Molly was the emotion that gummed up inside her when she remembered tackling him to the ground. There'd been a jolt of connection, like a flash of electricity, and, though it didn't make sense, she'd liked being tangled up with him in the snow. Probably just her own depraved desires. Things tended to get all bottled up when you kept them tamped down for a few years.

"Well, sounds like it was a harrowing experience for you," Fran said. "But I gotta say, he's lucky to be alive." She lowered her voice, adding, "Guys can be such assholes."

"I heard that," her husband, Keith, called from behind the tree, where he was checking a string of lights.

"But I love *you,* honey," Fran said.

"Ma, you owe a dollar to the swear jar." Fran's son Alex grinned from behind a box.

Fran waved him off. "I'll pay you later, and mind your business. You've still got a couple of bare spots on that tree."

Jo and her sister joined their mother in the kitchen, where meal preparations were in full swing and savory smells of roasted turkey, sage, and rosemary filled the warm air.

"Is that a wicked gorgeous turkey, or what?" Irene lifted the turkey from the oven, with a satisfied grunt.

"That's a big one, Mum. You sure you want to parade it around?" Jo asked.

"Of course. It's tradition." Armed in oven mitts, Irene hoisted the pan and walked carefully, passing through the dining room to the activity of the great room. "Hey! Look at this magnificent turkey!"

Peeking out of the kitchen, Jo smiled at the chorus of oohs and aahs, even from the little ones.

"If this family gets much bigger, we're going to need a

shopping cart to tote that thing around," Fran said from the fridge.

"But it's a great tradition." When Jo was a child, she'd taken all these rituals for granted. Now, with a child of her own, she embraced them, longing to pass down the full joy of family holidays to Ava.

Their mother returned and gratefully eased the pan back onto the counter. "Your father will start carving in a few minutes. I'll put you on the gravy, Jo. Fran, let's get this stuffing out of the bird."

Jo popped her sweet potatoes into the oven for one last warming, then set to work making gravy from the drippings while Fran spooned stuffing into a casserole dish.

Molly and her parents arrived just as the green beans were coming out of the steamer. Aunt Lisa took over mashing the potatoes, and soon Irene was calling everyone to dinner.

The family assembled around two tables, with some negotiation and shuffling of teenagers who'd been deemed ready to move from the "kids' table" to the main table.

Irene clanged a spoon against a glass to get everyone's attention, and her husband rose at the head of the big table, a glass of sparkling cider raised. Jo's brother Dave had joined Alcoholics Anonymous two years ago when he finally realized his drinking was out of control, and the entire family had joined him in refraining from drinking alcohol, in a move of solidarity.

"Let's raise our glasses in thanks," Pops said. "A wonderful family, a fine meal. We have so much to be thankful for. I'm grateful to be employed during these times. And I'm very happy to live in this beautiful neck of the woods. A nook of heaven." He turned to his wife. "Irene?"

"I'm thankful to have my health and all of you. Very

thankful that the teenagers will be helping me with the cleanup in the kitchen."

There was laughter at the adults' table and then the gauntlet was passed to Jo. She let her eyes sweep the room, landing on Ava, whose blue eyes sparkled in the candlelight of the kids' table. "I'm thankful to be here with my family. I'm so glad to live in this beautiful town that gives us all jobs. Sometimes I think they should call it Truman instead of Woodstock."

There were a few chuckles, and then Molly talked about how she was grateful that Cousins' Christmas Shop was doing stellar business. "And, by the way, how's the sign coming, Tommy?" she asked.

"I got it out in the garage," he said. "And let me say, I'm grateful that the auto repair business is going well. And happy for family and good food and all that."

Jo's stomach growled at the sumptuous food aromas, but no one ate until everyone spoke a word or two about what they were grateful for. Most of the kids said they were grateful that Santa was coming. Ava said she was grateful for Mommy and Santa.

After everyone added their two cents, Pops said a short prayer of thanks. "Lord, the kids are all excited about Santa coming, but we know the true celebration of Christmas is about you sending your son to save the world. As the scripture says, 'Today in the town of David, a Savior has been born to you. He is Christ the Lord.' Help us remember that that's what Christmas is about. And thank you, God, for the start of this joyous season. Amen."

Jo held back a grin. Leave it to Pops to tuck in a lesson when he had a captive audience.

"Amen!" came the chorus from hungry diners around the two tables, and Jo's sentiments gave way to the clatter of dishes and the buzz of conversation.

Chapter 6

Later, when the dishes were under control in the kitchen and Ava was sprawled on the floor by the Christmas tree dictating a Christmas list to her older cousin Laura, Jo headed out to the garage. Although Tommy had moved out years ago, he still kept his classic Mustang there, and Mum and Pops didn't seem to mind at all. "A restoration in progress," Tommy liked to say.

"Hey." She stepped into the cooler garage and noticed the string of colored lights over the workbench. The front of the car was up on blocks, and a light beamed out from under it. A radio played James Taylor's version of "Winter Wonderland."

"Okay if I enter the Man Cave?" she asked.

"You're safe to enter," Tommy said with a wry grin. "I keep the naked hula dancers down at the shop."

"Now you tell me," came another male voice from under the car. "I'm in the wrong garage."

Jo squinted at the car. Was that one of her brothers?

"Just find where the oil leak is coming from, okay?" Tommy answered.

"Really, Tommy." Jo folded her arms across her chest. "It's a wonder you have any employees left down at the shop when you talk to them that way."

"Yeah, Tommy." This time the voice under the car was clearly not one of her brothers'. "Show some respect."

"You got your turkey dinner, buddy. Time to sing for your supper."

Jo laughed. "Harsh, Tommy. But I came to check on my sign. Did you fix it yet?"

"Well, I did and I didn't." He picked up the sign leaning against the wall. It glistened with a new coat of polyurethane, though the letters underneath were blurred at the edges. "Some of the paint bled when I tried to waterproof it."

Jo frowned. "Ooh, that's not going to work. We're going to need a new sign."

"Yeah." Tommy hitched back his Red Sox cap and sighed. "I can cut the wood for you, but I'm no good with the painting."

"I can make you a sign," said the man under the car.

"Who's down there?" Jo asked.

Tommy's brows rose. "Sam Norwood from high school. Do you remember him?"

Hands on her hips, Jo stared down at the car. "Are you kidding me?" Sam Norwood had been Shane's best friend, the two of them inseparable.

"He's back from Afghanistan," Tommy added.

"Can't be the Sam Norwood I know," she said, digging her hands into the pockets of her jeans. "The guy I used to hang out with would never come back to town without calling me."

Tommy winced, scratching his chin.

"Someone has a pretty high opinion of herself." Sam's voice rose from under the car. "It's not like we were best friends."

"Nah, not best friends, but good friends," Jo said. "So I'm thinking this isn't the same Sam."

"It is indeed," Tommy said. "We were in the same grade in school."

"I'll believe it when I see his face," Jo said. She was going to order the soldier out from under the car, but her brother's frantic arm motions gave her pause. "What?"

Tommy shook his head and mouthed something. When he mimed his face being cut, she realized he was saying, *he was hurt.*

Oh. So was she supposed to be nicer to him? Of course she'd be nice to him . . . after the kidding.

"So what's the deal, Sam? You come back to town and don't pick up a phone?"

"I figured you'd be busy, and apparently you are with the shop and all. You always did have your hands full. Prom queen, snow bunny on the alpine team, and class president rolled into one."

"Yeah, all those school activities taught me about the real world. They prepared me to be a single parent and a working girl. How about you?"

"Eh. There isn't a lot of skiing in Afghanistan," he said.

Sam had been an excellent skier, training for the Olympics alongside Shane, though he'd withdrawn after Shane got killed. A great skier; but she remembered Sam as so much more. Agile and athletic, he was one of the few guys able to keep up with Shane.

But while Shane was flash and smiles, Sam was like one of those faceted stones that you could stare into for hours. He was artistic back in the days when it wasn't cool to illustrate or sculpt. His sculpture of a bobcat still stood in front of the high school, never defaced because it was so darned good.

And his illustrations could mirror life in a beautiful way. He could sketch a face, then make it whimsical or sad. And when he put color on a canvas, Sam could open up the world as quick as you'd crack a walnut. Yeah, Sam had the ability to make a wonderful sign for the shop.

But having grown up with three brothers, she knew that a guy like Sam didn't want to hear about his great qualities. So, instead, she said, "There's one of your achievements I'll never forget, Sam. Weren't you the guy who had twenty pizzas delivered the day of graduation practice?"

"That was you?" Tommy spun around. "Nobody told me that."

"You know, that may have been my ten minutes of fame." Sam snorted. "My ma was pissed when the principal sent her the bill. Two hundred bucks, but it could've been two million back then."

Just then the garage went dark and the radio died.

"Lights out," Sam said.

"Must be the wind," Tommy said as he scuffled in the pitch black.

From inside the house came the dramatic screams of children, followed by the laughter of adults.

"You'd think we never had a power outage before," Jo said.

As her eyes adjusted to the darkness, she sensed her brother moving at the workbench. A moment later, the beam of a flashlight shot to the far wall of the garage. "We got two flashlights here. You guys take one and I'll go inside and help them get the lanterns lit."

Jo took the flashlight from him and turned to the Mustang as her brother ducked through the door to the house.

"You okay down there? You should probably take this light."

"Nah. I'm just going to stay put right here where it's safe and quiet," he said. "If you want to go back inside, I understand."

"Did you hear the screams in there? I'm with you, sticking in here where it's safe and quiet." She moved to the side of the workbench, closer to the jacked-up front of the car. The floor gleamed under the beam of the flashlight, so clean you could eat off it. But then, Tommy had a reputation for being finicky clean about his stuff. "So . . . how long you been back?" she asked.

"Not too long. Just a few days."

"Shame on you for not calling."

"I didn't think I'd be sticking around, but now it looks like I am. When I ran into Tommy at the grocery store, he told me to head down to help him with the 'stang after dinner. Didn't know he'd smuggle a turkey dinner into the garage for me."

"Tommy's good that way." She felt like a teenager playing a stupid game, blindfolded and trying to come up with lame questions. She wished he would come out from under there.

"So . . . when did you get back on the ski patrol at Dare?" he asked.

"I'm not." What would make him think that?

She flashed to the other night on the mountain . . . the ski patrol jacket . . . the closed trail . . . the masked skier.

"Oh, come on! You were the guy with the mask?"

"What? I didn't say that . . ."

She turned to the front of the car and grabbed the fender. "Sam Norwood, I ought to knock this car right off its blocks . . . and right now I'm so freakin' mad at you, believe me, I've got the supercharged adrenaline strength to do it!"

"Calm down. Let's not get crazy there." Wheels whirred

as the dolly slid out from under the car, but he had moved to the driver's side, away from her.

"Do you have any idea how unnerving that was? I thought you were a dead man, going down that ridge . . ."

"I know. I'm sorry. It was a jackass move."

"Grrr!" She slammed a palm on the hood of the car and turned away. "You totally spooked me! It was my first time back on skis, and I looked up and I thought you were Shane!"

"Aw, Jo, I'm sorry. I didn't expect to see you there."

"Well, I sure as hell wasn't expecting Shane—or you!"

The door squeaked open and Tommy appeared, lantern in hand. "What drama queens!"

Jo felt caught in her flare of anger until she realized her brother was talking about the family inside.

"The power might be out awhile, and the house doesn't have a backup 'genny,' so Mum and Pop figured it's a good time to go caroling down the street. The Barrettos are here for the week, and Karen always has homemade cookies for the kids. I told Pops I'd come along."

"Okay, then." Jo could hear the telltale emotion in her voice, but hoped Tommy wouldn't notice.

He held the lantern up for a second. "You guys'll be okay in here, then?"

"Ay-yeah." She held up a hand, as if to ward off the light, though truth be told, she didn't want him to see the fury on her face. "We're good."

"Okay. We'll be back shortly." And Tommy was gone again.

Jo drew in a long, calming breath. "If I promise not to kill you, will you come out from under there and talk to me?"

"I'd rather not."

"Tommy said you got hurt. I'm sorry about that, but

the truth is, I can't see much of anything in here. I promise to keep the flashlight low if you'll just come out and sit. I don't like talking to a car. It's just too weird."

Silence. Then he groaned. "Yeah, okay. But you stay put and turn the flashlight off."

"Let me get situated." She turned an empty crate on its side by the workbench and sat down. "Aren't you afraid of walking into something? Falling over an engine block?"

"I know the dark."

She killed the light and sat, hugging her arms across her chest as he moved closer. For the first time, she wondered what terrible thing had happened to him in Afghanistan that made him so ashamed to be seen, and a pang of sorrow pinched her heart. Sam used to be a hottie; she couldn't imagine him without those proud, high cheekbones and that sexy square chin. Yeah, back in high school, she'd noticed. Even crazy in love with Shane, she'd still had eyes and a brain.

Concern for Sam mixed with anger as she felt the air stir beside her. She pulled her knees in, not wanting him to trip over them.

"You're okay," he said, and now the soft moonlight from the garage windows cast enough light to see raw forms in the darkness.

He stood over her, turned away from her, then slumped down beside her, his back against the workbench. "So what happened in Afghanistan?" she asked.

"There was an IED. My buddy got killed, and I got all messed up."

"I'm sorry about your friend. Are you in pain?"

"Not anymore."

"And you still ski like a champion."

"Yeah, but I look like a monster."

"I'm not going to argue with you, because that just doesn't seem right. What do I know? I can't see you." Jo wasn't one to offer false cheer or cling to denial. "But I do know that beauty is in the eyes of the beholder. So maybe you don't look so bad to other people."

"Mmm."

"What does your mum think?"

"She's just glad I survived, but you can't count on a mother for objectivity."

"True." Jo took a deep breath and let the cool air and familiar smell of engine oil calm her. "I gotta tell you, Sam, I was ready to strangle you a few minutes ago. I can't believe it was you impersonating Shane that night on the mountain."

"I wasn't trying to be him. Just trying to make some kind of peace with him."

"Really? Why would you need to do that? You guys were tight. Shane loved you. He didn't have a bad word to say about you."

"Ay yeah. He had my back. The problem was, I didn't have his that night, and I've always known it was my fault. I'm responsible for Shane's death."

"Cut it out." She tapped his arm with the back of her hand. "Everyone knows what drove him up to the top of Dare Mountain. He didn't want to be a father. He was freaking out over the responsibility, sure his future was going down the tubes. He didn't want to end up without two nickels to rub together, and he saw fatherhood as his ticket to poverty."

"You're way too philosophical. It wasn't his problems that drove him up the mountain that night. It was me. I knew where Les kept the keys to the cable car. I knew how to run it, from working the damned thing through high school."

"Sam, everyone knows that part. You helped Shane on his mission, but you didn't kill him."

"Taking a totally wrecked man to the top of a mountain on an icy night?"

"You didn't pour the whiskey down his throat, either."

Sam bowed his head and raked his hair back in frustration. When he lifted his head, she could make out the angles of his face: the high cheekbones, the strong jaw, the plane of his forehead. In this light, from this angle, he looked perfect. Handsome. Noble.

He certainly had the potential to break some more hearts.

"Say what you want about blame and guilt," Sam said, "but I can't shed the feeling that it was my fault. I've been carrying Shane's ghost on my back like a backpack of bricks. It's a heavy load, but the body adapts."

"I know what you mean." Jo leaned her chin on her hands. "I've always felt that the guilt was all mine. Getting pregnant was an accident, but once it happened, I couldn't undo it. Shane wanted me to end it, but I couldn't. I'm so glad I didn't. I made the right choice, but it may have killed Shane."

"You can't think that way. It's not your fault that he didn't man up and deal with it."

She pressed a hand to her heart. "Still, the guilt is there."

"I'd wrestle you for it, but after the way you tackled me the other night, you might win."

"Don't remind me. I'm still simmering inside about that. What the hell were you doing up there?"

"Trying to deal with shit."

"Yeah, yeah, the ghost on your back and all that. Did you really think you'd accomplish anything up on Dare Mountain on a night like that? Besides getting yourself killed?" She rubbed the softly worn knees of her jeans. "Thank God you didn't get hurt. I don't think I can bear another strike on my conscience."

"But that's the thing. Shane wasn't your fault. Shane was all about Shane, if you didn't realize that."

She turned to stare at him. In the pale shadows, she could barely make out his features, but she felt his sincerity, strong and true, like a weather front that stirs everything up. "He cared about the baby," she said levelly. "That's why he felt so bad about it."

"He cared about what people thought about him. That was the real issue." Sam rubbed his jaw, hesitating.

"What are you trying to say?"

"Shane took up with some chick on the Olympic alpine team. Lacey or Lucy, something like that."

A few years ago, those words would have injured Jo, but now it was as if she were listening to a story about strangers—some celebrity couple who didn't have a chance of making it together.

"Shane was planning to break up with you as soon as Olympic training was over, but once he heard about the baby, he freaked out about how it would make him look bad. He wanted to be a hero, like some White Mountain Superman, and he was afraid that dumping you with a baby would tarnish his image."

Jo shook her head, wishing she could shake off Sam's recollection as a pack of lies, though in her heart she knew it was true.

She remembered the night their relationship had turned. They'd spent the day hiking at Franconia Notch, near the spot where the Old Man of the Mountain used to be. She had planned to tell him she was pregnant with their baby, but every time she got into the conversation he managed to shift the focus back to his training, the Olympic games, or practicing Italian. At the end of the day, they'd been back at his house, getting ready to go out for pizza, except that Shane couldn't pull himself away from the mirror in the front vestibule.

"Do you think I should get a haircut before the Olympics or leave my hair longer?" he asked.

"I don't know," she said.

"I could try some thickening gel. And some of those colored contacts. Have you seen those? They would make my eyes a really intense blue. Unforgettable."

She was worried about their child, their future, their finances—and his greatest worry was his reflection in the mirror. When she finally got to tell him about the baby— good news, she thought—he fell into a funk.

"I'll help you pay the doctor's bill to, you know, take care of things," he'd said gently.

His calm demeanor had changed when Jo had told him she wasn't having an abortion. And after that, everything had fallen apart around her.

"Jo . . . I'm sorry." Sam's voice brought her back to the chill air and the oil smell of the garage. "I never wanted to tarnish Shane's memory, but I can't let you go on thinking you drove him to the edge. Shane contributed plenty to his own downfall."

"I should have known." She shook her head. "But I never suspected . . . I didn't know . . ."

"I'm sorry," he said again, and this time his right hand tapped her knee, a brotherly gesture.

Jo felt sick with anger, relief, and sadness. She had always thought that Shane's death was her fault, but, now, learning these circumstances, she wasn't sure at all.

"Wow." She took a deep breath. "I'm not sure if I should be relieved or pissed off at him all over again."

"Relief is probably good for now," he said.

"Thanks for telling me the truth." She squeezed Sam's fingers. "It's a huge relief to know the truth after all these years. I feel so wicked calm."

He nodded. "Good."

"I still don't get it, though. I would have let him off the

hook if he'd asked. I would have raised Ava alone, which is what I've ended up doing, with help from the family. But why'd Shane have to go and kill himself? For what? To save face? To be a hero? Yeah. Big hero. People in these parts know his name because he was notoriously reckless. Sad, isn't it?"

Sam didn't answer, but he squeezed back. Jo smiled, grateful for the human touch, grateful for the power outage that had given Sam the courage to get close to her.

"It's ironic," Jo said. "Both of us blaming ourselves for Shane's death. Both of us carrying around a burden that really doesn't belong to us."

"Thick with irony," he said.

"Maybe there really is magic in Christmas; we both get a chance to forgive ourselves."

"Let's not get too crazy." Sam removed his hand and stood up. "Maybe I'll try that flashlight. See if I can figure out this problem for your brother."

"When do you have to report back?" she asked, hoping she could see him again.

"I'm supposed to drive down to Concord for physical therapy, but other than that, the army is done with me. Too much damage for them to sew me back together and stick me out in the field again."

She rose, hope beating in her chest like a startled dove. "So you'll be around?"

"I'll be around."

She turned to him, her arms spread wide. "Thanks."

The hug was friendly, the sort of gesture she would share with one of her brothers. But as she pressed against his chest, the thrall of emotion between them was irresistible. Like a river flowing through a ravaged desert . . . a stream of sunlight breaking through pewter clouds after a turbulent storm.

When he pulled away, she wondered how he could bear to break the connection.

"I'd better get back to work," he said.

"Ay-yeah. Tommy is a taskmaster." She handed Sam the flashlight, then leaned back against the workbench as he turned away and went around the car, moving smoothly in the darkness.

The swelling song of the carolers outside told her that the family was back. "I should go. Ava turns into a screaming pumpkin when she stays up too late."

"See ya 'round," he called from under the car.

"Stop by the shop sometime," she said. She figured they'd talk again after the dust, nerves, and feelings settled.

It was something to look forward to.

Chapter 7

One week and no Sam.

Jo frowned at the page-a-day calendar on top of the desk and then let her eyes drop to the angel ornament she had been stringing together with fishing line. Three clear beads, one gold, and now she was ready to tie off the angel's skirt. These angel ornaments required some concentration, but people seemed to love them. She strung a few more beads, thinking that it would be easier to focus if she had a clear head about Sam.

Was it stupid to wait for him to call?

"Maybe I'm being silly," she said aloud.

Ava looked up from the book she was coloring on the floor. "Mommy's silly?" She giggled.

"Oh, I can be very silly." And insecure. Maybe she should call him . . .

"Mommy, did Daddy ever meet Santa?" Ava asked, frowning over the reindeer she was coloring.

"He did. More than once."

"Do you believe in Santa?"

"I am one of Santa's biggest fans." Jo looked down at

her daughter, adorable in her footy pajamas beside the small tree strung with lights. "You gotta believe."

The period of Santa's magic was so short for kids: At two, they just started to understand it, and, by seven, they were discovering the ruse. For Ava it would be over in a year or two, which was one of the reasons Jo encouraged lots of Christmas traditions like caroling with family, making cookies, taking canned goods to the church, and decorating their own little live tree each year.

"Sometimes I just wonder," Ava said sadly.

Jo tied off the ornament, climbed down to the carpet, and sprawled beside her daughter. "What's this about?"

"Why are there so many Santas everywhere? Aunt Molly said there's one coming to the shop, only he's not the real Santa."

"Hmm. Good point. I guess you could say all the Santas you see around town are helpers."

Ava wrote her name at the top of the page, then began to tear it out of the coloring book.

"What are you doing?" Jo asked.

"Can we send this to my other nanna?"

"Nanna Carol?" Shane's mother had moved to Maine to be closer to her sister last year, and though Ava only got to see her every few months, Jo tried to keep the relationship alive.

Ava nodded. "Nanna Carol doesn't have any kids at Christmas. Santa probably doesn't leave any toys under her tree." She frowned. "That makes me sad."

"I think Nanna Carol would love this picture. It's late now, but we can call her tomorrow and see how she's doing. And you know what? We can send her a little gift, too. Something she can put under her Christmas tree. And she can shake it and look at it every day, wondering what it is, until she opens it on Christmas morning."

Ava's eyes shone with her smile. "She would like that. Why don't we see her on Christmas?"

"Because she lives far away now." Of the many possible explanations, that was the easiest for Ava to understand. Jo wasn't sure she'd ever be able to tell Ava that her grandmother found it difficult to look at her because she saw her dead son in those cornflower blue eyes.

"But she loves you," Jo said with conviction, knowing that, despite Carol's cold demeanor, she cared deeply about her granddaughter.

Jo would never forget the day she received the letter in the mail with a whopping check for nearly half a million dollars. "This is from Shane's life insurance policy, through the Olympics," Carol had written. "You're a single mom now. I know how hard that is. And you're going to need money to take care of Ava."

"Nanna Carol is going to love this." Jo smoothed the colored page and removed a manila envelope from the desk drawer. "And we'll pick out a little gift for her tomorrow. But now, you need to brush your teeth and get to bed."

Shortly after Ava was safely tucked in, there was a knock on the door. Jo pushed the curtain aside to see her brother Tommy standing there, a wooden sign in his arms.

"Ho, ho! I've got an early Christmas gift for you," he said, his words forming white puffs in the cold, damp air.

"Come on in. Let's see what you did this time."

He stepped in and held the wooden placard up. "Nice, huh?"

It was a work of art.

COUSINS' CHRISTMAS SHOP was scrolled in thick black letters outlined in shiny gold to make them pop. The first "C" leaned into a ridge of puffy snow, balanced by a fat snowman at the far right. The bottom of the sign was lined with dancing Christmas trees, while snowflakes scattered through the purple sky at the top. It was warm yet wintry, cute but tasteful.

"Tommy! How the hell did you pull this one off?"

"I didn't. Sam made it."

"Of course he did." Jo should have recognized the animated trees from Sam's doodles in high school, when he could make anything from a school bus to a possum dance at the end of his pencil.

"I was tinkering with the old sign in the garage, and Sam said he thought he could come up with something better. You like?"

"I love it!" She took the sign from him and danced it around. "Can you hang it for me tomorrow?"

"What a taskmaster," he said. "I might be able to get over in the morning."

"I was wondering what Sam was up to." She leaned the sign against the wall. "You know, I haven't heard from him since our Thanksgiving is Ovah celebration."

"He's keeping a low profile."

"No profile is more like it."

"Sam doesn't like coming out. You know he got injured in Afghanistan."

"He mentioned that. How bad is it?"

"Some burns and whatnot from a roadside bomb. Side of his head and neck are bad. Shoulder, too. He's lost the hearing in his left ear, and it's pretty mangled."

She nodded. "I didn't notice anything the other night, but then, it was dark in the garage."

"I told him he's lucky to be alive, but he says that's debatable. Long story short, he thinks he looks like Frankenstein's monster."

"And because of that he doesn't leave the house?"

"He avoids being seen. When he does go out, he wears one of those caps with the earflaps."

"And where does he go? It's not like anyone has seen him hanging at the bar in Woodstock Station or Dunkin' Donuts."

Tommy put his hands on his hips. "So you've got the spy network looking."

"Maybe."

"He comes down to the shop a lot. And most nights he's right over in Ma and Pops's garage." He nodded toward the big house across the lane. "Been working on the 'stang. I think he found my oil leak."

"Sam was always good with mechanical stuff like that," Jo said, though she was thinking that those nights she'd been stuck wondering about him, he was probably just a few yards away in her parents' garage.

"He's real smart. Do you know he was in the bomb squad for the army? Trained to find and dismantle explosives."

"He's smart, all right," she said. Though the man didn't have the common sense to pick up a phone and call, or to stay off a closed trail at Dare Mountain.

And yet, he'd made her a sign—a magnificent sign.

Jo wasn't sure what to think . . . though she sensed that her feelings had already run ahead without looking back.

The next morning, as soon as she dropped Ava at school, Jo steered toward Tommy's shop, banking on Tommy's word that Sam had been hanging there.

She wasn't disappointed.

When she drove up, one garage bay door was open and Sam was one of three men who stood looking up at a car on the lift.

She parked her Jeep, suddenly self-conscious as the three men turned to her.

"'Morning, Jo." Chuck Arlan, the mechanic, nodded.

"Good morning," she said.

"Tell me you brought donuts," Tommy said.

"I brought my Jeep for an oil change," she said, hoping Tommy wouldn't point out that it wasn't due for one for another month yet. "Think you can handle it today?"

Although the question was meant for Tommy, her eyes went to Sam, who was watching her, his gray eyes intent beneath the brim of his cap.

Their eyes connected, and Jo went weak in the knees.

Oh, wow. Something wicked strong coursed between Sam and her. Although she wasn't sure she liked being caught in a feeling so intense, there was no denying it existed. She swallowed hard, trying to track the conversation.

"Guess we can squeeze you in," Tommy was saying. "Maybe if you promise to bring cookies when you pick it up this afternoon."

"I think I could handle that." Jo drew her eyes away from Sam, then lavished a second look at him. "Oh, and I wanted to thank you for the sign. It's perfect for the shop."

"No problem." Sam nodded, his dark eyes tugging on her resolve to act normal in front of her brother and his mechanic. His eyes made her think of their embrace, the way she'd nestled against his chest, the way her body fit against his.

She could imagine them doing that again . . . only the air around them would be warmer and they wouldn't be bothered by wearing so many outdoor clothes and . . .

"What time, Jo?" Tommy asked, knocking her out of her fantasy.

"Huh?"

"What time will you be back to pick up the car?"

"Oh. Four? No . . . make that two, so I can pick up Ava from school."

"You got it." Tommy held out his hand, and she dropped the spare key in his palm.

"I'll see you guys later," she said, backing away. When she nearly bumped into her Jeep, she realized she'd better take the sign. Grabbing it from the backseat, she called another good-bye and was on her way, walking the four blocks to the store with the new sign tucked under one arm.

As she approached the charming two-story Tudor that housed the bank, she remembered that they needed change for the shop. She stopped in and joined the line for the tellers, being careful not to whack Mr. Giordano, owner of GiGi's Pizza, with the plywood placard.

"That's a very beautiful sign. A new one for your shop?" he asked.

"It is. Hand-painted by a friend of mine."

"Hmm." He scratched the white whiskers on his chin. "He should make a business of it. I could use a new sign myself. What with the rain and snow and sun, the old one is so faded."

"I'll have Sam call you if you're interested."

"You do that."

Jo changed a hundred dollars into small bills and was on her way out when Emma Mueller, the bank manager, emerged from one of the private cubicles.

"How are you, Emma?"

"I'm fine." In boots, a tight wool skirt, and a fine knit sweater, Emma looked like she could have stepped out of the pages of a New England magazine. A few years older than Jo, Emma was never seen in public without a matching wardrobe and perfect makeup. "Just wondering if you're ready to invest some of that money you've got sitting in your savings account. We can get you a much higher yield on it."

"I'm not ready for anything risky yet," Jo said. "That's money for Ava when she gets older, so I don't want to take a chance investing it."

"I understand. If anything changes, you know where to find me."

Jo smiled. "I do."

"And what's the painting you have there?" Emma asked.

Jo showed her the sign and explained how Sam Norwood had made it for the Christmas shop.

"It's really charming. Makes me think that this building should have something like that. Wouldn't it be wonderful if every merchant in this complex had a placard like that? A uniform look, though every sign would be unique and individual. And that artist is so creative . . ."

"You know, Emma, that's a good idea."

A wicked good idea.

Chapter 8

He had it bad.

One visit from Jo, and the garage was no longer dark and gloomy. He didn't want to bite Chuck's head off every time the young mechanic dropped a wrench on the concrete floor. Tommy's jokes actually seemed funny again, and the snowflakes twirling through the air made him smile.

Yeah, he had it bad.

Two o'clock couldn't come soon enough.

"Hey, Sam!" When Tommy called, Sam closed the hood on the Jeep and ducked into the office, grateful for the distraction.

"Meet Nelson Dubinsky. He's looking for someone who knows explosives. Could be right up your alley."

"Sam Norwood." Sam shook hands with Dubinsky, a lean man with creases at the edges of his serious gray eyes. From his buzzed hair and squared-away clothes, Sam suspected he was former military.

Dubinsky's stern eyes swept over Sam quickly; he seemed satisfied with what he saw. "I'm looking for a munitions expert to supervise a local job. I hear you've got experience."

"Twenty-first Infantry in Afghanistan. Mine fields were my specialty. I worked at identifying and defusing IEDs, too, but I'm thinking that I'm done with that business."

The man nodded. "You from these parts, Sam?"

"I am. Grew up right here in Woodstock."

"Do you remember where you were the night the Old Man of the Mountain fell?"

"Of course." Sam thought of the rock face over at Franconia Notch, a fixture of his childhood. No one thought the huge face of the Old Man would ever come tumbling down. "That was a big deal around here. People were devastated. I think my mother cried."

"I cried," Tommy said from behind the counter. "Losing that old face was like losing family."

"A lot of people in this state would agree with you," Dubinsky said. "When you have an image on your state license plates and road signs, people get attached. It's a point of pride. That's why I'm here. I represent the foundation that wants to fund the re-creation of the Old Man."

"Really." Sam leaned against the counter.

"People are going to pay to rebuild it?" Tommy sounded dubious.

Dubinsky held his hands up. "It would be a monument. There's no way we could rebuild it exactly."

The Old Man of the Mountain . . .

Sam stared off past the dingy window of Tommy's office, and wondered what it would be like to be part of a project like that. Building something up, instead of blowing holes in the ground.

"I'd like to talk some more about your background." Dubinsky held out a business card. "It sounds like you could be an effective part of our team."

Sam looked at the card, shook his head. "You can save your card, sir. Not interested."

"Is that so?" The older man rose from the chair. "That's too bad." He made a point of placing his card on the counter. "I'll leave this here, just in case you change your mind."

"I won't."

"I'll be going, then. Gentlemen."

Tommy lifted a hand. "Take it easy." He watched as the man went out to his car. Once the car door slammed, he wheeled on Sam. "What the hell's wrong with you? That's not just a job, but the job of the century around here. Are you freakin' crazy, Sam?"

"Probably."

"Why would you not want to work for that man?"

Sam folded his arms across his chest. "I got no problem with Mr. Dubinsky."

"Is it about the explosives? Because I get that."

Sam shook his head. "That's just science and safety precautions. I can handle that."

"Then come on, man!" Tommy spread his long arms wide. "What's your problem?"

Sam shifted the ridiculous cap on his head, scratched under the earflap. Strange, but his hand still expected to find the lobe of his ear there. Instead, there was only a shiny knot of scar tissue.

"I got no answer," Sam said quietly.

"What?" Tommy wasn't backing down.

Sam shook his head. "Calm down, okay? As soon as I figure it all out, you'll be the first to know."

Tommy snorted. "Well, I'm keeping that guy's card for you." He shoved the card into the pocket of his coveralls and shuffled toward the door. "Excuse me, but I got an engine to flush."

* * *

For the rest of the day, work was work. Sam helped Tommy figure out why an old Volvo kept stalling, and did a brake job. When they took a break for lunch and watched a basketball game on ESPN, Tommy fell to his knees over a tiebreaker and they high-fived and laughed. That was the thing about guys. No one expected you to put it all out there.

After lunch Tommy went to hang the new sign at Jo and Molly's shop. When he returned, he had Jo with him, her cheeks pink and pretty and her hair smooth and shiny, like the girl in the shampoo commercial. Sam remembered how it felt, silky soft as it slid over the backs of his hands that night.

His left hand rose, his fingers tapping the flap of the cap. Everything was covered, at least for now.

"Have I got news for you!" Jo marched up to Sam and handed him a piece of white paper. "People love your sign. I told them it was handmade and now everyone wants one. The whole row of stores by the Christmas shop and all the businesses in the Tudor building around the corner. Isn't it amazing?"

"What's this?" he asked, scanning the list that included the pizza parlor, the Woodstock Inn, and the bank.

"It's a list of signs to be made. Molly and I double-checked the spellings. We didn't talk about money, but I floated the price of three hundred apiece, and no one even batted an eye!"

"That's a lot of oil changes," he said. And enough work to keep him in town for a few weeks. He didn't mind the work, but he wasn't so sure about the commitment. How long could he really stick around here, pining for Jo and knowing it was never going to happen?

"Ay-yeah. Pretty cool, huh?"

He nodded. "Pretty cool." He wished he could smile to

reassure her, but the stoicism that had fallen over him left steel in his blood.

"And this is just the beginning. Once people see these, I bet all the shops on Main Street will be ordering new signs. It'll add another level of quaintness to Woodstock, Sam. Thanks to you."

He shook his head. "You're the one, Jo. You work your magic on these people and they'll sign up to watch submarine races."

She laughed. "I don't think so, but I'm psyched about this, Sam. This could be big for you. Huge."

He scratched his jaw, not wanting to burst her bubble. "Could be."

"Is the price okay? If you think it's not enough, I'll throw another number out there."

"It's fine. It's generous."

She squinted at him. "You sure?"

"Absolutely. I just wasn't expecting anything like this."

She smiled. "I know. I love it when things fall together like this." She stepped closer, demanding that he face her.

When their eyes met, the light of joy in her face just about killed him.

"Thanks, Jo," he said quietly.

"You're welcome." She looked over her shoulder at the office. "I gotta run and pick up Ava. Tell Tommy I'll settle with him later, okay?"

"Will do." Sam watched as she drove off, even returned her wave. As the Jeep's taillights disappeared down the street, he wondered what bad luck Jo Truman had fallen into that made her keep entangling herself with the wrong guy.

Chapter 9

"I love Christmas parties, Mommy," Ava said as Jo led her by the hand toward the Woodstock Inn, where the white lights of the giant wreath gleamed beneath a dusting of snow.

Jo held back a grin. "I do, too, honey. But remember, this is a party for other people. Mommy is going to help serve the food, and you can help Nanna work the desk."

Tonight the inn would be rocking with three Christmas parties and a wedding, on top of the regular dinner traffic in the dining room. Pops had called in reinforcements, as he put it, asking for family members to help out, even if just for a few hours. Molly had volunteered to handle the shop so that Jo could work as a server for a few hours.

"Maybe I can fold napkins. I'm good at that."

"Maybe." The heavy door closed behind them as they stamped their feet on the entry rug to wipe off any snow.

Ava jumped up to peer through the beveled glass of the inner door. "Pops! I see Pops!" She flung the door open and raced inside.

By the time Jo pressed through the door, Ava was in

Pops's arms, chatting with the brawny man beside him, Earl Camden.

"Who's this little one?" Earl asked, winking at Ava. "Are you a Christmas angel?"

She giggled. "No. I'm just a girl."

"This is Ava, Jo's daughter." Pops nodded at Jo.

"I don't believe it!" Earl gasped. "You're a real girl!" He turned to Jo. "The last time I saw her, she was a wee little thing."

"They grow up so fast," Jo said. "It's good to see you in town, Earl. The inn misses you."

He waved dismissively. "Aw, your pops keeps it all under control. I'd like to get here more often, but it's hard with the grandkids in Baltimore and the condo in Boca. Wendy says she just can't take the cold anymore."

"Well, it's good to see you." Jo squeezed his arm. "Give Wendy our best."

"I will, and thanks for helping out tonight. I understand your pops sent an SOS out to the family."

"It's all good," Pops said, jiggling Ava in his arms. "Everyone can use the work this time of year."

"Good." Earl nodded. "If you'll excuse me, I think my dinner guests have arrived."

As he left them, Jo reached over to straighten her father's red bow tie. "You're really spruced up tonight, Pops."

"We have a wedding reception upstairs," he explained. "It's good to see Earl, right?"

"It is. Wasn't he just here last week?"

"I know . . . he stayed away for three months, and now two visits in two weeks. The rumor mill is churning."

"Saying what?"

"That he wants to sell the inn." When Jo winced, he shrugged. "Sounds crazy, I know. But Earl just said it himself. He just can't get here often enough." He tipped his face down toward his granddaughter. "Miss Ava, how would you like to help your nanna at the front desk?"

As Ava nodded contentedly and they all began to cross the lobby, Jo soaked up the ambiance of the old building, with its hand-hewn banisters, wide plank hardwood floors, and gas fireplaces.

How she loved this place.

Any time of year, the inn was the central pulse of Woodstock, but, now, decorated for Christmas, it surrounded her with its cozy embrace. The lobby was decked in garland speckled with twinkling white lights and clusters of red and purple Christmas balls festooned with fat ribbons. In the corner sat the tree that Jo and Molly had decorated, with its fat red poinsettias, embossed burgundy ribbons, and silver glass icicles.

She used to play hide-and-seek with her brothers in this lobby. They would race up the stairs to see who could deliver towels first. She learned how to bake with Earl's wife, Wendy, in the big industrial kitchen, and she and Fran had spent a few summers earning a quarter for each weed pulled from the gardens out back.

"Earl isn't going to sell this place," Jo told her father.

"I hope you're right, sport." He deposited Ava on a tall stool behind the front desk. Next to her, Irene was helping a guest with a phone reservation. She waggled her fingers at Jo, then turned back to the date book.

Jo kissed Ava's forehead. "You be a good girl and help Nanna, okay? I'm going to help Pops serve people their food."

"Okay, Mommy." Ava was already busy putting loose pens and pencils into a cup.

Jo turned away to follow her father through the dining room to the kitchen, but an elegantly dressed couple talking with Earl Camden at table four caught her eye. Although she couldn't see their faces, Jo noted the man's classic dark suit and the woman's blond hair swept back and held with a sapphire blue clasp, which glimmered in the lights. She wore the satin dress and high heels of a woman going ballroom dancing—certainly not a local who'd come to the inn for dinner.

Who were they?

Her question was answered a moment later as she followed her father across the dining room and saw the woman's face.

Clarice Diamond. And the man beside her was her husband, Sid; Jo recognized him from news photos.

"Pops . . ." Jo waited until they were in the loud clatter of the kitchen. "Did you see who Earl is having dinner with?"

He nodded. "Nice-looking couple."

"Pops, that man is Sid Diamond, the real estate mogul. Diamond Resorts?"

"Really? The big clubs that have ninety pools and hot tubs?" He seemed amused. "Earl never mentioned Sid Diamond."

She tied an apron behind her back. "Pops, I have a bad feeling about this."

"And as far as we know, that's just a feeling, Joanne," he said sternly. "Don't you go starting rumors." He wiped the back of his hand over his brow. "Diamond Resorts. Earl would never do that to us."

"You're probably right, Pops. Nothing to worry about now, right?"

He flashed a smile before ducking back into the dining room, but Jo could tell it was forced.

That night, after Ava was tucked in and Molly was in her room studying, Jo slipped out into the cold night and headed across the lane toward the main house.

She pulled her jacket closer, shivering. Stars glimmered in the night like a spilled satchel of diamonds—and she thought of Sid Diamond and his offer to buy the inn, which Earl had confirmed before she'd left that night. Sid Diamond and his super resorts . . . If he had his way, the inn would be torn down before the spring thaw.

One man held the power over so many lives. It just didn't seem fair.

The possibility of Woodstock losing its inn kept her from sleep, but she didn't want to disturb Molly from her studies. Although it was late, she had decided to take a chance and see if Tommy was right about Sam hanging out in their parents' garage most nights.

There was no answer when she knocked, and she realized how ridiculous it was to be standing here, at the outside door to her own parents' garage, knocking. She had turned away to go in the back door of the house when the door to the garage squeaked open.

"Jo?" Sam stood in the doorway, a baseball hat clamped over his head. "It is you. Is everything okay?"

"I just . . . I needed someone to talk to and Tommy said that you might be here working on the car."

"Yeah." His left hand rose to cover the side of his head. "Okay. Come on in, but watch your step. I'm going to kill the lights."

He hit the switch and the garage went dark, but for the string of colored lights above the workbench.

"Is Tommy here?" she asked, looking around. The Mustang was off the blocks, now supported by tires with fancy wheel rims.

"Nah, it's just me."

"Good." She knew Tommy would be equally upset about the uncertain fate of the inn, and she didn't want to burden him with it yet.

Sam edged over to the sink to wash his hands, hiding his left side as he moved. "I'd offer you a seat, but there's really nowhere to sit."

She glanced around. "You're right." She thought about going inside, but the idea of sneaking a boy into her parents' house after midnight seemed scandalous, even if she was in her twenties.

"Hold on." He circled the back of the car, then opened the driver's-side door. "This baby's off the blocks. We can sit in here."

She opened the passenger door and slid into the deep bucket seat. The silver Mustang charm on the dashboard gleamed against the smooth vinyl. "Hey, you guys have been working on the interior."

"A little Armor All does wonders."

"But you get the driver's seat?" She folded her arms across her chest.

"Of course. I'm the man." He ran his hands over the outer edge of the steering wheel, then gripped it at two and ten. "So what's up?"

Jo sank into the deep seat and stared through the windshield at the glowing colored lights. "Earl is looking to sell the Woodstock Inn, and the buyer is this big deal real estate developer who will probably turn it into a three-ring circus."

"The Woodstock Inn." He frowned. "That place has always been an institution around here. Wasn't the building originally the train station back in the day when the whole town was just a stop on the railroad?"

She nodded. "My father has been managing the inn for years, and it employs half of our family. This is going to kill Pops. We grew up in that place, had our run of it." She squeezed her eyes closed as she recalled the old days at the inn. "We can't let them tear it down."

She felt the warm pressure of Sam's hand on her thigh, and thought how bittersweet to feel the touch of a man in this low moment. Suddenly she felt drained of energy.

"I don't know why I'm taking this so personally. It's not as if I own the inn. And I'm so tired of working twenty-four-seven with nothing to show for it. But if we lose the inn, this town's as good as done."

"You can't give up yet," he said. "You've got to fight the battle. The inn is worth fighting for, right?"

"Of course, but how do you fight someone like Sid Diamond? He's got more power and money than the whole state of New Hampshire."

"So you need a strategy. You won't win against him. So you undermine him. Get to Earl. Find out what it would take for him to hold on to the inn. I know he thinks he's ready to sell, but he's got some attachments here. When push comes to shove, I don't think he'll give up on this town."

Jo thought of her brief exchange with Earl earlier, his praise of her father, the way he'd teased Ava as if she were his own granddaughter. "Earl is a great guy," she said. "We can at least try to talk to him."

"Right. That's a start. And if he doesn't budge, you still have options. The town won't go out without a fight, but you'd have to get people on board . . . the mayor and the merchants. Who's mayor now, anyway?"

"Steve Balfour. His construction company built half the condos at Loon Mountain. Remember him from high school?"

"Student body president, yeah. If Earl can't be swayed, you go to the people." Sam turned to her, his features barely visible in the dim light. Still, there was no mistaking that strong jawline and the spark in his eyes.

How she longed to run her hand along that jaw.

"You've given me some good ideas," she said. He reminded her of the Sam she used to know, solid and dependable. "It seemed so hopeless, but there are some alternatives."

"And if anyone can rally people around here, it's you. Who else could have sold a dozen personalized signs in one day?"

She snorted. "That's because I know everyone and their brother."

"Exactly." His hand moved down her thigh, squeezing just above her knee.

His touch felt so good. Maybe he meant it as a brotherly show of encouragement, but Jo's body was taking it seriously, her heart beating like a wild bird in her chest, a poignant want stirring deep within. Oh, to be in Sam's arms, to be falling through darkness in sync with him . . . the fantasy was so palpable in this moment, she had to call him on it.

"You know, when you touch a girl like that, it gets her thinking."

"Like this?" His hand moved up her thigh, straying dangerously close to the sweet spot, but circling around her hip pocket to squeeze her bottom.

No brotherly intention there. It was definitely sexual, and the reality stirred hot embers of fear and excitement for Jo.

"Oh, now you're really asking for it." She turned to face him, hoping to read his expression.

The spark of passion in his eyes defied the shadows. "I've always been asking, Jo."

The air between them was charged with energy, as he closed the space between their lips.

His kiss stole her breath and captured her spirit. She felt herself suspended, like a delicate leaf floating over the palm of his hand, as his mouth moved over hers, tantalizing and playful.

She reached up to hold on, anchoring herself to his shoulders as she slid into the kiss. Everything around them intensified—the charged air, their racing hearts, the heat firing up inside both of them. Jo didn't have to guess if Sam was right here with her; she could tell by the groan in his throat and the heat of his palms that he felt it, too.

Kissing Sam . . . what were the chances of the two of them landing in each other's arms?

A million to one. A bazillion to one.

But amazing things happened on God's good Earth.

One of his hands moved through the hair at the nape of her neck, sending tingles down her spine. With the other hand, he smoothed circles on her thigh, awakening sensations she had abandoned years ago. They were in their eighth or ninth heady kiss when Jo moved toward him and felt the gear shift between them. Damn!

The thought of more seemed delicious, but she knew that wouldn't happen anytime soon. Earning Sam's trust was going to take time. When a guy wouldn't let you see beneath his hat in the light of day, you had to know it would take some time for trust-building.

And that was fine by Jo's conscience. Hell, she couldn't really let him into her bed anytime soon, what with Ava to be taken care of. She figured she had a good thirteen years till Ava went off to college, and then maybe she could allow a romantic relationship into her life . . .

He ended the kiss and leaned back slightly. "Something tells me I've lost you."

He was right, but she didn't want to admit that she'd let her conscience get in the way. "We're steaming up the windows," she whispered.

"S'okay. We got Windex."

"Very funny." Her eyes opened to see his face just inches from hers. His steely gray eyes seethed with a passion, but they were full of that complex emotion as dark and deep as a spring lake.

"I try."

Realizing that she was holding onto his shoulders with a death grip, she relaxed her hands and gave a gentle massage. His left shoulder felt knotted and thick—the injury, she suspected.

"Oh . . . does it hurt when I do that?"

He shook his head. "But it hurts when we stop kissing."

She pressed her lips to his, loving the moist, warm contact. "Then we'll have to keep doing this. A lot. You can call it physical therapy."

"That's what I was thinking." He ran his hands up her back and held her in a solid, possessive embrace that made Jo feel as if he was claiming her for his own. "That's just what the doctor ordered."

Chapter 10

The next morning as Jo vacuumed the rug of the shop, she danced a little jump-step in time to a Christmas song on the playlist Molly had made, a rocking song in which a female singer lamented about not wanting to be alone for Christmas.

"All alone on Christmas!" Molly belted out as she hung slender silver icicles on a tree decked with white lights.

Jo switched off the vacuum and turned the sign to OPEN.

"Who does this song?" she called to her cousin.

"Darlene Love. Isn't it great?"

"Love it." As Jo used the vacuum hose to tidy up the window display, she visualized herself spending Christmas with Sam this year, all cozied up by the light of a tree. Crazy, yeah, but as she gave the snow globe of Woodstock a shake, she imagined the crackle of a warm fire and the smell of warm apple cider. There'd be a trace of cinnamon on Sam's lips as they . . .

The jingle of the door bells tweaked her out of the lovely daydream, back to reality. Pops's face was ruddy from the cold as he came in, but Jo was reassured by his cheerful grin. Snowflakes clung to his jaunty cap and dark coat.

"'Morning, girls. Brought you some coffees." He placed a cardboard tray with three cups on the counter.

"God bless you, Uncle Bob." Molly whisked a cup out of the tray. "I didn't get my morning jolt of caffeine yet."

Jo wheeled the vacuum to the back room. "Mum told you I called?"

When he nodded and took a sip from his cup, she added, "I was really bugged about the Sid Diamond thing last night, but I have a plan. I'm going to talk with Earl, but I figure we should do it together."

"That'd be a problem. Keith is driving him to the airport now. Taking the next flight back to Florida."

"What? He can't . . . I need to talk to him."

"I'm one step ahead of you, kiddo. Had a long conversation with the boss before he left." He removed his cap, smacked it against his knee. "You weren't the only one who lost sleep last night."

Molly abandoned her tree decorating and joined them at the counter. "What's going on?"

"Earl is thinking about selling the inn. He's got an offer from that developer Sid Diamond—the one whose wife was in here a few weeks ago?"

Molly nodded so vigorously her hair bobbed. "Yes, I remember. And . . . ?"

"Diamond has a reputation for building big spas. Super resorts . . . with casinos, if the local laws allow it." Jo pointed to the picture window of the shop. "Next year at this time, we could be looking out at a giant marquee with flashing lights."

"Really?" Molly's brows shot up. "Well, at least that'd give us something to do around here."

"Moll, have another sip of coffee and come to your senses. It would be tragic."

Pops frowned at his niece, nodding. "If the inn goes down, I guarantee your shop won't be too far behind. In fact, I can't imagine much of the businesses on our main street will stay alive. A resort like that changes the nature of a place. All-inclusive. People don't want to cross the street to use an ATM or grab a slice of pizza. They get it all under one roof. All delivered to their room, if they want."

"Oh." Molly's lips puckered. "I get it. It's about preserving Woodstock, which would be overwhelmed by something like that."

"Exactly. The Woodstock Inn holds this town together. It's the glue of this place." Pops smoothed the lining of his cap, his eyes lined by gray circles. "It'd be a tragedy for this town."

Jo was struck by his appearance. Despite his determination, Pops seemed a bit worn at the edges.

"So what did Earl say?"

"He told me the asking price. One point one million, which I think is a steal for a place like the inn, but Earl says he's looked around, and it's a fair deal."

A million dollars. Although it was an unimaginable sum for people in these parts, to Jo it seemed like a small price for the future of her hometown.

"I guess I'd feel better about it if the buyer wasn't a developer like Sid Diamond," Jo said. "Did you ask Earl if he could put the place on the market awhile, see who comes around?"

"That's the thing . . ." Pops turned his hat in his hand. "No one knew about it, but apparently the inn has already been up for sale for six months, listed on a special website for Realtors. Earl says that Diamond is the first person to make a solid offer, and he's afraid to let the fish slip away from his hook."

"Fish on a hook? Old Earl has been spending too much time fishing in Florida," Jo said, warming her hands on her coffee cup. "And it steams my clams to hear that he's had the place up for sale without telling anyone. Without telling you. That's just not fair."

"His intentions are good," Pops said. "But I can't get over the feeling that this is one of those crossroads that determines the fate for hundreds of people."

Her father was right; the inn was the lifeblood of this town. Which made Sid Diamond the Grim Reaper.

The door bells jangled, and four women in snow parkas entered.

Jo, Molly, and Pops turned and said, "Merry Christmas!" almost in unison. Then they turned back to face each other as the shoppers began to browse.

"Maybe Sid Diamond won't tear the inn down," Molly suggested. "I mean, it's a moneymaker, right?"

"It is, indeed. We sell out during summer and ski season. The rest of the year we're full on weekends, and the restaurant and catering business does well year-round. Yes, the inn earns a tidy profit."

"So maybe things will stay as they are," Molly said hopefully.

"That would be nice." Jo clutched her coffee cup, disappointed that it had grown cold. She liked Molly's optimism, but she couldn't trust that a man like Sid Diamond would do the right thing. "Pops, what are we going to do?"

"For now, we just sit tight. I'm going to have another talk with Earl, once he gets settled back in Boca. Your mother and I stayed up late, going over our finances and such. We could pull together enough money to match half of the asking price, but in these economic times, that's just not enough. We talked about selling the house—"

"Oh, Pops, not the house!" Built as a lodge in the 1800s and remodeled by Pops's father, who was a carpenter, the house had been home to many generations of Trumans. "It's the home of our hearts!"

"True, but if it's a matter of saving either the house on Bull Moose or the town, you know what we have to do." He leaned over the counter and pitched his cardboard cup into the trash. "It's just your mother and me in the house now, and it's worth a pretty penny, with the walnut paneling and built-in bookcases in the great room. If we bought the inn, your mother and I would have more than enough space in the owner's cottage. It's actually kind of cozy there."

Jo shook her head. "Pops . . ."

"I know, there's the matter of you girls renting the space above the old carriage house." He patted Jo's shoulder.

"I wasn't even thinking that far ahead. It's just that . . . the house. That's where our family gathers. We can't sell it off to strangers."

"Don't worry about it, sport. I don't know if it would even sell in this market. In the meantime, I put in a call to Emma Mueller, down at the bank, but I'm not too hopeful about it. We all know they're tight with loans these days."

"If it means saving the house, I could loan you some money," Jo offered.

"You know we'd never take from our children." He replaced his cap and winked at her. "Besides, you've got a little angel of your own. It will all work out. We'll figure a way. And speaking of the inn, I've got to get back to work."

Watching him cross the snowy street, Jo bit her bottom lip. Despite Pops's positive attitude, she could feel his hope draining. *Sit tight,* he'd said. But it was hard to sit back and watch as something you loved slipped through your fingers.

Jo's visits to the garage became a nightly occurrence, missed only on those rare occasions when Molly was out late—once for a celebration with other students after a semester final, and once for Christmas shopping down in Concord. Of course, Molly needed to be home for Ava. And Jo always waited until her little one was fast asleep before she tiptoed down the stairs to cross the snowpack of the lane.

A leading psychologist prescribed that single parents refrain from bringing a partner into their lives until their children were grown, and Jo saw the logic in that. Her Ava wasn't going to feel threatened by men her mom was seeing. There would be no "transient daddies" in their lives. Jo had a daughter to raise, and Jo could wait.

But Jo's heart trilled to have a secret love on the side.

On her end, Molly was the only one who knew about Jo's developing relationship with Sam, and she didn't ask nearly as many questions as Jo had anticipated. Jo suspected that her cousin understood how tenuous was the thread that connected them, and she gave Jo some space.

Since Tommy was never around at night, Jo suspected that Sam had hinted to her brother to keep his distance from the family garage. Tommy had never mentioned anything to her, but then again he did have a wife and kids at home, and it was Christmastime. Still, when they ran into each other, Tommy's quiet smile and averted eyes gave Jo the message. He knew, but thank God he wasn't saying anything.

For the most part, they talked. Although he didn't like to discuss it, she learned that his good friend, a guy nicknamed Cackalacky, had been killed in the explosion that had injured Sam. Sam seemed to think that Cackalacky had more to live for than he did, and somehow they should have switched places. Hearing that made Jo vow to show Sam that he had so much to live for.

She snuck him a plate of leftover meat loaf and mashed potatoes from dinner, and he gave her a Christmas gift for Ava, a sign specially made for Ava's room depicting a cow jumping over the moon, from her favorite nursery rhyme. Another night she brought him a tin of homemade cookies, and he assembled a small bicycle for Santa to put under the tree for Ava. She brought him a small decorated tree to take with him and cheer up his ma's house, and he brought a small space heater to take the chill off the garage attached to her parents' house.

Tonight he unrolled a sleeping bag on the floor of the garage and told her to stretch out, facedown, jacket off.

"Okay, this is a little weird," she said, peeling off her down jacket. "I'm not a camper, and spiders are not my friends."

"First off, this garage is cleaner than Betty Crocker's kitchen. Besides that, what species of spiders can live through a New Hampshire winter?"

"Point taken." She balled up her jacket and used it to cushion her face, then lay down. "But I'm still a little hinky about this."

"I'll stop whenever you feel uncomfortable. Just say uncle."

"Uncle." She punched her jacket and rolled to her side. "I'm not psyched about stretching out on the floor of the garage."

"Okay. I was going to give you a massage, but I'm not the kind of guy who pushes a woman to do anything . . ."

"A massage?" She flopped back onto her stomach. "Why didn't you say so in the first place? Giddyup." She felt a slight, warm pressure on her buttocks, and realized he had kneeled over her and lowered himself to straddle her. Such an intimate contact . . . intimate yet innocent for a massage.

"Giddyup is right." His voice was husky as his warm hands outlined her shoulder blades. "You are tight, just as I figured. You're letting this deal with the inn eat away at you."

"Yeah, I'm stressed. I can't help it. There's a lot at stake. But really—shouldn't I be the one massaging you? You're the one with the injured shoulder and all."

"I got plenty of that during physical therapy. It's pay-back time."

Even as he spoke, his hands melted the iron set of her shoulders, infusing warmth. "It's twenty degrees out there. How do you keep your hands so warm?"

"I run hot," he said. "Didn't you notice? I'm a hot guy."

"Mmm." She closed her eyes and imagined that her sweater and bra were stripped away. No boundaries between them. That would be great, but it was a little too chilly in here to go that far.

As he pressed into tender muscle, she took the fantasy a step further, with the two of them in her bed. Her head was pressed into the down of her pillow as he worked on her back.

Only, neither of them was clothed. And her tender nerves could clearly define every part of Sam as he strad-dled her . . .

"Does that feel okay?" he asked.

"It's amazing." A warm glow emanated through her entire body, fired by thoughts of what they could do in an-other place and time.

Was Sam thinking of that, too?

Did he wonder how their relationship was going to

progress beyond Mom and Pops's garage? Although he hadn't pushed her in any way, she sensed that he, too, wanted to take their relationship to the next level. Jo could think of nothing more delicious than a sensual romp with Sam, but she would have to be careful—and not just with birth control. Her relationship with Sam would have to remain a secret to protect Ava.

And that seemed okay with Sam, who had no interest in going out in public. So far he'd had her deliver all of the signs he'd made for Woodstock merchants, even for people he knew, like Carmine Giordano and Steve Balfour. Sam was content to be a hermit, and for the next few years, Jo would gladly visit his lair.

He rubbed his hands up and down her back, then ended by leaning over her so close she could feel his warm breath by her ear as he whispered, "How's that?"

"Wonderful." Every nerve in her body felt invigorated and alive—and aroused, too—but since she wasn't ready to take that step yet, she turned her head toward him, and said, "Now it's your turn."

"That's okay." He squeezed her shoulders, then lifted himself off her.

There was a chill in the air above her as she rose to her knees and faced him. "Really. I've given you space and privacy for a while now, but it's time." When he frowned, she reached out and gently pressed the left side of his neck. "I want to touch you, Sam. I want to learn your scars and your sensitive spots. I want to know you."

His face tensed. "You won't like what you see."

"No one wants to see how someone they care for got hurt, but now those scars are a part of you, Sam. I don't think they define you, but they're part of your body, and I don't want you to feel like you need to hide from me anymore. Our bodies are road maps of our lives, a history of where we've been. Show me. Show me where you've been."

"This is crazy." He sat back on his heels and undid the top button of his flannel shirt. "Look, I won't blame you if you want to turn and run out of here screaming."

Jo snickered. "That's not happening, so go on. Get your clothes off, man."

"Just the shirt and hat. I didn't get injured below the waist."

She rolled her eyes. "Now you're going to be a stickler for detail?"

He actually grinned for a moment, then sighed. "Okay." He pulled off the cap with the earflaps, raked up his hair, and turned so that she could see the left side of his head. She touched his cheek, where the skin was stubbly from a day's growth of beard. His face wasn't harmed, but under his hair was a rough patch of red raised skin where his ear should have been. Gently, her fingertips circled the shiny flesh and followed the scarring down the side of his neck, extending beneath the collar of his shirt.

"So you lost hearing on this side?"

"Yeah. The doctors were amazed that there wasn't some brain damage. I guess sometimes it pays to be hard-headed."

She drew back her hand and nodded. "Okay, buddy. Shirt off."

His eyes glistened, his gaze intent on her eyes as if eager for a reaction. "You're so demanding," he said as he finished unbuttoning and slid the shirt off.

His chest struck her first, and not because of any injury. Those were the very definition of six-pack abs, the rippled muscles evident even in the shadowed light. Unable to resist, she ran a hand between his pecs, down his belly.

"Easy, there. You're in the express lane. Missed your exit."

"Oh." She pulled her hand back, as if burned. "Sorry, but your abs are a huge distraction."

"My left shoulder." He turned toward the left. "The bomb shattered the bones, but the muscles stayed in good shape. I had to get a new joint, chrome and titanium. I've got a bionic shoulder."

She cupped the braided scar that capped his shoulder. "Does it hurt when I touch you?" she asked.

"No, I can't feel anything there because the nerves were severed. But I can feel things in plenty of other places."

She ran her hand back down his chest, then pushed him away. "You boys never grow up. Here I'm trying to dole out some tender loving care, and your mind goes right back to the sex thing."

"Nothing wrong with that," he said.

"Nothing wrong with it when two people are committed and responsible." As the intense moment eased, she leaned back and crossed her legs.

"You are one buff guy for someone who spent a year in rehab. Better put your shirt back on before I lose my senses and attack you."

He slid his arms into the sleeves. "I had access to a gym and plenty of time on my hands. What else was I going to do?"

"Well, apparently you weren't throwing a pity party and eating bonbons. Which is to say, you look great. I wish the scars didn't keep you from going out in public."

"I don't want to be a freak. The beast that scares little kids in grocery stores."

"Little kids see things through their own filters, and they are a lot less judgmental than most adults in the world. But that's another issue. I'm just saying, it doesn't look as bad as you think."

He nodded. "Whatever. I'm scheduled for another skin graft on the side of my head in the new year. That is, if I ever get down to Concord to the VA hospital to meet with the doctors. I haven't been too good about that since I landed here."

"Sam Norwood! You'd better take care of yourself. Get your butt down there this week."

"It's Christmas—they don't want to see me now, and it's all the way down in Concord."

"What is wrong with you? Concord isn't that long a drive."

"I've been busy. Got a job in an auto shop, and someone gave me a dozen signs to paint by hand."

"Those things can wait," Jo insisted sternly. "Your health comes first." She thought about Sam in the hospital alone, how he'd recovered through months of surgery and skin grafts. "And you'd better let me know when your procedure is scheduled, because I'm not letting you go through it alone this time."

"Going to hold my hand?" He sounded skeptical.

"I'll drive down with Molly. She's almost finished with her nursing degree, and she'll be able to make sure you're getting the best care."

Sam raked his hair back and stared at her, as if he didn't believe her promise. "That'd be good."

"We'll be there for you, Sam. I'll be there," she said, knowing that, in her heart, she was already committed to loving Sam.

It would just take a few years for the other details to fall into place.

Chapter 11

"What's the big deal?" Tommy asked across the engine of the truck. "You want an invite to Christmas dinner, I'm inviting you now. Don't wait on my sister, because the brain of a woman works entirely different than a man's, and you'll never understand what's holding her up."

Sam wiped oil off the stick and plunged it in again. "But I want it to come from her. I'm not going to just show up Sunday night."

"Why not? You know she wants you there. She's probably just freaked out about Ma and Pops finding out about you two. Jo hasn't dated much since Shane died." He tipped his hat back and scratched his head. "Actually, I don't think she's dated at all."

"It's okay, man. I'll wait till she asks."

"Just saying, you'll be waiting a long time, pal."

Sam released the hood of the truck and he and Tommy stepped back as it slammed shut. "And why is that? What's Jo afraid of?"

He had a theory, though he hoped it was wrong.

Their late-night meetings in the Trumans' garage were

magical, but you couldn't make out with a woman in the backseat of a classic Mustang forever.

They were two adult people, who were obviously attracted to each other. Jo rarely missed an evening with him, but during other times of the day, she was distant and inaccessible. It was almost as if she couldn't acknowledge him. They had to keep their voices down in the garage because she didn't want her parents to know about them, and though she had faced his scars without flinching, he was beginning to worry that it had soured her feelings for him.

Granted, his wounds looked hideous. He knew that. But still . . . he'd hoped that Jo would be the one person in this world who would see past the physical scars.

For whatever reason, Jo refused to be seen with him in public. She wouldn't associate with him beyond their late-night meetings in the garage.

"I don't know what's wrong with my sister," Tommy muttered, wiping his nose with the cuff of his coveralls. "You got a question for her, you'd better ask her yourself."

So much for insight from Jo's brother, Sam thought as he climbed into the truck and pulled it out of the garage bay. When he pulled into a spot in the lot, the car that pulled in beside him looked familiar. The man who stepped out had the look of a former marine, and Sam recognized him as the guy who was hiring a ballistics expert for the Old Man of the Mountain Monument.

"Sam Norwood." The man's steely eyes didn't miss a beat.

"You remembered my name."

"Your friend refreshed my memory." He nodded toward the shop, where Tommy stood in the doorway, talking on a cell phone. Seeing the man, Tommy gave a hesitant salute.

"I'm sorry, I forgot your name."

"Nelson Dubinsky."

"And you're working on the Old Man Monument."

"Right. I was about to extend an offer to a munitions expert from the Big Dig when I got an application that topped all. An application for you, Norwood."

Sam shook his head. "I don't know anything about that."

"Seems Thomas Truman has been working behind your back—with your mother, no less." He pointed a thumb toward his car. "I've got an application in there that shows you to be the perfect candidate for my project. The question is, do you want the job?"

Sam found it hard to believe that Tommy had the acumen to pull together such a feat, or that his mother cared enough to dig through his records and find all the crap that a job like this would ask for.

"I suppose they forged my signature, too?"

"The online application spared them that crime, though I don't appreciate being involved in their little scheme. My crew is geared up to start with planning at the end of February. We'll break ground after the spring thaw in March. Do you want to be part of the team, Norwood?"

Sam did.

He'd always wanted to build something that lasted, something that would stand long after he was gone, and few things in these parts were more beloved than was the Old Man of the Mountain.

But he wasn't sure he was ready to commit to staying in Woodstock. If things went south with Jo, life here would be unbearable.

"I didn't even know I'd been put in for the job," Sam said. "To be honest, it's a plum, but I'm not sure I'll still be here after Christmas."

Dubinsky squinted. "Got plans?"

"I'm just not sure my roots are strong enough to keep me here." Sam looked the man squarely in the eyes. "I'd like your job, but I can't commit right now. I'll know more after the holidays, but I understand if you can't wait."

Frowning, Dubinsky put his hands on his narrow hips. "I appreciate your honesty, but damned if you aren't a cagey bastard."

"I've been called worse."

"Haven't we all." Dubinsky turned to his car, then paused with his hand on the door. "Here's what I'll do. If I haven't heard from you by January fifteenth, I'll hire on my guy from the Big Dig. January fifteenth. If you want the job, call me before then." He extended a business card. "Fair enough, son?"

The light in the man's eyes had warmed.

"Thank you, sir." Sam took the card and shook the man's hand. "I appreciate your kindness."

"Bah . . ." Dubinsky waved him off. "You just call me by the fifteenth. Have a good Christmas."

Sam nodded, gooseflesh forming on the back of his neck as he recalled his father, who had died of a heart attack when Sam was twelve. No one had called Sam "son" since then. "Yes, sir."

As Dubinsky drove off, Sam realized this would be the Christmas that changed everything . . . for better or worse. If Jo could accept him, he'd have a life here and a job and a family.

If not, he'd heard there was work up in Alaska.

Chapter 12

December twenty-third, the day before Christmas Eve, Jo strolled down an aisle of sparkling trees in the store, savoring the sights, sounds, and scents of Christmas. She loved the last few days before Christmas: the excitement of the kids, the festive lights, the generosity of people in town, as evidenced by the overflowing boxes of food in the bank lobby. These were her favorite days of the year.

"O Come, O Come, Emmanuel" was playing, a version thick with brass trumpets that reminded her to stay on track for Christmas. When she wanted to get lost in the trappings, she reminded herself that it was a celebration of the Savior's birth, the promise of salvation for all mankind. Dad always told everyone that love is the center of the celebration.

Her only regret was that she wouldn't be spending much of the next few days with Sam. Christmas Eve was out, with all hands necessary to help out at the inn, and then the family tradition of midnight mass. She was hoping that she and Sam could get together Christmas night, after the family celebration. A brief snuggle in the glow of Tommy's Christmas lights in the garage would make the perfect ending for her Christmas.

Over at the counter, Molly was working with a customer, so Jo allowed herself a moment to bask in the glittering lights and ornaments. She thought of last night, the string of kisses that had ended their conversation; she pressed a finger to her lips. They'd seemed swollen with desire when she'd slipped out of the garage in a haze of passion. Sam had kissed her hard, with a fervor that said he wanted more.

She wanted it, too. It was something to look forward to in the new year, though she didn't know how they would swing the privacy issue. She did know she would use protection. Super-duper protection this time. But where could they go to get away from the family and prying eyes?

The image of Sam filled her mind—his stormy gray eyes, the strong jaw that tended to scratch her with stubble, the long fingers that moved over her with such tenderness. Sam would think of something. She had never met a guy who possessed such patience with other people.

"Jo? Yo, Joanne Truman," Molly called, grinning. "Get over here. Wow, for a minute there I thought we'd lost you to Christmasland or something."

Shrugging off embarrassment, Jo straightened her sweater and joined her cousin at the counter. "Just a holiday daydream. What's up?"

"Mrs. Porter is looking for some ornaments that kids can decorate at parties," Molly said, gesturing to the woman in jeans and a red knit poncho.

"How old?" Jo asked. When Mrs. Porter said they were all over ten, Jo guided her to glitter glue and ribbon and helped her with her purchase.

As the woman left the shop, Molly danced into the

open space in front of the counter and reenacted the scene.

"Okay, this is you, all wide-eyed and lovelorn. Really, Jo, I've never seen you like this, not even with Shane. Shane made his demands, but this guy Sam has bowled you over. You are just crazy in love with him, aren't you?"

"Both." Jo crossed her arms, hugging herself. "Crazy. And in love."

"I can't wait to meet him. Is he coming to Christmas dinner?"

"Of course not! I can't have him around the family, Moll. You know it's not healthy for Ava to be exposed to strange men her mother is dating."

"He's not a strange man, he's Sam, and you like him a hell of a lot. Ava's an easy sell. If you like him, she's bound to like him, too."

"Dr. Nora, that psychologist, says kids really suffer when a single parent brings a friend around. They might compete for attention or feel displaced. And when they do get attached to the boyfriend, it breaks their hearts when things don't work out for the couple."

"I know what Dr. Nora is getting at, but shit happens! You can't live in a bubble, and neither can Ava."

"I need to protect my child and let her know that I'm devoted to her."

"And live like a nun?"

Jo picked up an ornament that had rolled off a nearby tree. "I can date, silly. I just can't bring someone home or introduce him into our home life."

"Well, that's kind of useless."

"That's Dr. Nora's advice, and I'm sticking to it."

Molly hoisted herself onto the counter with a frown.

"That Dr. Nora has a bug up her ass. She's probably sneaking male strippers into her bedroom while her kids are asleep."

"Molly! Shut up!" Jo glanced around to see if anyone was listening.

"There's no one else in here," Molly said. "But that's about to change. Here comes trouble." She jumped off the counter and made herself busy in the back room so that Jo would have to deal with the customer.

Who could be that bad? Jo wondered as the door bells jingled, and Clarice Diamond stepped in.

"Hello," the elegant woman said, pausing in the doorway to brush snow from the shoulders of her cashmere coat. "Picturesque—but none of the songs ever mention what a sloppy mess it is."

"Merry Christmas." Jo tried not to let the animosity she felt, creep into her voice. "How's the tree working out at Cascade House?"

"It's perfect." Clarice stepped in, slipping off rust leather gloves as smooth as butter. "It really helped to make the place more homey. Of course, we haven't found a way to make the cooking any better, but I understand it's hard to get fresh ingredients up here in the winter."

Jo wanted to say that the owners of Cascade House were her friends and that Laura was one of the best cooks she knew, but she kept mum. Better to just take care of business and get Clarice Diamond out of here. "Can I help you find something?"

"I hope so. I'm sure you heard about Sid buying the inn."

"Right. Looks like we're going to be neighbors."

"Oh? Oh—you mean with this shop across the street?" Clarice frowned. "This whole block will probably be swept up in Sid's new spa."

Although Clarice kept talking, Jo was stuck on her last words. So their little shop would be swept away, a tiny shell under the tsunami that was Sid Diamond. And Clarice didn't understand how wrong that was? She had no sense of how it might hurt Jo and Molly to learn that their business was dispensable . . . utterly disposable?

"Anyway, when Sid told me the Camdens were waiting until after Christmas to make their decision, I wanted to send them a little gift to remind them of this town. That snow globe you sold me came to mind, but my son loves it. Do you have another one I can send to Earl and Wendy?"

"Of course." A sour knot lodged in Jo's throat and stuck there as she went to the back room and found a snow globe wrapped in bubble wrap.

Molly touched her arm, her eyes wide with alarm, but Jo just nodded and returned to the counter.

"The snow globe of Woodstock, right?" Jo asked. She wanted to tell Clarice Diamond that Jo's mother made these from ornaments that they special-ordered from Bavaria. And how Irene hand-painted the names of the shops, ever so tiny.

But she saved her breath, knowing the entrepreneur's wife wouldn't care. Besides, this time next year, the buildings depicted in the globe would be six feet under, all bulldozed over.

"That's it," Clarice nodded, removing a gold credit card from her slender wallet. "You'll ship it for me? Actually, I don't know their address down in Boca, but you can get it from the inn, can't you? As I hear it, you're all interrelated."

"Forty dollars extra for shipping," Jo said, doubling the usual fee.

"Not a problem."

As Jo processed the credit card transaction, the volume of the music rose—Molly at work. Jo bit her lower lip, noting that Clarice did not seem to appreciate the fine musical stylings of "Grandma Got Run Over by a Reindeer."

When the woman had left, Molly freaked.

"What the hell? I think Scrooge has been reincarnated!" Molly shouted.

"They're going to bulldoze our shop," Jo said, stunned.

Molly went to the display window and peered out. "Did you hear the crack about all of us being related? She made it sound like a scene from *Deliverance*!"

"I can't believe this is really happening." Jo looked at the snow globe of her beloved Woodstock and bit her lower lip. "They can't come in and ruin our little town."

"That woman is loony tunes," Molly said emphatically. "I say we don't ever let her in the shop again. Next time, we lock the door and duck. We can't let her ruin our Christmas."

"It's not just about Christmas," Jo said, peering at the miniature versions of the Christmas shop and the Woodstock Inn inside the snow globe. "She's going to ruin everything, she and her husband. They're going to ruin our lives."

Molly shook her head. "Much as I long to stray from the homeland, I'm starting to get this whole thing. I don't want to come home from Boston and find some resort with a golf course and hot tubs sitting where my parents' home used to be."

"And that's exactly what they plan to do."

"So we have to figure out a way to stop them. Have your parents made their offer on the inn yet?"

"They're waiting to get a loan approved from the bank."

"Well, somebody better call Emma down at the bank and have her crunch some numbers fast, before they take a wrecking ball to Main Street."

"Mum's working the desk at the inn today." Jo grabbed her coat from under the counter. "I'm going over to have a chat. Maybe we can light some fires under people at the bank." As the door bells jangled, she turned back to her cousin. "Sorry to stick you with minding the shop . . ."

"Just go . . . go!" Molly waved her off.

Jo held her coat closed, blinking against the falling snow as she crossed the street to the inn. "Proud old girl," she said, wondering how anyone could think of tearing down the majestic white building with its gables and wraparound porch, its white picket fence, old stonework, and towering pines. Sid Diamond had found success, but the man was blind to true beauty in this world.

The minute she walked into the lobby of the inn, Jo sensed that something was up. Was something wrong with her eyes, or were there small pink dots everywhere? And what was that floating from the old chandelier in the lobby?

Peering up at the grand light fixture, she moved closer, across the old Chinese carpet. A tag dangled from the chandelier. FOR SALE, it read. ASK AT THE DESK ABOUT MY PRICE.

"What?" Squinting, she swung around to the grandfather clock, where a sign read: FOR SALE. TAKE ME HOME.

"You've got to be kidding me." Jo tromped over to the mantel, which apparently was on the market for a steal at a thousand dollars. She suspected that if the mantel were removed, the entire wall would come tumbling down, but maybe that was the goal of the person selling the inn off. Demolition.

"Hey, Mum. What's the deal with the price tags?" She crossed the lobby to the main desk, but the seat behind the elaborate wood grillwork atop the marble counter was empty. "Anybody here?" It was not like her mother to leave the desk unattended on her watch.

"Oh, Jo. Thank goodness it's you, sweetie." Her mother's voice sounded thick and husky as she emerged from the cubby in the back. Irene Truman had been crying, something Jo did not remember ever witnessing before. Her face was drained of color and she pressed a gob of tissues to her red eyes. "I'm so embarrassed . . ."

"Mum, are you okay?" In an instant, Jo was behind the desk, helping her mother to a chair.

"I'll be fine. Not to worry, dear. It's just bad news. I need a few minutes to pull myself together."

"What?" Jo bent down beside her mother.

"I just got a call from Emma Mueller, and the bank has . . . has denied our loan." Irene's voice quavered at the last words.

"Oh, no. No, no." Jo touched her mother's shoulders. "I'm sorry, Mum."

"It's not the end of the world. In fact, your father and I have a plan B, which we decided on in advance, and he's already been on the phone, putting it into action." Irene sniffed. "We've put the house up for sale."

"What? Mum, you can't—"

Irene held up a hand to stave off Jo's objections. "I know it will be hard on all of us. We've had such a good run there, and it's always been your home. But the house on Bull Moose Road will fetch a small fortune. Half a million dollars, that's what Darlene Clark says. She's Larry Clark's daughter; got her Realtor's license now."

Jo didn't know Darlene, but Larry Clark Realty was an institution in Woodstock.

"The money from the sale of the house, combined with our savings, will be enough to buy the inn outright. A cash sale." She took a deep, calming breath. "I'll bet Mister Sidney Diamond isn't putting up that kind of cash."

The breath drained from her body as Jo rose and pressed against the walnut-paneled wall behind her, trying to gain some sort of balance.

Everything was spiraling out of control. Her home, her town . . . she pressed her clammy palms to the wall, trying to think of a way out of this box.

She held on tight as the old-fashioned phone jangled and Irene smoothed her collar over her blazer and picked it up.

"Yes, this is she. Oh, hello, Darlene. You do? Already? My, that was fast. Well, I'd be happy to show it today, but I'm working at the inn and I can't get away. Three holiday parties today. But if they're coming all the way from Concord, let me see if someone else can be there. Maybe one of the kids?"

She looked up, her eyes landing on Jo, assessing with that mixture of tenderness and prodding that mothers everywhere had perfected.

Knowing what was coming, Jo felt pinned against the wall.

"Jo, honey, Darlene's got a buyer on the hook. Driving up from Concord. Would you be able to meet them at the house this afternoon? A Miss Amy Loman and her client. You could do it on your lunch hour from the shop."

Helping to sell the house on Bull Moose was the last thing Jo wanted to do.

She had stuff to take care of. The Christmas shop would be crazy busy this afternoon, with Charlie Wilson playing Santa and lines of kids out the door.

She tried to decline, shake her head no. Instead, she glanced down at her mother, whose eyes were still red from crying, and nodded. "Sure, Mum. What time does Darlene want me there?"

Chapter 13

As Jo's Jeep bounced over the hardpack of snow on the lane, she took her foot off the accelerator and stared at the red and black atrocity stuck between snow-covered trees in her parents' yard.

FOR SALE, the sign said.

Seemed to be the theme of the day.

Clamping down on the brakes, she felt a strong urge to jump out of her vehicle and yank the sign right out of the ground. It hurt like a thorn in her side.

Instead she gave a grunt and hit the gas. She parked in front of the double garage—hallowed grounds for her these days—and slammed the door. Aside from the crunch of snow under her boots, the woods were silent.

She paused, listening carefully.

What was that lofty clink? Not the sound of Santa's sleigh, which was the first thing that came to mind, but more like the whisper of crystal glasses toasting in the distance.

A snowflake caught in her eyelashes and she knew. It

was the soft *ping* of millions of snowflakes finding their landing spots on trees, rooftops, and fences.

In the life span of a snowflake, there was no question about finding a place to land. Maybe it attached to other crystals or clung to a pinecone or melted on the warm hood of her Jeep, but it found its place. The process was more difficult for humans. Which was why it seemed so wrong to be selling this house. This place had been a home to her family. It was hard enough to find a place on this Earth, and now, to give it up . . .

Jo couldn't imagine it. She and her siblings had sledded down that hill behind the house for all their lives. The same hill Ava and her cousins used these days. She wasn't giving up the hill.

She unlocked the door and slipped out of her boots in the mudroom. James had wanted to convert the mudroom to a spa with a hot tub, but Mum wouldn't hear of it. "How do you keep a house clean without a mudroom?" she'd asked, and she'd been right.

The kitchen was neat as a pin, the warm copper of the granite counters inviting, the stained-glass piece in the window bright from the snow behind it. Would they leave the stained glass with the house? It had been made by Jo's great-grandfather more than fifty years ago, and they'd always joked that it was the family crest.

"I'll take it before some buyer comes in and tosses it off," Jo thought, though she had no idea where she would hang it. She would be out of her apartment in the carriage house if this house sold.

On impulse, she raced upstairs to her old bedroom. The stair rail, now decked with garland and white lights, reminded her of the Valentine's Day when she and Fran had taped a construction-paper heart to each post.

From the room that she had shared with Fran, Jo

looked out over the garage roof and marveled at her own idiocy for climbing out this window and shimmying down to meet Shane. She could have broken her neck! And the closet—a great spot for hide-and-seek: her personal hideaway, where she'd spent hours curled up in a ball, wondering how Shane could have been so selfish, worrying that she didn't have the courage to raise a baby on her own.

There were so many memories here.

Although she knew she would never be able to return to the room of her childhood, it was still hard to let it go. She wasn't so much concerned that a stranger would be sleeping here as that it would be left empty and dormant. Or worse, that the whole house would be dismantled to make way for a home with cathedral ceilings and columns, solar panels, and an in-ground pool.

Her throat was thick with a ball of emotion as she descended the stairs. She had left the great room for last. She smoothed her hand over the wide walnut mantel and plugged in the lights of the towering Christmas tree. With its fireplace, built-in shelves, and clusters of furniture, this was the room where the Truman family had spent most of their days. How many times had she wrestled on this floor with Tommy or played Monopoly with Fran and James? Dave and Chloe had been married in this room, right in front of the huge window with the spring trees as their glorious backdrop.

What if this was their last Christmas in the great room?

She skirted the giant tree, gazing up at the crystal star that caught the lights and refracted squares of gold, blue, red, and green on the ceiling. "Star light, star bright," she whispered, thinking back on the days when wishes held stock.

Tears stung her eyes, and she swiped the sleeve of her

jacket over her face. She didn't want the Realtor and her buyers from Concord to see her crying, and they would be arriving any minute now.

She glanced out the huge picture window toward the lane. No sign of a vehicle, but that red and black sign taunted her, a throbbing toothache.

A sob escaped her throat, and she pressed a hand to her mouth, trying to hold back the torrent of emotion.

"No." She would not lose it in front of the Realtor. She would be polite. She wasn't going to sabotage her parents' plans.

But that horrible sign . . .

Wheeling around, she skirted the tree and flew out the front door. The steps had been salted, but virgin snow lay around the trees. She sank down to her knees, and her wool socks did nothing to ward off the chill of raw snow.

Still, that eyesore had to go, and Jo took great delight in grabbing the post and giving it a tug. Not as easy as she'd anticipated. The post remained in place.

Leverage, she thought. Placing her snowy sock-clad foot at the top of the sign, she gave it a shove. It moved slightly. She kicked and pushed until it finally slouched to the side, enough for her to uproot it with a grunt.

Victory!

She held the sign high over her head, breathing hard with satisfaction.

The crunch of snow and a flash of red through the trees alerted her that a car was coming.

Jo lowered the sign as the red SUV slowed to a stop some ten yards away, visible through the bare trees.

The passenger-side window rolled down, and a man in a dark coat sat back as a woman leaned over from the driver's seat.

"Hi, there! I'm Amy Loman, from Loman Realty in

Concord. We're looking for fifteen-hundred Bull Moose, but I see you got here first."

Jo looked at the infuriating sign in her hands, but refused to feel remorse about ripping it out. "I did."

"Aren't you the early bird." Amy had a broad smile, which made it hard for Jo to completely hate her. "I should have known it was too good to be true. My client and I came as soon as the listing popped, but I guess we weren't fast enough."

"I guess not," Jo said, dropping the sign onto the snow. She wasn't tracking what Amy Loman was saying. Did they want to see the house or not?

"Well, let us know if your offer falls through," Amy said, flashing that smile again. "Happy holidays!"

Jo stood there staring, her toes beginning to freeze as the red SUV turned around in the driveway and headed back down the lane. Amy Loman thought Jo was Darlene? Since Jo had ripped out the sign, Amy had thought there was an offer on the house.

If only it were true.

If Jo had half a million, she would buy the place herself.

Ah, but you do.

Not in her checking account, but in savings. The money from Shane's life insurance. Of course, she'd put that aside for Ava, but she couldn't think of a better way to invest it than to buy the house outright. Ava would be guaranteed a chance to grow up in her family home and . . . and if they needed money down the road, Jo could refinance for a small amount.

"Oh, dear God . . ." Jo's heart began to race as she picked up the sign and hurried back toward the house. "Thank you, thank you, thank you!" she shouted, half prayer, half cheer.

This would be the best Christmas ever.

* * *

Sam buffed the dashboard of the Mustang, sat back in the seat, and tapped the steering wheel. Where the hell was Jo?

This garage romance was beginning to wear thin, with the cold, the smell of motor oil, and the limited access to Jo, which made him feel like a caged animal at times. He was supposed to wait here nights, while she had a life with Ava and her family, a life he wasn't allowed to be a part of because . . .

"Because of the way you look," he said, the words he'd been dreading all these weeks.

It was time to face the fact that he was damaged goods, even in Jo's eyes, and he wasn't going to be comfortable living within the bounds she'd set for their relationship.

The squeak of the outside door made him turn.

Jo stood there, her cheeks streaked with red, her eyes bright.

He got out of the car, closed the door. "You look like you ran all the way over."

"I did!" She parted her open coat, revealing flannel pajamas tucked into the tops of her rubber boots. "I just wanted to tell you that I can't stay. I'm working on a huge surprise for Christmas. Mom and Pops know about it, but I'm trying to get everything lined up so I can spring it on my family tomorrow, just before midnight mass."

"Really . . . can you give me a hint?"

"No way. I'll tell you tomorrow. Or . . . I won't see you tomorrow. How about Christmas night?"

His heartbeat seemed to be the loudest thing in the silence of the garage. He'd been holding onto hope, but this didn't sound like an invitation to Christmas dinner. "What are we talking about?"

"I don't know if you have a family thing with your mother—"

"She'll be having dinner with some family friends down in Portsmouth."

"Oh, so then you can meet me later? After all the family festivities die down?"

"Here?"

"Right here." She smiled, then bit her lower lip. "Sam, I'm sorry I can't hang here tonight, but this just came up all of a sudden and . . . and if I don't act now, it could all blow up in my face." The way her eyes danced with light, it was clear that her excitement outweighed any regrets.

She looked beautiful tonight, her face tinged with color and her eyes bright. It broke Sam's heart to know this would be his last chance to see her.

But he'd made himself a promise, and it was time to man up. It was all for the best.

Still, he'd never forget her. Bright eyes and silken hair. Quicksilver laugh and lips that set his senses on fire. His Jo.

"Kiss me good-bye," she said, stepping into his arms and pressing her body against his. "And I'll see you in my dreams tonight."

He would see her in his dreams tonight and every night, but he wouldn't ruin her Christmas now with the truth. Soon enough, she'd know how it was going to be.

For now, he dipped his head into the glow of her happiness, touched his lips to hers, and held Jo Truman one last time.

Chapter 14

The door bells jingled, and two little boys peered into the shop. "Is he here yet? Is Santa here?" the bigger kid asked eagerly.

"Not until noon," Jo called from behind the counter, where there was a line of customers three deep for last-minute gifts and stocking stuffers.

Ava went to the door and stared the boys down. "I told you. Santa will be here at twelve."

"Okay." They ducked away and closed the door, which they'd done half a dozen times before that morning.

"Where'd all these kids come from?" Molly asked.

"School's out, and Santa is going to be here soon," Jo said. "Also, the firefighters have one of the hook and ladder trucks on display next door. The kids are allowed to climb on it and ring the bell. All that stuff."

"So that's why I keep hearing sirens," Molly said as she wrapped a woman's purchase in holly-printed paper. She jumped when her cell rang loudly in her jeans pocket, hopping from one foot to another, Scotch tape on her fingertips, as she fished it out.

"Sorry about that," she said to her customer, "but it looks like Santa's calling. Hello, Charlie. How's everything? You're joking, right? But we've got kids already waiting to see you, and there's the gig at the inn tonight."

"Doesn't sound good," Jo said. She handed three dollars change to Mary Anne, a longtime employee of the grocery store.

Molly turned to Jo. "Charlie's sick."

Jo winced. "Poor Charlie."

"Something's going around," Mary Anne said. "Two of my kids missed school last week."

"Well, no, I don't want Santa to infect all the kids with strep throat," Molly said, causing Jo to turn to her.

"Little ears are everywhere," Jo reminded her cousin, though most of the little ones were over by the Matchbox car ornaments and the train track. But based on experience, Jo knew the shop would be loaded with kids by noon. In the last week before Christmas, the Santa Claus business had been quite lucrative for Cousins' Christmas Shop, doubling their sales. But today the priority wasn't sales anymore, but the kids. It would be awful to disappoint them.

Jo looked at the clock. In less than an hour, they would have a line of kids streaming through the door, eagerly awaiting a visit with Santa. The question was, who could fill the Santa suit in the back room?

"We need backup," Jo said, and she and Molly launched into a mad search for someone to fill the role. Molly couldn't reach her father, and Pops couldn't get away from the inn on Christmas Eve. Jo was unable to enlist any of her brothers. Their letter carrier Hal was busier than ever, and none of the leads customers gave them panned out.

With time ticking away, Jo called Sam. She figured it was a long shot, but she had to give it a try. But his voice mail kept kicking in. His phone was off. Molly suggested she run over and intercept him at home. Although Jo was hesitant, Molly persisted.

"We are running out of options," Molly said, her eyes wide with alarm. "Make sure you tell him that. And while you're at it, turn on the charm."

Jo knew the way to the house where Sam grew up. She and Shane had picked him up a hundred times for outings. And in the past few weeks, she had thought of stopping by more than once, but then gave Sam his privacy.

She slowed the Jeep as she approached his driveway and saw Sam standing outside his truck, stowing a duffel bag. Perfect timing.

"Stop right there!" She swung out of the Jeep, grinning like a fool at the sight of him. "I've got a proposition for you that I know you're going to hate, but if you do it, I'll love you forever." Quickly, she told him about their sick Santa, and how the kids had been lining up at the shop all week to visit with Santa. "You're my last hope, Sam."

Sam buried his hands in his jacket pockets, staring down at the ground. "I don't know why you even considered me. People don't want their kids exposed to a freak." He gestured to the left side of his head. "This is the sort of thing that'll give kids nightmares."

"Between the fur collar of the suit, the hat, and the beard, the side of your head and neck will be covered. No one will see your injuries, Sam. And think of all the kids you'd be saving from disappointment."

He frowned, shaking his head slowly.

"Oh, come on, Sam. It's Christmas Eve, the last chance these kids will have to see Santa this year." She moved closer and grabbed the lapels of his open jacket. "I know there's a warm heart inside here. Can't you share the love with some little kids this Christmas?"

He lifted his face, and when his eyes connected with

hers, she felt a jolt of fear. There was pain in his eyes; something had happened. "Sam . . . what's wrong?"

He winced, looking away. "I'll do it. I'll be your Santa."

"But that's not it. There's something you're not telling me." She looked beyond him to his truck, where coolers, a footlocker, and other assorted luggage were stacked. "You've been packing." All joy drained from her. This was serious. "Where are you going, Sam?"

His jaw clenched, and he nodded at her Jeep. "You're in a time crunch, right? We'll talk on the way."

Jo wasn't quite sure her legs would support her on the snowpacked driveway, but she made it to the driver's seat and slammed the door with a vengeance.

Sam got in beside her and stared out the window to his right.

"Seat belt on," she demanded. When she heard the click, she popped the Jeep into low gear and headed down the hill. "Looks like you're going on a trip, Sam. A long trip."

"That's right." His tone was neither proud nor regretful. "I'm heading out."

"What about your surgery?"

"I'll live without it."

The stoic approach. She swallowed, refusing to back down. "So where you headed? And when were you going to tell me?"

"I didn't want to ruin your Christmas, though from the look of things, I don't really matter enough to affect your Christmas. Telling me you can squeeze me in after all the other celebrations end? Ay-yeah. Thanks, but no thanks."

"But I wanted to see you on Christmas! Believe me, I daydream about it all the time. It's just not feasible right now. I've got a little girl to raise, and she has got to be my first priority."

"And everyone else can go to hell."

"I never said that. Sam—"

"Save it for someone who cares. We both know you don't want to bring a freak around to the family parties."

"That's not true!"

"I don't hold it against you, Jo. I can deal with the truth. But I can't wait around for you to fit me into your life. I can't be your garage buddy, hiding out in your parents' house. If I can't be in your life, Jo, then I'm out. Way out. I figure Alaska is far enough."

"You're going to Alaska?" She kept her face forward, hoping he didn't see the tears forming in her eyes. "What are you going to do there?"

"Blow some things up to build new highway."

She nodded, as if this were a run-of-the-mill conversation. "Wow. I didn't see this coming."

When he turned away, she quickly dashed the tears from her eyes. "For the record . . ." She cleared her voice. "For the record, I'm not ashamed of the way you look. It's important to me that you believe that, if nothing else. You're gorgeous, Sam." She sucked in a breath. "You always were. Still are."

"Then why do you keep me in the closet?" he asked.

"To protect Ava. Dr. Nora, you know, the famous psychologist? She says that single parents should never bring strangers into the home. It causes all kinds of problems for little kids like Ava, and it's my job to protect her. She's relying on me. So I promised myself I would keep her safe, and keep men out of the house, at least until she goes off to college."

"Really?" He raked his hair back. "That's like, thirteen or fourteen years away."

"I know, but she needs to feel safe in her home."

"And so you were going to try to keep me coming to the garage every night for the next thirteen years?"

"I don't know, Sam. I hadn't thought that far ahead. I just know that I like being with you, and I figured we'd find a way, work something out . . ."

"Were you ever going to discuss this with me?" His voice was flat and void of emotion. "Last time I checked, there were two people in this relationship."

That hurt, maybe because it was true. She felt her mouth pucker, her face twisting to hold back tears. She adjusted her grip on the steering wheel and stared through the windshield, wishing she could hide from him.

Sam was right; she'd treated him unfairly, thinking that he'd be happy waiting at her beck and call. And now, she'd lost him.

She drove into the dancing snow, heading toward a very bittersweet Christmas.

The afternoon was sweet torture for Jo. There was joy in spending time with Sam, watching him handle the rambunctious boys with ease and draw out the more shy kids with patience. Sam was a good listener, and the kids warmed quickly to his deep "Ho, ho, ho," and short stories of life in the North Pole.

They can tell he has a good heart, Jo thought.

And with each touching moment came the sad realization that Sam was leaving.

She'd caught him trying to slip out without saying good-bye. The image of Sam's truck, packed to the gills, made her queasy. She couldn't imagine nights without him.

But then there was Ava to love and protect, and no man was going to displace her daughter.

Her priority would always be Ava.

Ava, who right now was having a candid conversation with Santa Sam.

"Hold on, over there!" Jo called, trying to disentangle herself from wire ornaments. She had managed to keep them apart all afternoon, but now that Sam was on a short break in the back room, Ava seemed to think it her duty to fill him in on the world according to Ava.

"I'm not going to sit on your lap," she told him.

"Really? How come?" he asked.

"I know you're not the real Santa. You're Mommy's friend."

Jo's mouth dropped open as she approached. How did Ava know?

"I'm one of Santa's helpers," Sam told her.

"I know that. And I'm one of Mommy's helpers."

He looked her in the eye. "I know that."

She giggled, then squinted at him. "Oh, no!"

Jo gaped as her daughter reached out to touch Sam's neck.

Ava's slender fingers lifted the left side of Sam's beard so that she could see the red scar underneath. "What happened?"

"I got injured in the war," he said.

"Does it hurt?"

"Not anymore. But sometimes it makes me feel sad." His eyes didn't leave her face. "I can't use that ear anymore."

"Oh. It's a good thing you have the 'nother ear," she said wisely.

"Yeah, that's a good thing."

Ava suddenly noticed Jo watching them. "Mommy, can I have a juice box?"

"How many have you had today?" Jo asked.

"I think . . . three."

"How about some water?" Jo said, her eyes on Sam now.

With all the things she'd known about Sam Norwood, she'd had no idea he'd be so good with children. It made her wonder if Sam wanted kids of his own. Yes, he probably did.

And the thought of him starting a family with someone else killed her.

When Cousins' Christmas Shop closed, Molly, Ava, and Jo ushered Sam across the street to the Woodstock Inn.

"I thought this was about helping out your shop," he said, holding the padded belly in place as he trekked through the snow.

"You were a great help!" Molly said. "But we promised to send our Santa over to the inn to greet the Christmas Eve guests. It's a Woodstock Inn tradition to have Santa attend holiday dinners."

"Oh, goody."

"Don't worry, Sam." Ava took his hand to cross the street, surprising Jo again. "We'll be there with you."

"That will make it much better, Miss Ava."

As Jo stamped her feet on the carpet, she could see through the beveled glass of the front door that the lobby was packed with people. "Something's going on in there," Jo said.

"Another Woodstock Inn tradition?" Sam asked.

"Not that I know of." Jo opened the door, and a few people at the back of the crowd turned to her.

"Hey, Jo. Merry Christmas," Emma Mueller said, clapping her on the shoulder.

"It's wonderful news!" Carmine Giordano shook her

hand, then Molly's, then waved toward the front of the crowd. "Hey, Bob! We got your other daughter back here, along with Santa Claus!"

Laughter rumbled through the room as the crowd parted for the newcomers.

Jo took Ava's hand and ventured ahead, passing people she knew from the school and the grocery store. Her insurance agent beamed a smile at her, as did Mrs. Crisp, the librarian.

"What's going on?"

"Over here, sport." Bob Truman motioned her toward the desk, where he stood with his arm around his wife. Jo saw that the stairs, which swept in a curve over the desk, were covered with family members. Her siblings chatted with their spouses, and their kids elbowed and joked with each other.

"The good news spread like wildfire," Irene said. "People heard that we're buying the inn, and they came out to show their support.

"And I've been telling everyone that your brave action made it all possible, Jo. Not only did you help us raise the money to fulfill our dream, you're keeping the family home in the family. Thanks, honey. We love you."

"And we love the Trumans for keeping the inn open," Carmine Giordano shouted out. "Let's hear it for the Truman family."

In the thunderous applause, Jo turned in a circle and tried to take in the many faces of the community she'd grown up with. This was her town, these people her extended family. She thanked God for showing her a way to keep it all intact.

"Jo . . ." Molly grabbed her by the shoulders. "You didn't tell me. You're buying the house on Bull Moose Road? And Earl is selling the inn to your parents?"

Jo turned to her parents.

"Earl got back to Pops right away," Irene said. "It's a deal." The tears that glistened in her eyes were now tears of joy.

"It's wonderful!" Molly threw her arms around Jo, then around Irene and Pops. Thus began the hug fest.

"Thank you, everyone, for coming out on this snowy night." Pops's booming voice carried through the lobby as people began to talk and laugh in smaller groups. "And let's remember the joyous event we celebrate this season, the birth of our Savior. Merry Christmas!"

"Merry Christmas!" came the chorus of friendly voices.

Jo hugged Tommy, who hoisted Ava into his arms.

"How about a Shirley Temple to celebrate? Huh?" he said.

"Oh, Tommy." Jo winced. "The sugar and all that red dye. She'll be bouncing off the walls for hours."

"So? She's going to midnight mass, right?"

Ava's eyes grew wide. "Can I go, Mommy?"

"We'll see." Jo smiled as Tommy carried her daughter off, Ava waving over his shoulder.

"And Jo." Tommy turned back. "You might own the garage, but the 'stang is still mine."

"We'll see about that," she called after him.

When she turned back, Sam stood in her path, a wide swathe of red. Only, he had removed his head gear. Stripped of his hat and beard, he stood before her as Sam. Gorgeous, kind Sam. Great sense of humor. Sexy kisser. And, of late, her closest friend.

"Don't go." She pressed a fist to her mouth, then rushed toward him and grabbed his white fur lapel. "Please don't go. I've fallen in love with you, Sam, and . . . how often can a person get that lucky?"

"And you think you could love me as I am? Even when I'm not wearing that dorky cap?"

"Please . . . I'll burn that cap. I love the man you've

become. An artist and mechanic. My personal therapist. A patient guy. A funny guy. Tell me you'll stay."

"I'll stay, if you marry me."

"What?"

"It's not as if we just met, Jo. And you're right about protecting Ava. If you're going to bring me into your family, if she gets to know me, I want her to know she can count on me. I want to be her father. And I think she sort of likes me."

"She'll like you even more when she gets to know you."

"I'm counting on it." He plunked the Santa cap on her head and spoke into her ear. "And I'd like to give her some brothers and sisters."

"Oh my gosh, I was thinking that, too!"

He lifted her into his arms and their lips met in a bold, heady kiss. "I love you, Jo," he whispered as her feet left the ground.

"And I love you."

When she closed her eyes to kiss him again, she saw herself and Sam as if from afar, two people embracing inside the Woodstock Inn. She imagined God watching over their little town, as if looking into a snow globe where love, comfort, and joy fell like snow.

And it was good.

Christmas on Cape Cod

NAN ROSSITER

Every good gift and every perfect gift is from above . . .
—James 1:17

Chapter 1

"Dad, wake up!" There was a short pause and then the same soft voice whispered again with more urgency. "Dad . . . Dad, wake up! We have to go find a tree! You said we had to get up early." This time the plea was accompanied by gentle nudging and prodding. Asa Coleman opened one eye and squinted at the little face, which was inches from his nose. The face smiled. "Time to get up!" it announced cheerfully.

Asa closed his eyes, pulled his pillow over his head, and pretended to fall back asleep. He heard a small sigh of frustration and, from under the pillow, pictured the little boy standing in the middle of the braided rug with his hands on his hips, the arms and legs of his new pajamas rolled up to fit his small frame. To add to the boy's dilemma, Asa let out a loud snore. Almost immediately, there was a determined tug on the blanket . . . but Asa just pulled back and snored again.

It was quiet for a moment and he began to wonder what new plan was being hatched. He lay still, waiting, and felt the mattress press down under the weight of two small feet. He felt the two feet planting themselves firmly on either side of his legs and then he felt their weight shift as the small body leaned forward to take hold of the covers. Another moment passed and he could barely contain his laughter. But . . . just as the unsuspecting perpetrator was about to give the covers a tremendous heave . . . Asa threw off his pillow, spun around, and tackled him. The surprised boy giggled helplessly as Asa bounced him onto the bed and tickled him mercilessly.

"Stop, Dad! Dad, stop!" the squealing, squirming boy pleaded breathlessly. "I'm going to wet my pajamas!"

"What?!" Asa teased. "You mounted an attack on the enemy without going to the head first? What were you thinking, man?"

The little fellow giggled, shrugged, and sputtered, "I don't know!"

Asa picked him up and set him on the floor. "Go . . ." He watched the blond-haired boy run down the hall and wondered if he'd ever get used to being called "Dad." He looked out the window and glanced at his bedside clock—not even six yet—Noah certainly was an early riser! Just then, he came running back down the hall, full tilt, and bowled his father onto the bed, attempting to return the tickle. Asa laughed, feigning surrender and protest, and tried to protect himself. Noah just giggled, truly believing he had the upper hand—until Asa turned the tables and the little fellow found himself on the bottom again, getting the worst of it.

"Hey, what's the idea of waking up your old man before it's even light out?" Asa interrogated playfully.

Noah was trying to catch his breath, and sputtered, "You said we had to find a tree!"

"And . . . how can we find a tree in the dark?" Asa teased.

"Well, we have to have breakfast first," Noah explained matter-of-factly.

"We do?"

"And you said we have to pack."

"Pack what?" Asa continued to tease.

"Clothes . . . and Christmas presents!" Noah answered with a beaming grin.

"Oh . . . no need to worry 'bout that. . . . I think you're just getting coal for Christmas."

Noah looked dismayed.

"Well . . . have you been good?" Asa asked with a serious face.

Noah nodded. "Mm . . . hmm."

Asa cupped his chin thoughtfully. "I don't know . . . I guess we'll have to wait and see . . ."

"You're just teasing," Noah said hopefully.

Asa shrugged, raised his hands palms up, and smiled. Then he sat on the edge of the bed and yawned. "So, what're you making for breakfast?"

"Da-ad!" Noah moaned despairingly. "*You're* making breakfast!"

"I am? Well, what am I making?"

"Hmmm," Noah said, cupping his own chin in thought. "How 'bout French toast?"

"Are you goin' to help?"

"Sure!" Noah said, hopping off the bed and pulling Asa by the hand. Asa slowly relented, stopping only to pull on his jeans, and then shuffled to the kitchen.

"First things first," he said sleepily, reaching into the cabinet for the coffee.

"Okay," Noah said, opening the fridge and taking out the milk, orange juice, and butter. "How many eggs?" he asked.

"Two." Asa answered, absently measuring the coffee.

Noah balanced the eggs in one hand and then reached into the back of the fridge for a small jug of maple syrup.

"Gettin' low," he announced with authority.

"Is there enough for today?"

Noah shook the bottle and peered inside. Even though he couldn't really see how much was left, he answered with optimism, "I think so."

With the coffee perking cheerfully, Asa pulled out the pancake griddle, set it on the stovetop, and lit the burners. Then he reached for the bread. "How hungry?"

"Two," Noah answered with a nonchalant shrug. Asa took out four slices of bread and Noah pushed an old oak chair over to the counter. Asa set the bowl in front of him and Noah looked up in surprise.

"Go ahead . . . you know how."

Noah grinned and reached for an egg, but, just as he cracked it, there was a knock at the door. He looked up and the eggshell fell into the bowl. With egg still dripping from his fingers, he hopped down and went to the door and opened it, smearing the knob in the process.

Maddie peered around the door. "Am I too early?" Then she answered her own question as she unzipped her jacket. "Actually . . . looks like I'm just in time!"

Asa smiled at the rosy, freckled cheeks of his old friend and noticed that they were wet. "Is it snowing?" he asked.

"Just started . . . but not too hard." She closed the door behind her and then looked from her hand to the door-knob.

"Thank the chef," Asa said, smiling and nodding toward Noah, who was back up on his chair, fishing out the eggshells. Maddie rinsed her hands and Asa handed her a steaming cup of coffee.

"Mmmm, thanks. I knew there was a reason I liked you!" She blew softly on the coffee and a cloud of steam rose around her face. "Noah said I had to be here *very* early if I wanted to help pick out a tree—so, here I am!"

"Well, you're here just in time for my world-famous French toast!" Noah announced happily, pouring milk into the bowl.

"Easy there," Asa warned, watching the flow and wondering if Noah had picked up the phrase "world-famous" from his grandfather. He handed a third egg to him and took out two more slices of bread. "You should probably use a measuring cup," he said, but Noah just shrugged and cracked the last egg. "*And* you should probably wash your hands!"

Noah nodded, wiped his hands on his pajamas, splashed the eggbeater into the bowl, and began to churn with all his might. While he was still churning, Asa trickled vanilla into the mixture and sprinkled cinnamon on the froth of bubbles.

Noah stopped and looked up at him with a serious face. "*You* should probably be using a measuring spoon . . ."

Asa looked down at his little counterpart. "And *you* should be careful . . . or you might get another tickle!"

Noah grinned and continued beating, and Asa reached over his head for a sifter, which was kept on an old, chipped plate with a painting of Nauset Light on it. The purpose of the plate was to catch any confectioner's sugar that fell through the screen bottom. It was something Asa had learned in the kitchen of his childhood, but, even so, every time he reached for the sifter, he wondered if all sifters were kept on old, chipped plates. Still holding it in his hands, he looked at Maddie. "Maddie, where do you keep your sifter?"

Maddie, who'd been sitting at the old oak table in the cheerful kitchen, sipping her coffee and watching them work together, smiled at the odd question. "On a plate, of course."

"Does your plate have a chip in it?"

"Yup . . . and a painting of the Franklin Pierce Homestead on it. I don't think sifters work very well after they get wet. My mom washed hers once and, the next time she used it, brown rust sifted out."

Asa smiled . . . *mystery solved!*

Maddie stood up. "Here I am, not helping at all. Do you boys have a job for me?"

Asa glanced over his shoulder. "Want to set the table?"

"Okay," she said. Maddie set out plates, napkins, and silverware, poured orange juice, and then stood by and watched as Asa showed Noah how to turn the French toast. She smiled at his gentle patience and thought, *He makes a good dad.*

While it was still on the griddle, Noah cut the French toast diagonally, and then he arranged it in layers on a plate. He started to hand the plate to Maddie, but Asa stopped him. "Aren't you forgetting something?"

Noah looked puzzled for a second and then his face lit up. "Oh, yeah! Snow!" He hopped down and sifted confectioner's sugar onto Maddie's French toast. "Just like at the hotel on Lake Sunapee!" he said with a grin.

"Thank you!" Maddie said, kissing the top of his head. "It looks absolutely yummy!"

She sat down to wait for them, but Asa said, "Go ahead, while it's hot." She picked up the syrup, noted the light weight of the container, and drizzled it sparingly on her plate. She took a bite and, with a full mouth, said, "Oh my goodness, Noah, this is the best French toast I've ever had!"

Noah looked up at Asa and beamed. "It's world famous!"

After breakfast, Asa cleared the table and filled the sink with hot, sudsy water. Outside the kitchen window, patches of morning sun flickered through the trees and shimmered on the cold gray ribbon of river that wandered through the property. Tiny sparkles of snow danced in the chilly air and melted when they landed. Asa glanced up at the clock. "Noah, if you're finished, you need to get dressed, make your bed, and pack up. Don't forget warm socks and underwear—and the new pants and sweater for church tonight—In fact, why don't you just make a pile and I'll check it first."

Maddie refilled her coffee cup, slipped the dish towel from the oven handle, and stood ready to dry. Noah brought his plate over to the sink and pulled on Asa's shirt. Asa leaned down and Noah whispered, "Are we goin' to have time to go to the Birdwatcher's?"

Asa whispered back, "We will if we get going soon."

Noah grinned and raced down the hall. Maddie looked at Asa questioningly, but he just smiled. "It's a secret," he said. They stood side by side, washing and drying, and since Maddie knew her way around the kitchen, she put everything away as she went. As she reached for the last juice glass, she looked over at Asa's handsome face, lit by the sun. She recalled the many suppers and bottles of wine they had shared in his kitchen . . . and sighed softly. Even though they had often talked into the night, Maddie had never been there for breakfast . . . and she'd never seen Asa's face in the early morning sunlight.

As she dried the plates, she thought back to the rainy summer day when they'd first met. Asa had just finished his freshman year of college and Maddie had just graduated from high school. In the six years since then, they had both earned degrees in education. Asa had found a job almost immediately teaching English at the local high school; and Maddie, inspired by her brother Tim, born with Down syndrome, had focused on special education and had found a part-time position in the elementary school.

Noah's voice interrupted her thoughts. "Da-ad . . . got my pile!"

"Okay," Asa called back, rinsing out the sink. "Be right there." He smiled at Maddie. "Wish I could pack so quickly!" He dried his hands on the towel Maddie was holding. "Are you all ready, too?"

"Yup . . ." she answered. "I packed last night."

"Well," he explained with a grin, "men never pack 'til the morning *of* . . ."

"Well, you better hurry up." As she finished drying the silverware, she listened to Asa and Noah reviewing Noah's pile and, by the time she was hanging the damp towel back on the oven handle, he was lugging his duffel into the kitchen. He plopped it by the door with a thud. "All ready!" he announced matter-of-factly.

"Did you remember your dad's present?" Maddie whispered.

"Whoops!" Noah exclaimed, and ran back down the hall.

Twenty minutes later, Asa had taken a quick shower, thrown some clothes in a bag, and was locking the cabin. Meanwhile, Maddie was helping Noah pile their bags beside two big cardboard boxes already in the back of Asa's old Chevy pickup. "Must be lots of coal in these boxes," Noah said loudly, trying to peer inside.

Asa came over and eyed him. "Those are for Grandma and Grampa." At the mention of Noah's parents, Maddie suddenly remembered two pies she'd made the night before, apple and pumpkin, as well as the ingredients for the special holiday drink recipe that had been passed down for generations through her Swedish family. She retrieved everything from her car, and Asa and Noah peered inside the pie carrier. In unison, they expressed their anticipation for a taste, but Maddie quickly closed the top and wedged it into a corner of the truck bed. Asa cushioned it with his bag and then looked in the bag of drink ingredients—port wine and dried fruit.

"Hmmm . . . this looks interesting!" he said with a grin. He put the bag in the truck and looked around. "Well, is that everything?"

"Except for the tree!" Noah declared.

"Mmmm, except for the tree," Asa repeated to himself, wondering if there was going to be room for a tree . . .

They all piled into the cab with Noah in the middle, and Asa looked over Noah's head at Maddie. "What do you think? John is north of here . . . but not too far."

"If you think we have time."

Asa nodded and turned on the truck.

Maddie teased, "You just want to see Sadie!"

Asa smiled, knowing she was right.

Chapter 2

Asa had liked Maddie's brother from the moment he met him, but, even more than he liked John, he *loved* Sadie. Sadie was John's black Lab and she reminded Asa of Martha, the Lab he had growing up. Sadie, like Martha, was an old sweetheart with beautiful brown eyes. Whenever he went with Maddie to visit her brother and his family, Sadie would greet Asa with such unabashed abandon that, if she'd been a woman, her behavior would have bordered on embarrassing. After greeting him, Sadie would follow Asa around until he finally sat down, and then she would rest her chin on his thigh and gaze at him adoringly while he stroked her head. Asa would look into her intelligent eyes and see the same unconditional love and profound understanding with which Martha's eyes had glistened.

John would look at the two of them and say, "Asa, you should just take Sadie home with you. She's obviously head-over-heels . . . I mean, head-over-*paws* . . . in love with you . . . *and* she just mopes around after you leave."

Asa would laugh and consider the offer, but he knew

he could never take Sadie away from John and his family. So, instead, when he left, Asa would take Sadie's beautiful head in his hands, look in her loving eyes, and promise, "I'll be back, ol' girl . . . I'll be back." Then, he'd kiss her on top of her head. At these moments, the memory of the last time he'd said good-bye to Martha was never far from his mind.

They pulled up to the barn and Sadie was waiting, tail wagging, as if she'd been expecting them. John's two older sons looked up and smiled and John came out of the barn and waved. As soon as Asa climbed out, Sadie began to wiggle. Asa knelt down and greeted her, "My goodness! It's good to see you, *too*!" he said softly. She licked his face and hands and turned in happy circles, beating his face with her tail. Then she spied Noah getting out of the truck, too, and bounded over to him, just about knocking him over. It had become obvious to everyone in Maddie's family that ever since Noah had come to live with Asa, he had become a very close second in Sadie's book of true loves.

"Hi, Sadie!" Noah said as his face got washed.

Asa stood up and shook John's hand and the boys came over to shake hands, too. Then John gave his younger sister a hug. When they stepped apart, Maddie looked at her nephews. "Well, don't tell me you two are getting too old for hugs!" she said. They both grinned shyly and complied. Then Noah gave Mikey and John-John high fives and John a big hug. "Whoa," John exclaimed, hefting him up. "You are getting heavy! What the heck did you have for breakfast?"

"Just French toast and orange juice," Noah answered with an innocent grin.

John tousled his hair and turned back to his sister.

"So . . . you're not going to Ma's for Christmas?" Maddie shook her head and tried very hard to not reveal her regret in front of Asa. She had been so thrilled when he'd asked her to go to the Cape that she'd said yes without thinking. Afterward, though, it dawned on her that she'd never been away from home on Christmas . . . and, as the youngest of eight, she'd have seven siblings to answer to—not to mention four grandparents, two parents, several aunts and uncles, and thirteen nieces and nephews. The Carlson house was always full of excitement and people—especially on holidays!

Maddie tried to redeem herself by explaining that she'd already delivered all her presents and John smiled. "It's all right, Maddie. I'm just giving you a hard time." He looked at his boys. "Right, guys? We'll manage without Aunt Maddie . . . even though we'll probably have to endure Uncle Jesse playing the Christmas carols." The boys grimaced and Maddie laughed. She knew all about their brother's piano skills and it hadn't occurred to her that he'd be filling in. "I'm sorry," she said with a half smile. John put his arm around her. "I'm just teasing!" he said. "And I'm sure you'll have a good time with these two fellas." Maddie nodded and John kissed her on the head.

"So," he said, kneeling down in front of Noah, "are you here to pick out a Christmas tree?"

"Yes, sir," Noah answered, stroking Sadie's silky head.

"Well, then, you're going to have to find the hidden field. Only special people know about it."

Noah's eyes grew wide. "Is it really hidden?"

"Yup," John answered. "You have to go all the way to the top of the dirt road and look for an old wooden gate." He reached into his pocket and pulled out a worn key attached to an equally worn key ring with a pewter Christmas tree attached to it. "This key opens the gate." He smiled. "*But* . . . the key only works for special people." Noah nodded solemnly as John handed the key to him. "Don't lose it!"

"I won't," Noah said, clutching it tightly in his fist.

John stood and Maddie and Asa smiled at him.

"Will it be busy today?" Asa asked.

John nodded. "This morning will be . . . but it'll be quiet later." He looked down the valley and spied two cars already bumping along the dusty road. He turned to the boys. "You two better get up the hill with the saws."

Mikey and John-John nodded and gathered their tools. As they started to hike up the hill, Asa called, "Would you like a ride?" They grinned and hopped into the bed of Asa's truck instead.

Asa shook hands with John, thanked him, and wished him a Merry Christmas, and Maddie gave her brother another long hug. "Tell everyone Merry Christmas for me, too!"

"Will do!" he answered. "Merry Christmas to you, too!" He lifted Noah into the back of the truck with the boys and said, "Pick out a good one!" Noah nodded as Mikey and John-John made room between them.

John handed an old bow saw to Maddie. "Just hang the key and saw on the hook in the barn on your way down." Maddie nodded and climbed into the cab while Asa knelt to say good-bye to Sadie. They all waved to John, turned onto the dirt road, and headed up, passing field after field of Christmas trees. Asa marveled at the variety of sizes, shapes, and types, until Maddie pointed to a clearing with a large grassy area and they pulled in. The boys gave Noah another high five, picked up their tools, and hopped down.

They waved to Asa and Maddie, and Mikey hollered,

"Thank you," while John-John shouted, "Merry Christmas!" Then they trudged up to the staging area where a John Deere tractor was parked and a tree netter was set up near a wooden rack for the saws. Asa and Maddie called out, "Merry Christmas!" and then Asa looked in back to see if Noah was all right by himself. He gave him a questioning thumbs-up or -down, and Noah returned an affirmative thumbs-up and sank a little lower in the bed. They passed several more fields before the road narrowed, heading into the woods.

At the very top, just as John described, was a gnarled wooden gate, almost hidden by briars and fire bush. Noah hopped down, clutching the key, and Maddie climbed out to help him. The old lock was rusty, but, when Noah slid the key in and turned, it clicked open easily.

"*You* must be very special!" Maddie said with a smile. "That old lock never opens on the first try!" Noah grinned and tucked the key carefully back in his pocket and Maddie slipped the chain from around the gate and left it hanging on the post. Noah pushed the gate open and Asa drove through. Then Noah closed the gate and he and Maddie climbed back in the cab. They continued a little farther until the dirt road opened into a rolling meadow with a breathtaking view of the valley. The sky above was a vast, bright canopy of blue. Noah peered out the window and exclaimed, "Wow! You can see forever!" Then he looked across the meadow. "Holy cow! Look at the size of that Christmas tree! It looks like it belongs in Rockefeller Center!" Asa looked in the direction Noah was pointing and there, at the top of the meadow, seeming to overlook the entire world, stood a majestic, towering Norway spruce.

"Wow!" Asa agreed. "That tree must be ninety feet tall!"

"Have you ever asked the Rockefellers if they want it, Maddie?" Noah blurted out innocently.

Maddie laughed. "No, Noah, we haven't. All our friends ask that same question, but we could never cut it down. It's too old and beautiful. My great-grandfather planted it when my grandfather was born. There's a picture in the barn of him holding my grandfather and standing beside it when it was just a sapling." She paused. "The life span of a Norway spruce is about the same as a human being— eighty to a hundred years—but we're hoping it lives longer . . . it's still very healthy." She pointed to another magnificent tree nearby that was at least sixty feet tall. "My grandfather planted that tree when my dad was born. And, after that, my dad started planting trees for each of us! They're all marked—and not for cutting. But, at the rate our family's growing, I think all the trees up here will eventually be off limits!" Noah was very intrigued by the idea of having a tree planted in honor of one's birth.

"Where's your tree, Maddie?" he asked.

"I'll show you," she said with a smile. Asa turned the truck off and they climbed out. Maddie led them across the field to a group of eight trees, glistening in the morning sunlight, and gently touched the needles of the smallest one. And, although it was smaller than the others, it was still an impressive twenty feet. "This is it!" she announced proudly. There was a marker on the ground, engraved with her name and birth date.

"It's beautiful," Noah proclaimed, admiring the grand tree.

"Yes, it is," Asa agreed.

Noah looked at the marker and exclaimed, "My birthday's in June, too!"

"I know!" Maddie said, smiling at him. Then she looked at her watch. "Well, enough about family trees . . . we're here to find a Christmas tree!" She pointed down the hill. "And we can pick from any of those."

"Okay!" Noah called, sprinting down the hill. Maddie and Asa followed.

"How tall are you thinking?" Maddie asked.

"Only six or seven feet . . . the ceilings aren't very high."

Maddie nodded and they continued to walk, admiring the countless balsams, Frasers, and white firs as they passed.

They had just stopped to take a closer look at a six-foot balsam when Noah called from several rows over. "Dad, Maddie, how 'bout this one?"

They found him standing next to a tall, perfectly shaped blue spruce. "Its needles are kind of prickly, but it's beautiful!" he offered in his most convincing voice.

"It *is* nice," Asa agreed, "but I think it's a little too tall . . ."

"Oh," Noah said, disappointed.

Maddie had wandered down the row a little ways. "What do you guys think of this one?" Noah turned to Maddie. She was standing next to a fat, lush, dark green Douglas fir. "The needles aren't prickly and it's nice and full."

Noah nodded thoughtfully, walking toward her. As he reached out to touch the soft needles, his eye caught something hidden in the branches. He gently lifted the nearest branch and there, tucked safely away from wind and weather, was a small, meticulously woven nest. It even had a piece of the red fabric that was used to tag Christmas trees woven into it. "Look," he whispered in amazement.

Maddie looked and softly murmured, "Ohh . . ." She stepped back so Asa could see, too. Then she said, "My dad always says, 'If you find a nest in a Christmas tree, you will have a year full of blessings!' "

"Well, this is the one, then!" Noah exclaimed happily. "As long as the birds aren't using it anymore . . ."

"I'm sure they're done using it," Maddie assured him.

She held the saw out to Asa and he nodded to Noah. "Want to give it a try?"

Noah grinned and, taking the saw, crouched down beside the tree while Asa lifted the lower branches.

Twenty minutes later, after they had all taken a turn with the saw—and after a bit of rearranging in the back of the truck—the Christmas tree was loaded, the gate was locked, and they were bumping back down the road. When they passed the clearing where they'd dropped off the boys, Noah counted thirteen cars. "Looks like they're busy!" he surmised.

Asa stopped at the barn and Noah reached into his pocket for the key. Maddie said, "Be right back." She went into the barn hoping to find her brother. She hung up the saw, and found him setting up a cash box. She handed the key to him and asked if he still had any of the little saplings left that people often bought as gifts. He nodded and pointed to a table in the corner. "Any Norway?" she asked, a little disappointed by the selection. John pointed to a scraggly little tree and Maddie laughed. "That looks like a Charlie Brown tree!"

"It'll grow," he assured her.

"Okay." She hesitated. "Oh, and do you have any syrup?"

He took a quart jug off a shelf in back. "Anything else?" he teased. "Would you like my firstborn, too?"

"Sure," Maddie said with a grin. "I'd love to have Mikey around!" She paused, looking at the tree and syrup. "Actually, do you have something I can put all this in?"

John found a box and put some newspaper around the pot to keep it upright. Maddie closed up the box and gave her brother another hug. "Thank you for everything," she said softly.

"Have fun!" he said, looking in his younger sister's eyes. "And don't worry! One of these days, that boy will wake up and realize what a wonderful girl he has in front of him."

Maddie feigned confusion. "I don't know what you're talking about!"

John nodded with an easy smile. "I think you do . . ."

Maddie tried to be discreet as she tucked the box next to the pie carrier in the truck bed, but, when she got in the cab, Asa and Noah both looked at her questioningly. She just smiled and said, "It's a secret!"

As they turned onto the highway, Maddie looked out the window and thought about what John had said . . . *were her feelings that obvious?* Her mind wandered to the summer day when she'd first met Asa. She'd been working on a project in the Howe Library when she'd first noticed the slender blond-haired boy shelving books . . . but it wasn't until a couple of days later that she learned his name.

A young woman had come into the library looking for "Asa" and Maddie had overheard the librarian say that she expected him soon. The woman had asked if it would be all right to wait and the librarian had nodded. She'd found a seat in a faded Queen Anne's chair in the corner and seemed to be passing the time by reading, but as the minutes turned into hours, the woman had become increasingly captivated by the pendulum of the library's old Seth Thomas clock.

At last, she had stood, thanked the librarian, and said she had to leave. She tucked the note she'd written into a book she was carrying and, when she pulled on the heavy oak door, Maddie suddenly realized that the woman was pregnant . . . *and* that she seemed to be in pain. Soon after, Maddie had left the library, too. Almost immediately, she had encountered Asa and, when she stopped him to tell him that a woman had been waiting for him, his blue eyes had filled with dismay and sadness . . .

Chapter 3

"Should I wake him?" Maddie whispered over the wispy blond head that was nestled on her shoulder.

Asa looked over. "I guess you better. He said he wanted to be awake when we crossed the bridge . . . *and* he's not going to sleep tonight if he keeps napping."

Maddie shook Noah gently. "Noah, wake up," she said softly. Noah stirred and opened his eyes. "We're crossing the bridge."

Noah sat up and looked out at the canal and, as they reached the other side, he looked for the CAPE COD sign made out of evergreen bushes. "I just love that sign," he said with a contented sigh.

"Me, too," agreed Asa.

"How much longer?" Noah asked with a yawn.

"Less than an hour," Asa replied. "But don't fall back asleep."

"I won't," he said with a sleepy smile, and leaned against Maddie's arm again.

"Want to sing some Christmas carols?" Maddie suggested.

"Sure!" said Noah, perking up. "How 'bout 'Jingle Bells'?"

"Okay," agreed Asa, "but you two have to carry the tune."

As they drove along winter quiet Route 6, they sang every carol they could think of and, before they knew it, they were turning onto the rotary in Eastham. Asa stopped singing and looked over at Noah. "I think we better run our errand before we go to the house or they might not be open."

Noah looked out the window to see where they were. "Okay," he agreed as Asa turned off the rotary. A quarter of a mile down, they pulled into the parking lot of a long gray shop with a porch out front. The sign above the porch read THE BIRDWATCHER'S GENERAL STORE and had a painting on it of a cartoonish figure looking through binoculars.

"Can I come in?" Maddie asked.

Noah looked at Asa and Asa winked at him. "Well . . . you can . . . if you don't follow us . . ."

Maddie gave Noah a puzzled look. "Hmmm . . . what are you two up to?"

"Oh, nothing . . ." replied Noah with a shrug and a grin.

Asa held the door for them and Maddie noticed the store's funny hours: 9:03–5:57. Underneath was a hand-written addendum: "We will be closing at 2:33 on Christmas Eve . . . have a Merry!" She glanced at her watch—it was ten after two—*good thing they'd stopped . . . Noah would've been disappointed!* They went inside and Noah pointed to the left. "Maddie, they have really good books over there . . ."

Maddie smiled. "Well, you know me! I can never pass up a really good book!" Noah grinned at her, reached for Asa's hand, and pulled him in the opposite direction.

While she perused the collection of books, Maddie glanced over at them a couple of times and saw them conferring in a tucked away corner.

Moments later, they were by her side and Asa was asking, "Find anything?"

Maddie looked up. "I did . . ." She held up a little paperback titled *That Quail, Robert*. "It's a true story," she explained. "And it happened on Cape Cod! I thought I'd get it for my mom's birthday."

Asa read the synopsis and approved. "Looks good!"

He handed the book back to Maddie and she eyed the two of them suspiciously. "So, are you two sneaky people all set?" Noah nodded with his hands conspicuously behind his back. "Okay . . . well, let me pay for this."

"We'll wait in the truck," Asa said as Noah backed his way toward the door.

When Maddie climbed in next to them, she said, "It'd be nice to come back here again when we have more time." She eyed Noah. "I was only able to look at the books." Noah just grinned and looked out the window.

Asa turned the truck back onto Route 28 and soon turned left onto Beach Road. Maddie looked over at him. "I keep meaning to ask you . . . how come your parents aren't having Christmas at their summer place?"

Asa hesitated and glanced at Noah before answering. "Well, they thought about it and decided that Noah might enjoy having it at this house because this house was left to him when Nate died . . . and they don't want it to just sit empty until Noah's an adult. They want us to continue to use it."

Maddie nodded, silently wondering at the wisdom of the impromptu decision. She looked out the window and tried to grasp how complicated it must be for Noah to understand. *First, his mother dies in childbirth and, at barely six years old, he loses the wonderful man he's called "Dad" to a sudden heart attack . . . and, within days, another man steps into his life and gently tells him that he is his dad. What does a little kid do with all that?* Maddie looked at Noah leaning against Asa . . . *well, he certainly seems to be adjusting . . .* and she looked at Asa . . . *and he seems to be adjusting, too!* One of her mom's favorite sayings suddenly slipped into her mind—*the Lord works in mysterious ways . . .* it was definitely true in this case!

Asa turned onto the sandy driveway that led up to an old bow-roof Cape overlooking the ocean. He glanced up at the massive center chimney and felt his heart pound. He thought back to the last time he was there, and realized that it had also been for Christmas. . . . *Seems like a lifetime ago!* He parked the truck and looked up to see his dad standing in the doorway. Noah climbed out and raced to him, jumping into his arms. "Merry Christmas, Grampa!"

Samuel Coleman wrapped his little grandson in a big bear hug. "Merry Christmas to you!" he returned. "How's my little guy?"

"Great!" Noah exclaimed. "Come and see the Christmas tree we picked out—it's from Maddie's family's farm." Noah pulled him toward the truck, but Samuel released him so he could greet Maddie and Asa with hugs, too.

"Merry Christmas!" he said heartily. "It's so good to see you! You look great!" Over the years, Samuel had met Maddie on several occasions and he knew what a good friend she'd been to Asa. He had decided she was pretty special . . . and he often wondered when his son would wake up and take notice.

"You look great, too," Asa said with a warm smile. "Gettin' a little white," he teased, motioning to his father's snowy mane.

"Yes, I know . . . don't remind me!" Samuel replied, running his hand through his hair. "It's all thanks to you!"

"Grampa, come see the tree!" Noah called from the tailgate.

Samuel turned, "I'm coming!" He walked over and surveyed the tree, which filled the back of the truck. "Wow! That's a beauty!" He eyed Noah. "You sure know how to pick 'em!"

Noah grinned, nodded, and began to bubble over with the details of the search. "Maddie helped and . . . you know what else?" Samuel looked up. "There's a bird's nest in it! And Maddie said her dad always says that if you find a nest in a Christmas tree, the year ahead will be full of blessings—so we had to pick this tree!" Samuel nodded, completely caught up in his grandson's excitement. He was still smiling when Sarah came over, too, wiping her hands on her apron. "Grandma!" Noah shouted, jumping down and just about knocking her over with a hug. "Did you see the tree?" He began to recount the story again, this time adding the part about the magnificent tree that belonged in Rockefeller Plaza.

Asa looked at his dad and smiled. "He's a little excited . . ."

Samuel put his arm around his son. "He's supposed to be!"

An hour later, the handsome little tree was in a stand full of water in the corner of the living room with its best side out, and Maddie and Noah were sitting at the kitchen table, threading popcorn and cranberries for decoration, munching down almost as much popcorn as they threaded. Asa and Samuel took advantage of Noah being busy and made room in the closet under the stairs for the boxes of

Christmas gifts. They also carried in the duffels, Maddie's suitcase, the pie carrier, and Maddie's bag of secret ingredients. Samuel peered into the brown paper bag and raised his eyebrows. Sarah, for her part, suddenly noticed how much popcorn was being consumed, and asked if they'd had lunch yet. When Asa admitted that they hadn't, she eyed him in dismay.

"Why didn't you say something?"

Before Asa could protest, she was making roast beef sandwiches and coleslaw on rye bread and pouring tall glasses of sweet, cold cider. While they were still eating these, she also set out a plate of warm mincemeat cookies and brewed a fresh pot of coffee.

Asa reached for a cookie with his free hand and smiled at his mom. "You've been busy!" He took a bite and closed his eyes. "Mmmm . . . Maddie, have you ever had a mincemeat cookie fresh out of the oven?" Maddie smiled, amused by Asa's apparent rapture, and revealed that she hadn't. Noah picked one out for her and Maddie graciously accepted. Seemingly unaware that everyone was watching, she took a generous bite and tasted the sweet warm brandied fruit. "Mmmm!" she murmured, "Mrs. Coleman, these are wonderful."

Sarah smiled. "Thank you, Maddie. You can take some home with you." Asa looked up, feigning alarm, but Sarah laughed and assured him. "Don't worry, Asa, I'll fix a plate for you and Noah, too." Asa elbowed Noah with a grin and a thumbs-up and Noah returned the gesture and took a big bite out of his cookie.

Samuel reached over Noah's head and took a cookie, too. He looked at Asa. "By the way, which service would you guys like to go to? I know we usually go to the eleven o'clock, but there's also a service at eight for families. Your mother and I thought Noah might enjoy it. And then, of course," he eyed Noah and whispered with his hand cupped beside his mouth, "you-know-who can get to bed early . . . so you-know-who can come . . ."

Noah's eyes grew wide. "Who, Grampa? Do you mean Santa?"

"Santa?" Samuel said, feigning ignorance. "Who's Santa?" He looked at Sarah. "Are you expecting someone named Santa for dinner, dear?"

"Grampa, Santa doesn't come for dinner!" Noah sounded exasperated. *Didn't his grampa know who Santa Claus was?* "He comes for Christmas cookies . . . like these . . ." he explained, holding up a mincemeat cookie.

"He *likes* mincemeat?" Samuel asked.

"Mmm . . . hmm . . . ," Noah nodded.

"But they're *my* favorite. Couldn't we give him Fig Newtons or Oreos?"

Noah shook his head with authority. "No . . . they have to be *homemade* Christmas cookies . . . *and* eggnog."

"Eggnog, too?" Samuel began to sound perplexed.

"Yup, and carrots for the reindeer . . ."

"Carrots, too?! I don't know . . . I don't think we have any carrots . . . do we, dear?" He looked to his wife for support.

"Yes, we do," Noah said, hopping down and running to the fridge. Samuel tried to nonchalantly block the door, but Noah gently nudged him and said, "Grampa, let me show you." Sarah was enjoying their playful exchange and watched as Noah pulled open the fridge door and produced a big bag of carrots. "See? We have 'em!"

"I guess we do!" Samuel said, scooping Noah up and giving him a hug. "There're no flies on you, that's for sure."

Noah looked puzzled by his grandfather's funny observation, but gave him a big squeeze. "I love you, Grampa."

"I love you, too!" Samuel replied.

Asa watched his father set Noah down and noticed that there were tears in his eyes. "Hey, Dad," he said quietly, "the eight o'clock service sounds perfect."

Samuel nodded and wiped his eyes. "We better get going on the tree then!"

Chapter 4

Asa lugged a heavy cardboard box down from the attic, set it on the floor, and pulled on the flaps, which had been tucked under one another. Inside the tattered old box was a smaller box, simply marked, NOAH. He lifted it out just as Noah came in trailing a long string of popcorn and cranberries. "Dad, can you help me with this?"

"Yup . . . but I think you'll need a chair."

Noah laid the string carefully across the afghan blanket that was on the back of the couch and ran back into the kitchen. He returned with the chair and with Maddie, who was carrying another long string of popcorn.

"Dad, can we take the tree back with us and put it outside for the birds to hide in? That's what we used to do—they love the popcorn and berries."

"Sure," Asa replied with a smile . . . but suddenly feeling oddly sad. *That's what we used to do* . . . the innocent words had an odd sting . . . he hadn't thought of Noah's previous Christmas memories that didn't include him.

Maddie looked over at Asa and seemed to read his mind. "You and Noah will have lots of time to make memories of your own," she said as she passed the string back and forth with Noah around the tree.

Noah looked up from trying to untangle his end and said, "And you, too, Maddie!" Maddie paused thoughtfully . . . *I hope so, Noah! I hope so!*

They continued to work from top to bottom, gently draping the popcorn string over the limbs. Meanwhile, Asa tried to determine if all the lights worked and, when he was certain they did, they hung those on the tree, too.

"Moment of truth!" he declared as he plugged them in.

"Uh-oh, Dad!" Noah said in dismay. "The bottom ones aren't on."

Asa tried unplugging and plugging the string back in, with no better results.

"They were just working!" he exclaimed in frustration.

Maddie walked around the tree to see which light might be the culprit. She pulled out the first unlit bulb and the whole string came on.

"What did you do?" Asa asked in surprise.

"I just unplugged the first dead one," she said with a shrug. "Do you have any replacement bulbs?"

"I don't know," Asa answered.

"I'll go ask!" Noah said, running to the kitchen.

Maddie grinned at Asa and teased, "Guess you have to have the magic touch!"

"Hmmm," he surmised, "and I guess *you* do!"

Noah returned with Samuel in tow. "I think there are replacement bulbs somewhere in here," he said, squatting down next to the box. He started to look and then spied Noah's box. "Noah, here's your box. Why don't you open it?"

Noah knelt down next to his grandfather and pulled up the top of his box. "Hey!" he cried. "Here's my stocking!"

Asa watched Noah unfurl the soft red felt. "Dad," he said, hopping up, "can you help me hang it?" Asa nodded and lifted Noah so he could hang the stocking on a painted hook that was tapped into the mantel. He looked at Noah's name embroidered across the snowy white trim and thought back to the first time he'd seen that stocking . . . before a name was embroidered on it. He leaned on the mantel and closed his eyes. "What's wrong, Dad?" Noah asked.

"Nothin,' pal . . . just thinking . . ."

"Okay," Noah said, shrugging, and turned his attention back to his ornaments.

Maddie watched Asa and knew that he was struggling with long-ago memories . . . memories that she wasn't a part of. She began to wonder if it had been a mistake to come . . .

Samuel, sensing a somber mood descending on the room, turned to Maddie, handed her a new bulb, and said, "So, Maddie, tell me what you're cooking up with those potent ingredients."

Maddie laughed. "Oh, it's just an old Swedish recipe that my family always makes on Christmas Eve. I thought you guys might like to try it." Maddie slipped the new bulb in place and added, "It's called *Glug*."

Noah laughed. "Glug? That's a funny name! Can I try it?"

Maddie smiled. "*That* will be up to your dad!"

Asa looked up. "I don't know . . . I think you might just have to savor the fragrance."

"When are you making it, Maddie?" Noah asked.

"Probably when we get home from church."

Just then, Sarah came in and, spying the tree, proclaimed, "Oh, my! That tree looks beautiful!" She walked around it and admired it from every angle. Then she turned to Samuel, who'd recently found a seat in the rocking chair and appeared to be contemplating a nap. "Are you coming back to the kitchen, dear? I need you to make cocktail sauce."

He opened one eye. "Do you mean my *world-famous* cocktail sauce?"

Noah looked up with a grin. "Are we having shrimp?!" Sarah nodded and he let out a little whoop of excitement. "Can I help, Grampa?"

"You sure can!" Samuel replied.

Asa eyed Noah. "Watch out, Dad, he doesn't like to measure ingredients . . ."

"Coleman men don't measure!" Samuel said indignantly, resting his hands on Noah's shoulders. "We're going to make it so it puts hair on your chest! Right, Noah?"

"Right!" Noah agreed.

Maddie hung up the last two ornaments, folded tissue paper that was strewn about, laid it in the boxes, and stacked the boxes in a corner behind the piano. "Too bad we have to take all this down in a couple of days," she said gloomily. "That's the saddest part of Christmas . . . putting the ornaments away."

Asa nodded. He was quiet as he knelt down on the hearth and stacked kindling and small logs on the andirons.

Maddie sat on the couch and watched him. "I think it's harder for you to be here than it is for Noah." Asa didn't reply. He just finished tearing up an old egg carton, crumpling newspaper, and stuffing it all under the andirons. Then he brushed off his hands, stood up slowly, and sat next to her.

He gave her a half smile. "It *is* hard to be here. This old house is so full of memories . . . and not just memories of my relationship with Noelle . . . but memories of when I was Noah's age . . . when my parents' best friends, Nate and his first wife Annie were both still alive." He paused and looked around. "Maddie, this was *their* house and they used to hang Christmas stockings on those hooks for Isaac and me. We would sit right there," he motioned to the braided rug in front of the hearth, "and open their gifts for us . . ."

"Got some eggnog!" Noah announced cheerily, coming through the kitchen door. He stepped carefully around the couch and presented his offering to them on a tray. "Grandma put nutmeg on yours."

Maddie smiled and took a glass. "What service! Thank you!"

"Thanks, buddy!" Asa said, tousling Noah's hair.

"You're welcome!" Noah replied with a little bow, which almost upset the remaining glass on the tray. He put the tray on the coffee table, took a sip from the glass that didn't have nutmeg, and wiggled onto the couch between them.

Asa took a sip, too, and looked over at Maddie. "Hmmm . . . tastes like there's more in here than nutmeg." Maddie took a sip and nodded in agreement.

"When're you starting the fire, Dad?" Noah asked, noticing the wood.

"Oh, probably later . . . after church."

Noah suddenly looked worried. "Maybe you should wait 'til tomorrow."

"Why?" asked Asa in surprise.

"Well . . . because Santa's coming . . ."

Asa caught on to Noah's concern. "Oh, you don't have to worry about that. A fire in the fireplace won't stop Santa Claus."

"Are you sure?" Noah asked doubtfully.

Asa nodded. "Positive. When I was your age we always had a fire on Christmas Eve and it never stopped him from coming." Noah looked relieved, leaned back between them, jiggled his feet, and took another sip of his eggnog.

From the kitchen Samuel called, "Any volunteer taste testers in there?"

Noah's face lit up. "I will!" he hollered, sitting up so quickly that he spilled eggnog on his pants.

"Easy, Noah!" Asa scolded. He reached quickly for Noah's glass.

"I'm sorry, Dad . . ."

Asa looked up from the spill and realized that Noah was on the verge of tears. "It's okay . . . I only said to take it easy."

"I know . . ."

With a gentle smile, he handed Noah his glass. "Now, go make sure that cocktail sauce will put hair on our chests . . . I'm sure Maddie will appreciate that!" Noah nodded, put his glass on the tray, and carefully carried it back to the kitchen. Asa called after him, "And don't forget to bring some shrimp back with you!"

"Okay!" Noah hollered as the kitchen door swung closed.

Maddie looked at the tree and wondered if Asa would say anything more. She didn't want to press him. She never did. If he wanted to talk about it, she was always willing to listen. He smiled. "I'm sorry to be in a bit of a mood. I'm not very merry, am I?"

"That's all right," she consoled. "I know this house holds a lot of memories for you. It would be hard for anyone the first time they returned to . . ." she hesitated, not sure what to say.

Asa looked at the dark fireplace. ". . . to the scene of the crime . . ." he finished softly.

Maddie smiled gently. "Well, that's not what I was going to say . . ."

"It's true though. The relationship I had with Noelle when I was eighteen betrayed Nate, ended tragically, and changed all of our lives. It happened in this house . . . in this room . . . and the only good that came from it was Noah."

Just then, Noah came bumping back through the door with his replenished tray.

"Got shrimp!" he announced, stepping carefully around the couch and standing in front of them. Maddie reached for a napkin that was on the tray and wiped cocktail sauce from Noah's chin. "You've already had some," she surmised with a smile.

Asa studied him with a serious face. "Well, any hair on your chest?"

Noah put the tray down and pulled up his shirt, exposing his smooth baby skin. "Nope! Not yet." He pulled down his shirt. "Guess I'll just have to have another!" he said with a grin. He dipped a big fat shrimp into the cocktail sauce and began to lift it to his mouth. Maddie, realizing that another spill was imminent, hurried to slip her napkin under his hand. Almost immediately, a big red glob splattered onto it.

"Good catch!" Asa said, eyeing Noah. "Maddie just saved you!" Noah nodded, squeezing the tail like a pro and popping the whole shrimp into his mouth.

"Whew—that's hot!" he exclaimed, waving his hand in front of his mouth, and running back to the kitchen.

Asa held the tray out to Maddie. "You first!" Maddie took a shrimp, gave it a conservative dip, and took a dainty bite. Almost immediately, her eyes began to water. "What do you think?" Asa teased, eyeing the top of her blouse. "Any hair sprouting?"

Maddie blushed and shook her head. She took a sip of

her eggnog and looked away, embarrassed by the question. *Was he just teasing . . . or flirting?* She looked up and he was smiling. She was completely caught off guard by Asa's unexpected question. She laughed, trying to regain her composure. "I guess you'll never know!"

Asa popped a shrimp dripping with the spicy sauce into his mouth, and appeared to be completely unfazed. With a grin, he said, "I already have hair . . ."

Chapter 5

An hour later, Maddie was helping Sarah in the kitchen and supervising Noah as he arranged rows of marshmallows on top of the sweet potatoes. When he was finished, he popped the last one in his mouth, grinned at Maddie, and, with his speech impaired by the gooey substance, asked, "Doyooowanun?"

Maddie laughed. "No, thanks."

Asa peered around the kitchen door. "Would you ladies like a cocktail . . . or the whole rooster?"

Sarah smiled. "A glass of white wine would be good."

Asa nodded and looked questioningly at Maddie. She had never been posed this question before so she took advantage of the opportunity to speak her mind. "I'd like the *whole* rooster, please." Asa raised his eyebrows and she grinned at him. "White wine sounds good!" He nodded and, as the kitchen door swung shut, Maddie felt her cheeks blush and wondered if it was because the kitchen was so warm.

"Shall I put the sweet potatoes in the oven?" she asked.

Sarah looked up. "Yes . . . if you can find room!"

Asa returned with two glasses of wine and gave them to Maddie and to his mother. Then he looked at Noah. "And, what can I get for you, sir?"

Noah, who was still standing on a chair, put his finger on his chin thoughtfully and tried to remember the name of the drink he always had on special occasions. "I can't remember what Dad called it . . . I mean I can't remember what my other da . . ." He stopped short and his bottom lip quivered as his eyes filled with tears. Asa's heart ached at Noah's sudden grief and Sarah, realizing what he had just said, looked up.

She smiled gently. "Noah, honey, it's okay to have two dads." She wiped her hands on her apron, held his face in her hands, and looked in his eyes. "You can't forget someone you loved." She gave him a hug and whispered. "You can talk about your other dad anytime you want . . . especially if you're missing him. We miss him, too." Noah nodded. "Now, was that drink called a Roy Rogers?"

Noah looked relieved and wiped his eyes. "Yes! That's it." He looked at Asa. "I'll have a Roy Rogers."

"You got it!" Asa replied, giving him a thumbs-up and trying to shrug off the moment. He rejoined his father at the wet bar and started to make Noah's drink. "Do we have any cherries?" Samuel reached into the little refrigerator and took out a small jar. Asa popped open a can of Coke and poured it into a small fancy glass while Samuel looked for the grenadine.

"Asa, I've been meaning to talk to you about something."

Asa looked up with a puzzled expression and said, "Can I deliver this first?"

"Of course," Samuel replied.

When he came back in, there were two crisp Tangueray and tonics with lime on the bar. Asa eyed his father. "Do I need this?"

Samuel laughed. "No, no . . . it's nothing like that."

"Well, I think I might be sorry tomorrow . . . between gin, rum eggnog, and Maddie's recipe."

Samuel smiled. "That's true . . . I forgot you were such a lightweight. Even so," he said, holding up his glass in a toast, "Merry Christmas!"

"Merry Christmas, Dad." Asa replied, sitting on one of the stools.

Samuel cleared his throat and took a sip.

"Well, I've been meaning to tell you . . . or rather, *ask* you." He paused. "Your mother thinks we should have asked first . . . and she's probably right . . . but we wanted it to be a surprise for both of you. Now that the time is drawing near, though, I can see her point. We don't want it to be an unhappy surprise. So, she thought I better, at least, give you a heads-up." Samuel studied Asa's face to see if his message was getting across.

Asa's heart pounded as he absently wiped the condensation on his glass. "Dad, how 'bout you just tell me."

Samuel gave him a funny look. "I *am* telling you."

"Well, you're kind of beating around the bush," Asa said.

"Okay, well, it's just that your mother and I have a special Christmas present for Noah and . . ."

Just then, Noah pushed through the door hollering, "Okay, I'll tell 'em . . . Dad, Grampa, dinner's ready! Guess what we're having?" He waited until Asa responded appropriately and then went on. "Everyone is having their own chicken! Even me!"

"You mean Cornish hen?"

Noah nodded and pulled on Asa's hand. "C'mon! Grandma said, 'Right now or it's goin' to get cold.' "

Asa allowed himself to be pulled to the kitchen and Samuel followed. As he did, he clapped Asa on the shoulder. "Don't worry, son. You're gonna love it . . . it's noth-in' you can't handle."

Asa glanced over his shoulder. "Well, you still need to tell me . . ." Samuel just chuckled. He was obviously quite pleased with himself.

They sat down to dinner and reached around the table to hold hands. Samuel offered a long grace of thanks-giving and asked for a special blessing on Isaac and his family. When he finally said, "Amen," Noah looked up, puzzled, and asked, "How come Uncle Isaac didn't come here for Christmas?"

Asa passed the cranberry relish to Maddie and said, "Because he and Aunt Nina are spending Christmas in Providence." He scooped some sweet potato onto his plate and continued, "But they might be coming to our house for New Year's."

Noah nodded and held out his plate for a scoop, too. "Extra marshmallows, please." Asa reached over and plopped a big orange and white mountain on Noah's plate and then held up the serving spoon and looked around the table questioningly. "It's too hot to pass," he said. "Who wants some?"

Sarah held out her plate and said, "We're so glad you decided to spend Christmas with us, Maddie. It's not easy to be away from family. I know Isaac had mixed feelings about being with Nina's family." She looked at Samuel. "I think they're going to try alternating holidays so, hope-fully, they'll be with us next year."

Samuel nodded. "Well, I still miss seeing that cute lit-tle redhead."

Asa knew what his dad meant. Isaac and Nina had wasted no time starting a family and their little girl, Kate, was the cutest, most good-natured baby he'd ever met. It would've been fun to watch her open presents on Christmas morning. *Oh well, next year . . . and, since Nina was pregnant again, there'd be two little ones to watch.* Asa couldn't wait to see his brother with two babies. He knew Isaac was hoping for a son—he'd already announced that he wouldn't give up until he had one. But Asa would love it if his brother ended up living in a house full of women. *If anyone deserved such a blessing, it was Isaac!*

Sarah turned back to Maddie. "Does your mom cook a big dinner?"

Maddie nodded, as she passed the green beans to her. "Yes, everyone comes to my parents' house. It's quite an event."

"How many are there?"

Maddie thought for a moment, trying to calculate the size of her family. "Thirty-three . . . and there're two more on the way."

"Thirty-three people?!" Noah exclaimed. "Where does everyone sit?"

Sarah and Samuel both shook their heads in amazement and Maddie smiled. "Well, we have two big farm tables, and several card tables that all the kids like to sit at. Everybody helps and everyone brings food. Sometimes we serve it buffet style and other times we just keep passing."

"Wow!" Noah exclaimed. "Are there any kids my age?"

Maddie nodded. "There are two that are six, one that's five, and four that are seven . . . or maybe eight. Then there're some older and younger, too."

"How old are Mikey and John-John?"

"Mikey is fifteen and John-John just turned fourteen."

Noah grinned. "That sounds like a lot of fun!"

Maddie nodded. "It *is* fun!" Her voice sounded a bit nostalgic.

Noah was quiet for a minute and then added, "And don't forget Sadie."

Maddie agreed. "Yup, Sadie, too. There're lots of dogs in the family, but they don't all come to the house for Christmas . . . except for Sadie. John always brings her."

Noah looked at Samuel and Sarah and said, matter-of-factly, "Sadie is in love with Dad, and John says she's just gloomy when he leaves."

"What kind of dog is she?" Samuel asked.

Asa smiled. "She's an old black Lab . . . like Martha."

Samuel nodded and caught Sarah's eye. "Well, Asa's always had a penchant for Labs . . . and they, for him."

Noah looked puzzled. "Grampa, what's a *penchant*?"

Samuel smiled. "It's a fondness. It means he's always liked them."

"Me, too," Noah agreed. "I've always had a penchant for Labs, too."

Samuel nodded and took a sip of his drink . . . both he and Sarah tried to hide their smiles behind their drinks, but Asa looked suspiciously from one to the other. "Are you two okay?" he asked.

Samuel almost choked on the question and tried to keep a straight face. "Of course," he sputtered, picking up his knife and focusing on his hen. Sarah took her cue from her husband and did the same. And Asa just looked at Maddie and shook his head; the look on his face said, *I have no idea what's going on . . .*

Noah took a bite and said, "Grandma, this chicken's really good."

Maddie nodded in agreement. "Yes, Mrs. Coleman, everything's delicious."

Sarah smiled. "Thank you. The stuffing recipe is Annie's. I've always wanted to make it, but I never had the recipe before; I came across it when I was looking to see what spices I needed to bring over."

"Are there apricots in it?"

Sarah nodded. "Apricots . . . and Grand Marnier."

"Mmmm . . . I wondered what that flavor was," Maddie said. "It's very good. My mom would love it. She likes anything made with dried fruit."

"I'll give you the recipe," Sarah said, sounding pleased.

Noah leaned back in his chair, pushed his half-finished plate away, and groaned. "I'm stuffed!"

"I think you had too many shrimp," Asa said. "And I guess you won't have room for dessert either . . ."

Noah perked up. "Oh, yes, I will. I have a separate dessert stomach."

Asa laughed. "Where'd you hear that?"

Noah grinned. "That's what Grampa said *you* used to say."

Asa eyed his father. "I guess no secrets are safe with you!"

Samuel grinned. "Oh, I don't know 'bout that."

Maddie watched Asa interacting with his parents . . . his father teasing him . . . and his mother obviously just loving having him home. It was evident that his easygoing manner carried over into all of his relationships.

Before they'd met, Maddie had caught herself, on several occasions, watching Asa push his cart up and down the library stacks, and she'd found herself drawn to the easy manner in which he did things . . . the way he held several volumes in his hand, glanced at their call numbers, and slid each book back into place; the soft-spoken way he had with people who needed help finding something; and even the casual way his faded Levis and unironed oxford shirts hung on his slender frame. One time, he'd looked up and caught her watching him, but he'd just smiled and nodded, and she had smiled and quickly looked away . . . but not before noticing the color of his sky blue eyes. Maddie had never paid much attention to boys before Asa—she'd always been too busy with school and studying, so, when he walked into her home-town library that summer, she had been caught completely off guard.

Now, she smiled as she watched Asa put his arm around Noah. *They look so much alike,* she thought as he tousled Noah's hair. Noah grinned and leaned against him. Asa still had that same easygoing manner . . . but, in other ways, he had changed. His hair, still streaked with blond, was longer now and it fell over his eyes so that he had to sweep it back with his hand; his face, still young and boyish, conveyed that life's lessons hadn't always been easy; and his eyes, still blue and intense, revealed a sad wisdom that was older than his years. Asa looked up and saw Maddie watching him. He smiled and winked at her, and Maddie's heart sang . . . *oh, Asa, if you only knew* . . .

Sarah watched the silent exchange . . . and realized that the beautiful girl sitting across from her son was in love. The thought of Asa in a relationship with someone new warmed her heart and she wondered how long it would be before he realized it, too. She glanced up at the clock. "Oh, my goodness! When did it get so late?" she exclaimed, standing up and reaching for several plates to clear.

"I guess we'll have to wait on dessert," Samuel said, looking over his shoulder at the clock and standing, too. They hurriedly carried plates, silverware, serving dishes, and glasses into the kitchen. Sarah pushed dishes aside to make room on the counter for the last pile that Asa had in his hands, untied her apron, and said, "I think we should just leave everything. I'm sorry . . . I should've been pay-ing better attention."

Samuel smiled as he quickly covered several dishes with foil. "That's all right, dear, we forgive you." He looked at Asa. "Why don't you three go on ahead in the truck . . . your mother and I have a quick errand to run on the way home."

Asa eyed his father suspiciously. "I think I should probably go with you."

"Oh, no!" Samuel said with a grin. "You have to hurry back here so Maddie can start cooking." He nodded his head toward the door. "Go on . . . and save some seats. We'll be right along."

Chapter 6

"Dad, look! It's snowing!" Noah whispered. Asa looked out the window and nodded. The old New England church was filled to overflowing, but Asa, standing in the once familiar sanctuary after so many years, hardly noticed. He gazed at the falling snow and his mind filled with memories. He thought back to his boyhood summers on the Cape, sitting in church on Sunday mornings, longing to be on the other side of the magnificent many-paned windows . . . and then he recalled the sad occasion when he had stood there last . . . it had been for Noelle's funeral after she died giving birth to Noah. So lost in thought was he that Maddie had to nudge him twice before he realized his parents were standing in the aisle, waiting for him to make room.

As they squeezed into the pew, an older gentleman with white hair came over to greet them. Samuel stood to shake hands and they exchanged a few friendly words. The man turned to Sarah and took her hands in his. As they spoke, Asa tried to place the gentle smile and kind, gray eyes . . . and then he realized it was the minister who had served the church for many years.

The minister looked up, as if on cue, and nodded to Asa and Maddie, and then leaned toward Noah. "This must be Noah—all grown up!" Noah nodded shyly and the old gentleman continued. "How would you like to help with the service tonight?" Noah smiled and nodded again and the minister handed him a program highlighted with notes. He pointed to one of the highlights and then to the front of the sanctuary and explained what the job entailed. Noah listened carefully, clutching the program in his lap. The minister stood up and winked at him, clapped Samuel on the shoulder, and walked to the front of the church. Moments later, a hush fell over the sanctuary as the first chords of "O Little Town of Bethlehem" were played.

The service was beautiful and, just as Samuel predicted, perfect for young families. Carols were sung and passages from the New Testament were read; between each hymn and reading, a youngster from the congregation tiptoed to the front, picked up a small wooden hammer decorated with a red bow, and tapped a shiny brass Christmas bell that had been set out just for the occasion.

Noah followed the program carefully with his finger. There was an asterisk penciled in the space between the reading of Matthew 2:9–12 and the hymn, "We Three Kings of Orient Are." His heart pounded as he listened . . . "And having been warned in a dream not to return to Herod, they left for their own country by another road." Just as the reader finished, Maddie gently nudged Noah and he stood up resolutely and squeezed to the aisle.

The congregation watched expectantly as the little boy in the handsome red sweater made his way shyly to the front. He picked up the wooden hammer, hesitated briefly, feeling the weight of it, and then gave the bell a resounding clang. Everyone smiled at his enthusiasm and then there was a rustling of pages as they stood to sing. Noah hurried back to his seat, bursting with pride and delight. Asa gave him a thumbs-up and Noah returned the gesture with a grin that showed off his missing tooth. Asa smiled . . . still amazed that this little wisp of a boy, so full of love and excitement and promise, was *his* son.

After the hymn, Noah promptly put his head on Maddie's shoulder and listened to the final reading. . . . *But Mary treasured all these words and pondered them in her heart . . . and the shepherds returned, glorifying and praising God for all they had heard and seen* . . . A hush fell over the congregation as the lights dimmed. Each person held a small white candle and waited as the flame was symbolically passed from one to another. When his turn came, Noah solemnly tipped his candle into Asa's flame and then turned to Maddie and held his candle steady. She smiled gently as she dipped her candle into his. The candle illuminated her face in a soft warm glow and Asa suddenly felt as if he were seeing her for the first time . . .

Soon the entire sanctuary was shimmering in radiant light and a chorus of reverent voices joined together in singing "Silent Night." Maddie looked over and caught Asa's eye and noticed that he wasn't singing. She gave him a funny frown and he smiled and joined in softly . . . almost mouthing the words . . . so he could hear Noah's innocent voice mixed with her sweet soprano.

How is it, he thought to himself, *that I've known Maddie all these years . . . and I never realized she had such a beautiful voice?! Am I really so self-centered that I never paid attention?* He shook his head in dismay. *I must have learned a dozen new things about her today. How could that be? How did I not consider that she was missing a big family celebration to spend Christmas with us? Or that thirteen children who love her and call her Aunt were*

*counting on her to play Christmas carols . . . and would
miss her when they realized she wasn't coming? How is it
that I didn't know she had a Christmas tree planted in her
honor? Or that her mom liked things that were made with
dried fruit . . . or that her family always made a festive
drink on Christmas Eve? And . . . why in the world did
this sweet and selfless woman give all that up . . . to spend
Christmas with me?*

As Asa softly sang the last words of the beautiful
hymn, he looked around at the many faces illuminated by
candlelight . . . and realized that each one had a story to
tell. He was not the only one who had seen tragedy or
known heartache—the little church was overflowing with
people who had faced life's trials . . . and persevered. He
was surrounded by people who, despite the burdens they
carried, longed to celebrate the blessing of Christ's birth.
Asa gazed at all of the kind and weary, innocent and
solemn, reverent and peaceful faces around him . . . and
as he did, he felt an odd lightness fill his heart. It was as if
the burden of sorrow and guilt that, for so long, had per-
meated every aspect of his life . . . was lifting. Asa stood
in silence, watching the glistening snow fall outside the
window and realized, in amazement, that coming to this
sacred place . . . on this wondrous night . . . had brought
healing and peace to his heart.

The hymn ended . . . the candles extinguished . . . and
the congregation waited, shrouded in silent darkness and
wonder. A moment later, the chandeliers glowed brightly,
the organ came to life, and robust voices filled the air . . .
"Joy to the world, the Lord is come! Let earth receive her
King!"

From the balcony, the regal sound of a trumpet joined
in, declaring the majesty of the moment, and the little
New England church vibrated with joy and excitement.

Noah looked up in awe, grinning from ear to ear . . . and Asa smiled and brushed back his tears.

The organ continued to play as the congregation filed out into the snowy night. "Merry Christmas!" was repeated over and over as parishioners shook hands and gave hugs. The old minister shook Noah's hand and said, "You are, by far, the best bell ringer we've ever had!"

Noah nodded in agreement and said, "I know!"

Samuel laughed, picked him up, and gave him a big hug. They stood in front of the church and Samuel told Asa about a live Nativity that was out on Route 6. Asa eyed his father with suspicion. "Don't you want to see it, too?"

"Your mother and I saw it last night. Besides, we have an errand to run."

"Yes, I know. That's what worries me."

"You needn't worry," Samuel insisted. "We won't be long." Asa sighed resignedly. It was obvious he wasn't going to find out anything more.

There was a small crowd already gathered around the fenced-in area, but by the time Asa found a place to park, some folks were getting ready to leave.

Maddie climbed out and Noah jumped into her arms. "Wow! John's right. You *are* heavy!" she exclaimed.

"Wait until I have dessert!" he said with a grin. "I've got plenty of room now."

"Me, too," Asa agreed. "I can't wait for a piece of those pies."

Maddie smiled. "Well, I bought cream for whipped cream, but I'm afraid I left it home in the fridge."

"I bet we have some," Asa assured her.

Everyone at the fence was quiet as they walked over,

and Noah's eyes grew wide when he saw what they were looking at: there was a beautiful russet-brown cow contentedly munching on hay, and her speckled calf was curled up nearby; there were two curly white lambs nosing around in an almost empty grain trough, and a fuzzy goat was getting a drink from the water trough; under the sturdy wooden manger there were two geese curled up side by side . . . and right beside them was a duck with her head tucked under her wing. The humans in the crèche were not real but had been so beautifully made and illuminated that they appeared lifelike. The animals nosed about peacefully and seemed completely unaware of the gathering at the fence. Noah quietly watched the scene for several minutes and then whispered, "Was it snowing in Bethlehem that night?"

Asa smiled and said, "I don't think so." He picked Noah up and felt him shiver. "Are you cold?"

Noah nodded and Asa said, "Well, I guess we better get going then." When they got back to the truck, Asa pulled a blanket from behind the seat and Maddie tucked it around Noah . . . and, by the time they reached the house, he was sound asleep. Asa carried him inside, still cocooned in the blanket, and gently laid him on the couch in front of the fireplace. Then he knelt on the hearth, opened the damper, and struck a match to light the crumpled paper. As the flames curled upward and licked at the kindling, Asa swept the hearth with a small broom and fanned the tentative flame. Before long, a cheerful fire was crackling away, taking the chill from the air. Asa stood, took off his jacket, laid it on the end of the couch, and stood by the fire.

Maddie peered around the kitchen door. "Is Noah still asleep?" she whispered.

Asa nodded and followed her into the kitchen. He

looked around and saw that the dish drainer was already full. "Boy, you don't mess around!"

She smiled and held a towel out to him. "Problem is, I don't know where anything goes."

"Me neither, " he said with a grin.

She gave him a funny look. "You do so!"

He took the towel, still grinning, and began to dry. "So, what do you think my parents are up to?" he asked.

Maddie shook her head as she continued to wash. "I have no idea . . . but it seems like your father can hardly contain himself."

"I know . . . that's what has me worried," Asa said as he put a pile of dishes back on the shelf. They continued to work, side by side, and, as Asa reached for the utensils, he glanced at Maddie's pretty profile. She had pulled her chestnut-colored hair back into a ponytail and her cheeks were still rosy from the cold. With her freckles and petite figure, she looked more like a girl than a twenty-four-year-old woman. "By the way," he said, "I didn't know you played the piano."

"Yup," she said with a grin. "Eight long years of lessons . . ."

"Eight years?! Well, I'm sure the piano in the living room needs tuning—it's probably been at least twelve years, maybe longer, since it was last played. But you're welcome to give it a whirl. Noah would love it."

Maddie put the last glass in the dish drainer. "Are you going to wake him?"

"I think so . . . he'll be disappointed if he misses dessert . . . or when you make *Glug!*"

Maddie grinned. "Oh, I almost forgot! Where did you put the bag?"

"Right there." Asa pointed to a brown bag tucked behind the pie carrier.

"I'll need a big pot, too . . ."

Asa pulled one out of the drawer below the oven. "Anything else?"

Maddie dried her hands on the towel that Asa was holding and said, "Matches."

Asa looked puzzled. "Matches?"

"Yup!"

"Hmmm," he teased. "Sometimes, you're *so* mysterious . . ."

"I know," she said with a grin. "I like to keep you guessing . . ."

Chapter 7

Asa peered over the back of the couch. Noah was still sound asleep. He laid two more pieces of wood on the fire and reached for the matches on the mantel. As he did, he heard a commotion at the front door. He looked down the hall and saw his father trying to close the door and maneuver up the stairs with a cumbersome cardboard box. His mother was brushing snow from the sleeves of her coat, but, when she saw Asa, she smiled. "It's really coming down out there!"

"Is it?" Asa said with a suspicious smile. "So, what's Dad sneaking up the stairs with?"

"He's not sneaking, dear," she said with a smile. "If he was *sneaking*, he wouldn't be making so much noise." She hung up her coat and headed for the kitchen. "Did you go see the Nativity?" she asked, changing the subject.

"Yes, we did. It's pretty neat," Asa said, following her. "Does Mr. Thompson still own that farm?"

Sarah nodded. "He does, but his son does most of the work now." She pushed open the kitchen door and stopped suddenly. "Oh, my goodness! Maddie, I didn't expect you to do all this."

Maddie smiled at Asa. "I didn't do it alone . . . I had a helper."

"Well, thank you both *very much*!"

Samuel pushed the door open behind them, looked around at the kitchen, and shook his head. "You know, *you two,* we would've liked to have helped with this."

"No, you wouldn't have . . ." Asa teased.

Samuel was still shaking his head when he peered into the still-empty pot on the stove. "So, Maddie, what's in this Christmas drink?" he asked, and then using his best up-and-down dialect, added, "I know those *Svedes* like to keep *varm*!"

Maddie laughed. "That's true!" She reached into her bag and produced a half gallon jug of port wine and poured it into the pot. She turned on the burner and said, "I'm cutting the recipe in half because there're only four of us . . . and even that's probably going to be too much. But we can reheat it tomorrow, too . . . *if* you like it."

"I like it already!" said Samuel. Then, he looked around. "Where's Noah?"

"Asleep on the couch," Asa replied.

"He is? I didn't even see him."

"Yup . . . I think I better wake him, though," Asa said, and disappeared into the living room. A moment later, he came back with Noah in his arms, still rubbing his eyes.

Samuel took him from Asa and said, "C'mere, you!" Then he looked at Asa. "You're lucky he doesn't wake up in a mood like you used to do."

"I still *do* . . ." Asa said with a grin.

Noah peered around the kitchen. "Is Maddie making her stuff?" he asked.

"Yup . . . do you want to help?" she asked. He nodded

sleepily and Asa pulled a chair over near the stove, and Samuel set him on it.

Noah looked in the pot and yawned. "Do we have to measure?"

Maddie reached into the bag, took out the remaining ingredients, set them in front of him, and replied, "Nope, we just have to count." She opened a pint-size bottle that her father had given her and poured in the contents.

Samuel watched curiously and asked, "Now, what was that?"

Maddie held the bottle out to him. "It's called akvavit . . . or aquavit. It means 'water of life,' or some say it means 'water of the vine.' It's a Scandinavian vodka." Samuel nodded, handed the bottle back, and Maddie went on. "There are different recipes for Glug, but this is the one that my grandfather has always made."

She looked at her recipe and then at Noah. "Ready?" Noah nodded. "We need four prunes." Noah counted out the prunes, plopped them in, and watched them pop back up and float to the edge. "Next, we need three dried apricots and a handful of raisins . . ." With Maddie supervising, Noah dropped in the dried fruit, nuts, and spices. The last ingredient was a cinnamon stick. And then Maddie said, "Now we let it simmer."

Samuel smiled. "It smells pretty potent!"

Sarah agreed. "It's very fragrant . . . very Christmassy!"

And Asa asked, "What about the matches?"

Maddie grinned. "We haven't gotten to that part yet . . ."

"Well, while we wait, who's ready for pie?" Sarah asked.

"Me!" said Noah, hopping down from his chair.

Asa quickly whipped up a small container of cream while Maddie and Sarah cut the pies and put them on plates. "Is everyone having a slice of each?" Sarah asked. She needn't have asked because a resounding "Yes!" echoed through the kitchen.

They left the Glug to simmer and retreated to the living room to have dessert. Asa pulled a small stool up to the coffee table and Noah, carefully balancing his plate, sat down; he looked up at the tree and smiled. "I think that's the best tree we've ever had!" Then he took a bite of pie and, with his mouth full, said, "And this is the best pumpkin pie, too!" Everyone nodded in agreement, and the only sounds came from forks clinking on plates . . . and logs as they settled, snapped, and sizzled.

Finally, Asa scraped his plate clean. "Noah, do you think we should get Maddie to play the piano?" he asked.

Noah's eyes lit up and he nodded his head enthusiastically.

"Well, how 'bout we finish making the Glug first?" Maddie suggested.

"Okay!" Noah agreed.

"I think I might wait here," Samuel said sleepily, leaning back in the rocker and closing his eyes.

Asa stood, picked up the plates, and said, "If you do that, you're going to miss Maddie setting the house on fire."

Maddie grinned. "I hope not!"

Asa pulled on Samuel's hand. "C'mon, Grampa. You have to watch, too."

They gathered in the kitchen around the stove and Maddie brought the Glug to a gentle boil. She measured out a quarter cup of sugar, located the lid to the pot, and looked at Noah. "Would you like to turn off the light?" Noah hopped down, flipped the switch, and then climbed back onto the chair. Maddie paused thoughtfully, concerned about his close proximity to the pot. "Maybe you should back up a little bit."

Asa said, "I agree!" and hitched Noah onto his hip.

Maddie looked around again. "Everybody ready?"

Samuel teased, "Are you nervous?"

She laughed. "Well, to tell the truth, I've never done this part before."

"You can do it, Maddie!" Noah said encouragingly.

She grinned. "Okay! Here goes!" She spread the sugar across the top of the bubbling mixture, struck a match, and touched it to the air above the pot. A bright blue flame covered the surface of the liquid and Noah's eyes grew wide. "Cool!" he exclaimed. They watched the blue glow and Maddie couldn't help but wonder if her family was doing the same thing at home. She smiled and let it burn for a few seconds before covering it with the lid.

"Wow!" Noah said. "That was so cool!"

"Pretty impressive!" Asa agreed. "*But* . . . how does it taste?"

Maddie turned the stove light on and Samuel set out some mugs. "Are these okay?" he asked.

Maddie nodded and Sarah pulled a ladle from the drawer.

Maddie ladled some Glug into each of the mugs and Noah asked, "What about me?"

"I don't know if you're going to like it, hon," Sarah said. "Here, smell mine." Noah put his nose into the steam rising from his grandmother's mug and made a funny face. "How 'bout some eggnog, instead?"

"Okay!" Noah agreed.

Samuel watched Maddie cup her hands around her mug and breathe deeply. "Reminds you of home, doesn't it?" he asked. She nodded with a half smile. "Well, we are very glad you're here with us!" he said, putting his arm around her shoulder.

Asa smiled warmly. "Yes, we are . . ."

Samuel held up his mug and said, "Skoal!"

And then Maddie couldn't help but smile. "Skoal!" she replied. They clinked their glasses together and sipped their steaming drinks.

"Whew," Asa said, shaking his head. "That'll knock you for a loop!"

"Mmmm," Sarah said. "It's wonderful!"

Samuel just smiled and nodded. "Yup, we're going to need the recipe for this."

Samuel ushered Maddie and Asa out of the kitchen. "You've done enough. Go take the cover off that old piano and see if it still works," he commanded. "We'll finish up in here."

Noah eyed the fireplace as he settled on the couch. "Are you sure the fire won't bother Santa Claus?" he asked in a worried voice.

Asa laughed. "I'm positive!" He put his drink on the mantel. "Want to help me uncover the piano?"

"Sure!" Noah said, perking up. They pulled off the cover and Noah pushed down on some of the keys.

"Hmmm . . ." Maddie said thoughtfully. "You're right, it is out of tune." She sat down on the bench and began to play the "Für Elise" while Asa and Noah listened.

"Hey!" Noah exclaimed. "That's from *A Charlie Brown Christmas*!"

Maddie smiled and continued to play. "You're right . . . but it's really Beethoven."

Noah continued watching, mesmerized by Maddie's slender fingers dancing along the keys. "I wish I knew how to play," he said wistfully.

Maddie stopped playing and patted the bench. "C'mon over!" Noah grinned and slid in next to her. She took his right hand and shook it around a little bit. "You have to relax your hand," she said. Then she stretched his little fingers across five keys and rested her hand on top of them. "Okay, this is an easy one. Ready?" Noah nodded expectantly and Maddie pressed his middle finger down seven times.

"Hey, that sounds like 'Jingle Bells'!" he exclaimed as she continued to press down his fingers. When they got to the end, Noah said, "Let's play it again."

Maddie happily complied and, this time, said the notes out loud as they played . . . *eee eee egcde ffff eee dded g eee eee egcde ffff eee gfedc.*"

"Okay . . . let me try alone." Maddie took her hand away and Noah started to play. He got as far as *Oh what fun . . .*

Sarah and Samuel came in the room and quietly watched Noah as he concentrated on the keys. When he finished, they clapped and Samuel exclaimed, "Bravo! Bravo! Encore!"

Maddie whispered in Noah's ear, "*Encore* means they want you to play it again!" Noah grinned and placed his fingers back on the keys. Maddie looked up at Asa and said, "I think you might have a prodigy on your hands."

Asa laughed. "Well, he doesn't get it from me!"

Finally, after about the tenth playing of "Jingle Bells," Maddie suggested they try something different. She looked at Asa. "I know a few songs, but sheet music would really help. Do you know where there might be some?" They looked in the cabinets, but didn't find anything, so Maddie began to play "Deck the Halls" from memory. She stopped suddenly and said, "Noah, hop up." They both got up and Maddie lifted the seat of the bench. Right on top of a pile of papers was a book titled *Favorite Christmas Carols*. "Here we go!" she said. The room was quiet as she leafed through the book, so when a muffled sound came from upstairs, everyone heard it.

Noah's eyes grew wide. "*What* was that?"

Samuel glanced quickly at Sarah and put his mug down. "Probably nothing . . . but I'll go check." He disappeared up the stairs and Sarah encouraged Maddie to keep playing.

"Any requests?" Maddie asked.

Asa, who had wandered over to add a couple more logs to the fire, thought of the favorite carol Annie used to play when he was little. "How about "Rudolph the Red-Nosed Reindeer"? he asked.

"Yeah!" Noah agreed.

Maddie played "Rudolph" through twice . . . and then several more favorites before Samuel finally came back downstairs. He picked up his mug, shrugged, and shook his head. "Nothing . . . but, it *is* getting late," he said, glancing at the clock. "I think there's a certain *somebody* who needs to get to bed so Santa can come . . ."

Noah reached for Sarah's hand. "C'mon, Grandma, we have to put out cookies and carrots and eggnog."

Sarah followed Noah . . . and Samuel called after them, "Maybe Santa would prefer *Glug* on this snowy night!" Maddie and Asa both smiled . . . but Sarah and Noah had already disappeared into the kitchen.

Moments later, Noah returned with his treats for Santa carefully arranged on a plate. He looked around the room and placed the plate strategically on the coffee table. While Sarah waited, Noah gave hugs and kisses and whispered *good night* and *love you* . . .

"I'll take him up," Asa said.

"I don't mind," Sarah insisted. "I miss tucking little people in . . ."

Asa smiled and watched them go.

* * *

Samuel rocked slowly back and forth in the rocking chair, sipping his drink. "I think I need to warm this up a bit," he said. "Would anyone else like some more?"

Maddie looked in her empty mug. "Hmmm, I might . . ." She looked questioningly at Asa and he declined. "I think I'll wait."

Samuel disappeared into the kitchen and, when he returned with two fresh mugs, Sarah was just coming down the stairs. "Asa, don't you think those pajamas are a little big?" she asked.

Asa smiled. "Yeah, they are . . . but when they come in a package, it's hard to tell how big they are. Besides, he'll grow into 'em."

"Well, big or not, he was asleep before his head hit the pillow," she said.

"I'm not surprised," Asa said, yawning. "He was up at the crack of dawn." He looked over at Maddie. "This morning seems like forever ago, doesn't it?"

She nodded and leaned back on the couch, and Samuel handed her the warm mug. "Mmmm . . . thank you," she murmured.

As they sat gazing sleepily at the fire, an odd sound came from the room above them and Sarah looked over at Samuel. "I think you're going to have to tell them . . ."

Chapter 8

"Close your eyes . . ." Sarah said as Samuel came down the stairs.

"I thought this was—" Asa started to say, but before he could finish his sentence, he felt four small feet pressing on his lap. He opened his eyes and, standing there, looking up at him with gentle brown eyes, was a black Lab puppy. Asa reached out and lightly stroked the pup's silky ears and it plopped its bottom down on his lap and continued to gaze at him. Maddie watched the reaction they had to each other and smiled. Asa looked at his parents, his eyes shining. "I don't know what to say . . . I *never* expected this."

"Well, every boy needs a dog," Samuel said softly. "Especially Noah . . . *and you* . . ."

Asa picked the pup up and brought it to his face. It leaned forward and licked his salty tears and Asa smiled and pressed his cheek into the soft black fur. "Noah is going to love him," he said with certainty. Maddie reached over to pet him and, when she cupped his head in her hands, he climbed over onto her lap and curled up in contentment. "Hey!" Asa teased softly, leaning down to look in the pup's eyes. "Don't get any ideas there, mister!" But the pup just sighed and closed his eyes.

"I can't believe you did this . . ." Asa said with a smile. "Where'd you get him?"

Samuel looked at Sarah. "Well, we saw an ad in the paper when we were here last month and, when I called, we found out that the owner lived right in Eastham. She has the mother—a beautiful black Lab named Chloe—and she said she didn't even realize she was pregnant until she was nearly five weeks along. The woman isn't sure who the stranger in the night was . . . but she suspects a big yellow Lab named Tucker that lives up the road."

Sarah added, "And she's probably right—there were eight pups and they were all yellow—except for this little guy."

Asa looked at the pup and grinned. "Well, he must be the pick of the litter." Samuel and Sarah nodded, obviously pleased . . . and relieved . . . by Asa's positive reaction.

"We have a leash, bowls, and food. In fact, he's probably thirsty." Sarah looked at her husband. "Do you know where those bowls are?"

Samuel nodded. "They're up in that box . . . which happens to be wet. I'll get them." When he came back down, he dropped a new red leash and collar in Asa's lap. "He's not housebroken yet . . . *and* he's probably due to go out . . . so, let the fun begin!"

Asa smiled. "I knew there had to be a catch . . ."

He slipped the collar around the pup's neck, clipped the new leash to it, and looked at Maddie. "Want to come?"

"Oh . . . I don't know. I'm kind of comfortable right here," she said, leaning back on a cushion and stroking the sleepy black head on her lap. "*And* . . . it's kind of cold out there . . ."

"Oh, don't be a wimp," he teased. "Besides . . . I'll keep you warm." He stood up and put on his coat.

Maddie handed the pup to him and bundled into her coat and scarf. When they stepped outside, Asa put the pup down on the snow-covered ground and they watched as he gingerly picked up his oversized paws. Finally, curiosity got the best of him and he plowed his nose into the fluffy white stuff and then resurfaced with snow covering his head; then he shook it off, sneezed, and started racing in circles, sending snow flying everywhere. Maddie and Asa laughed at his antics and he looked up at them and sneezed again. They walked along the edge of the yard and listened to the surf thundering in the darkness. "I didn't realize the house was so close to the ocean," Maddie said.

Asa nodded. "There's a great view from upstairs and there's a path, or I should say, there *used to* be a path that wandered through the brush out to the beach. It's probably overgrown now . . . but we can look for it tomorrow."

Maddie gazed at the vastness of the sky, glittering with stars . . . and shivered. Asa put his arm around her and pointed to the brightest light. "Do you know what that is?"

Maddie laughed and guessed, "The Star of Bethlehem?"

"No, silly," Asa said with a smile. "It's Jupiter . . . and the smaller light up to the right is Venus."

Maddie nodded slowly. "I had no idea that planets looked like bright stars."

"Yup," Asa replied. "At this time of year, Jupiter and Venus are very bright." Asa felt Maddie lean against him and he pulled her closer. "I *am* really glad you're here," he said softly. Maddie felt her heart skip a beat . . . and didn't know what to say. He felt her shiver again and asked, "Are you ready to go in?" but she shook her head. They stood in silence, looking at the sky . . . until the pup at their feet had had enough and let out a little bark. Asa picked him up and said, "What's the matter, too much planet gazing for you?"

Sarah was putting presents under the tree, but looked up when she heard them come in. "Did he go?"

Asa looked puzzled as he unclipped the leash. "Did he go . . . ?" Then he realized what she meant. "Oh!" He looked questioningly at Maddie. "I don't know . . ."

She laughed. "I'm not sure either . . ."

Sarah looked at the puppy, who had just discovered an interesting bow to tug on, and said, "Well, I hope so!"

Samuel called from the hall. "Asa, shall I bring out these boxes?"

"I'll get them, Dad." Asa found his father with his head in the hall closet.

"I'm looking for the gift I have for your mother," he whispered. "I could've sworn I put it in here." Asa pulled the boxes out of the way and brought them into the living room. A moment later, Samuel came in, smiling and hiding something behind his back. When Sarah wasn't looking, he slipped it under the tree.

"What are we doing with this little guy tonight?" Asa asked, looking at the puppy who had now completely untied the bow.

"Well, we have a wrapped box with a top that lifts off to put him in in the morning, but tonight . . . I think he should stay down here," Samuel said.

"Well, I guess I'll stay with him." Asa looked at the time. "Is it really one o'clock?!"

"Yes, dear . . ." Sarah said wearily as she took down

Noah's stocking and dropped an orange into the toe. "Do you have anything to put in this?"

Asa nodded. "I have a few things . . ." He opened one of the cardboard boxes and pulled out some small, brightly wrapped gifts. "I have a couple of Matchboxes, some chocolate kisses, a chapstick, a set of jacks, *and* a limited edition Duncan yo-yo."

Sarah smiled at her son's thoughtful choices. "You're pretty good . . . for a beginner!"

"I also have an etch-a-sketch, but that won't fit in his stocking."

"It sounds like you're going to have more fun in the morning than he is!"

Asa laughed. "Maybe . . ."

Sarah handed the stocking to him and said, "I have a few more things, too." She disappeared into the kitchen and came back with a package of red string licorice, new mittens, and a small conch shell. "This is so he can hear the ocean when he's up in the mountains with you," she said with a smile.

Asa started to fill the stocking. "I don't know if this is all going to fit."

Sarah sighed, "Well, do the best you can. I'm going up to bed. There are clean towels and washcloths in the bathroom. Asa, you know where to find things . . . ?" It was more of a statement than a question. Asa nodded and then she looked at Samuel, dozing in the rocker. "Are you coming, dear?"

Samuel opened one eye. "Are you finally ready?" he asked, standing and stretching. "Good night, you two. Don't stay up too late."

Asa hung Noah's stocking back on the hook and wondered if the fabric would hold. "I hope the kisses don't melt." He started unpacking the rest of the gifts while Maddie found some ribbon and a gift bag for the syrup and the little tree. She had several wrapped gifts, too, and while she was arranging everything, Asa scratched his head and tried to remember where he had put the bag from the Birdwatcher's General Store. They did their tasks quietly, working around the little black mound that was asleep on a bed of shredded red ribbon.

When Asa finished, he considered putting another log on the fire . . . but decided against it. He turned to Maddie. "Would you like a little more Glug?"

"Okay," she said with a smile. "You also need to eat these cookies," she added, nodding toward the plate on the coffee table.

"Yup, I'm going to take care of that. Do you want the eggnog?" She shook her head and Asa drank it down. "Mmmm . . . nothing like warm eggnog." He left a small piece of carrot on the plate and scooped up the rest to put back in the fridge.

When he returned, he switched off all the lamps so that the room was lit only by the Christmas tree and the fireplace. Maddie was sitting on the couch with the puppy in her lap. "Noah is going to be so excited," she said as Asa handed a mug to her and offered one of the cookies. They each took one and Asa collapsed onto the couch, looked at the puppy, and said, "I wonder what we should name him?"

"I think you should let Noah name him," she said. "My brother Tim has always had the job of naming our barn cats and he takes it very seriously. He's come up with some pretty funny and appropriate names." She paused. "I'm sure Noah will come up with something good."

Asa watched the firelight dancing on the walls and reached for Maddie's hand. "How come you always know the right thing to say?"

She smiled and shrugged. "Oh, I don't always know . . . but I usually just follow my heart."

Chapter 9

"Dad?" a small voice whispered. Asa opened one eye and tried to remember where he was. "Dad, are you down there?" Asa heard small footsteps coming down the stairs and sat bolt upright, shook his head to clear the cobwebs, and glanced next to him at Maddie and the puppy. He cleared his throat. "Noah, don't come down just yet."

"Why?" the small voice asked.

Asa suddenly realized that calling back and forth wasn't going to work. He got up quickly and found Noah already halfway down the stairs. "Because Grandma and Grampa aren't up yet," he whispered, "and *you* are up kind of early . . . it's not even light out."

"I just wanted to see if Santa came . . ." Noah whispered back.

"Well, we have to wait for everyone to get up."

"Can I go wake them?" Noah asked hopefully.

Asa sighed and ran his hand through his hair. "Don't you want to go back to bed for a bit?"

"No!" Noah answered brightly.

"All right, you can wake them . . . but don't go jumping on their bed or anything. They were up pretty late."

"Okay!" Noah said cheerfully, bouncing back up the stairs.

Asa shook his head, found his boots and the leash, lifted the sleeping puppy off Maddie's still dry lap, and whispered, "Hey, you did pretty well . . . for a beginner!" He stepped out into the early morning air and let the puppy take care of business. Then he brought him back in and looked around for the box his parents had talked about.

"Maddie," he whispered softly. She looked so peaceful that he felt bad waking her. He sat down next to her and shook her knee. "Maddie . . ."

She opened her eyes and looked around. "Is it morning already?" she asked.

"Not really," Asa answered, "but Noah's awake and I can't find the box."

Maddie sat up and tried to clear her mind. "I thought I saw a box on the back porch last night."

Asa opened the door and looked. "You're right!" He brought the box in and then went to the bottom of the stairs to listen for his parents. There was definitely movement coming from their room and he could hear Noah talking. "I think I have time to make coffee," he said, putting the box on the couch and heading for the kitchen.

Five minutes later he heard his mother call softly, "Asa, are you ready for us to come down?"

"Just a minute . . ." he said. He put the box on the floor, and lifted off the top, and Maddie kissed the puppy and gently put him inside.

"Just for a few minutes, little fella!" she said as Asa put the top back on.

"Okay . . . ready!" he called.

They could hear Noah at the top of the stairs. "C'mon, Grandma . . . Dad said he's ready."

"Okay, honey, just a minute."

There were footsteps on the stairs again . . . and then Noah was standing there, grinning from ear to ear as he surveyed the scene. "Wow! I guess he *was* here!" He looked at the empty eggnog glass and the plate with just a piece of carrot left. "He *really* was here!" he whispered.

Samuel looked at Asa sleepily. "Did he make us a pot of coffee while he was here?"

Asa grinned. "He did . . . somehow he knew that was just what *you* wanted."

Noah looked up at his grandfather. "Is that really what you wanted, Grampa?"

Samuel tousled Noah's head and laughed. "I always—" but his sentence was interrupted by an odd sound.

Noah looked up in astonishment. "What was that?" he asked. It happened again . . . and then one of the boxes under the tree moved. Noah's eyes grew wide. "Dad, what's in that box?"

Asa smiled. "I don't know . . . maybe you should open it."

Noah reached for Samuel's hand. "C'mon, Grampa." Noah knelt down next to the box and started to unwrap it.

"Noah, I think you just have to lift off the top," Samuel said.

As soon as Noah did, the puppy jumped up against the edge, knocking the box over, and Noah fell backward, laughing in surprise. The puppy, sensing an advantage, climbed on top of him and started licking his ears and face . . . but Noah tried to roll away, giggling . . . and finally sputtered, "Stop! Stop! I have to go to the bathroom!"

Asa laughed, too, and lifted the puppy off of Noah so

he could escape and run to the bathroom. A moment later, he was running back . . . and bowling his grandparents over with the biggest hugs they'd ever had.

He sat on the couch between them, and Asa put the little black pup on his lap. The puppy gazed up at him and Noah asked, "What's his name?"

"He doesn't have one yet," Asa replied.

Samuel smiled. "A handsome pup like that needs a handsome name. We thought maybe you could come up with one."

Noah considered thoughtfully and gently stroked the pup's soft ears. "He's beautiful," he said softly. "His coat is so shiny and black . . . he's as black as coal."

He looked up at Asa. "How about 'Coal'?"

Asa smiled and nodded. "I think Coal is a perfect name."

"Coal is a great name, Noah," Maddie agreed. "I *knew* you would think of something good!"

Sarah and Samuel both smiled and nodded and Noah looked around at all of them. "Why are you crying? What's wrong?"

"Nothing, sweetheart," Sarah said softly. "We're just happy . . ."

Noah nodded. "Hey, Coal," he whispered. The puppy barked and Noah grinned. "I think he likes it, too!"

Samuel stood and wiped his eyes. "Okay, who's ready for coffee?"

Three cheerful "Me's!" replied.

Sarah looked up at Samuel. "Can you put the oven on four hundred, too?" Samuel nodded and disappeared into the kitchen.

Noah hugged the newly named pup and whispered, "This is the best present ever!" Then, remembering he had gifts to give, too, he turned to Asa. "Dad, can I give

Maddie her present?" Asa nodded and Noah handed Coal to Maddie and grinned. "That's not your present . . ." he said warningly.

"Are you sure?" Maddie teased as Coal nuzzled her hand. "I think he likes me."

Noah grinned. "I'm sure!" Then he searched around under the tree, looking for the present wrapped in brown paper with chickadees on it. He found two. "Dad, can I give Maddie yours, too?"

Asa sat down on the floor next to Maddie and nodded. Noah knelt in front of her with the two gifts and Maddie held one in each hand. "Which one should I open first?"

"Mine!" Noah replied, pointing to the one that appeared to be a box. Maddie carefully pulled away the pretty paper as Coal happily tugged on the ribbon. Noah was grinning as she lifted off the top of the box and peered inside. She pulled back the tissue paper and there nestled inside was an intricately carved Christmas ornament of a female cardinal. She lifted it out by its ribbon and Noah said, "You can hang it . . . or you could put it in the nest."

Maddie smiled. "Noah, it's just beautiful. Thank you!" She eyed him. "How did you know I like cardinals?" Noah just shrugged and grinned and Maddie handed Coal to Asa and stood up.

Noah held up one of the middle branches. "It's right in here."

Maddie reached inside the tree and gently nestled the cardinal into the nest. "You're right," she said admiringly. "She looks like she belongs there." Noah nodded.

They sat back down and Maddie began to open her gift from Asa. She pulled off the paper and Asa said, "I know you got a copy of this for your mom . . . but I had already gotten it, too. It must be good if we both picked it out!"

Maddie smiled and held up a slim paperback for Sarah to see.

She nodded. "Oh, yes. One of our neighbors gave me *That Quail, Robert* to read a couple of years ago . . . it's a very cute story."

Samuel came in with a tray of mugs and saw the book, too. "That's such a good book . . . even Noah would enjoy listening to it."

For the next hour, they sipped coffee and opened gifts and by the time they finished, the floor was covered with tissue paper, wrapping paper, and shredded ribbons and bows. Amidst the strewn-about boxes were one sleeping puppy, three wool sweaters, books of all shapes and titles, L.L. Bean boots for Asa and a quilt-lined flannel work shirt, new soft scarves for Sarah and Maddie, mittens and a hat for Noah . . . and a new jug of maple syrup that had made Asa laugh. When it seemed that everything had been opened and admired, Maddie reached into an unwrapped cardboard box and lifted out the tiny Norway spruce. She handed it to Noah with a grin. "I know it looks a bit like a Charlie Brown tree now, Noah, but if you plant it in a sunny spot, and take good care of it, it will grow to be as big as the Christmas trees in Rockefeller Center."

Noah took the little tree carefully. "Wow! Thanks, Maddie." He looked at Asa. "Dad, where should we plant it?"

Asa smiled. "Somewhere where there's plenty of room!"

Chapter 10

After a breakfast of cheese and sausage strata, sweet cinnamon buns, orange juice, and more coffee, Maddie and Asa were shooed from the kitchen.

"Why don't you two take the pup and his new owner for a walk?" Samuel suggested.

"Hmmm . . . that's an idea," Asa said, looking over at Maddie. "Are you up for a walk on the beach?"

"Sure," Maddie replied.

They bundled up, stepped outside, and discovered that it was surprisingly mild for Christmas Day. Asa was also surprised to find that Noah already knew all about the path through the brush . . . and he was astonished to find it better maintained than when he was a boy. "Dad kept . . . I mean *my other* dad kept it clear," Noah explained as he led the way with Coal in tow, seemingly at peace with his own words.

They slid down the dune onto the beach and were greeted by a chilly ocean wind. "Gee . . . it's not quite as tranquil out here!" Asa said with a grin. Maddie pulled her scarf snugly around her neck and looked up at the white wispy clouds racing across the blue winter sky. In spite of the strong headwind, the tide seemed to be ebbing, and the surf, although turbulent, was not as intimidating as an incoming tide. Noah ran ahead, laughing, with Coal, ears flopping, happily at his heels. Maddie and Asa walked along, watching them as they chased the waves . . . and as the waves chased them back. Coal splashed blissfully through the shallow remnants of each receding wave and seemed completely at case with the new experience of getting wet.

"Look, Dad," Noah shouted. "He loves the water."

"Of course he does!" Asa shouted back. "All Labs love water!"

Noah grinned and raced down the beach, putting his arms out as if he were flying, the wind billowing his coat.

"You know, that's not entirely true," Maddie ventured.

"What's not?"

"Not *all* Labs like water," Maddie explained with a slow smile. "My dad had a big yellow Lab named Mulligan and he didn't retrieve *or* like water!"

Asa was incredulous. "Are you sure he was a Lab?"

"Positive." Maddie nodded. "If he had to go out and it was raining, he would tiptoe through the puddles . . . it was pretty funny."

"No way!"

"Yup."

Asa looked up the beach and realized that Noah and Coal were getting a little too far ahead of them. "Noah!" he called out . . . but his voice was lost in the wind. They started to pick up their pace when, out of the corner of his eye, Asa noticed a rogue wave barreling inland—right toward the two small figures in the distance. Asa called again and started to run with Maddie right behind him, both shouting, "Noah, look out!"

Asa began sprinting—his heart pounding as he real-

ized he wasn't going to reach them . . . he could only
watch as Noah turned and saw the wave, too . . . he could
only watch as the small figure that he loved with all his
heart . . . ran toward the wave and, without hesitation,
scooped the little black pup into his arms and barely escaped its crushing force. When Asa reached them, Noah
had collapsed onto the dry sand with Coal on his chest.
The bottoms of his pant legs were soaked and his face
was getting a bath . . . *and he was laughing!* He looked
up at Maddie and his father with a grin and sputtered,
"Boy . . . *that* was close!"

"Too close!" Asa said, his heart still pounding. He
lifted the wet pup off of his son and pulled him to his
feet . . . and then he knelt down in front of him and
looked in his eyes. "Noah, you need to be more careful,"
he admonished.

Noah nodded at the look of concern in his father's
eyes. "It's okay, Dad," he said softly. "We're okay . . ."

Asa pulled the little boy into a hug, felt his slight frame
. . . and was suddenly overwhelmed with an aching desire
to always protect his son from all of life's dangers and
sorrows. Tears streamed down Asa's cheeks as his heart
swelled with a love that he hadn't fully understood before.
He buried his face in Noah's wispy blond hair, breathed in
the little boy's wonderful sweet scent, and whispered,
"You two are soaking wet. I think we'd better head back."
He wiped his eyes, felt Coal shiver, unbuttoned his coat,
and tucked him inside.

Noah put his hand gently on Asa's arm and repeated,
"It's okay, Dad. Nothin' happened . . ."

Asa smiled and wiped his eyes again. "I know, buddy,
I know." They walked back together. This time Noah
stayed nearby and ventured only far enough to gather
smooth stones that the tide had left behind. By the time
they reached the path through the brush, his pockets were

full and he looked longingly at the water. "Dad, can I skip some of these stones before we go in?"

"Aren't you cold?" Asa asked.

Noah shook his head and grinned hopefully.

"Okay," Asa relented. He watched as Noah reached into his pocket, pulled out a handful of stones, picked out the flattest ones, and hooked them, one at a time, expertly into the surf. Asa looked over at Maddie. "You're awfully quiet," he said, putting his arm around her shoulder.

"So are you," she said with a half smile.

Asa pulled her close and, as he did, Coal leaned out of his coat, stuffed his wet nose in her ear, and promptly snorted. Maddie laughed and turned her head away, but Asa gently turned her back to face him and searched her eyes. "Maddie, I'm sorry it's taken me so long," he said softly.

Maddie felt her heart pounding as Asa touched her cheek . . . and then pulled her head close to his and pressed his lips lightly against her forehead. Slowly, he moved down . . . kissing her eyelashes . . . and her nose . . . until he finally found her lips . . . and her soft, warm kiss in return. A moment later, another face joined in, nudging its cold wet nose between their chins and licking their cheeks. Maddie pulled back, laughing, and Asa grinned. "Well, you two have one thing in common . . . a cold nose!" Maddie laughed again and Noah looked over his shoulder at them.

"Dad, Maddie, look at this stone," he said, holding up a large black rock. "It looks like a piece of coal." He held it in his palm thoughtfully and walked toward them. "Hey, Dad . . . you said I might get coal for Christmas," he said, grinning as he reached up to stroke the puppy's silky black ears. "And I *did* get Coal for Christmas!"

They all laughed and Asa put his arm around him. "Yes, Noah, you sure did!"

* * *

For more on these characters, look for Nan Rossiter's novel *The Gin & Chowder Club*.

For an old Parson family recipe for *Glug*, visit www.nanrossiter.com